THE CLAY SANSKRIT LIBRARY
FOUNDED BY JOHN & JENNIFER CLAY

WWW.CLAYSANSKRITLIBRARY.COM
WWW.NYUPRESS.ORG

First Edition 2005

The Clay Sanskrit Library is co-published by
New York University Press
and the JJC Foundation.

Further information about this volume
and the rest of the Clay Sanskrit Library
is available on the following Websites:
www.claysanskritlibrary.com
www.nyupress.org.

ISBN-10: 0-8147-5707-3
ISBN-13: 978-0-8147-5707-9

Artwork by Robert Beer.
Typeset with Adobe Garamond in 10.25 : 12.3+pt.
Printed in Great Britain by St Edmundsbury Press,
Bury St Edmunds, Suffolk, on acid-free paper.
Bound by Hunter & Foulis Ltd, Edinburgh, Scotland.

THE EMPEROR OF THE SORCERERS VOLUME TWO

BY BUDHASVĀMIN

EDITED & TRANSLATED BY
SIR JAMES MALLINSON

NEW YORK UNIVERSITY PRESS
JJC FOUNDATION
2005

Library of Congress Cataloging-in-Publication Data
Budhasvāmin.
[Bṛhatkathāślokasaṅgraha. English & Sanskrit]
The emperor of the sorcerers / by Budhasvamin ;
edited and translated by Sir James Mallinson.– 1st ed.
p. cm. – (The Clay Sanskrit library)
In English and Sanskrit; translated from Sanskrit.
Includes bibliographical references and index.
ISBN-13: 978-0-8147-5701-7 (cloth : alk. paper)
ISBN-10: 0-8147-5701-4 (cloth : alk. paper)
1. Sanskrit literature–Early works to 1800.
2. Tales–India–Early works to 1800.
I. Mallinson, James, 1970- II. Title. III. Series.
PK3794.B84B713 2005
891'.21–dc22 2004014626
Volume Two
ISBN-10: 0-8147-5707-3
ISBN-13: 978-0-8147-5707-9

CONTENTS

A *sandhi* grid is printed on the inside of the back cover

SANSKRIT ALPHABETICAL ORDER

Vowels:	*a ā i ī u ū ṛ ṝ ḷ ḹ e ai o au ṃ ḥ*
Gutturals:	*k kh g gh ṅ*
Palatals:	*c ch j jh ñ*
Retroflex:	*ṭ ṭh ḍ ḍh ṇ*
Labials:	*p ph b bh m*
Semivowels:	*y r l v*
Spirants:	*ś ṣ s h*

GUIDE TO SANSKRIT PRONUNCIATION

a	b*u*t
ā, â	r*a*ther
i	s*i*t
ī, î	f*ee*
u	p*u*t
ū,û	b*oo*
ṛ	vocalic *r*, American p*ur*dy or English p*re*tty
ṝ	lengthened *ṛ*
ḷ	vocalic *l*, ab*le*
e, ê, ē	m*a*de, esp. in Welsh pronunciation
ai	b*i*te
o, ô, ō	r*o*pe, esp. Welsh pronunciation; Italian s*o*lo
au	s*ou*nd
ṃ	*anusvāra* nasalizes the preceding vowel
ḥ	*visarga*, a voiceless aspiration (resembling English *h*), or like Scottish lo*ch*, or an aspiration with a faint echoing of the preceding vowel so that *taiḥ* is pronounced *taih*^{i}
k	lu*ck*
kh	blo*ckh*ead
g	*g*o
gh	bi*gh*ead
ṅ	a*n*ger
c	*ch*ill
ch	mat*chh*ead
j	*j*og
jh	aspirated *j*, he*dgeh*og
ñ	ca*ny*on
ṭ	retroflex *t*, *t*ry (with the tip of tongue turned up to touch the hard palate)
ṭh	same as the preceding but aspirated
ḍ	retroflex *d* (with the tip of tongue turned up to touch the hard palate)
ḍh	same as the preceding but aspirated
ṇ	retroflex *n* (with the tip of tongue turned up to touch the hard palate)

t	French *t*out	*r*	trilled, resembling the Italian pronunciation of *r*
th	ten*t h*ook	*l*	*l*inger
d	*d*inner	*v*	*w*ord
dh	guil*dh*all	*ś*	*sh*ore
n	*n*ow	*ṣ*	retroflex *sh* (with the tip of the tongue turned up to touch the hard palate)
p	*p*ill	*s*	hi*ss*
ph	u*ph*eaval	*h*	*h*ood
b	*b*efore		
bh	a*bh*orrent		
m	*m*ind		
y	*y*es		

CSL PUNCTUATION OF ENGLISH

The acute accent on Sanskrit words when they occur outside of the Sanskrit text itself, marks stress, e.g. Ramáyana. It is not part of traditional Sanskrit orthography, transliteration or transcription, but we supply it here to guide readers in the pronunciation of these unfamiliar words. Since no Sanskrit word is accented on the last syllable it is not necessary to accent disyllables, e.g. Rama.

The second CSL innovation designed to assist the reader in the pronunciation of lengthy unfamiliar words is to insert an unobtrusive middle dot between semantic word breaks in compound names (provided the word break does not fall on a vowel resulting from the fusion of two vowels), e.g. Maha·bhárata, but Ramáyana (not Rama·áyana). Our dot echoes the punctuating middle dot (·) found in the oldest surviving forms of written Sanskrit, the Ashokan inscriptions of the third century BCE.

The deep layering of Sanskrit narrative has also dictated that we use quotation marks only to announce the beginning and end of every direct speech, and not at the beginning of every paragraph.

An asterisk (*) in the body of the translation (or Sanskrit text) marks the word or passage being annotated in the endnotes.

CSL PUNCTUATION OF SANSKRIT

The Sanskrit text is also punctuated, in accordance with the punctuation of the English translation. In mid-verse, the punctuation will not alter the *sandhi* or the scansion. Proper names are capitalized. Most Sanskrit metres have four "feet" *(pāda):* where possible we print the common *śloka* metre on two lines. In the Sanskrit text, we use French *Guillemets* (e.g. *«kva saṃcicīrṣuḥ?»*) instead of English quotation marks (e.g. "Where are you off to?") to avoid confusion with the apostrophes used for vowel elision in *sandhi*.

Sanskrit presents the learner with a challenge: *sandhi* ("euphonic combination"). *Sandhi* means that when two words are joined in connected speech or writing (which in Sanskrit reflects speech), the last letter (or even letters) of the first word often changes; compare the differing pronunciations of "the" in "the beginning" and "the end."

In Sanskrit the first letter of the second word may also change; and if both the last letter of the first word and the first letter of the second are vowels, they may fuse. This has a parallel in English when a nasal consonant is inserted between two vowels that would otherwise coalesce: "a pear" and "an apple." Sanskrit vowel fusion may produce ambiguity. The chart at the back of each book gives the full *sandhi* system.

Fortunately it is not necessary to know these changes in order to start reading Sanskrit. For that, what is important is to know the form of the second word without *sandhi* (pre-*sandhi*), so that it can be recognized or looked up in a dictionary. Therefore we are printing Sanskrit with a system of punctuation that will indicate, unambiguously, the original form of the second word, i.e., the form without *sandhi*. Such *sandhi* mostly concerns the fusion of two vowels.

In Sanskrit, vowels may be short or long and are written differently accordingly. We follow the general convention that a vowel with no mark above it is short. Other books mark a long vowel either with a bar called a macron (*ā*) or with a circumflex (*â*). Our system uses the macron, except that for initial vowels in *sandhi* we use a circumflex to indicate that originally the vowel was short, or the shorter of two possibilities (*e* rather than *ai*, *o* rather than *au*).

When we print initial *â*,	before *sandhi* that vowel was *a*
î or *ê*,	*i*
û or *ô*,	*u*
âi,	*e*

âu,	*o*
ā,	*ā* (i.e., the same)
ī,	*ī* (i.e., the same)
ū,	*ū* (i.e., the same)
ē,	*ī*
ō,	*ū*
āi,	*ai*
āu,	*au*

', before *sandhi* there was a vowel *a*

FURTHER HELP WITH VOWEL SANDHI

When a final short vowel (*a*, *i* or *u*) has merged into a following vowel, we print ' at the end of the word, and when a final long vowel (*ā*, *ī* or *ū*) has merged into a following vowel we print " at the end of the word. The vast majority of these cases will concern a final *a* or *ā*.

Examples:

What before *sandhi* was *atra asti* is represented as *atr' âsti*

atra āste	*atr' āste*
kanyā asti	*kany" âsti*
kanyā āste	*kany" āste*
atra iti	*atr' êti*
kanyā iti	*kany" êti*
kanyā īpsitā	*kany" ēpsitā*

Finally, three other points concerning the initial letter of the second word:

(1) A word that before *sandhi* begins with *ṛ* (vowel), after *sandhi* begins with *r* followed by a consonant: *yatha" rtu* represents pre-*sandhi* *yathā ṛtu*.

(2) When before *sandhi* the previous word ends in *t* and the following word begins with *ś*, after *sandhi* the last letter of the previous word is *c* and the following word begins with *ch*: *syāc chāstravit* represents pre-*sandhi* *syāt śāstravit*.

(3) Where a word begins with *h* and the previous word ends with a double consonant, this is our simplified spelling to show the pre-*sandhi* form: *tad hasati* is commonly written as *tad dhasati*, but we write *tadd hasati* so that the original initial letter is obvious.

COMPOUNDS

We also punctuate the division of compounds (*samāsa*), simply by inserting a thin vertical line between words. There are words where the decision whether to regard them as compounds is arbitrary. Our principle has been to try to guide readers to the correct dictionary entries.

WORDPLAY

Classical Sanskrit literature can abound in puns *(śleṣa)*. Such paronomasia, or wordplay, is raised to a high art; rarely is it a *cliché*. Multiple meanings merge *(śliṣyanti)* into a single word or phrase. Most common are pairs of meanings, but as many as ten separate meanings are attested. To mark the parallel senses in the English, as well as the punning original in the Sanskrit, we use a *slanted* font (different from *italic*) and a triple colon *(⁝)* to separate the alternatives. E.g.

yuktaṃ Kādambarīṃ śrutvā kavayo maunam āśritāḥ
Bāṇa/dhvanāv an|adhyāyo bhavat' îti smṛtir yataḥ.

"It is right that poets should fall silent upon hearing the Kadámbari, for the sacred law rules that recitation must be suspended when *the sound of an arrow⁝the poetry of Bana* is heard."

Soméshvara·deva's "Moonlight of Glory" I.15

EXAMPLE

Where the Deva·nágari script reads:

कुम्भस्थली रक्षतु वो विकीर्णसिन्दूररेणुर्द्विरदाननस्य ।
प्रशान्तये विघ्नतमश्छटानां निष्ठ्यूतबालातपपल्लवेव ॥

Others would print:

kumbhasthalī rakṣatu vo vikīrṇasindūrareṇur dviradānanasya /
praśāntaye vighnatamaśchaṭānāṃ niṣṭhyūtabālātapapallaveva //

We print:

kumbha|sthalī rakṣatu vo vikīrṇa|sindūra|reṇur Dvirad'|ānanasya
praśāntaye vighna|tamaś|chaṭānāṃ niṣṭhyūta|bāl'|ātapa|pallav" êva.

And in English:

"May Ganésha's domed forehead protect you! Streaked with vermilion dust, it seems to be emitting the spreading rays of the rising sun to pacify the teeming darkness of obstructions."

"Nava·sáhasanka and the Serpent Princess" I.3, by Padma·gupta

INTRODUCTION

THIS SECOND VOLUME of "The Emperor of the Sorcerors" *(Bṛhat/kathā/śloka/saṃgraha)* picks up the story at the beginning of the eighteenth canto. Nara·váhana·datta, the future emperor of the sorcerers who is both the hero and narrator of the story, has so far won three of the twenty-six wives about whom he is telling Káshyapa and the other sages at Káshyapa's hermitage. (The text breaks off when he is in pursuit of his sixth bride; unfortunately the rest of the poem is lost.) He is now in Champa, where he has just won the hand of Gandhárva·datta, Sanu·dasa's daughter, in a lute contest.

PLOT SYNOPSIS

Canto 18 (702 verses) The story of Sanu·dasa

vv. 3–702 Sanu·dasa tells his story. Dhrúvaka persuades Sanu·dasa to accompany him to his friends' picnic. Sanu·dasa is tricked into getting drunk and making love to Ganga·dattá. Devoted to decadence, he spends his vast fortune. His father dies, but still he spends his time with Ganga·dattá. His mother and children start living in a slum. Horrified, he vows not to return to Champa until he has made back his fortune four times over. He meets Siddhárthaka and sets off for Tamra·lipti with him and a caravan of traders. They are attacked and he makes his way to Tamra·lipti alone. He goes to the house of Ganga·datta, his maternal uncle. Ganga·datta offers him the money he has vowed to earn, but he refuses and runs away with a seafaring trader. He is shipwrecked and meets his erstwhile fiancée, Samúdra·dinná, another castaway. They fall in love, are rescued, and then are shipwrecked again. Sanu·dasa is separated from Samúdra·dinná and washes up in the land of the Pandyas. He journeys to the Máthura of the Pandyas, where he becomes a successful valuer of jewels. He has to flee Máthura when his house burns down. He meets travelers who have been sent to look for him by Ganga·datta and returns to Tamra·lipti with them. He then sets off for the land of gold with the merchant Achéra. He arrives at the hermitage of Bharad·vaja the Sorcerer and meets Gandhárva·datta.

543–561 Gandhárva·datta tells the story of how Bharad·vaja and Súprabha were her parents.

Bharad·vaja gives her to Sanu·dasa, along with vast riches, and tells him that she is to be won by the future emperor of the sorcerers in a lute contest. He returns to Champa with her. He discovers that he was set up all along, and is reunited with his mother, his first wife, Ganga·dattá and Samúdra·dinná.

636–702 Sanu·dasa's mother tells the story of how he was set up by her, his friends and the king.

661–697 Samúdra·dinná's brothers tell the story of how they found her after she had been shipwrecked.

684–690 Samúdra·dinná's story.

Canto 19 (204 verses) The tale of Nalínika, in the Winning of Ajínavati

Gandhárva·datta angers both Nara·váhana·datta and Vikáchika, an apprentice magician, thereby thwarting the latter's aims. Nara·váhana·datta goes to a festival and is captivated by a beautiful forest girl that he sees on the way.

62–202 Gandhárva·datta tells the story of Nalínika. Mano·hara, prince of Kánana·dvipa, goes to the Yaksha festival with his friends Bákula and Ashóka, and Sumángala, an expert in perfumery. He falls in love with the image of a *yakshi.* She returns to life, freed from Kubéra's curse, tells him to visit her at Shri·kunja, and disappears. Mano·hara hears about Shri·kunja from a seafaring trader and travels there by boat. He finds Sukumárika, his *yakshi,* and enjoys five days with her. She promises to visit him in Kánana·dvipa and does so, along with friends to keep Mano·hara's friends happy. A year passes.

Then Sukumárika has to return to Shri·kunja to serve Kubéra. Sumángala persuades Mano·hara and the others to follow in his boat. The boat sinks. Mano·hara finds himself on land and is rescued by a troop of horsemen who show him great respect. They take him to their king. Mano·hara finds that Sumángala is there, too.

171–195 Sumángala tells the story of how he and others were sent across the continents to find a suitable match for Nalínika, Puran·dara's daughter. Sumángala eventually came across Mano·hara, decided he was suitable and contrived to have him come to Naga·pura, Puran·dara's city.

Mano·hara and Nálinika fall in love, but Mano·hara is abducted by Sukumárika. Gandhárva·datta does not want the forest girl to make her like Nálinika: that is why she has told the story.

Canto 20 (438 verses) The Winning of Ajínavati

An old sorceress visits Champa and asks Dáttaka to give Ajínavati, her granddaughter, to Nara·váhana·datta. Nara·váhana·datta treats her with contempt and is abducted by a ghost. He is taken to the cremation-ground, where he meets the old lady. Ajínavati is the girl that Nara·váhana·datta saw on the way to the festival, and she is given to him. He is then taken in an aerial chariot to meet Chanda·simha, his new father-in-law. After landing at Chanda·simha City he goes to Ajínavati's house. They are married. One day the ladies are sobbing and Ajínavati's servant explains that she was promised to Vikáchika, a lowly sorcerer, and he has demanded a court hearing. Ajínavati and Nara·váhana·datta go to Sapta·parna·pura, where the court hearing is taking place. Chanda·simha wins the case. Vikáchika abducts Ajínavati. Chasing them, Nara·váhana·datta gets lost in the forest. He is taken in by a cowherd and sent on his way the next day. He comes across Go·mukha.

293–437 Go·mukha tells him what has happened since they were last together. After he had discovered that Nara·váhana·datta has gone, Ámita·gati and Végavati had arrived in the sky.

318–411 Ámita·gati's story. He recounts how Végavati secretly spied on Nara·váhana·datta in Champa and overheard him praising other women. She decided to kill herself, but reached Vatsa before she could.

357–401 Ámita·gati tells Végavati the story of the country rat and the town rat.

Udáyana sends an army to bring back Nara·váhana·datta. They are ambushed by robbers. Go·mukha flees and ends up at the village.

Canto 21 (172 verses) The story of destiny in the Winning of Priya·darshaná

Go·mukha and Nara·váhana·datta go to Varánasi. They stop in a ruined house and an ascetic and a student come in.

56–172 To prove that destiny is more powerful than human effort, the ascetic tells the story of Dridhódyama. A sage predicts that Dridhódyama's patron will have a daughter, Dridhódyama will marry her and she will be ill-omened and badly behaved. To avoid his fate, he flees the village. After twelve years he settles down in a village by the Ganga. He marries a girl called Tamálika and then finds out that she is the girl he was destined to marry. He flees and wanders the earth for another twelve years, in order to avoid the last part of the prediction. Then he goes to Varánasi, where he meets a Kapálika couple. The woman is his wife and she demands to live with him. A brahmin intercedes and gives Dridhódyama his daughter's hand. He and his wife live on the Ganga with Tamálika living nearby as a nun.

Canto 22 (312 verses) The story of human effort in the Winning of Priya·darshaná

1–312 The student tells a story to show how human effort is more powerful than destiny. Two merchants, Ságara·datta and Buddha·varman, meet on the sea. They agree to betroth their children to each other. Ságara·datta has a daughter, Kunda·málika, and Buddha·varman has a deformed son, Kurábhaka ("Freak"). Buddha·varman does not let on to Ságara·datta that his son is deformed, and messages pass between the two families for thirteen years. Ságara·datta's family becomes exasperated at not meeting Kurábhaka. Eventually Buddha·varman persuades Yajña·gupta, a brahmin boy, to pretend to be his son. When Kunda·málika finds out who her husband really is, she escapes dressed as a male Kapálika ascetic. She goes back to Yajña·gupta's house. She tricks him into believing that she has the divine power to find treasure, and he accompanies her on a pilgrimage. They go to Ujjain, where she returns home and has her father fetch Yajña·gupta. They live happily ever after.

Canto 23 (124 verses) The story of Nanda and Upanánda in the Winning of Priya·darshaná

Go·mukha and Nara·váhana·datta go to stay at Punar·vasu's house.

8–78 Go·mukha relates how he met Punar·vasu playing dice at the house of the royal chamberlain.

Punar·vasu brings Nanda and Upanánda to be cooks for Nara·váhana·datta and Go·mukha.

99–123 Go·mukha relates how Nanda and Upanánda knew that Nara·váhana·datta was the future emperor.

106–123 Nanda tells their story to Go·mukha. They are hereditary cooks to the king. Their father advised them to learn the signs of great men, hence they realized Nara·váhana·datta's identity.

Canto 24 (74 verses) Meeting Priya·dárshana

Go·mukha and Nara·váhana·datta see the nun, Rishi·datta. She complains to Punar·vasu that he is keeping his two guests to himself. They all go to the Jaina temple. Priya·dár-shana, the head of the guild, arrives for a concert. Nara·váha-na·datta sees him as a beautiful woman, and greets him thus. All are embarrassed. Several people play the lute beautifully, each better than the last. Go·mukha is surpassed by Priya·dárshana, and then Nara·váhana·datta amazes the gathering with his skills. Ganga·rákshita, the royal chamberlain, and Priya·dárshana both ask to be Nara·váhana·datta's pupils and Go·mukha accepts for him.

Canto 25 (109 verses) The wedding of Go·mukha in the Winning of Priya·darshaná

Go·mukha tells Nara·váhana·datta he has seen Hari·shi-kha's servant in the town and asks permission to search for him for a few days. He returns, seemingly drunk.

15–97 Go·mukha relates how he fell in love with Ri-shi·datta at first sight and has been visiting her. She asks him whether he knows of Go·mukha. He says yes, but does not let on that he is Go·mukha. She starts to cry and Go·mukha asks why.

34–63 Rishi·datta's story. She was betrothed to Go·mukha, her cousin, but kept falling ill and became a nun. Even though she has heard a rumor that he is dead, she still thinks of him all the time.

Go·mukha decides that he must marry her and puts a plan into action. Winning her sympathy by feigning an illness, he gets her alone in her bedroom and persuades her to embrace him. She is expelled from the community and they are married.

Canto 26 (51 verses) The glimpse of Priya·dárshana's breasts

Nara·váhana·datta sees Priya·dárshana taking off his coat and catches sight of a moonlike breast. He tells Go·mukha that he sees him as a woman.

20–40 Go·mukha asks him to be careful and tells the story of Satya·kaúshika and the floating rock to illustrate his point.

Nara·váhana·datta is unimpressed and falls lovesick. Priya·dárshana is ushered in.

Canto 27 (117 verses) The wedding to Priya·darshaná

He embraces her. She leaves and Nara·váhana·datta is summoned by the king.

25–50 Táraka·raja, the king's general, makes a speech. The king's friend Káliya died before his wife, Súmanas, bore their child. Súmanas lied that the child was a boy, causing Káliya to be reborn. He recently visited the king, told him what had happened and asked that his daughter be married to whomever she wants. She names Nara·váhana·datta.

They are married and Nara·váhana·datta congratulates himself on getting what he wanted.

69–115 Go·mukha informs Nara·váhana·datta of his role in the matter. When he was upset because Nara·váhana·datta had scolded him, Rishi·datta asked him what was going on.

75–94 Rishi·datta tells Go·mukha how a sorceress predicted that Priya·darshaná would be the wife of the future emperor of the sorcerers and gave her a locket to wear which meant that only he would see her as a woman; everyone else would see her as a man. Thus when Nara·váhana·datta saw Priya·dárshana as a woman, she realized that he was the emperor. She asks Go·mukha to bring about their union.

Go·mukha despairs, but meets a deformed child and puts a plan into action. He has the child pretend to be Káliya and go to the king. . .

Canto 28 (116 verses) The Winning of Priya·darshaná

A girl comes to Nara·váhana·datta bringing a present from the king's daughter. She addresses him as "glorious sir" and returns later to apologize on behalf of the princess for her presumptuousness. The princess tells Priya·darshaná to come to a feast with her. Nara·váhana·datta is angry at his wife being told to come to somebody else's house, but Go·mukha calms him down. She goes. On her return, she goes to bed with Nara·váhana·datta and the thread tying her girdle snaps. He asks her about it.

49–85 Priya·darshaná's story. She meets Bhagíratha·yashas in her garden. She is forced into having a massage. Looking at her body and its marks from lovemaking,

Bhagíratha·yashas pretends to be outraged by Nara·váhana·datta's behavior. Then she has Priya·darshaná put on her girdle.

Nara·váhana·datta surmises that Bhagíratha·yashas has designs on him and he is smitten. . .

SANSKRIT TEXT

The Sanskrit text printed here is based on Félix Lacôte's 1908 edition. He collated four Nepalese manuscripts: two from the twelfth century (denoted by A and B in his edition), and copies (*n* and *m*) made in 1906 of two undated manuscripts (N and M). A appears to be a direct copy of B. Lacôte has not been able to use stemmatic analysis to base his edition on a single manuscript, although a later hand has made several corrections and emendations to B and Lacôte always adopts his readings. When the evidence of this later hand is unavailable, he makes his own judgment as to which reading of all the witnesses is to be adopted, and he has a preference for the readings of *n* and *m*. In general, his text is very good: there are few places where it has been necessary to make corrections or emendations.

BIBLIOGRAPHY

Bṛhat/kathā/śloka/saṃgraha of Budhasvāmin. Ed. and tr. Félix Lacôte & Louis Renou. Paris. Imprimerie Nationale. 1908–1928.

Bṛhat/kathā/śloka/saṃgraha of Budhasvāmin with English Translation by Poddar, R.P. & Sinha, N. Varanasi. Tara Book Agency. 1986.

Keith, A.B. *A History of Sanskrit Literature.* Oxford University Press. 1920.

Lacôte, F. *Essai sur Guṇāḍhya et la Bṛhat/kathā.* Paris. 1908.

Maten, E.P. *Budhasvāmin's Bṛhat/kathā/śloka/saṃgraha. a literary study of an ancient Indian narrative.* Leiden. E.J.Brill. 1973.

Shastri, Hara Prasad. *Old Nepalese Manuscripts.* JASB LXII (1893) No.3 pp.254–5.

Van Buitenen, J.A.B. *Tales of ancient India.* Chicago. 1959.

CANTO 18
SANU·DASA

18.1 GANDHARVADATTAYĀ sārdhaṃ
divasān Dattakena ca
yathā Rati|Vasantābhyāṃ
Smaraḥ sukham ayāpayam.

atha Gandharvadattāyāṃ gatāyāṃ vandituṃ gurūn
Sānudāso namas|kṛtya vadati sma kṛt'|āsanaḥ:

«yuṣmākaṃ hi ‹sa|varṇ" êyam utkṛṣṭā v" êti› yan mayā
yūyaṃ vijñāpitāḥ pūrvaṃ tad etad avadhīyatām.

āsīd ih' âiva Campāyāṃ Mitravarm" êti vāṇijaḥ
n' â|mitro n' âpi madhya|sthaḥ sādhor yasy' âbhavad bhuvi.
18.5 tasya Mitravatī nāma nāmnā su|sadṛśī priyā
bhāryā maitr" îva sādhor yā śatror api hit'|âiṣiṇī.
tayor guṇavatoḥ putraṃ guṇavantam a|vindatoḥ
a|putrān ātmanaḥ paurāḥ sa|putrān api menire.

ekadā piṇḍa|pātāya Sānur nāma Dig|ambaraḥ
tri|rātra|kṣapaṇa|kṣāmo Vardhamāna iv' āgataḥ.
daṃpatibhyām asau tābhyāṃ prītābhyāṃ prīṇitas tathā
a|pṛṣṭo 'pi yath" ācaṣṭa dharmān Ṛṣabha|bhāṣitān.
praśn'|ādi|grantha|sāra|jñaś cittaṃ buddhvā tayor asau
ādideśa sphuṭ'|ādeśo bhāvinaṃ guṇinaṃ sutam.
18.10 yaś ca putras tayor jātas tasya nām' âkarot pitā
‹ādiṣṭaḥ Sānunā yat tat Sānudāso bhavatv› iti.
eka|putro 'py asau pitrā dur|labhatvāc ca vallabhaḥ
vidyāḥ śikṣayatā nīto bāla|līl"|ân|abhijñatām.
upādhyāyaiś ca s'|ôtsāhair vinītaḥ sa tathā yathā
sva|dārān eva sa|vrīḍaḥ para|dārān amanyata.

I PASSED THE DAYS happily in the company of Gandhárva· 18.1
datta and Dáttaka, like Kama with Rati and Vasánta.*

One day when Gandhárva·datta had gone to pay her respects to her elders, Sanu·dasa bowed to me, took a seat and said:

"I told you before that the girl is either of the same caste as you or superior. Now listen why.

Here in Champa there used to be a merchant called Mit-
ra·varman. He was a good man and no one in the world was
inimical or even indifferent to him. His dear wife Mítravati 18.5
"Rich-in-friends" was true to her name:* like a personification of the benevolence of a good man, she wished well
on even her enemies. Because this virtuous couple failed to
have a son to add to their virtues, the citizens, even those
with sons, considered themselves without.

One day a naked Jaina ascetic called Sanu came begging for food. Haggard from a three-day fast, he looked like Vardhamána.* The kindly couple pleased him so much that even without being prompted he preached the precepts taught by Ríshabha.* He had mastered works on divination and read the couple's minds. He then made a clear prediction that they would have a virtuous son.

The son that was born to them was named by his father 18.10
thus: 'Sanu predicted him, so let him be called Sanu·da-
sa.'* Since he was an only son and was cherished because
he had been difficult to obtain, his father schooled him
so thoroughly that he knew nothing of childish pastimes.
Zealous teachers made him so reserved that he treated his
own wife as bashfully as if she were someone else's. This

ten' âti|vinayen' âsya loka|bāhyena pārthivaḥ
pitarau suhṛdo dārā na kaś cin n' ākulī|kṛtaḥ.
ādiṣṭaḥ Sānunā yo 'sau tayoḥ putraḥ su|vṛttayoḥ
aham eva sa vo dāsaḥ Sānudāsas tathā|guṇaḥ.

18.15 mama tu Dhruvako nāma dhruva|maitrī|sukhaḥ sakhā
sa ca mām abravīn ‹mitra kriyatāṃ tad bravīmi yat.
udyāna|nalinī|kūle sa|dārāḥ suhṛdas tava
anubhūta|jala|krīḍāḥ khādanti ca pibanti ca.
bhavat" âpi sa|dāreṇa tatra gatvā mayā saha
sāphalyaṃ kriyatām adya rūpa|yauvana|janmanām.
dharm'|ârthayoḥ phalaṃ yena sukham eva nirākṛtam
viphalī|kṛta|dharm'|ârthāt pāpa|karmā kutas tataḥ?
janm'|ântara|sukha|prāptyai yaś ca dharmaṃ niṣevate
tyakta|dṛṣṭa|sukhaḥ so 'pi vada ko nāma paṇḍitaḥ?
18.20 na c' âpi sv'|ârtha|siddhy|arthaṃ mayā tvaṃ vipralabhyase
tathā hi Bhīmasenasya vākyam ākarṇyatāṃ yathā.
«pratyupasthita|kālasya sukhasya parivarjanam
an|āgata|sukh'|āśā ca n' âiṣa buddhimatāṃ nayaḥ».›

mayā tu sa vihasy' ôktas ‹tuccha eva prayojane
idaṃ saṃrambha|gāmbhīryam! śaṅkām iva karoti saḥ.
yadi pītaṃ na vā pītaṃ sva|dāra|sahitair madhu
lābhaḥ kas tatra hānir vā? rāgo 'yam abhivāsitaḥ.
rāg'|âgniḥ prāṇināṃ prāyaḥ prakṛty" âiva pradīpyate
tam indhayati yan mitra tatra kiṃ nāma pauruṣam?
18.25 yas taṃ viṣaya|saṃkalpa|sarpir|indhanam uddhatam
vairāgya|vacan'|âmbhobhir nirvāpayati sa kṣamaḥ.

excessive and antisocial reserve of his worried everyone, including the king, his parents, his friends and his wife. The man predicted by Sanu, the son of that virtuous couple, is none other than me, your servant Sanu·dasa, and those are the qualities I have.

I have a friend called Dhrúvaka, who enjoys a firm friend- 18.15
ship with me. He once said to me, 'My friend, please do as I tell you. Your friends and their wives are at the lotus pool in the park. They have been playing around in the water and are now eating and drinking. You and your wife must accompany me there and reap right now the rewards of your good looks, youthfulness and birth! What greater sinner is there than he who renders his religious merit and material gains fruitless by rejecting their reward, happiness? Tell me, is he really a wise man who acquires religious merit to attain happiness in a subsequent life, but has given up happiness
after experiencing it in this one? And I am not deceiving 18.20
you for my own ends. Listen to the words of Bhima·sena: "To reject present happiness in the hope of happiness yet to come is not the way of the wise."'

But I laughed and said to him, 'Such intense gravitas in such a trifling matter! Bhima·sena is arousing my suspicions somewhat. What is gained or lost if one does or does not drink wine with one's wife? This is but veiled talk of passion. The fire of passion is kindled naturally in almost every living being. Where is the manliness in making it burn brighter,
my friend? Once kindled, it is fueled by the oil of sensual 18.25
desire; it is the man that extinguishes it with the waters of the doctrine of dispassion who is capable. If the reward of religious merit were said to be that sort of happiness, then

phalaṃ yadi ca dharmasya sukham īdṛśam iṣyate
dharmasy' â|bhāvanaṃ bhūyāt tat|phalasya sukhasya ca.
yāṃ yathā|sukham āsīnām aśnantīṃ ca striyaṃ prati
n' ēkṣyate pratiṣedhāt sā katham evaṃ viḍambyate.
goṣṭhī|maṇḍala|madhya|sthā mad'|ôpahata|cetanā
viṣa|mūrcchā|parīt" êva bhartur bhāryā viḍambanā.
atha vā gacchatu bhavān yathā|sukham ahaṃ punaḥ
na yāsyāmi na dhāsyāmi dāraiḥ saha sabhām› iti.
18.30 sa tataḥ sthira|saṃkalpaṃ māṃ dṛṣṭvā pratyavasthitam
haste sa|smitam ālambya sa|viṣāda iv' âvadat.
‹suhṛdām agrataḥ kṛtvā pratijñām aham āgataḥ
«Sānudāso 'yam ānītaḥ sa|dāro dṛśyatām» iti.
ten' ôpahasitasy' ôccaiḥ suhṛdbhir vadanaṃ mama
pratijñā|khaṇḍana|mlānaṃ kathaṃ śakṣyasi vīkṣitum?
tat prasīd' āsatāṃ nāma dārā yadi virudhyate
tvay" âikena pratijñāyāḥ sāphalyam upapādyatām.
sa|doṣaṃ yadi pānaṃ ca svayaṃ mā sma pibas tataḥ
suhṛdaḥ pibataḥ paśya sa|dāra|tanayān› iti.
18.35 tatas tat sahito gatvā pur'|ôpavana|padminīm
tāṃ tadā dṛṣṭavān asmi sa|kalatrāṃ suhṛt sabhām.
nindit'|êndr'|āyudha|chāyaiḥ kusum'|ābharaṇ'|âmbaraiḥ
kṣipt'|âmbhaḥ|padminī|chāyāṃ sthalī|kamalinīm iva.
tataḥ sa|mañjarī|jālair mādhavī|cūta|pallavaiḥ
kalpitaṃ Dhruvako mahyam uccam āharad āsanam.
apaśyaṃ tatra c' āsīnaḥ suhṛdaḥ pāyita|priyān
pibataś ca madhu prīta|priyā|kara|tal'|ârpitam.
kva cid vasanta|rāgaṃ ca veṇu|tantrī|rut'|ânvitam
gīyamānaṃ śṛṇomi sma rudantāś c' âli|kokilāḥ.

there would be no more production of religious merit, nor of its reward, happiness. It is forbidden for a wife to be seen when she is relaxing or eating: why should she be insulted thus? A wife who is drunk in the midst of a group of friends and appears to be overcome by intoxication is a disgrace to her husband. You go if you want, but I will not go, nor will I take my wife to the gathering.'

When he saw that I was firmly opposed to what he had 18.30
said, he smiled, took my hands and said dejectedly, 'I came here after promising my friends that I would bring you and your wife for them to meet. After my friends have laughed loudly at me, my face will be sad because I have broken my promise: how will you be able to look at it? So, please, if it is a problem for her, leave your wife and fulfil my promise by coming alone. And if you consider drinking to be wrong, then don't drink yourself but watch my friends drinking with their wives and families.'

So I went with him to the lotus pool in the city park and 18.35
saw the gathering of my friends and their wives. With flowers, ornaments and clothes whose beauty put the rainbow to shame, they looked like an earthbound bed of lotuses, their beauty surpassing that of the lotuses in the water.

Then Dhrúvaka offered me a raised seat made from sprigs of *mádhavi* and mango with abundant blossoms.

I saw some friends sitting there who had given drinks to their sweethearts and were now drinking wine offered to them from the palms of their happy lovers. I heard a spring song being sung somewhere to the accompaniment of a flute and a lute, and the buzzing and cooing of bees and *koyal*s.

18.40 hitvā kurabak'|âgrāṇi varṇa|saṃsthāna|cāruṣu
patitāḥ karṇikāreṣu lūna|nāsā iv' âlinaḥ.
ā|mūla|śikharaṃ phullās tilak'|âśoka|kiṃśukāḥ
a|sārasya hi jāyante naṭasy' âty|utkaṭā rasāḥ.

atha kardama|digdh'|âṅgaḥ śaival'|āvila|śāṭakaḥ
utthitaḥ puruṣaḥ ko 'pi sa|rasaḥ sarasas tataḥ.
ādāya nalinī|pattra|puṭaṃ ken' âpi pūritam
‹bhoḥ puṣkara|madhu prāptaṃ may" êti› ca mud" âvadat.
pratiṣiddhaḥ sa c' âikena ‹mūrkha mā caṇḍam āraṭīḥ!
na puṣkara|madhu prāptaṃ tvay" ân|artho 'yam arjitaḥ!
18.45 yadi tāvad idaṃ sarve pibanti suhṛdas tataḥ
param'|âṇu|pramāṇo 'pi bindur aṃśo na jāyate.
dīyate yadi vā rājñe dur|labhaṃ pārthivair api
aparaṃ so 'pi yāceta ratna|gṛddhā hi pārthivāḥ.
taṃ ca karṇe|japāḥ ke cid vakṣyanti priya|vādinaḥ
«rājann aparam apy asti tatra prāptam idaṃ yataḥ.»
«etāvad eva tatr' āsīn n' âtiriktam» iti bruvan
a|bhāvam atiriktasya ken' ôpāyena sādhayet?
iti protsāhitaḥ pāpair labdh'|āsvādaś ca pārthivaḥ
haret sarva|svam asmākaṃ tasmāt tasmai na dīyate.
18.50 kiṃ tu rasyatar'|āsvādaṃ na ca madyaṃ yatas tataḥ
idaṃ puṣkara|madhv eṣa Sānudāsaḥ pibatv!› iti.
dur|labhatvāt tatas tasya suhṛd|abhyarthanena ca
‹na ca madyam› iti śrutvā pītavān asmi tan madhu.
āsīc ca mama ‹ko nāma ṣaṇṇām sa raso bhavet?
lakṣyate na hi sādṛśyam etasya madhur'|ādibhiḥ.

The bees had abandoned the *kurábaka* buds and descended 18.40
upon the beautifully colored and shaped *karni·kara* flowers as if their noses had been chopped off!* Blossoms covered the *tílaka*, *ashóka* and *kim·shuka* trees from root to crown, for just as it is the actor who has no personality that produces the most intense emotions, so the tree with no core produces the most sap.

Then someone appeared out of the pond, dripping wet. His limbs was smeared with mud and his robe was dirty with duckweed. He was carrying a lotus-leaf bowl filled with something and joyfully announced, 'Hey! I've found some blue-lotus nectar!'*

Someone rebuffed him, saying, 'Don't shout so loudly, you fool! It is not blue-lotus nectar that you have found
but misfortune! If all your friends drink it, their share won't 18.45
even be a drop the size of an atom. Even sovereigns find it hard to come by, and if it is given to the king he may ask for more because kings are greedy for precious things. Some sycophantic informers will tell the king that there is more where this came from. How might one convince him that there was this much only and no more? After having had a taste of it, the king, urged on by evil men, might take away everything we own, so it shouldn't be given to him.
On the other hand, this delicious liquid is blue-lotus nectar 18.50
and not wine, so Sanu·dasa here can drink it!'

Because of its rarity and my friends' insistence that it was not alcoholic, I drank the nectar. I said to myself, 'Which of the six flavors could this be? It does not seem to have any similarity with sweet or the others* and I can't work out

na c' âhaṃ ṣaḍbhir ārabdhaḥ saṃhatya madhur'|ādibhiḥ
sarva|jñair api dur|jñānā yen' âsminn ekaśaḥ rasāḥ.
tena manyata ev' âyaṃ saptamaḥ su|rasaḥ rasaḥ
rasite 'mṛtam apy asmin gacched virasatām!› iti.
18.55 tatas tad|rasa|gandhena tṛṣā ca gamita|trapaḥ
‹bādhate māṃ pipās" êti› śanair Dhruvakam abruvam.
tena dattaṃ tu tat pītvā sva|bhāv'|âpoḍha|mānasaḥ
tat pur'|ôpavanaṃ vegāc cakravad bhramad abhramam.
tataś ca tāra|madhuraṃ dīrgha|veṇor iv' ôṣasi
dīna|mantharam aśrauṣaṃ pramad"|ākrandita|dhvanim.
atha gatvā tam uddeśam apaśyaṃ mādhavī|gṛhe
striyaṃ sākṣād iv' āsīnāṃ mādhavī|vana|devatām.
ākhyāyikā|kathā|kāvya|nāṭakeṣv api tādṛśī
varṇyamān" âpi n' âsmābhiḥ kadā cit pramadā śrutā.
18.60 tatas tām abravaṃ sāmnā ‹bhadre yadi na duṣyati
duḥkhasy' âsya tato hetur mahyam ākhyāyatām› iti.
tataḥ rudita|saṃbhinnaṃ nīcakair uditaṃ tayā
‹duḥsahasy' âsya duḥkhasya nanu hetur bhavān› iti.
lajjā|prahva|śiraskena tato nīcair may" ôditam
‹yad' îdaṃ mat|kṛtaṃ duḥkhaṃ bhīru mā tvaṃ rudas tataḥ.
yad anantam anant'|ârghaṃ tan manye draviṇaṃ tṛṇam
śarīrakam ap' îdaṃ me kva cid vyāpāryatām!› iti.
ath' âvocad asau smitvā harṣ'|âśru|kaluṣ'|ēkṣaṇā
‹anen' âiva tvadīyena śarīreṇ' âham arthinī!
18.65 ahaṃ hi Gaṅgadatt" êti yakṣa|kanyā nabhaś|carī
saṃkalpa|janman" ân|alpaṃ saṃkalpaṃ kāritā tvayi.
tad ehi gṛham asmākaṃ satyaṃ mantrayase yadi
śarīrasy' âsya te tatra viniyogo bhavatv!› iti.

what combination of the flavors it might be: the individual flavors in this drink would be hard for even the omniscient to recognize. Therefore this must be considered to be a delicious seventh flavor, on tasting which even the nectar of immortality seems insipid!'

Its taste and bouquet, together with my thirst, dispelled 18.55
my inhibitions, and in a soft voice I said to Dhrúvaka, 'I'm parched.' But when I drank what he gave me, my mind became unhinged and I staggered about the city park, which was spinning like a wheel. Then, like the shrill, sweet sound of tall bamboo at dawn, I heard the sad, soft sound of a young woman crying. When I headed in its direction, I saw a woman in a *mádhavi* bower. It was as if the goddess of the *mádhavi* forest was sitting before my eyes. Even in fables, stories, poems or plays I had never heard a description of such a girl.

In a soothing voice I said to her, 'Good lady, if you do 18.60
not mind, please tell me why you are sad.'

In a whisper punctuated with sobs she replied, 'But you yourself are the cause of this unbearable sorrow!' I bowed my head in shame and said quietly, 'If I have caused this sorrow, sweet lady, then do not cry. I consider infinite inestimable wealth to be but a blade of grass. Let even this pitiful body of mine be put to work, if needs be!'

At this, she smiled and tears of joy misted up her eyes
as she said, 'It is your body that I desire! I am called Gan- 18.65
ga·dattá. I am a yaksha maiden and a sky-rover. The god of love has brought about in me a great desire for you. So, if you mean what you say, come to my house and put this body of yours to use there!'

kṛṣyamāṇas tayā c' âhaṃ pāṇāv ādāya mantharam
asur'|ântaḥ|pur'|ākāraṃ prāviśaṃ bhavan'|ēśvaram.
tatr' âpaśyaṃ striyaṃ gaurīṃ sit'|â|sita|śiro|ruhām
sthūl'|ôdara|valī|lekhāṃ śuddha|sūkṣm'|âmbar'|āvṛtām.
sā mām arghyeṇa saṃbhāvya mūrdhni c' āghrāya sādaram
abravīd ‹adhva|khinno 'si putra viśramyatām› iti.
18.70 ādṛtā c' ādiśat preṣyāḥ ‹Sānudāsaḥ pipāsitaḥ
tat puṣkara|madhu svādu śīghram ānīyatām!› iti.

mama tv āsīd ‹dhruvaṃ yakṣī Gaṅgadatt" ânyathā kutaḥ
gṛhe puṣkara|madhv asyā duṣ|prāpaṃ mānuṣair?› iti.
gandhena puṣkara|madhu|prabhaveṇ' âdhivāsitam
vasanta|kusum'|ākīrṇaṃ prāviśaṃ vāsa|mandiram.
pītvā ca puṣkara|madhu prītayā sahitas tayā
asyai pūrva|pratijñātaṃ sva|śarīram upāharam.
sva|śarīra|pradānena mahyaṃ pūrv'|ôpakāriṇe
s" âpi pratyupakārāya sva|śarīraṃ nyavedayat.
18.75 āsīn me ‹yan mayā dattvā śarīraṃ puṇyam arjitam
tasya kanyā|śarīr'|āptyā sadyaḥ pariṇataṃ phalam.›
iti tatra ciraṃ sthitvā pṛcchāmi sma priyāṃ ‹priye
kim idānīṃ suhṛd|goṣṭhī karot' îty› atha s" âbravīt.
‹yadi te draṣṭum icch" âsti may" âiva sahitas tataḥ
gatvā paśya suhṛd|goṣṭhīṃ mad'|âtiśaya|vihvalām!
may" ālambita|hastaṃ tvāṃ na kaś cid api paśyati
ten' â|dṛṣṭaḥ suhṛd|goṣṭhyā viśrabdhaḥ paśyatām› iti.

gatvā tatas tad udyānaṃ Gaṅgadatt"|âvalambitaḥ
paśyāmi sma suhṛd|goṣṭhīṃ smita|vyāvartit'|ānanām.
18.80 atha svābhāvika|mukhaḥ suhṛt kaś cid abhāṣata
‹na dṛśyate Sānudāsaḥ kva nu yāto bhaved?› iti.
apareṇ' ôktam ‹āścaryam a|dṛṣṭaṃ kiṃ na paśyasi?

She took my hand and led me gently along. I entered a magnificent house that resembled the harem of an *ásura*. Inside I met a fair woman with graying hair and folds of fat on her stomach. She was wearing bright white clothes of fine cloth. She welcomed me with an offering of water, and kissed me respectfully on the head before saying, 'My
son, you are tired from your journey—you must rest.' The 18.70
venerable lady told her maidservants, 'Sanu·dasa is thirsty. Quickly, bring some delicious blue-lotus nectar!'

I said to myself, 'Gangadatta must indeed be a *yakshi*, otherwise how could there be blue-lotus nectar in her house when it is so hard for humans to obtain?' I went into a bedroom scented with the bouquet of blue-lotus nectar and strewn with spring flowers. I drank the blue-lotus nectar with the delighted girl and gave my body to her as I had promised earlier. By giving my body I was doing her a favor,
and to return it she offered hers. I said to myself, 'In receiving 18.75
this girl's body, the merit I have earned by giving mine has instantly come to fruition!' I stayed there for a long time and then asked the lovely girl, 'What will all my friends be up to now?' and she replied, 'If you want to see, then come with me and take a look at the party; they are reeling from too much wine! When I hold your hand, nobody can see you, so you can watch without worry, unseen by the party.'

So, with Ganga·dattá holding my hand, I went to the park
and saw my friends. They averted their smiling faces. One 18.80
friend then said with a straight face, 'I can't see Sanu·dasa. Where might he have gone?' Another replied, 'What? You don't see the hitherto unseen miracle? Sanu·dasa has brought

Sānudāsena duḥ|sādhyā sādhitā yakṣa|kanyakā!
yakṣy" âvalambitaḥ pāṇāv a|dṛśyo dṛśyatām ayam
Sānudāsaḥ suhṛn|madhye vicaran puṇyavān!› iti.
Gaṅgadattām ath' âvocam ‹a|dṛśyo yady ahaṃ tataḥ
bhadre katham anen' ôktam «a|dṛśyo dṛśyatām!»?› iti.
tataḥ saṃrudhyamāno 'pi yatnena jana|saṃsadā
pravṛttaḥ sahasā hāsaḥ salil'|âugha iv' ôlbaṇaḥ.
18.85 teṣām anyatamo nṛtyan sa|tāla|hasita|dhvaniḥ
mām avocad ‹a|dṛśyāya yakṣī|bhartre namo 'stu te.
kva puṣkara|madhu kv' âtra dur|labhā yakṣa|kanyakā
drākṣā|madhu tvayā pītaṃ sādhitā ca vilāsinī!
sarvathā duś|cikitso 'yaṃ bhavato vinay'|āmayaḥ
suhṛd|vaidya|gaṇen' âdya kuśalena cikitsitaḥ!
sa bhavān Gaṅgadattāyā gṛhaṃ yātu nir|āmayaḥ
suhṛdo 'pi kṛta|sv'|ârthāḥ sarve yāntu yathā|yatham!›
aham tu puṣkara|madhu|cchadmanā chalito 'pi taiḥ
jñāta|kānt"|āsava|svādo na tebhyaḥ kupito 'bhavam.
18.90 āsīc ca mama ‹te dhīrā ye sv|abhyasta|madhu|priyāḥ
vidūṣita|madhu|sparśāḥ pravrajanti mumukṣavaḥ.
ahaṃ tu sakṛd āsvādya pramadā|madirā|rasam
na prāṇimi vinā tasmād dhiṅ nikṛṣṭaṃ ca mām› iti.
atha gacchati sma ravir asta|bhū|dharaṃ
vasati|drumān adhi śakunta|paṅktayaḥ
mada|mandam ātma|bhavanāni nāgarāḥ
priyayā sah' âham api tan|niveśanam.

a wayward yaksha girl under his control! Look at lucky Sanu·dasa! With the *yakshi* holding his hand, he wanders invisible among his friends!'

I said to Ganga·dattá, 'Good lady, if I am invisible then how can he have said, "Look at the invisible man!"?'

At this, despite their efforts to hold it back, laughter suddenly burst forth from the party like a raging torrent of
water. One of them was dancing, clapping and laughing. 18.85
He said to me, 'O invisible one, husband of the *yakshi*, hail to thee! There never was any blue-lotus nectar, nor any unobtainable yaksha girl: you have drunk wine made from grapes and seduced a courtesan! Your reserve was a disease that was almost incurable, but today it has been cured by a crafty band of doctors—your friends! Now that you are better, go to Ganga·dattá's house. As for your friends: they have achieved what they set out to do, so they may all be on their way!'

Even though they had deceived me with the fake blue-lotus nectar, I had experienced the tastes of both a loving
woman and wine, and was not angry with them. I said 18.90
to myself, 'They are strong-willed men indeed who, after regularly enjoying beautiful girls and being contaminated by contact with wine, renounce the world in the quest for liberation. I, on the other hand, having tasted the pleasures of young women and wine just once, cannot live without them. Shame on lowly me!' Then the sun went to sunset mountain, flocks of birds went to their nests in the trees, citizens ambled drunkenly to their houses, and I went with my beloved to her home.

tatra prasannayā kālaṃ priyayā ca prasannayā
prasannaḥ Dhruvak'|ādīnām suhṛdām atyavāhayam.
daśabhir daśabhir yāti sahasrair divasa|vyaye
dhana|rāśiḥ parikṣīṇaḥ kālena mahatā mahān.
18.95 kadā cic c' âham āhūya nīto dārikayā gṛham
duḥ|śravaṃ śrāvito mātrā pituḥ svarg'|âdhirohaṇam.
guruṇā guru|śokena pīḍyamānaṃ ca māṃ nṛpaḥ
samāhvāyy' âvadat ‹putra Mitravarm" âham eva te.
kula|putraka|vṛttena sthātavyam adhunā tvayā
sa h' îha para|loke ca sukhāya prāṇinām› iti.
alaṃ|kṛtāya sa ca me bhūṣaṇ'|âmbara|candanaiḥ
pitryaṃ śreṣṭhi|padaṃ kṛtvā ‹gṛhaṃ yāh' îty› abhāṣata.
kāla|stoke prayāte ca sa|dainyaḥ Dhruvako 'bravīt
‹sa|śokā Gaṅgadatt" âpi sā samāśvasyatām› iti.
18.100 mayā t' ûktam ‹idānīṃ me bāla|kālaś calo gataḥ
anya ev' âyam āyātaḥ kuṭumba|bhara|dāruṇam.
kva veśa|vanit"|āsaktiḥ kva kuṭumba|parigrahaḥ?
na hi vānara|śāvasya yuktā syandana|dhuryatā!
adhunā Gaṅgadattāyā bālatā lolatāṃ gatā
mārgam āsevatāṃ s" âpi mātṛ|mātā|mahī|gatam.
dur|ācār" âiva sā veśyā ciraṃ yasyāḥ satī|vratam
na hi Vedam adhīyānaḥ śūdraḥ sadbhiḥ praśasyate.
«sa|doṣam api na tyājyaṃ saha|jaṃ karma sādhubhiḥ»
it' îdaṃ vacanaṃ Viṣṇoḥ s" âpi saṃmānayatv› iti.

Happy with Dhrúvaka and my other friends, I passed the time there drinking with my happy sweetheart.* My vast wealth went at a rate of tens of thousands of coins every day, and after a long time it had disappeared completely.

One day I was summoned by a maid and taken home. 18.95
My mother told me the terrible news of my father's ascent to heaven. While I was grieving heavily for my father, the king summoned me and said, 'My son, I am Mitra·varman to you. Now you must behave like the scion of a respectable family, for that is how people attain happiness in this world and the next.' He then decorated me with ornaments, clothes and sandalwood paste, gave me my father's position as chief of the merchant's guild, and told me to go home.

A short while later Dhrúvaka, looking upset, said to me, 'Ganga·dattá is also grieving: you must console her!'

I replied, 'My fleeting childhood is now over. A different 18.100
time has come: the grave responsibility of family life. How can one reconcile devotion to a courtesan with having a family? The young of monkeys cannot be yoked to a chariot! Ganga·dattá's childishness has now turned to greed. She should follow the path traveled by her mother and grandmother. A courtesan who spends a long time as a faithful wife is only behaving badly: good men do not praise a low-caste man who studies the Veda. "Even if they are sinful, hereditary obligations are not to be given up by good people." She, too, should respect these words of Vishnu.'

18.105 ten' ôktaṃ ‹gaṇik"|āsaktiḥ pratiṣiddhā kuṭumbinām
na tu śok'|ôpataptāyā gaṇikāyāḥ sabhājanam.
tad bravīmi samāśvasya Gaṅgadattāṃ sa|mātṛkām
ayam āgata ev' âsi tyaja niṣṭhuratām› iti.

tasyām udbhūta|rāgatvād Dhruvak'|âbhyarthitena ca
doṣam utprekṣamāṇo 'pi gata ev' âsmi tad|gṛham.
atha sā mad|viyogena mad|duḥkhena ca karśitā
krandat|parijanā kṛcchrāt parisaṃsthāpitā mayā.
may" âiva ca saha snātā nirupta|salil'|âñjaliḥ
śarāvaṃ madirā|pūrṇaṃ nyasyati sma gṛh'|âṅgaṇe.
18.110 mātā tu Gaṅgadattāyā gṛhīta|caṣak" âvadat
‹putra duḥkha|vinod'|ârthaṃ tarpaṇaṃ kriyatām› iti!

mama tv āsīt ‹prapañco 'yaṃ viṣamaḥ prastuto 'nayā!
nūnam asmān iyaṃ vṛddhā mugdhān ākṛṣṭum icchati.
īdṛśī ca vaco|dakṣā sa|dākṣiṇyaś ca mādṛśaḥ
nir|dākṣiṇyā ca devī Śrīr iti jāto 'smi śaṅkitaḥ.
a|vaśyaṃ ca madīyā śrīr Gaṅgadattāṃ gamiṣyati
prāyaḥ samāna|śīleṣu sakhyaṃ badhnanti jantavaḥ.
atha vā Gaṅgadatt" âiva kṣetraṃ dānasya pūjitam
dānaṃ hi tatra dātavyaṃ yatra cittaṃ prasīdati.›
18.115 iti c' êti ca niścitya trās'|āsvādita|cetasā
tri|phalā|viras'|āsvādaṃ pānam āsevitaṃ mayā.
‹na vartate sakṛt pātum atas triḥ pīyatām!› iti
gaṇikā|mātur ādeśam ‹om› iti pratyapūjayam.
yathā yathā ca māṃ mandam ārohan madirā|madaḥ

He replied, 'Attachment to a courtesan is forbidden for family men, but civility to a courtesan stricken by grief is not. I'm telling you, it won't take a moment for you to cheer up Ganga·dattá and her mother and be back here. Stop being cruel!' 18.105

Because of my passion for her, and Dhrúvaka's insistence, I went to her house even though I thought it was wrong. Our separation and her grief for me had made her thin, and she was surrounded by crying women. With difficulty I got her to stand up. After taking a ritual bath with me and offering the ancestors a libation of water from her joined palms, she placed a bowl filled with wine in the courtyard of the house.

With a cup in her hand, Ganga·dattá's mother said, 'My son, to assuage your sorrow, make a libation!' 18.110

I said to myself, 'It is an unfair trick that she is playing! Surely this old woman is trying to entrap foolish me. A silver-tongued woman like her, a kind man like me, and the unkind goddess of fortune—all this is making me nervous. My goddess of fortune is undoubtedly going to go to Ganga·dattá: people tend to make friends with those of similar natures. But perhaps Ganga·dattá is a worthy recipient of charity, for when giving charity one should follow one's heart.'

Vacillating thus, and with my mind tinged with trepidation, I drank the drink, which had an unpleasant taste similar to that of *tri·phala*.* The courtesan's mother told me, 'It does not do to drink once, so drink thrice!' and I consented. Thus drunkenness slowly overtook me, and even my overwhelming grief for my father abated. Then, 18.115

pitṛ|śoko 'pi balavān avārohat tathā tathā.
ataḥ paraṃ mad|ādeśān madīyāḥ paricārikāḥ
madirā|mandirān madyam āharanti sma saṃtatam.
tadīyāś ca madīyāś ca gata|śokam avekṣya mām
gāyanti sma hasanti sma ke cit tatr' ârudann api.
18.120 iti vismāritas tābhiḥ pitṛ|śokam ahaṃ tadā
divasān gamayāmi sma surā|smara|parāyaṇaḥ.
ekadā gaṇikā|mātrā preṣitā gaṇik" âvadat
‹śvaśrūs tvām āha rūkṣo 'si gātram abhyajyatāṃ tava.
Gaṅgadatt" âpi paruṣā jātā sneha|vivarjanāt
tasmād iyam api sneham aṅgeṣu nidadhātv› iti.
śāṭakaṃ c' âharan mahyaṃ sthūlaṃ taila|malīmasam
skandhaḥ kaṭuka|tailena mrakṣitaś ca tayā mama.
uktaś c' âsmi punar ‹yāvad dārikāyā muhūrtakam
abhyaṅgaḥ kriyate tāvad bhavān avataratv iti.›
18.125 ath' ôpari|purāt ṣaṣṭham an|antaram avātaram
śilpinas tatra c' âpaśyaṃ ratna|saṃskāra|kārakān.
sa|saṃbhramaiś ca tair uktaḥ kṛt'|âñjali|puṭair aham
‹śreṣṭhi|putra pravīṇo 'si tvatto lajjāmahe vayam.
sarva|vidyā|kalā|śilpa|kovidasya puras tava
sarva|jñānām api trāsāt prasaranti na pāṇayaḥ!
tasmād avataratv asmād dīrgh'|āyuḥ pañcamaṃ puram
alaṃ|karaṇa|karm' êdam āśu niṣṭhāṃ vrajatv› iti.
evaṃ ca pariśeṣebhyaḥ kramāc citra|kar'|ādibhiḥ
pañcebhyo 'pi purebhyo 'ham upāyair avatāritaḥ.
18.130 s'|ântaḥ|karmārikābhiś ca ghaṭa|dāsībhir aṅgaṇāt
‹sicyase gomay'|âmbhobhir› iti nirdhārito bahiḥ.

at my command, my servants kept fetching drink from the wine-store. Seeing that my grief was gone, the maidservants, both mine and hers, sang and laughed; some people there cried too.

After the women had thus made me forget my grief for 18.120
my father, I devoted my days to drinking and lovemaking.

One day the courtesan's mother sent a girl to me. She said, 'Your mother-in-law says that your skin has become dry, so your body must be rubbed with oil. Ganga·dattá has stopped using oil, so her skin has also become dry: she, too, must put oil on her body.' She brought me a coarse, oil-stained towel and rubbed my shoulders with pungent oil. Then she asked me to go downstairs for a moment while
she massaged her mistress. I went down from the top floor 18.125
to the next, the sixth, and there I saw craftsmen making jewelry. Flustered, they put their palms together and said to me, 'O son of the president of the guild, you are an expert and we are embarrassed before you. In front of you who are skilled in all sciences, arts and crafts, even the gods are so nervous that their hands will not work! So please go from this floor to the fifth, venerable sir, in order that we may quickly finish making these ornaments.'

In this way the painters and so forth used their wiles to
have me descend the remaining five floors one by one. The 18.130
servant girls and water-carriers kept me out of the courtyard, saying that I would be sprinkled with the purificatory mixture of water and cow dung.

śrūyate sma ca tasy' âiva prāsādasy' ôpari dhvaniḥ
bandinaḥ paṭhataḥ ślokam uccakair uccarann iti.
‹jaya rāja|siṃha para|danti|maṇḍalaṃ
vijit" âiva vādi|mṛga|saṃhatis tvayā
parimaṇḍala|graha|pati|prabhā|prabhair
guṇa|kesar'|âṃśu|visaraiś ca rājase.›
cintitaṃ ca mayā ‹manye praviṣṭaḥ ko 'py ayaṃ viṭaḥ
raṇḍā|putrasya yasy' âite śrūyante bandibhir guṇāḥ.
kuto 'sya guṇa|gandho 'pi yena lajj" âiva khāditā
veśa|nārī|graha|sthena svayaṃ khyāpayatā guṇān.›
18.135 ity asūyann ahaṃ tasmai lajjā|varjita|kaṃdharaḥ
sva|gṛh'|âbhi|mukhaṃ prāyāṃ paura|dhik|kāra|kāritaḥ.
ya eva māṃ suhṛt kaś cid apaśyat saṃ|mukh'|āgatam
sa ev' âmīlayad dṛṣṭiṃ ‹hā! kiṃ dṛṣṭam?› iti bruvan.
yen' âṅgaṇena yāmi sma saṃstutasy' âitarasya vā
tatra gomaya|pānīyaṃ pātayanti sma nāgarāḥ.
evaṃ|prāya|prapañcābhir janatābhir jugupsitaḥ
a|pūrva|puruṣ'|ākrāntaṃ sva|gṛha|dvāram āgamam.
tena ca praviśann eva pūrv'|âbhyāsād a|śaṅkitaḥ
‹tiṣṭha tiṣṭh' êti› ruṣṭena dvāra|pālena vāritaḥ.
18.140 tatas taṃ pṛṣṭavān asmi śaṅkā|mandī|kṛta|trapaḥ
‹bhadra sarvaṃ na jānāmi tattvam ākhyāyatām› iti.
ten' ôktam ‹īdṛśaṃ tattvaṃ na tvaṃ para|gṛhaṃ punaḥ
tiṣṭhad|dauvārika|dvāram a|śaṅkaḥ praviśer› iti.
may" ôktam atha s'|âsūyaṃ ‹kiṃ ca Mitravatī mṛtā›
ten' ôktaṃ ‹kaccid āyuṣmān Sānudāso bhavān› iti.
ahaṃ tu kaṭuk'|ālāpas tasmān madhura|bhāṣiṇaḥ
lajjamānaḥ sthitas tūṣṇīm atha ten' ôditaṃ punaḥ.

From the top of the building I heard the sound of a bard loudly reciting a verse: 'O lion among kings, may you be victorious over your elephant-like enemies! You have conquered your detractors as if they were a herd of deer! With your mane of fine virtues resembling the radiant orb of the moon, you are resplendent!'

I thought, 'Some debauchee must have turned up and the bards are singing the whoreson's praises. This man does not have even a whiff of virtue about him—he has swallowed his very shame and is having his virtues proclaimed while
in the grasp of a courtesan!' As I grumbled about him like 18.135
this, I walked toward my house to cries of 'Shame!' from the citizens and hung my head in embarrassment. Every friend that saw me approaching closed his eyes and said, 'Oh! What have I seen?' People poured cow dung mixed with water over every courtyard that I walked through, whether that of an acquaintance or a stranger.

After being publicly abused like this, I reached the door to my house, where a man I had never seen before was standing guard. I went in without hesitating, as usual, but was obstructed by the angry guard, who was saying 'Stop!
Stop!' My reserve diminished by dismay, I asked him, 'Good 18.140
sir, I have no idea what is going on; please tell me.' He replied, 'This is what's going on: when a guard stands at the door you don't walk straight into someone else's house.'

I indignantly said, 'What? Has Mítravati died?' and he replied, 'Might you be Master Sanu·dasa?' I had addressed him harshly, so when he answered politely I was embarrassed and remained silent. He continued, 'Even though she is living, sir, your mother Mítravati is as good as dead. She

‹jīvaty eva mṛtā tāta mātā Mitravatī tava
spṛhayaty an|apatyābhyo yā strībhyaḥ putravaty api.
18.145 eken' âiva pravṛddhena kāmen' ā|gantunā tava
saṃhatāv api dharm'|ârthāv ucchinnau sva|kul'|ôcitau.
gṛhaṃ vikrīya niḥ|sāram a|nāthā jananī tava
saha pautreṇa vadhvā ca kutr' âpy anyatra tiṣṭhati.
yo 'yaṃ prathama|kakṣāyāṃ kurute karma vardhakiḥ
āste Mitravatī yatra tad ayaṃ pṛcchyatām› iti.

sa ca gatvā mayā dṛṣṭaḥ pratyabhijñāya māṃ cirāt
‹hā kaṣṭam› iti kṛtv" ôccair duḥkha|skhalitam abravīt.
‹hṛt'|ârtha|jana|dāridryāt tvat|prasādāt saha snuṣā
daridra|vāṭake tāta jananī tava tiṣṭhati.
18.150 daridra|vāṭakaṃ pṛṣṭaḥ ‹kutr' êti› sa mayā punaḥ
‹caṇḍāla|vāṭak'|â|dūraṃ dakṣiṇen' êty› abhāṣata.
śanaiḥ saṃcaramāṇaś ca daridra|grāma|rathyayā
daridrān dṛṣṭavān asmi kṣaya|kṣīṇān mṛt'|ākṛtīn.

atha nimba|taror mūle Dattakaṃ nāma putrakam
dṛṣṭavān asmi bahubhir bālakaiḥ parivāritam.
bālakānām ayaṃ rājā te 'nye mantry|ādayaḥ kila
dadāti sma tatas tebhyaḥ svāḥ sa kulmāṣa|piṇḍikāḥ.
yas tu teṣāṃ pratīhāraḥ saḥ rāj'|âṃśaṃ prakalpitām
kulmāṣa|piṇḍikāṃ hṛtvā kṣudhitatvād abhakṣayat.
18.155 Dattako 'pi hṛta|sv'|âṃśas tāraṃ mātaram āhvayan
agacchat kuṭikām ekāṃ saṃkāra|sthagit'|âjirām.
kaṭaiḥ kṛta|parikṣepāṃ jarad|virala|vīraṇaiḥ
ananta|paṭala|chidra|praviṣṭ'|ātapa|candrikām.

envies childless women, even though she has a son. A single 18.145
intense and unsolicited love affair of yours has destroyed all
the merit and wealth to which your family is accustomed.
Your widowed mother has sold her empty house and is
staying elsewhere with her grandson and daughter-in-law.
There is a carpenter working in the first room. Ask him
where Mítravati is staying.'

I went and found him. After a long pause he recognized
me and cried, 'Oh dear!' before saying in a voice choked with
sorrow, 'Thanks to you, sir, your mother is poor and has
no money or servants, so she is staying with her daughter-
in-law in the slum.' When I then asked him where the 18.150
slum was, he said that it was to the south, not far from the
outcastes' settlement. As I slowly walked along the road to
the poor people's village, I saw wretches so emaciated that
they looked like corpses.

Then, at the foot of a neem tree, I saw my young son
Dáttaka surrounded by several children. He seemed to be
the king of the children and the others were his ministers and
so forth. He was sharing his little balls of barley gruel with
them. The boy among them that was playing the doorkeeper
took the ball of barley gruel allotted to the king and hungrily
ate it. His share having been taken, Dáttaka called loudly 18.155
for his mother, and went to a small hut whose yard was
covered in rubbish. Its fence consisted of old and tattered
straw mats, and the countless holes in the roof let through
the light of the sun and the moon.

pṛṣṭato Dattakasy' âhaṃ gatas tat kuṭik"|âṅgaṇam
dāsyā ca pratyabhijñāya Mitravatyai niveditam.
sā tu niṣkramya saṃbhrāntā mām āliṅgya tathā|vidham
gāḍha|nidrā|prasupt" êva n' âkampata na c' âśvasīt.
sadyaḥ putreṇa saṃyuktā svāminā ca vinā|kṛtā
an|uṣṇ'|â|śīta|saṃsparśair mām asnāpayad aśrubhiḥ.

18.160 nilīnāṃ ca kuṭī|koṇe paśyāmi sma kuṭumbinīm
alaṃ vā vistaraṃ kṛtvā mūrtām iva daridratām.
sa|tuṣaiḥ kodrava|kaṇair apanītaṃ mam' âṅgataḥ
tad|duṣṭa|ceṭikā|dattam ādarāt svayam ambayā.

lākṣ"|āvṛta|bahu|chidrā khaṇḍ'|âuṣṭhī śīrṇa|tālukā
ānīt" ôṣṇ'|ôdakaṃ dātum ālukā para|gehataḥ.
snapayantyā ca māṃ bhagnā karma|karyā pramattayā
ath' âsyāḥ svāminī caṇḍam ākrandat tāḍit'|ôdarī.
‹ayi tvayi vipannāyām ālukā|devi gomini
śūnyam adya jagaj jātam adya mātā mṛtā mama!
18.165 mama mātur vivāhe tvaṃ labdhā jñāti|kulāt kila
tena tvām anuśocāmi dvitīyāṃ jananīm iva!›

vilapatyai tathā dīnaṃ karuṇ'|ārdrī|kṛt'|āśayaḥ
śāṭakaṃ pāṭayitv" âham ardhaṃ tasyai vitīrṇavān.
puṣkariṇyāṃ tataḥ snātvā pibant" îva viṣāṇakāḥ
kāñjika|vyañjanaṃ kṛcchrād bhuñje kodrav'|âudanam.

atha v" âlam idaṃ śrutvā daridra|caritaṃ ciram
śrūyamāṇam api hy etad duḥkhāy' âiva bhavādṛśām.

I followed Dáttaka into the hut's front yard. A servant girl recognized me and informed Mítravati. She hurried out and embraced me just as I was. Then she stopped moving and breathing, as though she had fallen into a deep sleep. Suddenly united with her son after being widowed, she bathed me with tears that were neither hot nor cold.

I saw my wife lying in a corner of the hut. Suffice it 18.160
to say that she looked like poverty incarnate. My mother carefully used whole *kódrava* grains to remove from my body whatever it was that the mischievous masseuse had put on me.

A small water pot was brought from someone else's house to provide hot water. Its many holes were covered with resin, its rim was broken and its lid cracked. While she was bathing me the careless servant girl broke the pot. Its owner beat her breast and wailed terribly: 'Oh, my pot princess, my queen! Now that you are destroyed, my world is empty and my
mother dead! You were a present from relatives when my 18.165
mother was married, so I shall grieve for you as though you were a second mother to me!'

As she sobbed miserably, compassion melted my heart. I tore my cloak in two and gave one half to her. Like an elephant drinking from a lotus pond in which they have bathed, I struggled to eat a porridge of *kódrava* grains mixed with rice gruel.*

But enough of listening to this long tale of the exploits of poor people—even hearing it leads only to discomfort for people like you.

so 'haṃ katham api kṣiptvā varṣa|lakṣ'|āyatāṃ kṣapām
jāta|dur|vāra|vairāgyaḥ prāto mātaram abravam.
18.170 ‹tataḥ prakṣapitād dravyād upādāya catur|guṇam
gṛham mayā praveṣṭavyaṃ na praveṣṭavyam anyathā.
tasmād a|jāta|putr" êva māto mṛta|sut" êva vā
duḥkha|karma|vinodena gamayer divasān› iti.
tay" ôktaṃ ‹mā gamaḥ putra! tvāṃ sa|dāraṃ sa|dārakam
jīvayāmi sukh'|āsīnaṃ karmabhir garhitair› iti.
may" ôktaṃ ‹vṛddhayā mātrā jīvyate duḥkha|karmabhiḥ
yaḥ śaktaḥ puruṣas tasya ślāghyam ekasya jīvitam!
ten' âlam avalamby' êmām amba kātaratāṃ tava
nanu tātasya dārāḥ stha Sumeru|guru|cetasaḥ?›
18.175 ity avasthita|nirbandhaḥ praṇamya jananīm aham
daridra|vāṭakād ghorān nirayāṃ nirayād iva.
ambā dūram anuvrajya hitaṃ mahyam upādiśat
‹Tāmraliptīṃ vrajeḥ putra yatr' āste mātulas tava.
narāṇāṃ hi vipannānāṃ śaraṇaṃ mātṛ|bāndhavāḥ
tyājyās tu nija|śatrutvāt prājñena pitṛ|bāndhavāḥ.›
evam|ādi samādiśya dattvā c' âudana|mallakam
sā nivṛttā pravṛtto 'haṃ pathā prāg|deśa|gāminā.
paśyāmi sma ca vaideśāñ jarjara|chattra|pādukān
skandh'|āsakta|jarac|carma|sthagikā|pacan'|ālikān.
18.180 evam|ādi|prakārās te tat|prakāraṃ nirīkṣya mām
karuṇā|gaś|carī|bhūtam abhāṣanta parasparam.
‹aho kaṣṭam idaṃ dṛṣṭam asmābhiś ceṣṭitaṃ vidheḥ

Somehow I struggled through a night that lasted a hundred thousand years. An unshakable melancholy came over me and in the morning I said to my mother, 'I shall return 18.170
to this house only when I have amassed the wealth that I squandered four times over. So, mother, like a woman who has no son or whose son is dead, you should make the days pass by distracting yourself with hard work.'

She replied, 'Don't go, my son! I shall keep you, your wife and your son in comfort by doing menial work.' I said, 'An able man sustained by the hard work of his aged mother? What a commendable life such a singular fellow would have! Mother, do not be frightened: are you not the widow of my father, a man who was as resolute as Mount Suméru?'

I stuck to my guns. After bowing to my mother, I left 18.175
that horrible slum like I was escaping from hell. My mother accompanied me for a long way and gave me some good advice: 'My son, you should go to Tamra·lipti, where my brother lives. For men who are destitute, their mother's family is their refuge. Because of their innate enmity, a wise man should avoid his father's kinsmen.'

After giving me this and other advice, and a parcel of cooked rice, she turned back. I carried on along the road that leads to the east. I saw people from foreign lands with tattered parasols and shoes. From their shoulders hung cooking pots and old leather knapsacks. I looked like them and 18.180
when they saw me they took pity on me, saying to one another, 'Oh! Look at this terrible twist of fate. How could the goodly Sanu·dasa have ended up like this? But he needn't be grieved for: he has not lost his fortune, for when great men

kva sādhuḥ Sānudāso 'yaṃ kv' êyam etādṛśī daśā?
atha vā n' âiva śocyo 'yam a|vipanna|mahā|dhanaḥ
a|vipanna|guṇānāṃ hi kiṃ vipannaṃ mah"|ātmanām?›
māṃ c' âvocan ‹vayaṃ sarve bhavataḥ paricārakāḥ
etasmād a|sahāyatvān mā sma śaṅkāṃ karor› iti.
atha māṃ ramayantas te ramaṇīya|kathāḥ pathi
agacchan kaṃ cid adhvānam a|cetita|patha|klamam.
18.185 saṃkocita|jagac|chāye pratāpena visāriṇā
sarv'|ôpari sthite bhānau saṃprāpaṃ su|mahat saraḥ.
vañcayitvā tu tad|dṛṣṭiṃ dūre snātv" â|mṛt'|ôpamam
tat kodrav'|ânnam a|sneha|lavaṇaṃ bhuktavān aham.
te 'pi plutair udāttaiś ca vyāhāraiḥ parito diśam
‹Sānudāsā kva yās' îti› vyāharan māṃ sa|saṃbhramāḥ
uktavantaś ca.
māṃ dṛṣṭvā nirvṛtta|snāna|bhojanam
‹dhik pramāda|hatān asmān! bhavatā chalitā vayam!
asmābhiḥ kāritaṃ kandau khāditavyam an|ekadhā
bhavatā ca na saṃbhuktam etad asmād an|arthakam.
18.190 idānīm api yat kiṃ cit tvayā tatr' ôpayujyatām
anyath" âsmābhir apy adya sthātavyaṃ kṣudhitair!› iti.
tatas tad|arthitaḥ kiṃ cid bhakṣayitvā sah' âiva taiḥ
sāy'|âhne prasthito grāmam agacchaṃ Siddhakacchapam.
tatra māṃ rathyay" āyāntaṃ kaś cid dṛṣṭvā kuṭumbikaḥ
praṇipaty' âbravīd ‹ehi sva|gṛhaṃ gamyatām› iti.
anujñātasya pathikaiḥ praviṣṭasya gṛhaṃ mama
svayaṃ prakṣālayat pādau vārito 'pi kuṭumbikaḥ.
abhy|aṅg'|ôcchādana|snāna|gamit'|âṅga|śramāya me
dhātu|raktam adāt sthūlaṃ prakṣālaṃ paṭa|śāṭakam.
18.195 tataḥ kṣīr'|âudana|prāyaṃ bhuktvā navata|kājjhake
śayanīye niṣaṇṇaṃ mām avocat sa kuṭumbikaḥ.

still have their virtue, they have lost nothing!' To me they
said, 'We shall all wait upon you, so do not worry about
having nobody with you.'

They amused me along the way with entertaining stories,
and we traveled quite some distance without feeling any
fatigue from the journey. When everyone's shadows had 18.185
shrunk to nothing in the overarching glare and the sun had
reached its zenith, we arrived at a large lake. Avoiding the
gaze of the others, I took a bath some distance away and
ate the dry, unsalted *kódrava* porridge, which was like the
nectar of immortality. They were worried and called for me
with shrill, extended cries: 'Sanu·dasa, where are you?'

When they found me and saw that I had finished bathing
and eating, they said, 'Shame on us for being so careless!
You have tricked us! We have made lots of food in the pot,
but because you haven't eaten any, it will go to waste. Please 18.190
eat something from it now, or today we will have to go
hungry!'* At their request I ate a little with them.

Setting off in the evening, I arrived at a village called
Siddha·kácchapa. A householder there saw me coming along
the road. He bowed and asked me into his house. When I
had taken my leave of the travelers and gone into the house,
the householder, despite being asked not to, washed my feet.
After removing my fatigue with an oil massage and a wash,
he gave me a thick red bathrobe. I ate a hearty meal of rice 18.195
pudding, and afterward, when I was sitting on a bed covered
with a woollen blanket, the householder said to me, 'Sir, I
am aware of everything that has happened to you: who does
not notice an eclipse of the sun? Thanks to Mitra·varman,
whose wealth was like that of Mount Meru and the ocean,

‹tvadīyas tāta vṛtt'|ântaḥ sarvaḥ saṃvidito mayā
bhānoḥ svar|bhānunā grāsaḥ kasya n' ēkṣaṇa|gocaraḥ?
Meru|sāgara|sārasya prasādān Mitravarmaṇaḥ
sahasrāṇi samṛddhāni mādṛśām anujīvinām.
ahaṃ Siddhārthako nāma vaṇig bhṛtyaḥ pitus tava
tena tvadīyam ev' êdaṃ yat kiṃ cid draviṇaṃ mama.
mūlam etad upādāya vardhantāṃ te vibhūtayaḥ
bahu|sattv'|ôpakāriṇyaḥ śākhā iva vanas|pateḥ!
18.200 dina|stokeṣu yāteṣu sārthena sahito mayā
Tāmraliptīṃ prayāt" âsi tāvad viśramyatām iti.›
   ath' ôpapannam āh' êti vicārya saha cetasā
prātiṣṭhe saha sārthena tena Siddharthakena ca.
tato vicitra|śastrāṇāṃ harṣeṇa sphuṭatām iva
śṛṇomi sma pracaṇḍānāṃ ḍiṇḍikānāṃ vikatthitām.
‹śrūyatāṃ dhātakī|bhaṅga|pratijñā|parvata|sthirāḥ
Khaṇḍacarm" êti me nāma muṇḍāḥ Pāśupatā vayam!
sahasram api caurāṇāṃ śūrāṇāṃ yuddha|mūrdhani
na nayeyaṃ yadi svargaṃ gaccheyaṃ nirayaṃ tataḥ!
18.205 taskarān yadi paśyāmas tatas tvāṃ devi Caṇḍike
praty|agrais tarpayiṣyāmo mahiṣa|chāga|śoṇitaiḥ!›
   iti gatv" âṭavī|madhye nadīṃ gambhīra|kandarām
āvasāma kṛt'|â|puṇyāś caṇḍāṃ Vaitaraṇīm iva.
kṛṣṇa|pakṣa|kṣapā|kālī praṇāda|parihāriṇī
Kāla|rātrir iv' â|sahyā Pulinda|pṛtan" âpatat.
   tathā kathitavantas te tām āloky' âiva ḍiṇḍikāḥ
apākrāman parityakta|śastra|lajjā|yaśo|dhanāḥ.
luṇṭhyamānāt tv ahaṃ sārthāt prāṇa|trāṇa|parāyaṇaḥ
saṃbhrama|bhrānta|dig|bhāgaḥ kāndiśīkaḥ palāyitaḥ.

thousands of people like me, his dependents, have become rich. I am a merchant called Siddhárthaka and I worked for your father, so what little wealth I have here is all yours. May your riches use it as a root and grow like the broadly
beneficent branches of a great tree! In a few days you will 18.200
set forth for Tamra·lipti with me and a caravan of traders. In the meantime you must rest.'

I thought about what he had said and, deciding that it was right, I journeyed on with Siddhárthaka and the caravan of traders. I heard the boasting of the fearsome mendicant mercenaries with their strange weapons—they seemed to be bursting with excitement: 'My name is Khanda·charman and we are shaven-headed Páshupatas, as resolute as mountains in our promise to defeat highwaymen! If in the first fight I fail to despatch a thousand brave bandits to
heaven then may I go to hell! O goddess Chándika, if we 18.205
come across any robbers then we shall make you happy with offerings of the fresh blood of buffaloes and goats!'

We reached a steep-sided river in the middle of a forest and halted, like sinners halting at the fearsome Vaitárani.* As dark as a moonless night and as inexorable as the black night of doomsday, a gang of Pulíndas silently fell upon us.

The mercenaries who had been talking earlier took one look at them and ran away, abandoning their weapons, their shame, their reputation and their belongings. I was intent on saving my life and ran away from the caravan while it was being plundered, losing my way in the confusion.

18.210 ‹taskaro 'yam› iti bhraṣṭaḥ sārthikād api dhāvataḥ
gahan'|ântaṃ din'|ântena van'|ânta|grāmam āsadam.
tasya madhyena gacchantaṃ māṃ pariṣvajya vṛddhikā
iti roditum ārabdhā vṛddhatā|ghargharа|dhvaniḥ.
‹putra niṣṭhura|citto 'si yo mām utsanna|bāndhavām
vṛddhāṃ duḥkhitakām a|svāṃ tyaktvā deś'|ântaraṃ gataḥ!
mādṛśīṃ mātaraṃ dīnāṃ tyaktvā yad upacīyate
tat Prayāga|gaten' âpi na pāpam apacīyate.
tīrtha|yātrā|kṛtaṃ pāpam ataḥ kṣapayatā tvayā
mām ārādhayamānena sva|gṛhe sthīyatām!› iti.
18.215 mama tv āsīd ‹aho kaṣṭam aparo 'yam upadravaḥ
manye mūrti|matī k" âpi vipattir iyam āgatā.
mādṛśāṃ hi pramattānām a|pramattā vipattayaḥ
saṃtatāḥ saṃnidhīyante prājñānām iva saṃpadaḥ.›
atha māṃ ciram īkṣitvā tay" ôktaṃ lajjamānayā
‹putra sva|putra|sādṛśyāt tvaṃ may" êtthaṃ kadarthitaḥ.
atha vā putra ev' âsi mam' êty› uktv" ānayad gṛham
tatr' âkarod a|khedaṃ māṃ aṅg'|âbhyaṅg'|āśan'|ādibhiḥ.
prabhāte prasthitaś c' âinām abhivādy' âham abravam
‹Campāyāṃ Sānudāsasya gṛham amba vrajer› iti.
18.220 śrānta|śrāntaś ca viśrāntaḥ pṛṣṭvā panthānam antare
Tāmraliptīṃ vrajāmi sma paribhūt'|Âmarāvatīm.
‹bhoḥ sādho Gaṅgadattasya gṛham ākhyāyatām› iti
yaṃ yam eva sma pṛcchāmi sa sa ev' âivam abravīt.
‹Tāmraliptyāṃ pure bhrātas tvatto dhūrtataro janaḥ
dur|vidagdha|jan'|ālāpo grāmya|nāgarako bhavān.›

I thought that the caravan-leader was a robber when he ran into the dense jungle and became separated from him too. By the end of the day I had reached a village on the edge of the forest. As I walked through it, an old woman embraced me and started to sob in a voice that creaked with age: 'My son, you are cruel-hearted to have left me—a sad, destitute old woman with no relatives—and gone to another country! Not even a visit to Prayága can remove the sin accumulated by abandoning a poor mother like me! So, to get rid of the sin incurred by your pilgrimage to the holy sites, you must stay at home and worship me!' 18.210

I said to myself, 'Oh dear, here's more bad luck. It seems as though some embodiment of misfortune has arrived in the shape of this woman. A constant series of misfortunes seems carefully to find its way to careless people like me, just as fortune finds its way to clever people.' 18.215

She looked at me for a long time before saying with embarrassment, 'Child, I scolded you like that because you look like my son. But, anyway, you are as good as a son to me!' On saying this, she took me to her house and refreshed me with a massage, food and such like. I set out in the morning, and when I bade her farewell I said, 'Mother, you should visit Sanu·dasa's house in Champa.'

Resting when tired and asking the way when necessary, I reached Tamra·lipti. It put the city of the gods to shame. Everyone that I courteously asked to tell me where Ganga·datta's house was would answer by saying, 'The people of the city of Tamra·lipti are more cunning than you, brother. You talk like a fool and are very rustic for a man-about-town!' 18.220

iti saṃpṛcchamānāya yadā mahyaṃ na kaś ca na
ācaṣṭe sma tadā khinnaḥ sann upāviśam āpaṇe.
tatra māṃ pṛṣṭavān eko vaṇik pāṇḍara|mastakaḥ
‹udvigna iva vicchāyaḥ kiṃ nimittaṃ bhavān?› iti.
18.225 may" âpi kathitaṃ tasmai s'|ânukampāya pṛcchate
udvegasya nimittaṃ tat ten' âpi hasit'|ôditam.
›tvām amī kuṭil'|ālāpaṃ manyante Tāmraliptikāḥ
gṛhaṃ hi Gaṅgadattasya na pṛcchanti yathā|sthitāḥ.
paurṇamāsī|śaśāṅkasya yo na jānāti maṇḍalam
na sa jānāti dhūrto vā Gaṅgadattasya mandiram.
atha vā dharma|kām'|ârthān kūṭa|sthān yatra paśyasi
pravṛddhāṃś ca viśuddh'|âṃśu Gaṅgadattasya tad gṛham.
atha vā gaccha mugdh' êti› māṃ uktvā svayam eva saḥ
Gaṅgadatta|gṛha|dvāram anayat prīta|yācakam.
18.230 tasmān mām āgataṃ śrutvā dauvārika|paraṃparā
antaḥ|kakṣ'|āntara|sthāya mātulāya nyavedayat.
Gaṅg"|âughasy' êva patatas tuṣāra|giri|gahvare
ath' ântas tāra|gambhīraḥ pravṛttaḥ krandita|dhvaniḥ.
tataḥ sa|dāra|bhṛtyena tasmān niryāya mandirāt
Gaṅgāyāṃ Gaṅgadattena pitre dattaṃ jalaṃ mama.
tatr' âham upabhuñjānaḥ s'|ântar|duḥkhaṃ mahat sukham
kāla|stokaṃ nayāmi sma viṣa|bhinnam iv' âmṛtam.
ekadā labdha|viśrāmaṃ mām abhāṣata mātulaḥ
‹bhāginey' ârthaye yat tvāṃ tad anuṣṭhātum arhasi.
18.235 yad an|antam a|kupyaṃ ca draviṇaṃ mama paśyasi
guṇa|draviṇa|rāśes tad utpannaṃ Mitravarmaṇaḥ.
svasmāt svasmāt tad ādāya pratijñātāc catur|guṇam
draṣṭuṃ tvad|viraha|mlānāṃ mātaraṃ parigamyatām.

When nobody would answer my question, I became dejected and sat down in a shop. A white-haired merchant inquired of me, 'You are pale and seem depressed, sir. Why?'
He was asking sympathetically, and I told him why I was 18.225
upset. He laughed and said, 'The inhabitants of Tamra·lipti think that you are not being straight with them, for people don't normally ask after Ganga·datta's house. Only a man who doesn't recognize the orb of the full moon or someone playing a joke wouldn't know Ganga·datta's house. You see that place where religious merit, pleasure and wealth are flourishing? That's Ganga·datta's gleaming white house. You might as well come with me, silly.' After addressing me like this, he himself took me to the door of Ganga·datta's house, where the beggars are happy.

When they heard of my arrival, word was passed along 18.230
a series of porters to my maternal uncle, who was in his private apartments. Then, like the sound of a torrent of Ganga water falling into an icy mountain defile, a loud low lament issued forth from inside. Ganga·datta came out from the house with his wife and servants and offered water to the Ganga for my father. I spent a few days there enjoying great happiness accompanied by inner grief, like nectar mixed with poison.

One day when I was resting, my uncle said to me, 'My
nephew, I beg you to do as I ask. This unlimited wealth 18.235
of gold and silver of mine that you see was born of Mitra·varman's vast wealth and virtue. It's yours. Take from it four times what you lost, as promised, and go back and see your mother, who is distraught at being separated from you. When that runs out, more riches will come to you, for

tasmiṃś ca kṣīṇa ev' ânyā gantrī te dravya|saṃhatiḥ
a|kṣaya|prabhavo hy asyā Gaṅgāyā Himavān iva.
sve svasmin sati c' ân|ante lips" ânyasmin vigarhitā
vijñāta|s'|âṅga|Ved'|ârthaḥ kaḥ paṭhen mātṛkām?› iti.
anuśāsatam ity|ādi Gaṅgadattam ath' âvadam
‹sāre 'rthe dṛḍha|nirbandhaṃ mā māṃ vyāhata mātula.
18.240 pravartyo gurubhiḥ kārye yatra bālo balād api
svayam eva pravṛttas tair nivartyeta kathaṃ tataḥ.
yac c' ôktaṃ «māmakair arthaiḥ kuṭumbaṃ jīvyatām» iti›
etat sa|hasta|pādāya mādṛśe n' ôpadiśyate.
mātulād dhanam ādāya yo jīvati sa|mātṛkaḥ
nanu mātula|mātreṇa klība|sattvaḥ sa jīvyate.›
sthira|sattvaṃ sa buddhvā mām ālāpair evam|ādibhiḥ
āptair akārayad bhṛtyaiś cakṣū|rakṣitam ādṛtaiḥ.
‹palāyamānaṃ kaḥ śakto mriyamāṇaṃ ca rakṣitum?›
iti lokād idaṃ śrutvā palāyana|paro 'bhavam.
18.245 atha sāṃyātrikaṃ kaṃ cid gamiṣyantaṃ mah"|ôdadhim
a|dṛṣṭaḥ kena cid gatvā vinayen' âbhyavādayam.
tasmai ca kathayāmi sma prakṛṣṭān ātmano guṇān
tṛṣṇā|dāsī|vidheyā hi kiṃ na kurvanti pātakam.
‹ahaṃ Campā|niveśasya tanayaḥ Mitravarmaṇaḥ
sarva|ratna|parīkṣ"|ādi|kalā|kula|viśāradaḥ.
yuṣmābhiś ca sa|nāthatvam aham icchāmi sādhubhiḥ
tvādṛg|nātho hy a|natho 'pi mukhyo *nāthavatām* iti.›

their source is unending, like the Himálaya for the Ganga. When one already has a limitless fortune, desire for another is contemptible. What man who knows the Vedas and its ancillaries would study the alphabet?'

Ganga·datta went on giving me advice like this, but I interrupted, saying, 'Uncle, my resolve in this important matter is unswerving, so don't deter me. A young man should 18.240
be made—even forced—by his elders to do his duties, so why would they obstruct him when he is doing them of his own accord? And you said that I should support my family with your money. An able-bodied man like me should not be given advice like that. Surely a man who takes money from his uncle and stays with his mother is emasculated, living off his uncle alone.'

From conversations like this he realized that I was determined, and ordered some trusted and diligent servants to keep an eye on me. But I knew the proverb 'No one can safeguard a man who is running away or dying,' and I became intent on running away. A certain seafaring trader was 18.245
about to set out on the ocean. Unseen by anyone, I went to him and greeted him courteously. I told him that my skills were first-class, for what sin will those in the sway of the demoness desire not commit? 'I am the son of Mitra·varman, resident of Champa, and I am expert in a whole range of skills, including the examination of gemstones. I want to have your good self as my patron, for with a man like you as his patron even an orphan would stand out among those who have *parents : patrons*.'*

sa Mitravarmaṇo nāma śrutv" âiv' ānanda|vihvalaḥ
śraddadhāti sma duḥ|sādhyāṃ mayi sarva|jñatām api.
18.250 avocac ca ‹pur" âbhūma sa|nāthā Mitravarmaṇā
adhunā bhavatā tāta! tataḥ prasthīyatām!› iti.

atha deva|dvi|ja|gurūn arcitvā maṅgal'|ôjjvale
praśaste tithi|nakṣatre bohittham amucad vaṇik.
taraṅga|jala|d'|ālayaṃ Makara|Nakra|cakra|grahaṃ
Pinākadhara|kaṃdhara|prabham an|antam a|prakṣayam
mah"|ârṇava|nabhas|talaṃ lavaṇa|sindhu|nau|chadmanā
viyat|patha|rathena tena vaṇijas tataḥ prasthitāḥ.

kathaṃ vā na vimānaṃ tad yena mānasa|raṃhasā
locan'|ônmeṣa|mātreṇa yojanānāṃ śataṃ gatam.
tato jala|gaj'|êndreṇa jalād unmajjat" āhataḥ
viśīrṇa|bandhanaḥ potaḥ paṭṭaśaḥ sphutati sma saḥ.
18.255 ‹yasya keśeṣu jīmūtā› iti gītām anusmaran
daivāt phalakam ālambya prāpaṃ toya|nidhes taṭam.

kṣaṇaṃ viśramya tatr' âhaṃ ‹hā! kiṃ vṛttam?› iti bruvan
udbhrānt'|ôdbhrānta|dikkatvād bhrāntavān sindhu|rodhasi.
candan'|âgaru|karpūra|lavaṅga|lavalī|vanaiḥ
yatr' ākrāntāḥ saritvantaḥ śail'|ôpāntāḥ samantataḥ.
kadalī|nāri|ker'|ādi|phalina|druma|saṃkaṭāḥ
āraṇyakair araṇyānyo bhajyante yatra kuñjaraiḥ.
śil"|âpihita|pūrv'|ârdhe darī|dvāre tataḥ kva cit
śil"|âpihita|pūrv'|âṅgīm aṅganām asmi dṛṣṭavān.
18.260 tato yathā|pramāṇena nir|nimeṣeṇa cakṣuṣā
ṛjutā|nir|vikāratvān mām asau trastam aikṣata.

As soon as he heard Mitra·varman's name he was overcome with joy and believed me to possess a rare omniscience.
He said, 'In the past, Mitra·varman was our patron, now, 18.250
sir, it's you! Let's go!'

After worshipping the gods, brahmins and elders, the merchant weighed anchor on an astrologically auspicious day with clearly favorable omens. In an oceangoing boat that looked like an aerial chariot, the traders set out for the sea, which, infinite, eternal and as blue as Shiva's throat, its waves like clouds and its wheeling dolphins and crocodiles like the spinning constellations of Mákara and Nakra, could just as well have been the sky!

And why not believe it was an aerial chariot when, with the speed of thought, it crossed one hundred *yójana*s in the blink of an eye? Then a huge whale emerged from the water and struck the boat. Its keel was smashed and it splintered
into pieces. I thought of the song that begins, 'In whose 18.255
hair the clouds...,' and fate had me cling to a plank and reach the shore.*

I rested there for a moment and then wandered about the beach saying, 'Oh! What has happened?' with no idea of where I was going. There were rock-pools everywhere, surrounded by sandal, aloe, camphor, clove and *lávali* groves. The forests were thick with banana, coconut and other fruit trees, and frequented by wild elephants. Then, at the door of a cave whose upper part was obscured by a rock, I saw a woman. The top of her body was hidden behind the rock.
She looked at me with wide-open, unblinking eyes and the 18.260
intensity of her stare frightened me.

āsīc ca mama ‹k" âpy eṣā dānavī devat" âpi vā?
na hi rūpaṃ mayā dṛṣṭaṃ nāryāḥ kasyāś cid īdṛśam!
atha vā kṣudhitā k" âpi devatā|rūpa|kañcukā
mām ih' âikākinaṃ dṛṣṭvā prāptā naktaṃ|car'|âṅganā?
rākṣasyo hy apsaro|rūpā mādṛśeṣu pramādiṣu
randhreṣu praharant' îti yat tan mām idam āgatam.
tasmād asmād ahaṃ deśāt palāye sa|bhayād› iti
prasthitaś cintayitvā ca sā ca mām ity abhāṣata.
18.265 ‹bhoḥ sādho! mā bhavat te bhīr n' âhaṃ naktaṃ|car'|âṅganā
bohittha|vyasana|bhraṣṭāṃ viddhi māṃ mānuṣīm› iti.
atha śrutv" êdam utkṛṣṭāt sādhvasād ūrdhva|mūrdha|jaḥ
trātārau jagato vande Pārvatī|Param'|ēśvarau.
āsīc ca mama ‹divy" êyam iti saṃprati niścitam
nir|nimeṣā yato yac ca para|citta|jña|mānasā.
yady eṣā rākṣasī tasmāt kva gataḥ syāṃ palāyitaḥ?›
niścity' êti parāvṛtya bibhyantīm idam abravam.
‹yadi tvaṃ mānuṣī satyaṃ darī|dvārād itas tataḥ
nirgaty' ātmānam ācakṣva divyā cet pāhi mām!› iti.
18.270 atha hrīt" êva sā kiṃ cin netre saṃmīlya s'|âśruṇī
śil"|ânuṣṭhita|vastr'|ârdhe pūrva|kāye nyapātayat.
tataḥ saṃmīlite dṛṣṭvā tayā netre mam' âbhavat
‹nanu mānuṣa|yoṣ" âiva varāky eṣā nir|ambarā.›
tataḥ parāṅ|mukhī|bhūya sva|śātakam apāṭayam
‹idaṃ vassv' êti› tām uktvā tasyai tasy' ârdham akṣipam.
chādita|chādanīy'|âṅgī bāhu|vastr'|ârdha|mūrdha|jaiḥ
tataḥ sva|jaghana|sphītām adhyaśeta śilām asau.

I said to myself, 'Who is this—a demoness or a goddess? I have never seen such beauty in any mortal woman! Or is it some famished nightwalking ghoul who saw me here alone and came along disguised as a goddess? For demonesses take the form of heavenly damsels to abduct careless people like me into caves. That's what has happened to me here, so I must flee this terrifying place!'

No sooner had I made my mind up and started on my way
than she spoke to me: 'Hello, good sir! Do not be frightened, 18.265
I am not a nightwalking demoness; I am a woman who has been shipwrecked.'

When I heard this, my terror intensified and my hair stood on end. I prayed to the saviors of the world, Párvati and Shiva. I said to myself, 'Now it is certain that she is divine: she does not blink and she can read the minds of others. If she is a demoness, I have no escape.' At this realization, I turned around. She was terrified and I said to her, 'If you really are a woman, then come out of the doorway of the cave and introduce yourself. If you are divine, spare
me!' Then, seeming somewhat embarrassed, she fluttered 18.270
her eyes, which had tears in them, and glanced down at the front of her body, part of which was concealed by the rock. When I saw her close her eyes, I said to myself, 'She is but a poor mortal woman, and she has no clothes!' I averted my face, tore a strip off my robe and threw her half of it, telling her to put it on. With her naked body covered by her arms, the piece of cloth and her hair, she sat her voluptuous behind on a rock. Afraid that she might be someone else's wife, I kept my distance. Looking down, I asked her,

atha n' âti|samīpa|sthaḥ paritrastaḥ para|striyāḥ
‹bhadre kasy' âsi kā v" êti› tām apṛccham avāṅ|mukhaḥ.
18.275 mānuṣī mānuṣaṃ dṛṣṭvā deśe dur|labha|mānuṣe
labdha|bandhur iv' āraṇye viśrabdh" ārabdha bhāṣitum.

‹sādhu|dharm'|ârtha|sarv'|ârthaḥ sārtha|vāho 'sti Sāgaraḥ
Rāja|rāja|gṛh'|ākāra|gṛhe Rājagṛhe pure.
Yāvanī|nāmikā yasya jāyā Yavana|deśa|jā
yā prakṛṣṭe 'pi saubhāgye patiṃ devam iv' ârcati.
tayoḥ Sāgaradinn'|ākhyaḥ putraḥ pitror guṇaiḥ samaḥ
jyeṣṭhaḥ Samudradinnaś ca tat sa|nāmā ca kanyakā.
Campā|bhūṣaṇa|bhūtasya sat|pater Mitravarmaṇaḥ
sutāya Sānudāsāya sā ca pitrā pratiśrutā.
18.280 Sānudāsaś ca rūpeṇa Smareṇa sadṛśaḥ kila
sa|kalaṃ ca kalā|jālaṃ ved' êti jagati śrutiḥ.
atha vā na kalā|jālaṃ jālaṃ veda sa kevalam
ko hi nāma kalā|śālī karma tādṛśam ācaret.
sa hi veśy"|āhṛt'|â|śeṣa|guṇa|draviṇa|saṃcayaḥ
sama|brāhmaṇa|caṇḍālaiś cauraiḥ sārtha|vadhe hataḥ.

tac ca vaiśasam ākarṇya Sānudāsasya duḥ|śravam
Sāgarasya kuṭumbaṃ tat prasthitaṃ Yavanīṃ prati.
yāna|pātra|vipattau ca vipannaṃ lavaṇ'|âmbhasi
medinī|maṇḍala|dhvaṃse jantūnām iva maṇḍalam.
18.285 y" âsau Samudradinn" êti kanyā nindita|lakṣaṇā
na tasyai nir|dayen' âpi sindhunā dattam antaram.
Sāgareṇa ca yā kanyā Sānudāsāya kalpitā

'Good lady, who is your husband and who are you?' Seeing 18.275
a man in a place where humans were rare, it was as though the woman had found a relative in the jungle. Emboldened, she started to talk:

'In the city of Raja·griha, where the houses look like Kubéra's palace, there is a merchant called Ságara, all of whose wealth is used to benefit virtuous men and religion. His wife was born in Greece and is called Yávani. Even though she is very happily married, she worships her husband like a god. Their eldest son is called Ságara·dinna and is as virtuous as his parents. Their second son is called Samúdra·dinna and their daughter has the same name: Samúdra·dinná. She was promised by her father to Sanu·dasa,
the son of the great Mitra·varman, jewel of Champa. Sa- 18.280
nu·dasa was renowned throughout the world for being as beautiful as the god of love and knowing all the arts. But in fact he did not know the arts, only deception. For what cultured man would do what he did? His virtues and wealth were taken by a prostitute and he was killed when his caravan was ambushed by thieves to whom brahmins and outcastes are the same.

When they heard about Sanu·dasa's terrible demise, Ságara's household set out for Greece. The boat sank and everyone perished in the ocean, just as all the creatures of
the earth perish at the end of the world. The ill-fated girl 18.285
Samúdra·dinná, however, was not taken in by the cruel sea. The luckless girl destined by Ságara for Sanu·dasa and rejected by the sea is none other than me!* Keeping myself occupied by thinking about what to do, where to go, what has happened and what is happening, I stay here, happy

sāgareṇa nirastā ca manda|bhāgy" âham eva sā.
«kiṃ kartavyaṃ kva gantavyaṃ
kiṃ vṛttaṃ kiṃ nu vartate?»
iti cintā|vinod" âham
ih' āse priya|jīvitā.
śuktīnāṃ taṭa|bhinnānāṃ māṃsair dāv'|âgni|sādhitaiḥ
prajñātaiḥ phala|mūlaiś ca puṣṇāmi vi|phalāṃ tanum.
lubdhatvāc ca vaṇig|jāter āhṛty' āhṛtya saikatāt
mauktikasya guhā|koṇe rāśiḥ prāṃśur mayā kṛtaḥ.
18.290 mama tāvad iyaṃ vārttā tvadīy" ākhyāyatām!› iti
iti pṛṣṭasya me cittam iti cittam abhūt tayā.
«Sānudāso 'ham ev' êti» yady asyai kathayāmy aham
anyad eva kim apy eṣā mayi saṃbhāvayiṣyati.
saṃbhāvayatu nām' êyam! ahaṃ punar imāṃ katham
vipan|magnām upekṣeyaṃ puruṣaḥ san striyam satīm?
api c' êdaṃ smarāmy eva tāta|pādair yathā vṛtā
pitrā c' êyaṃ pratijñātā tena vyarthā vicāraṇā.›
ath' êtthaṃ kathayāmi sma ‹Campāyām abhavad vaṇik
Mitravarm" êti yaḥ sva|stho yaśas" âdy' âpi tiṣṭhati.
18.295 yasya Mitravatī jāyā Sānudāsaḥ sutas tayoḥ
sa tābhyām eka|putratvāj jñāpitaḥ sakalāḥ kalāḥ.
asau c' âlīka|pāṇḍityād loka|vṛtta|parāṅ|mukhaḥ
suhṛdbhir dhūrta|citta|jñair dāsyā saṃgamitaḥ saha.
Sānudāsaḥ sa ev' âhaṃ sarva|svaṃ me tayā hṛtam
s" âtha m" ân|arthakaṃ jñātvā nirvāsayitum aihata.›
ath' âsminn antare sā māṃ bhāṣamāṇam abhāṣata
‹kiṃ cit pṛcchāmi yat tan me yūyam ākhyātum arhatha.
snāna|śāṭakam ānīya sthūlaṃ taila|malīmasam
prāsād'|âgre yad uktāḥ stha dāsyā tat kathyatām› iti.

with my life. I nourish my useless body with meat from oysters broken on the shore that I cook on forest fires, and fruits and roots that I recognize. With the greediness of one born to a trader, I have collected pearls from the beach and made a large pile of them in the corner of the cave. So that 18.290
is my story; tell me yours!'

When she asked me this, I thought, 'If I tell her that I am Sanu·dasa she will presume that there is more to come from me. But let her presume! For how can I, as a man, disregard this virtuous woman who has been plunged into misfortune? Moreover, I can clearly recall how my revered father chose her and she was promised by her father in return, so deliberation is pointless.'

I told her the following: 'There was a merchant in Champa called Mitra·varman, who, through his fame, lives on even today. His wife was Mítravati and their son was Sanu· 18.295
dasa. Because he was their only son, they taught him all the arts. His puffed-up scholarship made him turn away from the ways of the world, and his friends, expert tricksters, paired him off with a courtesan.

I am that Sanu·dasa. The girl took all my property, and then, when she ascertained that I had no money left, she did her best to throw me out.'

At that point she interrupted me: 'I have one small question. Please answer it for me. Tell me what the servant girl said to you when, on the top floor of the mansion, she brought the rough, oil-stained towel.'

18.300 mayā t' ûktaṃ ‹tay" ôkto 'haṃ «dārikāyā muhūrtakam
abhy|aṅgaḥ kriyate tasmād bhavān avataratv» iti.›
s" âth' âpṛcchat ‹pure ṣaṣṭhe ratna|saṃskāra|kārakaiḥ
kim uktāḥ śilpibhir yūyam› iti pratyabruvaṃ tataḥ.
‹tair ukto 'haṃ «pravīṇo 'si tvatto lajjāmahe vayam
tasmād asmāt purāt ṣaṣṭhat pañcamaṃ gamyatām» iti.›

ity|ādi yat tayā pṛṣṭaṃ vṛttaṃ vṛttaṃ may" â|khilam
sārtha|dhvaṃs'|âvasān'|ântaṃ pratyuktaṃ sakalaṃ mayā.
atha kūrm'|âṅgan" êv' âṅgair aṅge līn" âpi lajjayā
māṃ āliṅgad apāṅgena s" ân|aṅg'|âbhy|aṅga|cāruṇā.
18.305 tatas tāṃ pṛṣṭavān asmi ‹bhīru kiṃ kriyatām?› iti
s" âtha prasārayat svinnaṃ sphurantaṃ dakṣiṇaṃ karam.
gambhīraṃ dhvanati tataḥ samudra|tūrye
gāyatsu śruti|madhuraṃ śilī|mukheṣu
nṛtyatsu sphuṭa|raṭiteṣu nīla|kaṇṭheṣv
ālambe karam ibha|tālu|tāmram asyāḥ.

tatas tat tādṛśaṃ duḥkhaṃ pota|bhaṅg'|ādi|hetukam
sarvam eka|pade naṣṭaṃ sādhāv apakṛtaṃ yathā.
pāṣaṇḍino gṛha|sthāṃś ca mokṣa|svarg'|âbhikāṅkṣiṇaḥ
cintitāṃs tān hasāmi sma pratyutpanna|mahā|sukhaḥ.
mīna|kūrma|kulīr'|ādi|vṛṣya|vāri|car'|āmiṣaiḥ
nārikel'|ādibhiś c' âṅgam apuṣāv' ôpabṛṃhibhiḥ.
18.310 pulinaiḥ sindhu|rājasya muktā|vidruma|saṃkaṭaiḥ
rāja|haṃsāv iv' ôtkaṇṭhau prītau samacarāvahi.
kadā cit kuñja|śikharair a|calānāṃ sa|nirjharaiḥ
sa|phala|druma|saṃnāhaiḥ kareṇu|kalabhāv iva.

I replied, 'She told me that I should go downstairs because 18.300
she was going to massage her mistress for a while.' She then asked me what the craftsmen on the sixth floor who were making jewelry had said to me, to which I replied that they had told me that because I was such an expert they were embarrassed in front of me and could I please go from the sixth floor to the fifth.

She questioned me like this about everything that had happened, and I told her the whole story up to its dénouement in the destruction of the caravan. Then, even though she was embarrassed and had drawn her limbs close to her body like a tortoise, she embraced me with a side glance from her beautiful love-drenched eye.

I asked her, 'Sweet lady, what is to be done?' and she ex- 18.305
tended her moist and trembling right hand. With the drumbeat of the ocean resounding deeply, the bees singing their sweet song, and the peacocks dancing and calling loudly, I held her hand, which was as pink as an elephant's palate.

All the distress brought about by the shipwreck was destroyed in an instant, like a sin in a virtuous man. When I thought of sectarians and householders who strive after liberation and heaven, I laughed at them, and a great happiness arose in me. We lived off the stimulating flesh of aquatic creatures like fish, turtles and crabs, as well as coconuts and
other invigorating fruits. Like a couple of amorous swans we 18.310
joyfully roamed about the beaches, which were covered in pearls and coral. Sometimes we were like a pair of young elephants, wandering about the lush mountaintops with their waterfalls and mantles of fruit trees. Aphrodisiacs such as cloves, areca, camphor and betel were in abundance and

lavaṅga|pūga|karpūra|tāmbūl'|ādyair a|dur|labhaiḥ
nityam aṅgam an|aṅg'|âṅgaiḥ samaskurva sa|candanaiḥ.
guhā|latā|gṛh'|āvāsau vasita|druma|valkalau
devam ātma|bhuvaṃ dhyāntau jātau svaḥ kāma|yoginau.
tato Samudradinnā mām ity avocat kadā cana
‹bhinna|pota|vaṇig|vṛttam arya|putra samācara.
18.315 divā prāṃśos taror agre prāṃśur ucchrīyatāṃ dhvajaḥ
jvalano jvālyatāṃ rātrau tuṅge sāgara|rodhasi.
kadā cin nāvikaḥ kaś cid āloky' âvāntaraṃ dvayoḥ
sva|deśam ānayed āvāṃ dharmo 'yaṃ vaṇijām› iti.
‹yuktam āh' êti› nirdhārya tath" âiva kṛtavān aham
āptānām upadeśo hi pramāṇaṃ yoṣitām api.
tatas tuṅgeṣu raṃhantī bhaṅga|śṛṅgeṣu bhaṅgiṣu
madgu|paṅktir iv' âgacchad upanauk" âruṇ'|ôdaye.
tāṃ dvi|niryāmak'|ārūḍhām ārūḍhaḥ paṭu|raṃhasam
prāg|vātālīm iv' âmbhodaḥ prātiṣṭhaṃ dūram antaram.
18.320 paśyāmi sma tataḥ sindhau bohitthaṃ sthiram a|sthire
kātarāṇām iva vrāte sthira|sattvam avasthitam.
tatra vāṇijam adrākṣaṃ mahā|draviṇa|bhājanam
Kailāsa iva śubhr'|âgraṃ Mahāpadma|mahā|nidhim.
abhivādayamānaṃ ca māṃ dṛṣṭvā tena sa|spṛham
bāṣpavad|dṛṣṭi|kaṇṭhena bhāṣitaṃ praskhalad|girā.
‹«kiṃ jātiḥ? kasya putro 'si? kiṃ vā māt" êti» sarvathā
kiṃ tvayā tāta pṛṣṭena Mitravarma|suto bhavān!
kathaṃ punar amuṃ deśam āgato 's' îti› pṛcchate
vistareṇa mayā tasmai sarva|pūrvaṃ niveditam.

every day we adorned our bodies with a mixture of them and sandalwood paste. Living in caves and creeper bowers, wearing bark and meditating on the self-born god, we became yogins of love.*

Then one day Samúdra·dinná said to me, 'Darling, you must do what shipwrecked merchants always do. During 18.315
the day, fly a big flag from the top of a tall tree, and at night light a fire on the highest part of the beach. One of these days a sailor might see one or the other of the two and take us to his country. That is what merchants do.'

I decided that she was right and did exactly that—the advice of reputable people is authoritative, even if they are women. At dawn a ketch appeared, surfing the crashing crests of the tall waves like a raft of cormorants. It was a swift craft, manned by a crew of two, and after I climbed aboard I journeyed far, as if I were a cloud in an easterly gale.

Then I noticed a boat hove to on the rolling sea, like 18.320
a brave man in a crowd of cowards. I saw a merchant on board, a repository of great riches like the gleaming peak on mount Kailása where the Great Lotus treasure is found. He looked at me intently as I greeted him. His eyes and throat filled with tears and he said in a faltering voice, 'There is absolutely no need to ask after your caste or your parents, sir: you are Mitra·varman's son! But how did you come to be in this country?' When he asked me this, I gave him a detailed account of everything that had happened.

18.325 ten' ôktam ‹asi dīrgh'|āyur jāmātā tanayaś ca me
ātmā Sāgaradattaś ca Mitravarmā ca me yataḥ!
gaccha Sāgaradattasya tanayāṃ tac ca mauktikam
bahu|nāvikayā nāvā taṭād ānīyatām iha.
anyac c' â|siddha|yātro 'haṃ kiṃ ca potaṃ na paśyasi
avagraha|hṛt'|âmbhaskaṃ taḍāgam iva riktakam?
mam' êdaṃ vahanaṃ riktaṃ voḍhavyaṃ sāravat tava
naṣṭ'|âśva|dagdha|rathavad yogaḥ ślāghyo 'yam āvayoḥ!
mūlyaṃ tasya ca yat tan nau sama|bhāgaṃ bhaviṣyati
pūrvaṃ saṃmantrit'|ârghas tvaṃ dharmo 'yaṃ vaṇijām› iti.
18.330 tac ca mauktikam ānīya potas tena prapūritaḥ
Samudradinnayā pādau vāṇijasya ca vanditau.
tasyai daśa|sahasrāṇi vastrāṇy ābharaṇāni ca
tena dattāni vadatā ‹vadhūs tvaṃ me sut" êti› ca.
kṛtaṃ c' âti|prasaṅgena! saṃkṣepaḥ śrūyatām ayam
preritaṃ yāna|pātraṃ ca tad vipannaṃ ca pūrvavat.
jīvite 'pi nir|āśena yāna|pātre nimajjati
nigṛhītāḥ śikhā|madhye muktāḥ katipayā mayā.
tāś ca vijñāpayāmi sma ‹parasmin mama janmani
bhagavatyaḥ sadā bhaktam upatiṣṭhata mām!› iti.
18.335 evaṃ|prāye ca vṛtt'|ânte taraṃg'|ântara|tāraṇī
paṭṭa|śliṣṭā mayā dṛṣṭā saṃnikṛṣṭ" āgatā priyā.
mām upāhūyamān" âiva sā prasārita|pāṇikā
capalena taraṃgeṇa balād apahṛt" â|balā.
tasmai kruddhas taraṃgāya mahā|moham ahaṃ gataḥ
cetaye yāvad ātmānaṃ loṭantam udadhes taṭe.
kāntām uktvā ‹vimuktā tvam!› priyā|viśleṣa|viklavaḥ
prakrāman vilapāmi sma nir|jane nir|avagrahaḥ.

He replied, 'May you live long: you are my son-in-law 18.325
and my son, for Ságara·datta and Mitra·varman were both
like my own self to me! Take a boat with a company of sailors
and fetch Ságara·datta's daughter and the pearls from the
shore. One more thing: my journey has been unsuccessful—
do you not see how the boat is empty, like a pond that has
dried up in a drought? I have this empty vessel and you have
a valuable cargo. Our meeting is to be celebrated, like that
of a man who has lost his horses with one whose chariot has
been reduced to ashes! We shall split the profit equally after
you have agreed on a price. That is what merchants do.'

The pearls were fetched and they filled the boat. Samúd- 18.330
ra·dinná greeted the merchant by touching his feet. He gave
her a fantastic quantity of clothes and ornaments, saying,
'You are my daughter-in-law and my daughter!'

To cut a long story short, the boat set sail and sank like
the last one. Even though I had no hope of survival, while
the boat was sinking I put some pearls in my topknot. I
begged them, 'O blessed ones, in my next life return to me,
your eternal devotee!'

As this was happening, I noticed my sweetheart draw 18.335
near, floating between two waves while clinging to a plank.
At the very moment that she called for me, holding out her
hand, a sudden wave snatched the poor girl away. Furious
with the wave, I fell into a deep faint. When I came to, I
found myself rolling about on a beach. I said to my beloved,
'You are free!' and as I wandered about the desolate spot,
distraught at being separated from my sweetheart, I wailed,
'Homage to thee, blessed oblivion, bestower of the bliss of
liberation! Shame on thoughtless consciousness: it has no

‹namas te Bhagavan moha nirvāṇa|prīti|dāyine!
kāl'|â|kāla|vidā|śūnyāṃ cetanāṃ dhig a|cetanām!
18.340 mauktikaṃ gṛhyatāṃ nāma tat te svaṃ svaṃ mah"|ôdadhe
sādho sādhvī vipad|bandhuḥ priyā me mucyatām!› iti.
yāś ca tāḥ śirasi nyastā muktāḥ pote nimajjati
siraḥ kaṇḍūyamānena tāḥ spṛṣṭāḥ pāṇinā mayā.
tāḥ parīkṣitavān asmi tan|mātra|draviṇas tadā
tat kiṃ parīkṣitaṃ tāsāṃ yā na dṛṣṭāḥ parīkṣakaiḥ?

sa śokas tāsu dṛṣṭāsu yat satyam abhavat tanuḥ
yad etad draviṇaṃ nāma prāṇā hy ete bahiś|carāḥ.
śāṭak'|ânte ca tā baddhvā dṛḍhayā granthi|mālayā
velā|kūlena yāmi sma dhīra|dhīr draviṇ'|ôṣmaṇā.
18.345 kadalī|phala|cikkhalla|praskhalac|caraṇaḥ kva cit
nārikela|jal'|ôcchinna|pipāsā|vedanaḥ kva cit.
elā|marica|tāmbūla|vallī|vellita|pallavaiḥ
panasa|kramuk'|ārāmair nīta|dṛk phala|bandhuraiḥ.
golāṅgūl'|ādi|vikrānta|viśīrṇa|kusumeṣu ca
kva cic campaka|ṣaṇḍeṣu gamayan gamana|śramam.
din'|ânte kapiś'|âṅge ca divas'|ânta|divā|kare
dhāvad|dhenu|dhan'|ôddhūta|dhūlīkaṃ grāmam āsadam.

tatas tatra vasaty|arthaṃ yaṃ yaṃ yāce sma kaṃ|cana
‹dhanninuṃ collit!› iti ca bravīti sma hasan sa saḥ.
18.350 ath' âikena dvi|bhāṣeṇa gṛhaṃ nītvā kuṭumbinā
jāmāt" êva cirāt prāptaḥ priyaḥ prīty" âsmi sat|kṛtaḥ.
taṃ ca sva|śayan'|āsannam apṛcchaṃ rajanī|mukhe
‹deśo 'yaṃ katamaḥ sādho katamad v" âtra pattanam.›

sense of timing! O kind ocean, please take these pearls— 18.340
they belong to you—but give up my sweetheart, my faithful companion in misfortune!' While scratching my head, my hand touched the pearls that I had stashed there when the boat was sinking. They were all the wealth I had and I examined them. But what was the point of examining them when they had not been seen by expert valuers?

When I looked at them, my sorrow did in fact subside, for what is wealth but an external manifestation of the breath of life? I tied them in the hem of my robe in a series of tight knots and walked along the beach emboldened by the
glow of wealth. In some places I lost my footing in a mire 18.345
of rotting bananas; in others I quenched my thirst with coconut water. My gaze was drawn to the groves of breadfruit and areca trees, bending under the weight of their fruit, their branches entwined with cardamom, pepper and betel creepers. Elsewhere, in groves of *chámpaka* trees strewn with flowers scattered by bounding cow-tailed monkeys and other animals, I rid myself of the fatigue of walking. At the end of the day, in the red evening sunlight, I reached a village where the dust had been disturbed by droves of dashing cows.

Everyone I asked there for somewhere to stay would
laughingly say, '*Dhánninum chollit!*' Then a bilingual house- 18.350
holder took me into his house, and I was welcomed with affection, like a beloved son-in-law returning after a long time. In the evening when he was sitting on his bed I asked him about the country and the village we were in. He replied, 'This is the country of the Pandyas, on the southern seaboard, where seeing a beggar would be as amazing

ten' ôktaṃ ‹Pāṇḍya|deśo 'yam anu|dakṣiṇa|sāgaram
Mahāpadma|nidhi|prāpti|ramyaṃ yatr' ârthi|darśanam!
itaś ca Pāṇḍya|Mathurā grāmān mṛduni yojane
viśramya rajanīm atra prāto gant" âsi tām› iti.
suptena priyayā sārdham a|supten' ârtha|cintayā
saṃkṣiptā ca nirastā ca yāpitā yāminī mayā.
18.355 prātaḥ krośa|dvay'|âtītaḥ kadalī|ṣaṇḍa|saṃvṛtam
pāntha|saṃhāta|saṃbādham apaśyaṃ sattra|maṇḍapam.
paśyāmi sma ca vaideśān kriyamāṇa|kṣura|kriyān
abhy|aṅg'|ôcchādan'|ācchāda|bhojan'|ādyaiś ca sat|kṛtān.
kṛta|kṣaur'|ādi|karmā tu labdha|vastr'|ôttam'|āśanaḥ
pṛṣṭo 'smi sattra|patinā śayyā|sthaḥ śarvarī|mukhe.
‹kva cit kaś cit tvayā dṛṣṭaḥ prājño vāṇija|dārakaḥ
Sānudāsa iti prāṃśuḥ śyāmas tāmr'|ânta|locanaḥ?›
tatas taṃ pṛṣṭavān asmi ‹Sānudāsena kiṃ tava
kasya vā Sānudāso 'sāv› iti ten' ôditaṃ tataḥ,
18.360 ‹Gaṅgadatt'|âbhidhānasya Tāmraliptī|vibhūṣaṇaḥ
guṇavān bhāgineyo 'sau gataḥ potena sāgaram.
sa ca potaḥ kil' âmbhodhau prabhañjana|parāhataḥ
praviśīrṇaḥ payaḥ|pūrṇaḥ payodhara iv' âmbare.
vārttā c' êyaṃ prasarpantī mūrch'|âtiśaya|dāyinī
krūr'|āśī|viṣa|yoṣ" êva Gaṅgadattam amūrchayat.
ten' âpi sarva|deśeṣu kāntāreṣu tareṣu ca
pravartitāni sattrāṇi velā|taṭa|pureṣu ca.
kadā cit Sānudāsasya pot'|âpetasya jīvataḥ
pānthaḥ kaś cit kva cit sattre pravṛttiṃ kathayed iti.
18.365 tat te yadi sa dīrgh'|āyur āyuṣmat darśanaṃ gataḥ
ācakṣva nas tato dīnā janatā jīvyatām› iti.

as obtaining the Great Lotus treasure! The Máthura of the Pandyas is only a short distance from this village. Stay the night here and you can go there in the morning.' The night passed quickly for me when I was asleep and in the company of my sweetheart, but dragged on when I was awake and worrying about money.

In the morning, after I had gone about four miles, I saw 18.355
in the middle of a banana grove a rest house crowded with travelers. I saw foreigners being shaved and treated to oil massages, clothes, food and so forth. When I had washed and shaved, I was given a robe and food. As I lay on my bed in the evening, the keeper of the rest house asked me, 'Have you seen anywhere a clever young merchant called Sanu·dasa, who is tall and dark and has eyes that are red around the edges?'

I asked him, 'What do you want with this Sanu·dasa? Whose son is Sanu·dasa?' to which he replied,

'He is a good man, the nephew of someone called Gan- 18.360
ga·datta and the jewel of Tamra·lipti. He went to sea in a boat and apparently the boat capsized in a storm and broke into pieces, like a cloud full of water bursting into the sky. Winding its way like a cruel venomous vipress, this heart-stopping news stunned Ganga·datta. He has set up rest houses in every country, on forest roads, at river crossings and in coastal towns, in the hope that some traveler in one of the rest houses might bring news that Sanu·da-
sa escaped the ship and is alive. So, sir, if you have seen 18.365
that worthy gentleman, tell us and bring relief to his poor family.'

mama tv āsīt ‹pratijñāyāḥ kiyat saṃpāditaṃ mayā
asmai yad aham ātmānam ācakṣe 'pahata|trapaḥ?
tasmād iti bravīm' îti› viniścity' êdam abravam
‹Sānudāsaḥ punaḥ potam āruhya gatavān› iti.

prātaś ca Pāṇḍya|Mathurām āścarya|śata|śālinīm
prāyaṃ pūrita|sarv'|êcchāṃ cintā|maṇi|śilām iva.
tasyām adhyāsi bhinn'|ābha|ratna|pañjara|saṃkulam
Agastya|pīta|pānīya|sāgar'|ākāram āpaṇam!

18.370 tatr' âlaṃ|kāram ādāya dvāv upāgamatāṃ narau
tasya c' âikataraḥ kretā vikret" ânyataras tayoḥ.
tau taṃ vāṇijam abrūtāṃ ‹ratna|tattva|vidā tvayā
ucitaṃ bhūṣaṇasy' âsya mūlyam ākhyāyatām› iti.
ten' âpi tac ciraṃ dṛṣṭvā ‹na jānām' îti› bhāṣite

tau māṃ niś|calayā dṛṣṭyā dṛṣṭavantam apṛcchatām.
‹niś|cala|snigdhayā dṛṣṭyā suṣṭhu dṛṣṭam idaṃ tvayā
manyāvahe vijānāti mūlyam asya bhavān› iti.

an|āsth"|ôttāna|hastena tataḥ smitvā may" ôditam
‹n' âiv' êdam ati|dur|jñānaṃ kiṃ mudh" êv' ākulau yuvām?
18.375 koṭir asya samaṃ mūlyaṃ ratna|tattva|vido viduḥ
tasmād adhikam ūnaṃ vā kretṛ|vikrāyak'|êcchayā.›

atha vikrāyakas toṣān mukt'|âśrur mām avocata
‹yad' îdaṃ mūlyam etasya dhanaṃ dhanyās tato vayam!
«api bhūṣaṇam etan me koṭi|mūlyaṃ bhaved» iti
sad" âiva me manasy āsīd ayam eva mano|rathaḥ!›

I said to myself, 'I have amassed too little of the amount that I promised for me to introduce myself to him without embarrassment. Very well, this is what I shall say...' After deciding thus, I said the following: 'Sanu·dasa has again gone off by boat.'

In the morning, I reached the Máthura of the Pandyas, which abounds in hundreds of marvels and, like the philosopher's stone, can fulfill all wishes. I sat down there in a shop full of cabinets containing gems of various hues; it looked like the ocean after Agástya had drunk all the water!

Two men approached with a piece of jewelry. One of 18.370
them was the buyer, the other the seller. They said to the merchant, 'You are an expert on gemstones: tell us the right price for this piece of jewelry.' He looked at it for a long time before saying, 'I do not know.'

I had been staring at it and they inquired of me, 'You have been staring at it with a fixed and interested gaze: we think you know its worth.'

Nonchalantly turning up my palms, I smiled and said, 'This is really not very difficult to work out. Why are you
needlessly troubling yourselves? Those who know about 18.375
gems know that ten million is a fair price for this, give or take a little depending on the wishes of the buyer and seller.'

The seller was so happy he was crying and said to me, 'If it is worth that much then I am rich! I had always wished my jewel might be worth ten million—my wish has come true!'

athʼ êti krāyakeṇʼ ôktaṃ ‹mamʼ âpy āsīn mano|rathaḥ
«api nāma labheyʼ âham idaṃ koṭy" êti» cetasi.›
tatas tāv astuvātāṃ māṃ ‹namas te Viśvakarmaṇe!
ko hi mānuṣa|dur|bodham idaṃ budhyate mānuṣaḥ.
18.380 kraya|vikraya|kāmābhyām āvābhyāṃ bahuśaḥ purī
dravyasyʼ âsya parīkṣʼ|ârthaṃ parikrāntā samantataḥ.
«pṛthivī mūlyam asyʼ êti» kaś cid āha parīkṣakaḥ
ajānan «kākin" îty» anyo «na kiṃ cid» iti cʼ â|paraḥ.
tvat|kṛtena tu mūlyena janitaṃ nau mahat sukham
etad ekʼ|ârthayor āsīd abhīṣṭam ubhayor api.›
ity|ādi tau praśastāya prādiṣātāṃ sa|saṃmadau
ayutaṃ me suvarṇānāṃ sa|sārʼ|ābharaṇʼ|âmbaram.
atha vārttām imāṃ śrutvā nṛ|peṇʼ āhūya sādaram
parīkṣito ʼsmi ratnāni varjitāni parīkṣakaiḥ.
18.385 bahu|bhṛtyaṃ bahu|dhanaṃ bahu|vṛttʼ|ânta|niṣkuṭam
viśālaṃ bahu|śālaṃ ca prītaḥ prādāt sa me gṛham.
ataḥ param ahaṃ tasyām āsaṃ puri parīkṣakaḥ
dharmeṇʼ âiva ca māṃ kaś cin na parīkṣām akārayat.
evaṃ ca vasatas tatra mamʼ êyam abhavan matiḥ
‹kena nāmʼ âlpa|mūlyena mahā|lābho bhaved?› iti.
upalabhya tato lokāt ‹karpāso guṇavān› iti
tasya Kailāsa|kūṭʼ|ābhān sapta kūṭān akārayam.
dhik karpāsa|kathāṃ tucchāṃ! sarvathā mūṣakeṇa te
pradīpa|śikhayā kūṭā gamitā bhasma|kūṭatām.
18.390 Mathurāyāṃ ca maryādā ‹gṛhaṃ yasya pradīpyate

Then the buyer said, 'I too, had hoped that I might get it for ten million.'

The two of them praised me: 'Homage to thee: you must be Vishva·karman, for this is beyond the scope of human intelligence—no mortal man could know it!* In our desire 18.380
to make this transaction, we have traveled around the city several times trying to have this thing valued. One valuer said it would cost the earth, another, not recognizing it, said it was worth a penny, while another said it was worth nothing at all. The value fixed by you has made us both very happy. It was what we both wanted.' They were both overjoyed and after singing my praises some more they gave me ten thousand gold coins and some expensive ornaments and clothes.

When the king heard what had happened, he politely summoned me and had me value some gemstones that had confounded his valuers. Satisfied, he gave me a huge house 18.385
with lots of rooms, lots of servants, expensive contents and extensive pleasure gardens. I became established in the city as a valuer, and nobody had me carry out any valuations for charity!

While I was living there in this fashion, I wondered how I might make a big profit for a small outlay. I discovered that people were saying that cotton was a good investment and I amassed seven mounds of it, like the peaks of Mount Kailása. . . But curse this stupid cotton story! With the flame of his lamp, a thief turned those mounds into nothing but mounds of ash. The custom in Máthura is that if some- 18.390
one's house is on fire, he and his household are thrown into

prakṣipyate sa tatr' âiva sa|kuṭumbaḥ raṭann› iti.
atha hasta|dvitīyo 'ham! ‹iyaṃ dig!› iti saṃbhraman
udīcīṃ diśam uddiśya kāndiśīkaḥ palāyitaḥ.

dhāvitvā ca tri|yām'|ârdham ahar|ardhaṃ ca raṃhasā
dur|gād utkramya supto 'haṃ vaṭa|mule mahā|śramaḥ.
ath' âṃśumati śīt'|âṃśau praśānta|prabala|śramaḥ
janatā|dhvanim aśrauṣam abhito vaṭam utkaṭam.

āsīc ca mama ‹hā kaṣṭaṃ! hanta naṣṭo 'smi saṃprati
jvalati jvalane kṣipto nirghṛṇair draviḍair› iti.

18.395 atha kanthā|jarac|chattra|pāduk"|ādi|paricchadān
adrākṣaṃ pathik'|ākalpāñ jalpataḥ Gauḍa|bhāṣayā.
‹hā māto jīvito 'sm' îti› tān āloky' âśvasaṃ tataḥ
rakṣo|mukto hi n' āśvasyāt ko vā dṛṣṭvā narān naraḥ?
āstīrṇa|parṇa|śayyās te tato nyasta|paricchadāḥ
parito mām upāsīnāḥ samapṛcchanta viśramāḥ.
‹āgacchati kuto deśān nagarād vā bhavān?› iti
may" âpi kathitaṃ tebhyaḥ ‹Pāṇḍya|deśa|purād› iti.

atha taiḥ sa|spṛhaiḥ pṛṣṭaṃ ‹Mathurāyāṃ tvayā yadi
Sānudāso vaṇig dṛṣṭas tato naḥ kathyatām› iti.
18.400 may" ôktaṃ ‹Sānudās'|ākhyo vaṇik tatra na vidyate
bhavantaḥ katamat tatra pṛcchant' îty ucyatām› iti.

it, screaming. So now I had nothing but my hands! Confused and unsure where to go, I fled northward, thinking, 'This way!'

After running as fast as I could for half a night and half a day until I was out of danger, I fell asleep, exhausted, at the foot of a banyan tree. When the sun's rays were cool and I had recovered from my exhaustion, I heard people talking loudly near the banyan tree.

I said to myself, 'Oh dear! What a pity! I am done for now. Merciless southerners are going to throw me into a blazing fire.'

Then I saw that they looked like travelers: they had ragged 18.395
clothes, well-worn umbrellas, sandals and so forth, they carried traveling paraphernalia, and they were talking in the language of the country of Gauda. On seeing them I thought, 'Oh mother, I am saved!' and breathed a sigh of relief, for what man would not breathe a sigh of relief on seeing men after escaping from demons? They spread out leaves for their beds and put down their traveling paraphernalia. They sat around me and, once comfortable, they asked, 'What country or city have you come from, sir?' I told them I had come from the capital of the country of the Pandyas.

They became interested and said, 'If you saw Sanu·dasa the merchant in Máthura, please tell us.'

I replied, 'There is no merchant called Sanu·dasa there. 18.400
Please tell me why you are asking about him.'

tatas te kathayanti sma, ‹Tāmraliptyāṃ vaṇik|patiḥ
Gaṅgadatto guṇān yasya na na veda bhavān api.
ye guṇān na vidus tasya sa|dvīpāt prāṅ|mah"|ôdadheḥ
vyāpinyā kīrtitān kīrtyā na jātās te 'tha vā mṛtāḥ.
svasrīyaḥ Sānudāso 'sya pota|bhaṅgāt kila cyutaḥ
adhyāste Pāṇḍya|Mathurāṃ kṛta|karpāsa|saṃgrahaḥ.

Gaṅgadattas tu pānthebhyaḥ pravṛttim upalabhya tām
āhūy' āha sma suhṛdaḥ prītāṃś ca paricārakān.
18.405 «ye me śoṇitam āyānti gṛhītvā dakṣiṇā|pathāt
tān ahaṃ suhṛdaḥ sphītais toṣayāmi dhanair» iti.
tad vayaṃ Gaṅgadattena tam ānetuṃ visarjitāḥ
yadi c' âsau tvayā dṛṣṭas tad ācaṣṭāṃ bhavān› iti.

mama tv āsīd ‹varaṃ kṣiptas tatr' âiv' âhaṃ vibhāvasau
na tv a|pūrṇa|pratijñena mātur ānanam īkṣitum.›
ath' êtthaṃ kathayāmi sma ‹Sānudāsas tapasvikaḥ
karpāse jvalati kṣiptaḥ Pāṇḍyair niṣ|karuṇair› iti.

tatas tāḍita|vakṣaskās tāram āraṭya te ciram
iti saṃmantrayante sma viṣāda|kṣāma|vācakāḥ.
18.410 ‹Gaṅgadatt'|ârthitā yūyaṃ Sānudās'|ârtham āgatāḥ
tasmai tan|mṛtyu|vṛtt'|ântaṃ kathaṃ śakṣyatha śaṃsitum?
vārttāṃ c' êmām upaśrutya Vaivasvata|has'|â|śivām
Campāyāṃ Tāmraliptyāṃ ca jīvitavyaṃ na kena cit.
tad ātmānaṃ parityajya svāmino bhavat' ân|ṛṇāḥ
Gaṅgadatto 'pi tad|vārttām anyato labhatām› iti.

te kāṣṭha|skandham ādīpya praveṣṭu|manasas tataḥ
stuvanto devatāḥ svāḥ svāḥ paryakrāman pradakṣiṇam.

They replied, 'The chief merchant in Tamra·lipti is Ganga·datta, of whose virtues even you must be aware. Those who do not know of his virtues—their renown reaches across the continent to the eastern ocean—are either not yet born or already dead. His nephew Sanu·dasa survived a shipwreck and has settled in the Máthura of the Pandyas, where he has built up a stock of cotton.

When Ganga·datta heard about this from some travelers, he summoned his friends and favored servants and said, "I 18.405
shall reward with great riches the friends that bring my relative back from the south." So Ganga·datta sent us out to bring him back. If you have seen him, sir, please tell us.'

I thought to myself that I would have preferred to have been thrown into the fire than to have to see my mother's face before fulfilling my promise, so I said, 'Poor Sanu·dasa: his cotton caught fire and he was thrown into it by the merciless Pandyas.'

At this they beat their chests and lamented long and loud. Then, their voices choked with despair, they said to one another, 'At Ganga·datta's request we came to find Sa- 18.410
nu·dasa; how can we bring him tidings of his death? This news is as ill-omened as a laugh from the god of death; when they hear it, nobody in Champa or Tamra·lipti will want to live. Therefore we must kill ourselves and be free of our debt to our master. Let Ganga·datta learn the news from someone else.'

They lit a pile of wood and, intent on entering it, they ceremoniously circumambulated it, each singing praises to his own god.

mama tv āsīd ‹aho kaṣṭaṃ! baddho 'haṃ nara|śambaraḥ
s'|ôtsāhair api dur|laṅghyaṃ jālaṃ jālmaiḥ prasāritam!›
18.415 ath' ôccair āraṭāmi sma ‹bhoḥ! bhoḥ! tyajata sāhasam!
Sānudāsaḥ sa ev' âhaṃ vidheyo bhavatām› iti.
viṣādena tatas teṣām asavo niryiyāsavaḥ
asmat|saṃprāpti|harṣeṇa jātāḥ kaṇṭh'|ôpakaṇṭha|gāḥ.
śeṣatvād āyuṣas te 'pi vinivṛtta|priy'|âsavaḥ
harṣ'|ārdrāḥ samakūrdanta tāla|kṣobhita|kānanāḥ.
te stuvantas tato hṛṣṭāḥ Sugataṃ Saugatā iva
bahu|kṛtvaḥ parikramya mām avandata mūrdhnibhiḥ.
te 'tha māṃ śibik"|ārūḍhaṃ n' âti|dīrghaiḥ prayāṇakaiḥ
nidhi|lābhād iva prītāḥ Tāmraliptīm aneṣata.
18.420 atha kṣiti|pateḥ putraṃ pariṇetum iv' āgatam
hṛṣṭaḥ pratyudagacchan māṃ mātulaḥ sphīta|ḍambaraḥ.
Vyāsen' âpi na śakyo 'sau vyāsen' ākhyātum utsavaḥ
samāsena tav' ākhyāmi vāk|kuṇṭhānām ayaṃ vidhiḥ.
tiṣṭhantu tāvad a|kalaṅka|kuṭumbi|dārāḥ
śīt'|âṃśu|bhāsvad|anilair api ye na dṛṣṭāḥ
sindūra|pāṭalita|khaṇḍa|naṭair naṭadbhir
nagn'|âṭakair api nar'|êndra|patheṣu gītam!
vidyā|vṛttais tato viprair Gaṅgadattaḥ svayaṃ ca mām
madhurair upapannaiś ca vacanair ity abodhayat.
‹pitā me dhriyate bhartā bhṛtyān āttena kiṃ mama
ātman" ā|yāsiten' êti prāg abhūs tvam upekṣakaḥ.
18.425 adhunā jananī|jāyā|prajā|guru|jan'|ādibhiḥ
a|vaśya|bharaṇīyaiś ca rakṣyaiś ca paravān bhavān.

I said to myself, 'Oh dear! I am trapped like a deer. These
poor fellows have cast a net from which it is impossible
to escape, however hard I try!' I then shouted, 'Hey! Hey! 18.415
Don't be so hasty! I am Sanu·dasa, and I am at your service!'

Their despair had brought their life-breaths to the point of leaving, but the joy of having found me brought them back to their throats. Because their dear life-breaths had returned and they had more life to live, they jumped for joy and made the forest quake with their clapping. Blissfully singing my praises like Buddhists to the Buddha, they circumambulated me many times before prostrating themselves at my feet.

They then put me in a palanquin and took me in short
stages to Tamra·lipti, as happy as if they had found a treasure. My overjoyed uncle came to meet me with great pomp, 18.420
as though I was the son of an emperor coming to get married. Even Vyasa would not be able to describe in detail
the celebrations. I shall describe them for you in brief:
such is the way of the tongue-tied. Forget the immaculate
matrons who had never been seen by the moon, the sun
or the wind: even naked ascetics—terrible dancers daubed
red with vermilion—were singing and dancing in the main
streets!

Then, via learned brahmins and his own kind and fitting
words, Ganga·datta gave me a lecture: 'In the past, you
thought that because your father was alive and supporting
his dependents there was no point in exerting yourself, and
you became apathetic. Now you have obligations toward 18.425
people whom you have to care for and support, including
your mother, your wife, your children and your elders. You

tad bhavad|bhartṛke tatra varge proṣita|bhartṛke
a|sārathāv iva rathe dhruvaṃ yan na bravīmi tat.
tasmād utkaṇṭhay" ôtkaṇṭhaṃ tvayi tāta didṛkṣayā
sva|kuṭumbam an|utkaṇṭhaṃ kuru yāhi gṛhān› iti.

ekadā kaṃ cid adrākṣam Aceraṃ nāma vāṇijam
suvarṇa|bhūmaye yāntam anantaiḥ saha vāṇijaiḥ.
tair gatvā saha potena kaṃ cid adhvānam ambudheḥ
taṭe bohittham ujjhitvā prātiṣṭhāmahi rodhasā.
18.430 ath' âbhraṃ|liha|śṛṅgasya pādaṃ pāda|pa|saṃkaṭam
āvasāma nag'|êndrasya lohitāyati bhāsvati.
tatas tatr' āhṛt'|āhārān niṣaṇṇān parṇa|saṃstare
ity asmān anuśāsti sma sārtha|vāhaḥ kṣapā|kṣaye.
‹tridhā pṛṣṭheṣu badhnīta pātheya|sthagikā dṛḍham
grīvāsu taila|kutupān samāsajata vāṇijāḥ.
etāś ca komalāḥ sthūlāḥ śoṣa|doṣ'|ādi|varjitāḥ
hastair vetra|latā gāḍham ālamby' ārohat' â|calam.
latām an|īdṛśīṃ mohād yaḥ kaś cid avalambate
pramīto himavaty asmin sa prayāti parāṃ gatim.
18.435 eṣa «vetra|patho» nāma sarv'|ôtsāha|vighāta|kṛt
suvarṇ'|āśā|pravṛttānāṃ mahān iva vināyakaḥ.›

evam|ādi tataḥ śrutvā viṣaṇṇair asmad|ādibhiḥ
hema|gardha|graha|grastais tath" âiva tad anuṣṭhitam.

ath' âiko dūram ārūḍhaś chinna|vetra|latā|śikhaḥ
kṣura|prakṣurita|jyākaḥ kṣoṇīṃ śūra iv' âgamat.
vayam ev' â|cal'|âgraṃ tad āruhya paridevya ca
nirupya ca jalaṃ tasmai tatr' âiv' âneṣmahi kṣapām.

are the family's protector, and a family whose protector is away is like a chariot without a driver—surely I don't have to tell you that. So, my boy, your family misses you and wants to see you; go home and remove their longing.'

One day I met a merchant called Achéra, who was going to the land of gold with several other merchants. After traveling together by boat for some distance across the ocean, we disembarked from the vessel onto a beach and set out along the coast.

When the sun was turning red, we stopped in thickly 18.430
wooded country at the foot of a mountain whose peak kissed the clouds. We ate there and slept on beds of leaves. At the end of the night the leader of the caravan gave us instructions: 'Merchants, use a triple knot to tie your knapsacks firmly onto your backs and hang your oil bottles around your necks. Climb the mountain by holding on tightly to those cane creepers which are soft and thick, and not dry or otherwise defective. Anyone who mistakenly holds on to any other kind of creeper shall die on the mountain and
proceed to the ultimate destination! This is called the "cane 18.435
path." It obstructs every effort, but is like a great guide to those who set out in the quest for gold.'

On hearing all this and more, I and the others were disheartened, but, gripped by a ghoulish greed for gold, we did exactly what we had been told.

A long way up, the tip of one man's cane creeper snapped and he fell to earth like a brave warrior whose arrow's barb has severed his bowstring. The rest of us climbed to the top of the mountain. After mourning our companion and making offerings of water to him, we spent the night there.

prāto mahāntam adhvānaṃ gatv" âpaśyāma nimna|gām
gav'|âśv'|âj'|âiḍak'|ākāra|pāṣāṇa|kula|saṃkulām.
18.440 ath' Âceraḥ puraḥ sthitvā pānthān uccair avārayat
‹mā mā spṛkṣata vāry etad! bhoḥ! bhoḥ! tiṣṭhata! tiṣṭhata!
mūḍhaiḥ spṛṣṭam idaṃ yair yais te te pāṣāṇatāṃ gatāḥ
atha vā svayam ev' âināṃ suhṛdaḥ kiṃ na paśyatha?
vaṃśān paśyatha yān asyāḥ parasmin saritas taṭe
arvāk|kūlaṃ nudaty enān paṭuḥ para|taṭ'|ânilaḥ.
kārśya|kaumala|saṃkotha|śoṣa|doṣ'|â|vidūṣitam
eṣām anyatamaṃ gāḍhaṃ gṛhṇīdhvaṃ maskaraṃ karaiḥ.
vāte mantharatāṃ yāte maskarāt tuṅgatāṃ gatāt
parasminn āpa|ga|pāre śanakair avarohata.
18.445 kotha|śoṣ'|ādi|doṣaṃ tu yo 'valambeta maskaram
sa tataḥ patito gacchec chaila|sthira|śarīratām.
eṣo «veṇu|patho» nāma mahā|patha|vibhīṣaṇaḥ
kuśalaiḥ kuśalen' āśu nir|viṣādaiś ca laṅghyate.›
yath" âsura|bilaṃ bālaḥ śāsanān mantra|vādinaḥ
praviveś' â|vicāry' âiva tath" âsmabhis tad īhitam.
teṣām ekaṃ kṛśād vaṃśād viśīrṇād apatat tataḥ
śilā|bhūtāṃ tanuṃ tyaktvā gatiṃ Māheśvarīm agāt.
avatīrya tu vaṃśebhyas tyaktvā dūreṇa tāṃ nadīm
tasmai salilam anyasy' âmadāma nyavasāma ca.
18.450 vāhayitvā ca panthānaṃ yojana|dvayasaṃ prage
bhujaṃgasy' âtisaṃkṣiptām adrākṣaṃ padavīṃ tataḥ.
tasyāś c' ôbhayato bhīmam a|dṛṣṭ'|ântaṃ rasātalam
andh'|ândhakāra|saṃghāta|vitrāsita|tamonudam.

In the morning, after covering a good distance, we saw a
river full of rocks shaped like cows, horses, goats and sheep.
Achéra was in front and blocked the travelers' way, calling 18.440
out, 'Hey! Hey! Stop! Stop! Don't touch the water! Those
who have been foolish enough to touch it have turned to
stone. Can you not see it for yourselves, my friends?

Look at those bamboos on the other bank of the river. A
strong wind from the opposite bank is bending them over
to this one. Get a good grip on a bamboo that is neither too
thin, too bendy, too rotten, nor too dry. When there is a lull
in the wind and the bamboo straightens up, get down gently
on the other bank. Whoever hangs on to a piece of bamboo 18.445
that is rotten or dry or otherwise unsound will fall and his
body will turn to stone. This is called the "bamboo path." It
is as terrifying as the path to the next world, but is quickly
and easily crossed by men who are able and intrepid.'

Like the fool who unblinkingly entered the demon's cave
at the sorcerer's bidding, we attempted the crossing. One of
the travelers held on to a bamboo that was thin. It snapped
and he fell. His body turned to stone; he left it and departed
for Lord Shiva. After we had climbed down from the bamboos and left the river far behind, we made offerings of
water from another river to him and stopped for the night.

The next morning, after we had traveled about one *yó-* 18.450
jana, I saw an extremely narrow and serpentine path. On
either side of it was a terrifying bottomless abyss, so dark
that it terrified the sun.

ath' Âcero 'vadat pānthān ‹dāru|parṇa|tṛṇ'|ādibhiḥ
ārdra|śuṣkair araṇyānī sa|dhūmā kriyatām iyam.
etāṃ dṛṣṭvā sa|paryāṇāñ śārdūl'|âjina|kaṅkaṭān
chāgān vikretum āyānti kirātāḥ parito diśaḥ.
tān krīṇīyāta kausumbha|naila|śākalik'|âmbaraiḥ
khaṇḍa|taṇḍula|sindūra|lavaṇa|snehanair api.
chāga|pṛṣṭhāni c' āruhya gṛhīt'|āyata|veṇavaḥ
atigāhata c' âdhvānaṃ Kāla|bhrū|daṇḍa|bhaṅguram.
ādāya yadi c' ânye 'pi kāñcanaṃ kāñcan'|ākarāt
anen' âiva nivarteran pathā pānthāḥ kadā cana.
tatas tair asmadīyaiś ca saṃmukhīnair ih' ântare
rasātalaṃ praveṣṭavyaṃ sa|suvarṇa|mano|rathaiḥ.
na mahā|saṃkaṭād asmān mārgād utkramya vidyate
chāga|paṅkter avasthānaṃ na nivartitum antaram.
tasmād abhyasta|kuntena vīreṇa pratibhāvatā
anubhūta|samīkena paṅkteḥ prasthīyatāṃ puraḥ.
samarthas tādṛg eko 'pi hantuṃ para|paraṃparām
na parābhāvyate yāvad apareṇa pareṇa saḥ.
ayaṃ c' âja|patho nāma śrūyamāṇo vibhīṣaṇaḥ
dṛśyamāno viśeṣeṇa Bhṛguḥ pāt'|ârthinām iva.›

ity Acere bruvaty evaṃ prāṃśu|kodaṇḍa|maṇḍalā
āgacchan mleccha|pṛtanā chāga|pūga|puraḥ|sarā.

teṣu tu pratiyāteṣu niṣkārya kraya|vikrayau
snātv" âvandanta krandantaḥ pānthāḥ Śaṃkara|Keśavau.
atha pānth'|āsthitā dīrghā prasthitā chāga|saṃtatiḥ
raṃhasiny api niṣkampā nivāte naur iv' âmbhasi.
tasyāś ca pathika|śreṇyāḥ saptamaḥ paścimād aham
Aceraś c' âbhavat ṣaṣṭhaḥ pṛṣṭhato 'nantaro mama.

Then Achéra said to the travelers, 'Fill the forest with
smoke by burning damp wood, leaves and grass. When they
see it, the tribesmen of the forest will come from all around
to sell goats with saddles and tiger-skin coverings. You must
buy them in exchange for clothes dyed with safflower, indigo
and *shákala*, or even sugar, rice, vermilion, salt and oil. Ride 18.455
on the backs of the goats and carry long staffs to negotiate
this path, which zigzags like the brow of Death. If there
happen to be any other travelers bringing gold from the gold
mine and returning by the same path, then, when we meet
face-to-face on it, they and we, together with our desires for
gold, will have to fall into the abyss. The path is too narrow
for a line of goats to stand aside, nor is there space to turn
around. Therefore a man experienced at wielding a spear, a
powerful warrior who has seen action, must be put at the
head of the column. Even one such man can slay a line of 18.460
enemies, as long as he is not overcome by a superior foe.
This is called the "goat path." It is terrifying when heard
about and particularly so when seen, like Mount Bhrigu for
those who seek to kill themselves by jumping from it.'

As Achéra was saying this, a troop of tribesmen with long curved bows arrived, driving a herd of goats.

When the bartering was over and they had gone, the
travelers bathed and made loud invocations to Shiva and
Krishna. They sat on the long train of goats and it set off.
Even though it moved quickly, it was as steady as a boat
on calm water. I was seventh in line from the rear of the 18.465
caravan, and Achéra was sixth, immediately behind me.

evaṃ|prāye ca vṛtt'|ânte dūrād āśrūyat' ôccakaiḥ
vaṃśānāṃ tāḍyamānānāṃ puraḥ ṣṭhā|ṣṭh"|ôdita|svanaḥ.
chāgānāṃ puruṣāṇāṃ ca dhīrāṇām api sādakaḥ
majjatāṃ dhvānta|jambāle ‹me me hā h" êti› ca dhvaniḥ.
sarvathā kṣaṇa|mātreṇa prakṣīṇā para|vāhinī
eka|śeṣ" âsmadīyā yā saptama|pramukhā sthitā!
atha mām avaśāsti sma grāma|ṇīḥ ‹kim udāsyate?
ekakaḥ puruṣaś c' âyaṃ paraḥ svo nīyatām!› iti.
18.470 paras tu vaṃśam ujjhitvā baddhvā mūrdhani c' âñjalim
hata|sva|pāntha|sārthatvād a|nātho mām anāthata.
‹eka|śākh" âvaśeṣasya mad|vaṃśasy' âvasīdataḥ
śākhā|chedena n' ôcchedam atyantaṃ kartum arhasi.
eka eva priyaḥ putraḥ pitror aham a|cakṣuṣoḥ
andha|yaṣṭis tayos tasmād bhrāto māṃ mā vadhīr!› iti.
āsīc ca mama ‹dhik prāṇān pāpa|pāṃsu|vidhūsarān!
dhig dhig eva suvarṇaṃ tat prāpyaṃ prāṇi|vadhena yat!
tasmān nihantu mām eṣa varākaḥ priya|jīvitaḥ
prāṇā yasy' ôpayujyante pitror duś|cakṣuṣor› iti.
18.475 atha roṣa|viṣādābhyām Aceras tāmra|niṣ|prabhaḥ
ambū|kṛtam avocan māṃ vācā niṣṭhura|mandayā.
‹are bāla|balīvarda! kāl'|â|kāl'|â|vicakṣaṇaḥ
kva kṛpāṇ'|ôcitaḥ kālaḥ kva kṛpā kṛpaṇ'|ôcitā.
aho kāruṇikatvaṃ te siddhaṃ siddh'|ânta|vedinaḥ
ekasya kṣudrakasy' ârthe yaḥ ṣoḍaśa jighāṃsati!
sa|chāge nihate hy asmiñ jīvitāḥ syuś caturdaśa
a|hate tu sah' ânena bhavatā ca hatā vayam.

As we proceeded like this, from far in front we heard the loud knocking sound of bamboo staffs clashing together, and the noise, terrifying even to the brave, of the bleating and screaming of goats and men plunging into the dark defile. Almost instantly the enemy's forces were completely destroyed, but for one man. As for us, the seventh from the rear was now at the front!

Our leader ordered me, 'What are you waiting for? The enemy is down to a single man: dispatch him to heaven!'

But my foe put down his staff and touched his joined 18.470
palms to his head. His caravan had been destroyed, so he had no one to protect him and he begged me, 'I am the only branch of what remains of my disappearing family. Don't destroy it forever by cutting off its last branch! I am my parents' one dear son. They are blind and I am their guiding stick—don't kill me, brother!'

I said to myself, 'Shame on a life stained with sin! To hell with gold that is to be had by murder! Let this wretch kill me! His life is dear to him and, alive, he can help his blind parents.'

Achéra was red with rage and ashen with disappointment. 18.475
In a stern low voice he spat at me, 'Oh you silly ox! You have no idea of timing. At a time fit for fighting you deem a rogue worthy of compassion! What a sound basis there is to your compassion, you, the master logician who wants to end sixteen lives for the sake of one miserable wretch! If he and his goat are killed, fourteen lives will be spared, but if you do not kill him, all of us will die, including him and you. One should not give up one's own precious life to save a scoundrel. "On the contrary, one should always protect

«na c' âpi rakṣituṃ kṣudram ātmānaṃ dus|tyajaṃ tyajet
ātmā tu satataṃ rakṣyo dārair api dhanair api.»»

18.480 ity|ādi Bhagavad|gītā|mātraṃ daṇḍakam īrayan
saḥ Pārtham iva māṃ Viṣṇuḥ karma krūram akārayat.

ath' âhaṃ prabala|vrīḍo garhamāṇaś ca karma yat
caraṇeṣu para|chāgaṃ su|kumāram atāḍayam.

chāga|pote tatas tasmin dhvānta|sindhau nimajjati
pāntha|sāmyātriko magnaḥ sah' âiva dhana|tṛṣṇayā.

vayaṃ tu dur|gamān mārgāt prakṣīṇa|svalpa|sainikāḥ
Bhāratād iva saṃgrāmāt sapta|śeṣa hat'|ôdyamāḥ.

taṃ ca deśaṃ parikramya prāpya Viṣṇupadī|taṭam
aśru|miśrāṃ pramītebhyaḥ prādāma salil'|âñjalim.

18.485 tatas tat tādṛśaṃ duḥkhaṃ bādhitaṃ no bubhukṣayā
śarīra|vedanā n' âsti dehināṃ hi kṣudhā|samā.

athā saṃpādit'|āhārān parṇa|śayy"|âdhiśāyinaḥ
manda|nidr"|ākul'|âkṣān naḥ prabodhy' āha sma nāyakaḥ.

‹amī chāgāḥ pramāpyantāṃ tatas tan māṃsam adyatām
sīvyantām ajinair bhastrās teṣāṃ viparivartitaiḥ.

tathā ca paridhīyantāṃ muktvā vighna|kṛtaṃ ghṛṇām
yathā tāsām asṛk|klinnam yad antas tad bahir bhavet.

pakṣavanta iv' âhāryā darī|dārita|cañcavaḥ
hema|bhūmer imāṃ bhūmim āgacchanti vihaṃ|gamāḥ.

18.490 māṃsa|piṇḍa|dhiyā te 'smān nabhas" ādāya cañcubhiḥ
suvarṇa|bhūmaye yānti tat tat saṃpādyatām› iti.

ath' âham abravam ‹brūte janatā yat tath" âiva tat
«tyajyatāṃ tat suvarṇaṃ yac chinatti śravaṇe» iti.

yen' âhaṃ dur|gamān mārgād dharmeṇ' êva tu dur|gateḥ
tāritaś chāga|nāgena hanyāṃ taṃ nir|ghṛṇaḥ katham?

one's own life, even with one's wife or wealth."' Reciting this 18.480
and other verses, he gave a sermon as long as the *Bhagavad*
Gita, and, just as Krishna did Árjuna, had me do the cruel
deed.*

Deeply ashamed and reproaching myself for what I was
doing, I tapped the enemy's goat lightly on the feet. With
his boat, a goat, sinking in the ocean of blackness, the road-
going sea merchant drowned along with with his thirst for
wealth. As for us, after that treacherous path our small force
was decimated; we were like the seven disheartened sur-
vivors of the *Maha·bhárata* war. We crossed the country
and reached the bank of a Ganga, where we offered the
dead a handful of water mixed with tears. Then our grief, 18.485
severe as it was, gave way to the desire to eat; for living
beings there is no physical pain like hunger.

After we had eaten, we lay down on beds of leaves. Our
eyes were bulging from lack of sleep when our leader woke
us up and said, 'These goats must be killed. Their flesh is
to be eaten and the skins turned inside out and sewn up to
make bags. You must abandon squeamishness, which will
be a hindrance, and put them on so that their blood-soaked
insides are on the outside. Birds like winged mountains,
with gaping beaks like caves, come to this land from the
land of gold. Thinking we are pieces of meat, they will take 18.490
us through the air to the land of gold, so do as I say.'

I said, 'People are right when they say one should throw away golden earrings if they hurt. How could I be so heartless as to kill this fine goat that saved me from the perilous path, like merit saving one from hell? That's it: I've had

tasmād alaṃ suvarṇena prāṇair ev' âtha vā kṛtam
yena ten' âiva dattebhyas tebhyo hanyāṃ suhṛttamam.›
 ath' Âcero 'vadat pānthān ‹ajaḥ svaḥ svaḥ pramāpyatām
ayaṃ tu Sānudāsīyaḥ su|dūre mucyatām› iti.
18.495 teṣām ekatamaḥ pānthas tam ajaṃ kv' âpi nītavān
daṇḍ'|ālambita|kṛttiś ca pratyāgaty' êdam uktavān.
‹chāgena Sānudāsasya may" ânyaḥ parivartitaḥ
tadīyaṃ c' êdam ānītam ajinaṃ dṛśyatām› iti.
 mayā tu pratyabhijñāya tasy' âiv' âjasya carma tat
uktaṃ ‹n' âsau tvayā muktaḥ prāṇair muktaḥ priyair!› iti.
 ath' āpta|vacanād bhīmaṃ samudra|taraṇād api
yukti|hīnaṃ tad asmābhir nabho|gamanam iṅgitam.
tato dur|bhaga|nihrādaiḥ pāṇḍu|chavibhir aṇḍa|jaiḥ
śāradair iva jīmūtaiḥ sāśam ākāśam āvṛtam.
18.500 tat|pakṣati|marut|piṣṭa|guru|skandha|nago nagaḥ
Śakra|śastra|śikhā|kṛtta|pattra|cakra iv' âbhavat.
atha kaṇṭha|gata|prāṇān asmān ādāya khaṃ kha|gāḥ
ākrāman sapta sapt' âpi Garutmanta iv' ôragān.
 pariśiṣṭo 'paras teṣāṃ sa ca mad|grāhiṇo balāt
nir|aṃśatvān nir|āśaṃso mām ev' ācchetum aihata.
atha raudram abhūd yuddhaṃ
 gṛdhrayoḥ sv'|ârtha|gṛddhayoḥ
yath" âmbara|cara|trāsi
 Daśa|kaṇṭha|Jaṭāyuṣoḥ.
paryāyeṇ' âham ākṛṣṭaś cañcoś cañcau patatriṇoḥ
kaccic ca skhalitas tasyāḥ kha|stho Śaṃkaram asmaram.
18.505 vajra|koṭi|kaṭhorābhiś cañcū|caraṇa|koṭibhiḥ

enough of gold and, what's more, I'm done with a life for which I'd have to kill the fine friend who has just saved it!'

Then Achéra told the travelers to kill each of their goats and release mine a good distance away. One of the travelers 18.495
took it off somewhere and returned with a skin hanging from a stick. He said, 'I swapped Sanu·dasa's goat for another, whose hide I have brought here. Take a look.'

But I recognized it as the skin from my goat and said, 'You did not set it free—it was set free of its precious life-breath!'

At the command of our trusted leader, we prepared ourselves for the crazy aerial journey, which was even more terrifying than crossing the ocean. Then the sky was filled in every direction with pale birds making ominous sounds, like clouds in autumn. The heavy tree trunks on the moun- 18.500
tain were laid waste by the wind of their flapping wings, so that they looked like circles made by leaves torn off trees by bolts of lightning. Our hearts were in our mouths as seven birds came and carried us off into the sky, like seven Gárudas carrying off serpents.

There was one more bird. Frustrated at not getting its share, it tried to snatch me away from the bird that was holding me. A terrifying battle between the two vultures ensued; they were both bent upon getting what they wanted and it was as terrifying for the creatures of the air as the battle between Rávana and Jatáyu.* I was snatched back and forth between the two birds' beaks. Now and then I would fall from one; when I was in the air I thought of Shiva. Their 18.505
beaks and claws were as sharp as diamond points; they tore at the goatskin with them and it became as perforated as a

kuṭṭitaṃ tat tayoś carma jātaṃ titaü|jarjaram.*
tato niṣkuṣitaś c' âhaṃ kuṭṭitāc carma|kañcukāt
patitaḥ sarasi kv' âpi śobhā|vismita|mānase.
tatra śoṇita|śoṇāni ghṛṣṭvā gātrāṇi paṅka|jaiḥ
snātas tarpita|devaś ca paścād amṛtam āharam.
tat|taṭe kṣaṇam āsitvā niṣadya ca gata|śramaḥ
a|pūrva|bahu|vṛtt'|ântaṃ dṛṣṭavān asmi tad vanam.
yatra vismṛtavān asmi duḥkhaṃ bhāruṇḍa|yuddha|jam
asi|pattra|van'|âpetaḥ saṃcarann iva Nandane.
18.510 śīrṇa|durvarṇa|parṇo vā vidyud|dāha|hato 'pi vā
a|puṣpaḥ phala|hīno vā yatr' âiko 'pi na pāda|paḥ.
kadamba|mālatī|kunda|mādhavī|mallik"|ādayaḥ
bhṛṅg'|ânīkaiḥ sadā yatra kṛṣṇa|kalmāṣa|pallavāḥ.
catur|aṅgula|tuṅgaiś ca Nīlakaṇṭha|gal'|âsitaiḥ
śaśorṇa|su|kumāraiś ca tṛṇair bhūṣita|bhū|talam.
yatra kesari|śārdūla|śikhaṇḍi|bhujag'|ādayaḥ
vratayanti dayāvantaḥ parṇa|puṣpa|jal'|ânilān.
a|nivṛtta|didṛkṣaś ca kānanaṃ parito bhraman
kasy' âpi caraṇaiḥ kṣuṇṇām adrākṣaṃ padavīm iva.
18.515 tayā saṃcaramāṇaś ca mantharaṃ dūram antaram
vāman'|ôbhaya|rodhaskām a|gambhīr'|âmbhasaṃ nadīm.
tāṃ ca kāñcana|gāh'|ādi|ratna|kāñcana|vālukām
uttīry' ācarya ca snānam ārciṣaṃ devatā|gurūn.
sarit|taṭ'|ôpakaṇṭhe ca kadalī|kānan'|āvṛtam
tapaḥ|kānanam adrākṣaṃ baddha|paryaṅka|vānaram.
tatr' â|cira|dyuti|piśaṅga|jaṭaṃ mun'|îndram
aikṣe nikharva|kuśa|viṣṭara|pṛṣṭha|bhājam
ājy'|āhuti|stimita|nīrasa|dāru|yoni|
kuṇḍ'|ôdar'|āhitam iv' āhavanīyam agnim.

sieve. Then I slipped out of the tattered skin-bag and fell into a lake whose beauty was astonishing.

I scrubbed my bloodstained limbs with lotuses in it, bathed, offered water to the gods and then drank the ambrosial liquid. I sat on the shore for a while and rested. My exhaustion gone, I noticed the forest and its many unique wonders. Like a man who has escaped from the hell paved with swords and is wandering about Indra's paradise, I forgot the anxiety brought about by the birds' battle. There 18.510
was not a single tree with withered or discolored leaves, nor one that had been burned by lightning, nor one without flowers or fruits. The blossoms of the *kadámba, málati, kunda, mádhavi, mállika* and other trees were constantly speckled black with swarms of bees. The ground was carpeted with grass that was four fingers high, as dark as Shiva's throat and as soft as rabbit fur. Carnivorous beasts like lions, tigers, peacocks and snakes were merciful, and had vowed to live off leaves, flowers, water and air.

My curiosity unabated, I wandered about the forest and came across what looked like a path trampled by someone's
footsteps. I slowly followed it a long way into the forest and 18.515
came to a river with low banks and shallow water. Its bed was golden, its pebbles precious stones and its sand gold dust. I crossed it, bathed and worshipped the gods and the elders.

Near the riverbank I noticed a penance grove in the middle of a banana glade where monkeys were sitting in meditative postures. Sitting there on a bed of short grass, I saw a great sage with matted hair as yellow as lightning. He looked like a sacrificial fire in the middle of a fire-pit containing dry wood moistened with an oblation of ghee.

tam̩ vanditum upāsarpam utsarpat saumya|candrikam
s'|ânta|sam̩tāpaka|sparśam uṣṇ'|âm̩śum iva haimanam.
ath' âsau sam̩mad'|âsr'|ārdra|kapolo mām abhāṣata
‹kuśalam̩ Sānudāsāya śreṣṭhine bhavatām!› iti.

mama tv āsīt ‹tato nāma divyam̩ cakṣus tapasvinām
sarvam̩ paśyati yen' ârtham̩ mām̩sa|cakṣur|a|gocaram.
yan me yādṛcchikam̩ nāma yac ca vyāpāra|hetukam
tat kīrtitam anen' âdya na kadā cid api śrutam!›

iti vicintitavantam̩ mām āsthit'|ādiṣṭa|viṣṭaram
vrīḍā|mantharam āha sma smitv" êti muni|pum̩gavaḥ.
‹tvayā yac cintitam̩ tāta tataḥ prati tath" âiva tat
nāma|mātra|kathā n' âti|citram̩ hi tapasaḥ phalam.
Dhruvak'|ādyair yathā madyam upāyaiḥ pāyito bhavān
yathā vadhukay" ôdyāne sam̩gataḥ Gaṅgadattayā.
yāvad bhāruṇḍa|sam̩grāmād Yama|dram̩ṣṭr'|ântarād iva
vimuktas tvam iha prāptaḥ sarvam̩ tad viditam̩ mama.
anubhūtā tvayā tāta yāna|pātra|vipattayaḥ
laṅghitāś ca su|dur|laṅghyāḥ śaila|kāntāra|nimna|gāḥ.
yad artham̩ c' âyam āyāsaḥ prāptaḥ kṛcchratamas tvayā
Mitravaty eva tat sarvam̩ mātā te kathayiṣyati.
sakalaś c' âyam ārambhaḥ suvarṇa|prāptaye tava
tac ca sam̩prāpta|deśīyam ato mā viṣadad bhavān.
tvādṛśaḥ sthira|sattvasya mādṛś'|ādeśa|kāriṇaḥ
su|prāpam̩ prājña|s'|ôtsāhaiḥ suvarṇam̩ kva gamiṣyati.
parṇa|śāl'|āśayen' âtaḥ pāda|p'|âvayav'|āśinā
ahaḥ|katipayāny asminn āśrame sthīyatām› iti.

When I went to greet him he was radiating a gentle white light, like the sun in winter when its burning rays have cooled. His cheeks were wet with tears of joy as he said to 18.520
me, 'Hail to thee, Sanu·dasa, best of merchants!'

I said to myself, 'Ascetics really do have divine sight: he sees everything that is beyond the scope of normal vision. He has just said my name, which could have been anything, and my occupation, without ever having heard them!'

After I had thought this, he indicated a grass seat and, embarrassed, I slowly sat down on it. The great sage smiled and said to me, 'Your thoughts are quite correct, my son. However, the telling of a mere name is not the most amazing fruit of asceticism. Your being tricked into drinking wine by 18.525
Dhrúvaka and the others, your meeting with the girl Ganga·dattá in the park, right up to your escaping from the battle of the birds as if from the jaws of death and your arriving here: I know it all. You have experienced shipwrecks, my son, and crossed impassable mountains, jungles and rivers. None other than your mother, Mítravati, will tell you all about why you have suffered so terribly. Your entire enterprise has been for the attainment of gold. You have almost got it, so do not lose heart. Gold is easily obtained by those who are 18.530
clever and keen. If a strong-willed man like you follows the instructions of a man like me, where is his gold going to go? So stay for a few days in this hermitage, sleeping in a leaf-hut and living off parts of trees.'

ath' âbhilaṣit'|āsvādaṃ mṛj"|âujaḥ|puṣṭi|vardhanam
vāneyam āharann annaṃ kṛṣṭa|pacyam ahaṃ dviṣan.
parṇa|śāl'|ântar|āstīrṇe śayānaḥ parṇa|saṃstare
tuṅga|paryaṅkam adveṣaṃ Gaṅgadattā|niveśanam.

iti vismṛta|duḥkho 'pi sukh'|āsvādair a|mānuṣaiḥ
daridra|vāṭaka|sthāyāḥ satataṃ mātur adhyagām.
18.535 ākāśa|patha|yān'|ântāḥ praśaṃsāmi sma c' âpadaḥ
suvarṇa|prāptaye prāptā yā vipat saṃpad eva sā.

ekadā taṃ mah"|ātmānam abhitaḥ prāptam ambarāt
mūrtaṃ puṇyam iv' âdrākṣaṃ vimānaṃ Meru|bhāsvaram.
kanyās tasmān nirakrāmat dyuti|dyotita|kānanāḥ
s'|êndra|cāpād iv' âmbhodāt krāntā saudāmanī|latā.
tatas tāḥ saṃparikramya praṇamya ca yati|prabhum
vihāyas|talam ākrāmann indor iva marīcayaḥ.

ekā tu na gatā tāsām aṅkam āropya tāṃ muniḥ
pramoda|gadgad'|ālāpaḥ pramṛṣṭ'|âkṣīm abhāṣata.
18.540 ‹putri Gandharvadatte 'yaṃ Sānudāsaḥ pitā tvayā
asmān api tiras|kṛtya śraddhay" ārādhyatām› iti.

taṃ c' âham ati|sat|kāram amanye 'ti|viḍambanām
vandyamāno Mahāgauryā krīḍayā pramatho yathā.
sā kadā cin mayā pṛṣṭā ‹ko 'yaṃ kā vā tvam ity› atha
‹śrūyatām› iti bhāṣitvā tayor vṛttam avartayat.

Eating that delicious forest food, which was purifying, invigorating and nourishing, I developed a distaste for cultivated fare. Sleeping on a layer of leaves spread inside the leaf-hut, I developed a distaste for Ganga·dattá's house with its high beds.

But even though the experience of unearthly pleasures like these made me forget my troubles, I kept thinking of
my mother in the slum. I began to treasure the calamities 18.535
that had culminated in the journey through the sky, and as far as my quest for gold was concerned, the misfortune that had befallen me was in fact a blessing.

One day I saw in front of the great saint a sky-chariot as brilliant as Mount Meru: it was as though his merit had taken physical form and arrived from the sky. Maidens emerged from within, and their radiance lit up the forest like a streak of lightning coming from a rainbow-tinted cloud. They walked reverentially around the majestic ascetic and bowed to him before flying into the sky like moonbeams.

One of them, however, did not leave, and the sage sat her on his lap. In a voice choked with happiness, he said to
her after she had wiped his eyes, 'Gandhárva·datta, my girl, 18.540
this is your father, Sanu·dasa. You must turn your back on me and serve him faithfully.'

I took her excessive courtesy to be tomfoolery, as if I were one of Shiva's attendants being saluted in jest by Párvati. One day I asked the girl about the sage and her. 'Listen,' she said, and told their story.

‹Bharadvāja|sa|gotro 'yam upadhānaṃ tapasvinām
vidyā|dhara|Bharadvājo yad vidyā|sādhan'|ôdyataḥ.
mahatas tapasaś c' âsya vyathamānaḥ Puraṃ|daraḥ
āsanen' â|cal'|ābhena calatā calitaḥ kila.
18.545 Śacy|āliṅgana|kāle 'pi dhyātvā kaṃ cit tapasvinam
viṣād'|ākula|cetasko duḥkhaṃ jīvati Vāsavaḥ.
Nāradāt tu Bharadvājam upalabhya tapasvinam
Hariṇā Suprabh" ādiṣṭā gandharv'|âdhipateḥ sutā.
«rūpa|yauvana|saubhāgyair garvitām Urvaśīm api
atiśeṣe tvam ity eṣā pratītiḥ piṣṭa|pa|traye.
Bharadvājam ato gatvā tvam ārādhaya sundari
tathā te rūpa|saubhāgye sa|phalī|bhavatām» iti.

Suprabh" âtha muner asya vacaḥ|prekṣita|ceṣṭitaiḥ
śṛṅgārair aicchad ākraṣṭuṃ sa|tattv'|ālambanaṃ manaḥ.
18.550 yadā n' âśakad ākraṣṭum abdair bahu|tithair api
tadā karma|karī|karma nirvedād akarod asau.
puṣp'|ôccaya|jal'|āhāra|kuṭī|saṃmārjan'|ādibhiḥ
toṣito 'yam avocat tāṃ «varaḥ kas te bhavatv» iti.

tay" ôktaṃ «spṛhayanti sma yasmai Tridaśa|yoṣitaḥ
tan me Bhagavatā dhairyāt saubhāgyaṃ dur|bhagī|kṛtam.
niṣ|prayojana|cārutva|bhūṣaṇa|srag|vilepanam
saubhāgya|mātrakaṃ strainaṃ kāma|kāmeṣu bhartṛṣu.
tena vijñāpayāmy etat prītaś ced dayase varam
jagato 'pi varas tasmād bhavān ev' âstu no varaḥ!
18.555 taruṇīnāṃ hi kanyānāṃ cetoja|kṣuṇṇa|cetasām

'He is of the lineage of Bharad·vaja and a most excellent
ascetic. Because he has striven to master sorcery, he is known
as Bharad·vaja the Sorcerer. His great austerities made Indra afraid that he might be toppled from his throne, which,
despite looking like a mountain, had begun to shake. Even 18.545
when in the embrace of Shachi, Indra lives uneasily: thinking of this or that ascetic, his mind is filled with anxiety.
Indra learned about the ascetic Bharad·vaja from Nárada
and gave Súprabha, the daughter of the king of the Gandhárvas, the following instructions: "Úrvashi is proud of her
beauty, youth and grace, but everyone in the three worlds
believes that you surpass even her. Therefore go to Bharad·
vaja, beautiful lady, serve him and have your beauty and
charm bear fruit!"

With her coquettish words and glances, Súprabha tried to
attract the mind of the sage, which was fixed on the ultimate
reality. When she had been unable to seduce him, even after 18.550
several years, she was so disappointed that she started to do
the work of a servant. She did chores like gathering flowers,
fetching water and cleaning the hut. He was pleased by this
and asked her what she would like as a boon.

She said, "My charms were coveted by the wives of the
gods, but with your resolve Your Holiness has made a mock-
ery of them. Beauty, decorations, garlands and makeup have
no bearing on the measure of women's charms; it is found in
their husbands' desire for love. So I ask this: if you are happy
to grant me a boon, then may you, the finest man in the
world, be my husband!* For what, to tender young women 18.555
overcome by desire, is a finer boon than a husband who
pleases both their hearts and their eyes? Therefore, blessed

cetaś|cakṣu|priyāt puṃsaḥ kīdṛśo 'nyo varād varaḥ?
tasmād a|priya|rāgo 'pi bhagavān anukampayā
vaśitvād rāgam ālambya saubhāgyaṃ me dadātv» iti.

anurodhāc ca ten' âsyām ek" âiva janitā sutā
ciram ārādhito bhaktyā virakto 'pi hi rajyate.
sā tu Suprabhayā nītvā pitryaṃ Viśvāvasoḥ puram
vardhitā ca vinītā ca vidyāsu ca kalāsu ca.

atha gandharva|rājas tām ānīya duhituḥ sutām
abhāṣata Bharadvājaṃ «nām' âsyāḥ kriyatām» iti.
18.560 «astu Gandharvadatt" êyaṃ mahyaṃ dattā yatas tvayā»
iti tasyāḥ kṛtaṃ nāma Bharadvājena s'|ârthakam.
Suprabhāyāṃ tu yā kanyā Bharadvājād ajāyata
nāmnā Gandharvadatt" êti vitta mām eva tām!› iti.

ekadā kṛṣṇa|śarvaryāṃ paśyāmi sma śil"|ôccayam
jāta|rūpa|śilā|jāla|jyotir|ujjvalita|drumam.
mama tv āsīd ‹ayaṃ śailo hiraṇmaya|śilaḥ sphuṭam
kalyāṇaṃ kāñcanaṃ c' âsminn! asmat|kalyāṇa|kāraṇam!›
nirdhāry' êti suvarṇ'|āśā|pāśa|yantrita|cetasā
viśālā parṇa|śāl" âsau śilābhiḥ pūritā mayā.

18.565 tās tu prātaḥ śilā dṛṣṭvā pṛṣṭaḥ Gandharvadattayā
‹kim etad?› iti tasyai ca yathā|vṛttaṃ nyavedayam.
tayā tu kathitaṃ pitre mām āhūya sa c' âvadat
‹āyuṣman na hiraṇmayyaḥ śilā eva hi tāḥ śilāḥ.
oṣadhīnām idaṃ jyotir dhvānte hāṭaka|sa|prabham
bhāsvad|bhās'|âbhibhāvinyā muktaṃ rātrau vijṛmbhate.
dṛṣṭavān asi sauvarṇās tat saṃparkād imāḥ śilāḥ
paśyante ca diśaḥ pītās tṛṣṇā|timira|mīlitāḥ!
aham eva suvarṇaṃ ca Campāṃ pratigamaṃ ca te

lord, even though you dislike desire, be so kind as to give in to it and grant me the good fortune of being your wife."

He complied and fathered a single daughter by her, for even the passionless become enamored when solicited with devotion for a long time. Súprabha took the girl to the city of her father, Vishvávasu, where she brought her up and schooled her in the arts and sciences.

Then the king of the Gandhárvas brought his granddaughter to Bharad·vaja and asked him to name her. Bha- 18.560
rad·vaja gave her an appropriate name, saying, "May the girl be called Gandhárva·datta, because she was given to me by you." The girl called Gandhárva·datta who was born to Súprabha and fathered by Bharad·vaja is none other than me!'

One dark night I noticed a mountain on which the trees glowed with the light from numerous golden rocks. I said to myself, 'This mountain is clearly made of rocks of gold. How lucky that there is gold on it! It will make my fortune!' At this realization, my mind was ensnared by the desire for gold and I filled a large leaf-hut with the rocks.

When she saw the rocks in the morning, Gandhárva·dat- 18.565
ta asked me what was going on, and I told her what I had done. She told her father, who summoned me and said, 'Dear fellow, those rocks do not contain gold, they are just rocks. In darkness, the glow of the herbs resembles gold. It disappears in the overpowering light of the sun, but is visible at night. You saw these rocks as golden because of their proximity to that glow; moreover, those whose eyes are clouded with greed see everything as golden! It is I who before long shall provide you with gold and arrange for your

18.570 a|cirāt saṃvidhāsyāmi tat tyaj' ākulatām› iti. yāś ca tās tuṣṭa|
tuṣṭena muhūrten' āhṛtāḥ śilāḥ
tā mayā duḥkha|duḥkhena sarv'|āhṇena nirākṛtāḥ.

ekadā kacchapīṃ vīṇāṃ mahyaṃ dattv" âvadan muniḥ
‹yad bravīmi tad ākarṇya tvam anuṣṭhātum arhasi.
Gandharvadattayā yas te mad|vṛtt'|ânto niveditaḥ
sa tath" âiva yatas tasmād asmākam iyam ātma|jā.
vidyā|dhara|pateś c' êyaṃ bhāvino bhāginī priyā
na hi sāgara|janmā Śrīḥ Śrī|pater anyam arhati.
tena Campām iyaṃ nītvā deyā te cakra|vartine
cihnair yaiś ca sa vijñeyaḥ kriyantāṃ tāni cetasi.
18.575 ṣaṣṭhe ṣaṣṭhe bhavān māse gandharvān saṃnipātayet
puras teṣām iyaṃ gāyād geyaṃ Nārāyaṇastutim.
yas tu saṃvādayet kaś cid gandharvas teṣu vīṇayā
vādayet tac ca yas tasmai dadyāḥ sva|tanayām› iti.

sarvathā bhavatāṃ yad yad vṛttaṃ gandharva|saṃsadi
vīṇā|vādana|paryantaṃ tat tat tena niveditam.

ath' āvāṃ munir āha sma ‹khinnau sthaḥ putrakau ciram
khed'|ôcchedāya tac Campāṃ pratiṣṭhethāṃ yuvām!› iti.

tatas taṃ praṇipaty' âhaṃ calitaḥ pracalo mudā
yāma|trayaṃ tri|yāmāyā yāpayitvā prasuptavān.
18.580 ath' â|mānuṣam aśrauṣaṃ dāravī|mātra|vīṇayoḥ
sa|veṇu|nisvanaṃ svānaṃ manaḥ|śravaṇa|vallabham.
sa|tāmra|śikha|rāsāni tāraṃ maṅgala|vādinām
nidrā|tyājana|dakṣāṇi bandināṃ vanditāni ca.
ātmānam atha nir|nidro jāta|rūp'|âṅga|pañjaram

return to Champa, so stop being impatient.' It took me all 18.570
day piling sorrow upon sorrow to remove the rocks that I
had so happily gathered in an instant.

One day the sage gave me a lute with a bowl shaped like
a tortoise-shell and said, 'Listen to me and do as I say. The
story Gandhárva·datta told you about me is true: she is my
daughter. She is lucky enough to be destined to become
the bride of the future king of the sorcerers: Lakshmi, the
daughter of the ocean, deserves none other than Vishnu!
So take her to Champa that she might be betrothed to
the emperor. Take note of the signs by which he is to be
recognized. Every six months you shall host a gathering 18.575
of musicians. In front of them the girl is to sing the song
called the Hymn to Naráyana. You should betroth her as
your daughter to whichever musician accompanies her on
the lute and sings the hymn.'

He then related everything that you did in the gathering of musicians, up to your playing of the lute.

Then the sage said to the two of us, 'You have been bored for a long time, my children. To alleviate your boredom, set forth for Champa!'

After prostrating myself before him, I went on my way
trembling with excitement. I did not sleep until the end
of the night. Then I heard the unearthly sound of two 18.580
wooden lutes accompanied by a flute, delightful to the mind
and ears, and, mixed with the crowing of cocks, the shrill
salutations—perfect for waking one up—of bards singing
benedictions. I got up and found myself sitting on a golden
bed sparkling with precious stones. A colorful silk carpet was
spread across an inlaid crystal floor under a cloth canopy

paryaṅkam adhitiṣṭhantam adrākṣaṃ ratna|piñjaram.
citra|cīn'|âṃśuk'|āstīrṇam ambaraṃ svaccha|kuṭṭime
mṛṣṭa|hāṭaka|daṇḍ'|ālī|taṭite paṭa|maṇḍape.
nīla|ratna|śil"|ôtsaṅge vitān'|āvṛta|bhāskare
vīṇā|paricaya|vyagrām āsīnāṃ Suprabhā|sutām.
18.585 vicitr'|ôjjvala|varṇaṃ ca su|veṣ'|ākāra|bhartṛkam
goṇībhir hema|pūrṇābhiḥ pūrṇaṃ paṭa|kuṭī|kulam.
krīṇato maṇi|hem'|ādi vikrīṇānāṃś ca vāṇijān
samāhitaiś ca sīm'|ântān saṃkaṭān auṣṭrak'|âukṣakaiḥ.
sarvathā duṣ|karaṃ mandair alaṃ kṛtv" âti|vistaram
svapne 'pi na narair dṛṣṭā samṛddhiḥ kaiś|cid apy asau.

Bhāradvājīm ath' âpṛcchaṃ ‹mātaḥ kim idam adbhutam
Gandharva|nagaraṃ māyā svapno v" âyaṃ bhaved?› iti.

‹Bharadvāj'|ârjitasy' êdaṃ tapa|kalpa|taroḥ phalam
a|prameya|prabhāvaṃ hi sadbhiḥ su|caritaṃ tapaḥ.
18.590 tasmād idam an|antatvād dhanam icch"|âvyaya|kṣamam
bhūmer anyatra sarvatra sat|pātr'|ādau nidhīyatām!
āya|cintāṃ parityajya vyaya|cintā|paro bhava!
āya|sthānaṃ hi te 'sty eva muni|kāñcana|parvataḥ!
«kadā paśyāmi jananīm» iti c' ākulatāṃ tyaja
sārtha|sthānād itaḥ Campā nanu krośeṣu pañcasu.›

sa ca me svapna|māy"|ādi|viṣayaḥ saṃśayas tayā
niścay'|ātmikayā sadyaḥ prajñay" êva nivartitaḥ.

atha Dhruvakam adrākṣaṃ vailakṣyān namit'|ānanam
dhūrtaṃ tādṛg|vidhair eva suhṛdbhiḥ parivāritam.
18.595 tam utthāy' âtha paryaṅkāt parirabhya ca s'|ādaram
adhyasthāpayam ātmīyāṃ śayyāṃ gata|vilakṣatam.
saṃbhāṣaṇa|pariṣvaṅga|śāta|kumbh'|āsan'|ādibhiḥ
suhṛd|gaṇam anu|jyeṣṭham udāraiḥ paryatoṣayam.

supported by rows of polished golden poles. Gandhárva·datta was busy practicing the lute, sitting on a bench of sapphire shaded from the sun by an awning. There were 18.585
several small brightly colored tents filled with sacks of gold guarded by handsome well-dressed men. Merchants were buying and selling gemstones, gold and so forth, and at the edges of the camp were crowds of camels and bulls. There is no point in trying to describe it in too much detail—an altogether impossible feat for the dull-witted! No man has ever seen such opulence, even in his dreams.

I asked Gandhárva·datta, 'Good lady, what is this marvel? Is it the city of the Gandhárvas? Is it a mirage? Is it a dream?'

She replied, 'This is Bharad·vaja's reward from the wish-fulfilling tree that is asceticism: performed well by virtuous
people, it has unlimited power.* Because they are infinite, 18.590
these riches can be spent at will. Don't bury them in the ground; spend them everywhere and start with those who deserve them! Stop worrying about acquiring wealth and concentrate on spending it! Your treasury is the sage's mountain of gold! Don't worry about when you will see your mother. Champa is but ten miles from this caravansary.'

Like wisdom, the essence of which is certitude, she instantly removed my doubts about whether or not it was a dream, or a mirage or any other such fantasy.

Then I saw that rogue Dhrúvaka. He was hanging his
head in shame, surrounded by friends doing just the same. I 18.595
stood up, embraced him courteously, and had him sit on my bed, thereby removing his embarrassment. By offering them kind words, embraces, golden seats and the like according to their rank, I cheered up his friends.

ataḥ param a|śeṣ" âiva naṭan|naṭa|puraḥ|sarā
pravṛddha|pramad'|ônmādā Campā taṃ sārtham āvṛṇot.
praharṣ'|ôtkarṣa|vicchinna|niśvās'|ânila|saṃtatiḥ
amṛt' âiva janaḥ kaś cic! cirāt kaś cid udaśvasat.
su|svāden' ânna|pānena ratna|vāsaḥ|srag|ādibhiḥ
sphītair hem'|âti|sargaiś ca paura|śreṇim avardhayam.
18.600 yaiś ca gomaya|pānīyaṃ kṣiptaṃ mama puraḥ|saram
uddhṛtās te viśeṣeṇa dāridrya|nirayān mayā.

atha Dhruvakam ābhāṣe ‹bhadra raudratar'|ākṛteḥ
daridra|vāṭakād ambā svam ev' ānīyatāṃ gṛham.
yāvan|mātreṇa vikrītaṃ draviṇena tad ambayā
tataḥ śata|guṇen' âpi kretur niṣkretum arhasi.
tādṛśīm īśvarām ambāṃ daridra|kuṭikā|gatām
draṣṭuṃ śaknoti yas tasya kṣudrakān dhig asūn!› iti.

tatas tena vihasy' ôktaṃ ‹kva devī kva daridratā?
kena Bhāgīrathī dṛṣṭā vicchinna|jala|saṃhatiḥ?
18.605 tad eva bhavanaṃ devyāḥ samṛddhiḥ s" âiva c' â|calā
ujjvalā tu tvay" êdānīṃ kumudvatyā iv' êndunā.›

iti tat kṣaṇa|saṃkṣiptaṃ kṣiptvā sa|kṣaṇa|daṃ dinam
su|prātaḥ prāviśaṃ Campāṃ dhan'|âdhipa iv' Âlakām.
rathyābhir viśikhābhiś ca śreṇi|śreṇi|puraḥ|saraḥ
gatvā nar'|êndram adrākṣaṃ sur'|êndram iva bhāsvaram.
vandanāya tato dūrād dharaṇīm aham āśliṣam
asāv api mud" āhūya mām āśliṣad a|kaitavam.
sāravadbhir anantaiś ca mām asau bhūṣaṇ'|âmbaraiḥ
sat|kṛty' ājñāpayat ‹putra jananī dṛśyatām!› iti.
18.610 tataḥ Sumeru|sāreṇa ratna|kāñcana|rāśinā

Then, with dancers at their head, all of Champa surrounded the caravan in a frenzy of exhilaration. Some people were so overjoyed that they were unable to breathe and
died! Others took an age to get their breath back. I made the
townspeople happy with delicious food and drink, presents
such as jewels, clothes and garlands, and copious gifts of
gold. In particular, I saved from the hell of poverty those 18.600
people who had had to throw the purificatory cow dung
paste after me.

Then I said to Dhrúvaka, 'My friend, please take my
mother away from the awful slum and bring her to her own
house. You must buy it back from the man who bought it,
even for a hundred times the amount he paid my mother.
Shame on the pathetic life of a man who can look at a
goddess of a mother like her in a poor person's hut!'

He laughed and said, 'That fine lady in poverty? Who
has ever seen the torrent of the Ganga stemmed? She has the 18.605
same house and the same vast fortune. But now, thanks to
you, she will blossom like a lotus pond in the moonlight.'

A day and a night passed in the blink of an eye, and I
entered Champa early in the morning like the lord of wealth
entering Álaka. With a vanguard of the various guilds, I
traveled along roads and avenues. Then I saw the king; he
was as splendid as the king of the gods. In salutation, I
prostrated myself on the ground at a distance. He joyfully
called me over and openly embraced me. He welcomed me
with endless precious jewels and clothes, and then ordered
me to go and see my mother. I filled the king's unfillable 18.610
chasm of greed with a pile of jewels and gold as valuable

duṣ|pūraṃ pūrayāmi sma rājñas tṛṣṇā|rasātalam.
nar'|êndra|parivāreṇa pratīten' āvṛtas tataḥ
paṭhadbhiś ca tato viprair ātmīyam agamaṃ gṛham.
manda|dhvani|mṛdaṅg'|ādau tasminn uddāma|tāṇḍave
paurair harṣa|kṛt'|ôtsāhair na kṣuṇṇaḥ katham apy aham.
ambām ath' ârgha|jala|pātra|bhṛtaṃ
nirīkṣya dūrād apāsarad asau janatā vihastā
pūrṇād iv' ândha|tamasāni tuṣāra|kānter
āryāt pṛthag|jana|śatāni hi saṃbhramanti.
labdh'|ântaras tataḥ pādau śirasā mātur aspṛśam
s" âpi sārdha|payaḥ|pātrā patati sma mam' ôpari.
18.615 cirāc ca labdha|niśvāsā mām udasthāpayat tataḥ
anayat pāṇin" ākṛṣya gṛh'|âbhyantara|maṇḍapam.
deva|dvija|gurūṃs tatra sa|dur|gata|vanīpakān
sphītaiḥ parijanaṃ ca svaṃ vibhavaiḥ samayojayam.
tato nivartit'|āhāra|paryanta|karaṇa|sthitiḥ
prāviśaṃ mātur ādeśād āvāsaṃ guru|cārutam.
tatr' āsīnaś ca paryaṅke mahī|tala|sam'|āsanām
apaśyaṃ prathamāṃ jāyāṃ kara|śākh'|āvṛt'|ānanām.
tasyāḥ karuṇayā netre mārjatā saṃtat'|âśruṇī
Gaṅgadattā mayā dṛṣṭā śliṣṭa|bhittiḥ parāṅ|mukhī.
18.620 vāṅ|mātreṇ' âpi yat satyaṃ na sā saṃmānitā mayā
smaranti hi tiras|kārān munayo 'pi garīyasaḥ.
tac c' āvāsa|gṛhaṃ dṛṣṭvā kusuma|sthagita|kṣiti
sindhu|rodhaḥ smarāmi sma phulla|nānā|latā|gṛham.
Samudradinnayā sārdham anubhūtaṃ ca tatra yat
sthita|prasthita|gīt'|ādi viśrabdh'|ācaritaṃ mayā.

as Mount Suméru. Surrounded by a retinue of the king's trusted servants and chanting brahmins, I went home.

Somehow I managed to avoid being trampled by the exuberant citizens as they danced wildly to the deep beat of the *mridánga* and other drums. But when the crowd saw my mother in the distance carrying a jug of water with which to welcome me, they dispersed in embarrassment, for the common herd runs away from an aristocrat like darkness from the full moon.

Now that I had the chance, I touched my mother's feet
with my head and she, jug of water in hand, fell on top of
me. At last she got her breath back and let me stand up. 18.615
She took me by the hand and led me into the inner hall of the house. I gave sumptuous gifts to the gods, brahmins and elders, as well as to the luckless beggars and my own servants. When I had completed my duties and eaten a meal, my mother showed me into the beautiful bedroom.

I sat on the bed and saw my first wife sitting on the floor, hiding her face with her fingers. While I was taking pity on
her and wiping the flood of tears from her eyes, I noticed
Ganga·dattá leaning against the wall, her face averted. I 18.620
did not grace her with so much as a word, for even sages remember when they have been gravely abused. And when I looked at that bedroom with its floor carpeted in flowers, I thought of the ocean's shore with its bowers of flowering creepers and the carefree life of sitting, walking, singing and so forth that I lived there with Samúdra·dinná.

mama tv āsīd ‹varaṃ duḥkham anubhūtaṃ mahan mayā
hṛdayād vyāvṛtād yena kv' âpi priyatamā gatā.
duḥkha|śūnyaṃ tu tad dṛṣṭvā randhr'|ânveṣaṇa|tat|parā
adhunā nir|anukrośā sā praviṣṭ" â|nivāritā.
18.625 praviṣṭā hṛdayaṃ sā me yath" āvāsa|gṛhaṃ tathā
praviśed api nām' êyaṃ dur|ghaṭo 'yaṃ mano|rathaḥ.
sā hi mām āhvayaty eva «paritrāyasva mām» iti
taraṃga|pāṇin" ākṛṣya hṛtā pāpena sindhunā.›
iti cint"|āturaṃ sā māṃ harṣa|tyājita|dhīratā
praviśya tvaray" āliṅgad aṅgais tuṅga|tanū|ruham.
atyant'|ân|upapannaṃ tu dṛṣṭvā tasyāḥ samāgamam
tām eva dhyātavān asmi sindhu|bhaṅg'|âgra|tāraṇīm.
vismṛt'|âpara|vṛtt'|ântas tad|āsakta|manastayā
tām ev' āśvāsayāmi sma ‹mā sma bhīrur bhaver!› iti.
18.630 atha bhīt" êva s" âvocat ‹sva|gṛhe vartate bhavān
vipanna|vahanaḥ kaṣṭe na tu kṣār'|âmbudhāv› iti.
tataḥ kṣār'|âmbudher bhīmāt pratyāhṛta|manās tayā
gṛhaṃ tat paritaḥ paśyann apaśyaṃ vanitā|dvayam.
smaratā ca sad|ācāraṃ sa|patnī|jana|saṃnidhau
vakṣaḥ|sth" âpi satī n' âsau dorbhyām āliṅgitā mayā.
ath' âvasth"|ântare tasmin dāra|saṃnidhi|saṃkaṭe
a|śrāvitā mam' āgacchad amb" â|trās'|ākul'|ēkṣaṇā.
Samudradinnayā sārdham ucchrite saṃbhramān mayi
ambā śayanam adhyāste śeṣās tv āsata bhū|tale.
18.635 tataḥ kiṃ cid iv' âmbāyai yat satyaṃ kupito 'bhavam
a|kāla|jñā hi māt" âpi putreṇa paribhūyate.

I said to myself, 'It is better that I face up to my great sadness rather than turn my heart away because my dearest has disappeared, for she has seen it empty of sorrow, and, intent on finding a way in, she has now cruelly entered it
unchecked. I have the impossible wish that just as she has 18.625
entered my heart, so might she enter my bedroom, for the moment that she called out to me to save her, that sinner the ocean, with waves for hands, dragged her away.'

While I was troubled by these thoughts, she could not contain her excitement any longer, and ran in and hugged me, and I tingled all over. But when I saw her come in so utterly unexpectedly, I could only think of her as floating on the crest of an ocean wave.

Forgetting everything else that had happened, my mind was fixed on that vision and I tried to reassure her, saying, 'Don't be scared, my darling!'

Now she did seem frightened, and said, 'You are in your 18.630
own house, not shipwrecked in the perilous salty sea!' She brought my mind back from the terrifying salty sea and as I looked around the house I saw both my wives. Remembering to conduct myself correctly in front of my rival spouses, I did not put my arms around Samúdra·dinná, even though she was against my chest. The presence of both my wives made this situation delicate, and into it my mother arrived unbidden, her eyes showing no trace of anxiety. I and Samúdra·dinná quickly got up, and my mother sat on the bed
while the rest of us sat on the floor. I was in fact a little angry 18.635
with my mother, for a son can be embarrassed by even his mother if she has no sense of timing.

ath' âmbayā vihasy' ôktam ‹a|kāla|jñ" êti mā grahīḥ
nanu sarva|jña|kalpasya bhāry" âhaṃ Mitravarmaṇaḥ?
tvad|bhāryā|saṃnidhāv asmin n' âgamiṣyam ahaṃ yadi
vyanaśiṣyan mahat kāryaṃ tac c' êdam avadhīyatām.
āyācita|śatair jātaḥ putraḥ putra tvam āvayoḥ
vardhitaḥ śikṣitaś c' âsi pitrā vidyā|catuṣṭayam.
Parivrāṭ|Śākya|Nirgrantha|granth'|âbhyāsāc ca sarvadā
kuṭumba|pālan'|ālāpas tava jāto 'ti|dur|bhagaḥ.
18.640 tataḥ sa|mantrinā rājñā saṃmantrya gurubhiś ca te
suhṛdbhir Dhruvak'|ādyais tvam udyāne madhu pāyitaḥ.
Gaṅgadattā ca tair eva yojitā bhavatā saha
tayā tathā kṛtaś c' âsi yathā vettha tvam eva tat!
prakāreṇa ca yena tvaṃ gṛhaṃ nivāsitas tayā
jananyai Gaṅgadattāyāḥ kathito bhū|bhṛt" âiva saḥ.
daridra|vāṭake yac ca rātriṃ|divam asi sthitaḥ
tad ev' âikam asau rājñā kalpitaṃ cāraṇ'|ādibhiḥ.
jānāty eva ca dīrgh'|āyuḥ kva Campā kva daridratā
paurṇamāsī kṣapā kena dṛṣṭā dhvānta|malīmasā?
18.645 sarvad" âiva hi Campāyām asmin balini pālake
Balāv iva mahī|pāle Bali|rājyaṃ na dur|labham.
yāṃ ca rātriṃ bhavān suptas tasmin dur|gata|vāṭake
mama khaṭvā|tale tasmiñ śayitaṃ Gaṅgadattayā.
tasyāḥ prabhṛti bhīmāyā yāvad adyatanīṃ niśām
atr' ântare niṣaṇṇ" êyaṃ mat|khaṭvā|tala|bhū|tale.
yac ca tad dhanam etasyai tvayā dattaṃ tad etayā
bhāṇḍ'|āgāre tava nyastam a|śeṣaṃ kṛta|lekhakam.

My mother laughed and said, 'You mustn't think that I have no sense of timing. Am I not the wife of Mitra·varman, who was virtually omniscient? If I had not come to see you and your wives, an important matter might have ended in disaster. Listen! My child, you, our son, were born to us as a result of hundreds of prayers. Your father nurtured you and taught you the four sciences.* Because of your constant study of the books of Brahmin, Buddhist and Jaina renouncers, talk of raising a family became repellent to you.

After discussing it with the king, his ministers and your 18.640
parents, Dhrúvaka and your other friends had you drink wine in the park. They made you get together with Ganga·dattá, and you alone know what she did to you! The way she made you go home was proposed to Ganga·dattá's mother by the king himself.

And when you spent a day and a night in the slum, the king had used actors to stage it just for that period. For, my long-lived son, you know full well that there is no poverty in Champa. Who has seen the full-moon night sullied by darkness? As long as our powerful king, who is as generous 18.645
as King Bali, is reigning in Champa, a rule like that of Bali is not beyond our grasp.

And when you spent the night in the slum, Ganga·dattá was lying at the foot of my bed. Ever since that terrible night, she has been sleeping here, on the floor at the foot of my bed. She has put the money that you gave her into your treasury and written accounts for it all. She loves you and wants to see you. Don't treat her with contempt because you remember her contemptuous behavior: it was put on.

tad iyaṃ s'|ânurāgatvād bhavad|darśana|kāṅkṣiṇī
smṛtvā mithyā|tiras|kāraṃ na tiras|kāram arhati.
18.650 bhavatā paribhūtā ca sa|patnī|jana|saṃnidhau
kātarā pramadā|bhāvāt prāṇān api parityajet.

etan manasi kṛtv" ârtham a|kāle 'py aham āgatā
sīdad|gurutar'|ârthānāṃ kaḥ kālo nāma kāryiṇām?

eṣa te Gaṅgadattāyā vṛtt'|ântaḥ kathito 'dhunā
vadhūḥ Samudradinn" âpi yath" āyātā tathā śṛṇu.
daridra|vāṭakād yais tvaṃ pathikaiḥ saha nirgataḥ
prayuktās te nṛpeṇ' âiva sa ca Siddhārthako vaṇik.
antare yac ca te vṛttaṃ sārtha|dhvaṃs'|ādi bhīṣaṇam
Tāmraliptī|praveś'|ântaṃ śiṣṭaṃ Siddhārthakena tat.
18.655 bhraṣṭena vahana|bhraṃśād bhrāmyatā jaladhes taṭe
yathā Samudradinnāyāḥ pāṇir ālambitas tvayā.
punaś ca bhinna|potaś ca Pāṇḍya|puryāṃ ca yat tava
vṛttaṃ karpāsa|dāh'|ântaṃ Tāmralipty|āgamaś ca yaḥ.
Gaṅgadattena tan mahyaṃ saṃtatair lekha|hāribhiḥ
khyāpitaṃ yāvad Acero bhavantaṃ kv' âpi nītavān.
ataḥ paraṃ bhavad|vārttāṃ vicchinnatvād a|vindatī
nairāśya|kṛta|nirvedāt para|lok'|ôtsuk" âbhavam.

evaṃ|prāye ca vṛtt'|ânte dauvārika|niveditau
Samudradinnayā sārdhaṃ syālau prāviśatāṃ tataḥ.
18.660 prayukt'|ârghy'|ādi|sat|kārau kṣaṇaṃ tau gamita|śramau
vilakṣy' â|vīkṣamāṇau mām ābhāṣy' êdam avocatām.
«tava putrāya pitrā nas tanay" êyaṃ pratiśrutā
sa ca yauvana|mūḍhatvāt svī|kṛtaḥ Gaṅgadattayā.
tayā ca svī|kṛta|svasya gacchato mātul'|ālayam

If you insult her in front of your wives, the fainthearted girl, 18.650
as is the wont of young women, might even give up her life.

It was with this in mind that I came here at a seemingly inappropriate moment, but, when they have important matters at stake, what is the appropriate moment for those who have a case to plead?

That is Ganga·dattá's story. Now hear how my daughter-in-law Samúdra·dinná also came to be here. The travelers with whom you left the slum, as well as the merchant Siddhárthaka, were employed by the king himself. Everything that happened to you, from the terrible loss of the caravan until your entry into Tamra·lipti, was reported by Siddhárthaka. How you took Samúdra·dinná's hand after being 18.655
shipwrecked and wandering lost about the shore, and how you were shipwrecked again, and what happened to you in the city of the Pandyas, up to the cotton catching fire and your arrival in Tamra·lipti—Ganga·datta had it all reported to me through a constant flow of messengers until Achéra took you away. Then, because I was cut off and not getting any news of you, despair made me inconsolable and I wanted to go to the next world.

With the situation thus, the doorkeepers announced that two men had arrived, and your two brothers-in-law came in with Samúdra·dinná.

They were welcomed with offerings of water and so forth, 18.660
and rested for a moment. Embarrassed, they spoke without looking at me when they said the following: "Our father promised this girl, his daughter, to your son, but he, in the foolishness of youth, was won over by Ganga·dattá. She took his wealth and he left for his maternal uncle's

na śakyate yad ākhyātuṃ Pulindaiḥ kila tat kṛtam.
vaiśasaṃ duḥ|śravaṃ śrutvā tat sūnor Mitravarmaṇaḥ
niṣ|pratyāśaṃ kuṭumbaṃ naḥ prasthitaṃ Yavanān prati.
atha bohittham āsthāya pūjita|dvija|devatāḥ
saṃbhāvya|vyasana|dhvaṃsaṃ samagāhāma sāgaram.
tataḥ prajavinaṃ potaṃ taṃ pracaṇḍaḥ prabhañjanaḥ
mṛg'|êndra iva nāg'|êndraṃ prasphurantaṃ prabhinnavān.
vayaṃ tu karma|sāmarthyāt taraṃgaiḥ śara|gatvaraiḥ
ārūḍhāḥ paṭṭa|pṛṣṭhāni prāpitā jaladhes taṭam.
vadhūs tv ek'|ârṇav'|âmbhodhau lola|kallola|saṃkule
bhrānta|megha iv' ôdbhrāntā vyomni sārasa|kanyakā.
muktvā Samudradinn"|āśām arth'|āśāṃ ca mah"|âśrubhiḥ
Yavana|stham agacchāma mātāmaha|gṛhaṃ tataḥ.
tatr' âsmākaṃ kuṭumbaṃ tad dūrād utsukam āgatam
samṛddhe saras' îv' āsīt tṛptaṃ haṃsa|kadambakam.

atha yāte kva cit kāle pitā vām ittham ādiśat
‹āsāte kim udāsīnau bhavantau sthavirāv iva.
taruṇau sakalau svasthau vārttā|vidyā|viśāradau
sva|jan'|ânnena jīvantau kim ucyethe janair yuvām.
tasmān muktā|praval'|ādi sāraṃ sāgara|saṃbhavam
gṛhītvā yāna|pātreṇa sindhur uttāryatām› iti.

‹tath" êti› ca pratijñāya tath" âiv' āvām akurvahi
śliṣṭa|paṭṭām ath' âdrākṣva tarantīṃ rudatīṃ striyam.
‹a|spṛśantaḥ karair enāṃ para|strīm upanaukayā
āropayata bohittham› ity avocāva vāhakān.
tāṃ c' ārūḍhām apṛcchāma para|str" îti parāṅ|mukhau

house. We cannot bear to relate what is said to have been done to him by Púlindas on the way. When we heard the terrible news of the calamity that had befallen Mitra·varman's son, our family had nothing left to live for and set out for Greece. We boarded a boat, worshipped the brahmins and the gods, and set sail for the ocean, where disaster and
destruction are always to be expected. Then, like a lion 18.665
ripping open a trembling bull-elephant, a terrifying storm dashed the speeding boat to pieces. Driven by destiny, we climbed on top of the timbers and were propelled ashore by waves as swift as arrows. Your daughter-in-law, however, was lost in the huge ocean with its rolling waves, like a crane disappearing up into a sky filled with tumultuous clouds. Amid many tears, we gave up hope for Samúdra·dinná and our goods, and went to our maternal grandfather's house in Greece. Once there, our family was as happy as a flock of swans that has eagerly arrived from afar at a well-stocked lake.

After some time had passed our father said to us, 'Why 18.670
are you two sitting around doing nothing, like two old men? You are young, able-bodied, healthy and skilled in the science of business. Do you want people to say that you are living off your family? Take a valuable cargo of pearls, coral and other marine goods, and sail across the ocean!'

We agreed and were as good as our word. Floating in the water, clinging onto a plank, we saw a woman crying. We told the sailors to use the tender to get her up into the boat, but not to touch her with their hands, because she
was another man's wife. When she was on board, thinking 18.675

«mātaḥ kasy' âsi kā v"» êti
sā ca nīcair avocata,
‹vācā pratyabhijānāmi ciram abhyastayā yuvām
kaccit Sāgaradattasya bhavantau tanayāv iti?›
tatas tasyāś cir'|âbhyastaṃ pratyabhijñāya tad vacaḥ
‹kaccit Samudradinn" âsi sundar' îty› avadāva tām.
ākrandantī tatas tāram āvayor vāma|dakṣiṇe
s" â|parāṅ|mukhayor jaṅghe bāhubhyāṃ gāḍham āśliṣat.
abhāṣata ca ‹hā tāta! hā mam' âmbā priy'|ātma|jā!
dhik|kāraḥ sāgaraṃ pāpaṃ yena tau kv' âpi yāpitau!
18.680 h" ârya|putra kva yāto 'si? hata|sneha vihāya mām?
āpanna|priya|dārāṇāṃ n' âiṣa dharmaḥ satām!› iti.
ath' ārya|putra|śabdena bhaya|saṃśaya|hetunā
niḥ|snehī|kṛta|cetaskāv abhāṣāvahi tām iti.
‹alaṃ sundari kranditvā jīvataḥ pitarau tava
ārya|putraḥ punar yas te sa nau niścīyatām› iti.
tataḥ śruta|pitṛ|kṣemā sā śok'|ôjjhita|mānasā
āvāṃ ‹mā bhaiṣṭam› ity uktvā svaṃ vṛttaṃ vṛttam abravīt.
‹asty ahaṃ vahanād bhraṣṭā bhrāmyantī jaladhes taṭe
yasmai datt" âsmi yuṣmābhis tam adrākṣaṃ vipad|gatam.
18.685 saṃvādita|sva|vṛttena gṛhītas tena me karaḥ
jāyante hi su|puṇyānām utsavā vyasaneṣv api.
sa māṃ alālayad bāla|nārī|lālana|peśalaḥ
tathā yathā priyatamau n' âsmaraṃ pitarāv api.

she was someone else's wife we averted our faces and asked her, 'Madam, who is your husband and who are you?'

She replied softly, 'I recognize you by your voices, which are very familiar to me. Might you be Ságara·datta's two sons?' We recognized her voice, which was very familiar to us. We asked her, 'Beautiful lady, might you be Samúdra·dinná?'

We turned to face her, and, sobbing loudly, she wrapped her arms tightly around the left leg of one of us and the right leg of the other. She said, 'Oh Father! Oh my Mother, so devoted to your children! Curse the wicked ocean for
taking them away! Oh my husband, where have you gone? 18.680
Has your love died, that you have abandoned me? This is not the way that good men behave when their dear wives are in trouble!'

The word 'husband' was a cause for fear and worry, and made us cold-hearted when we spoke to her: 'Stop crying, beautiful lady. Your parents are alive. But tell us about this husband of yours.' When she heard that her parents were well, her mind was freed from sorrow, and, after saying that we needn't worry, she told us everything that had happened to her:

'When I was shipwrecked, I wandered about the shore and came across the man to whom you had betrothed me;
he was in a sorry state. We told each other our stories and 18.685
he took my hand in marriage. For those of great merit, occasions for celebration happen even in times of misfortune. He was expert at romancing young ladies, and romanced me in such a way that I forgot even my beloved parents. Today we boarded a ship that appeared by chance, and set

ath' âdya potam āruhya samāyātaṃ yadṛcchayā
prasthitau svaḥ sva|deśāya vipannaḥ sa ca pūrvavat.
sa ca vāṃ bhāginī|bhartā s'|ākrandāyāḥ puro mama
saṃpraty eva taraṃgeṇa gamitaḥ kv' âpi vairiṇā.
nabhovaj|javanair bhaṅgair bhaṅgurair āvṛtaḥ sa ca
a|kasmāj jāta|śatrubhyāṃ bhavadbhyāṃ c' âham uddhṛtā.
18.690 satvathā tad|viyog'|âgni|taptāny aṅgāni sāgare
śīte śītalayiṣyāmi muñcataṃ māṃ yuvām!› iti.

upapannair ath' ālāpair janita|pratyayau tayā
utpanna|param'|ānandāv āliṅgāma parasparam.
‹vipanna|potayor āsīd yuvayoḥ saṃgamo yathā
bhaviṣyati tathā bhūyaś citraṃ hi caritaṃ vidheḥ.›
evam|ādibhir ālāpaiś ceto|vikṣepa|hetubhiḥ
parisaṃsthāpayantau tām atarāva mah"|ôdadhim.

tac ca muktā|praval'|ādi guru|mūlyaṃ yad āhṛtam
sahasra|guṇa|lābhaṃ tad āvābhyāṃ parivartitam.
18.695 vadhūḥ Samudradinnā te guru|sāraṃ ca tad dhanam
sarvam arpitam āvābhyāṃ tubhyaṃ tat parigṛhyatām.
vahana|dhvaṃsa|muktānāṃ sametānāṃ ca bandhubhiḥ
evaṃ Samudradinnā ca tvat|putrasya nidarśanam.
pūrvavat Sānudāso 'pi muktaḥ pota|vipattitaḥ
āgamiṣyati tad devi muñca kātaratām» iti.
ity uktvā sa|dhana|skandhāṃ nikṣipya bhāginīṃ mayi
su|sat|kāra|prayuktau tau yath"|āgatam agacchatām.
evaṃ Samudradinn" êyam āgatā bhavato gṛham
daiva|pauruṣa|yuktasya Śrīr iva ślāghya|janmanaḥ.

out for our own country. It sank like the first one. Your sister's husband was just now taken away by a cruel wave as I looked on, screaming. He was swamped by crashing breakers as swift as the wind, and you became my enemies when you suddenly saved me. My body is burning up with 18.690
the fire of separation from him; I shall soothe it in the cool ocean. Let me go!'

Her words were seemly and reassured us. We were blissfully happy and embraced one another. 'Just as the two of you met after you had both been shipwrecked, so it could happen again, for the ways of fate are strange.' Consoling her with these and other words designed to distract her, we crossed the ocean.

We then sold our valuable cargo of pearls, coral and so forth for a thousand-fold profit. Here is your daughter-in- 18.695
law Samúdra·dinná and that precious fortune. We offer it all to you. Please accept it. As an example of someone who has escaped from a shipwreck and been reunited with her family, Samúdra·dinná is an indication that the same will happen to your son. Just as before, Sanu·dasa will survive the shipwreck and return, so do not despair, good lady." With these words, they handed over their sister and their fortune to me. After being very hospitably looked after, they left the way they had come. That is how Samúdra·dinná came to be in your house, just as Lakshmi comes to the house of a nobleman who is both lucky and bold.

18.700 tad etān bhavato dārān dharma|cāritra|rakṣitān
rakṣantyā guru|māninyā carite caritaṃ mayā.
vrīḍita|Draviṇ'|ēśasya samṛddhyā divyay" ânayā
‹pitrā tulyo bhavatv› eṣa śāpo n' ā|śaṃsitas tava!
tasmād dhanam idaṃ bhuñjan bhuñjānaś ca yath"|āgamam
devatānāṃ pitṝṇāṃ ca yātv ānṛṇyaṃ bhavān› iti.»

iti Bṛhatkathāyāṃ Ślokasaṃgrahe Sānudāsa|kathā.

So here are your wives. I have considered myself their mother and behaved accordingly, looking after them so that their virtue and reputation have been safeguarded. You put Kubéra to shame with this divine wealth, and I shall not make the wish that you be the equal of your father, because it would be a curse! Therefore enjoy this wealth yourself and make use of it according to scriptural law so that you can be free of your obligations to the gods and ancestors.'"* 18.700

Thus ends the story of Sanu·dasa in the
Abridgement into Sanskrit Verse of the Long Story.

CANTO 19
NALÍNIKA

19.1 SNIGDHAIR DĀRAIḤ suhṛdbhiś ca
maitrī|mātra|nibandhanaiḥ
Campāyāṃ ramamāṇasya kālaḥ
kaś cid agān mama.
ekadā prāsakaiḥ krīḍan saha Gandharvadattayā
sahasā pramadā|veṣam apaśyaṃ puruṣaṃ puraḥ.
kapāla|śikhi|piñchābhyāṃ virājita|kara|dvayam
ā|yukt'|êndra|dhanuś|chāya|śṛṅgāra|gala|kaṇṭhikam.
Gandharvadattayā c' âsau datta|sv'|āsanayā svayam
prakṣālya caraṇau bhaktyā sv'|âlaṃ|kārair alaṃ|kṛtaḥ.
19.5 tac ca me guru|gāmbhīryaṃ kv' âpi nītam asūyayā
yathā kesari|śāvasya gandha|hasti|jighāṃsayā.
mam' āsīd «iyam ev' âtra sa|doṣā kula|māninī
eṣa strī|puruṣaḥ śocyo yo na strī na pumān!» iti.
mām uddiśya tatas tena krodh'|âruṇita|cakṣuṣā
vadatā «nihato 's' îti» vimuktaḥ śikhi|picchakaḥ.
sa me keśa|kalāp'|âgram īṣad āmṛśya yātavān
nāg'|êṣur iva Karṇ'|âstraḥ kirīṭ'|âgraṃ Kirīṭinaḥ.
svayam eva ca tat tasya kapālam apatat karāt
niḥ|sthāmnaḥ kuñjarasy' êva vidhānaṃ vinaśiṣyataḥ.
19.10 so 'tha grāmeyaken' êva dhiyā dhūrto 'tisaṃdhitaḥ
dhūmra|chāyaḥ śanair jalpan «dhig! dhiṅ mām!» iti nirgataḥ.
atha Gandharvadattā māṃ dīpt'|āmarṣam a|śaṅkitā
sa|vāḍavam upāsarpan nimna|g" êva mah"|ârṇavam.
mama tv āsīd «aho strīṇām a|trāsam a|trapaṃ manaḥ!
yat pur" êva pragalbh" êyam upasarpati mām» iti.

WITH A LOVING WIFE and friends who were bound to 19.1
me by affection alone, time passed pleasurably for me in Champa.

One day I was playing dice with Gandhárva·datta when suddenly I saw before me a man dressed as a woman. In his hands were a skull and a peacock feather, and he was wearing a delicate necklace that looked like two rainbows joined together. Gandhárva·datta gave him her seat, respectfully washed his feet herself, and adorned him with her own ornaments.

At this my usually steadfast composure was removed by 19.5
irritation, like that of a young lion being removed by the urge to kill a rutting elephant. I said to myself, "It is my wife that is at fault here. This pitiful man-woman is neither man nor woman!"

His eyes reddened by rage, he threw the peacock feather toward me, saying, "You're dead!" It lightly brushed the edge of my hair, just as Karna's weapon, the snake-arrow, brushed the top of Árjuna's crown. Then the skull fell from his hand of its own accord, like a piece of food falling from
the trunk of a weak and dying elephant. Looking like a 19.10
villain who has met his match in base cunning, he turned pale and departed, muttering, "Shame! Shame on me!"

I was burning with rage but Gandhárva·datta approached me fearlessly, like a river going down to an ocean ablaze with the submarine fire.

I said to myself, "How free of fear and shame are women's minds! She is so brazen that she approaches me as if nothing had happened."

sā mām avocad bhīt" êva «śītalī|bhavata kṣaṇam
kiṃ cid vijñāpayāmy eṣa yātu vaḥ krodha|pāvakaḥ!
ayaṃ Vikaciko nāma Gaurī|śikhara|vāsinaḥ
vidyā|dhara|pater bhrātā Gaurimuṇḍasya sādhakaḥ.
19.15 Bhūta|vrataṃ ca nām' êdaṃ bahu|vighnaṃ caraty ayam
samāpte 'sminn a|vighnena vandhyāḥ syur no mano|rathāḥ.
yā ca pūjayate taṃ strī Gaurī|vrata|vicāriṇam
tasyai varaṃ mahā|Gaurī dayate śāpam anyathā.
vijñāpayāmi saṃkṣiptaṃ krodhād anyo mahā|balaḥ
vihantā sarva|siddhīnāṃ n' âsti vighna|vināyakaḥ.
siddha|kalpaṃ ca tasy' êdaṃ khaṇḍayatyā mahā|vratam
tuṣṭayā toṣitā Gaurī mayā yūyaṃ ca roṣitāḥ.
tad etasy' âsya yuṣmabhyaṃ
kruddhebhyaḥ krudhyatas tathā
Gaurī|bhraṣṭā mahā|vidyā
vidy" êva tanu|medhasaḥ.
19.20 tena yuṣmākam ev' êdaṃ kāryaṃ kurvāṇayā guru
yan mayā roṣitā yūyam etan me mṛṣyatām» iti.

sa ca krodha|grahaś caṇḍaḥ śanakaiḥ śanakair mama
dayitā|mantra|vādinyā hṛdayād apasarpitaḥ.
iti saṃjanit'|ôtsāhas tay" âhaṃ mantra|sādhanaiḥ
āsīnaḥ Sānudāsena kadā cid iti bhāṣitaḥ.

«āsīd ih' âiva Campāyām iṣṭa|bhāryo mahī|patiḥ
tena dohadakaṃ pṛṣṭā bhāry" âvocat trapāvatī.
‹krīḍan|makara|kumbhīra|kulīra|jhaṣa|kacchape
krīḍeyaṃ saha yuṣmābhir jale jala|nidher› iti.

She did seem a little scared as she said to me, "Calm down for a moment, I have something to tell you—stop your burning rage! The fellow is called Vikáchika. He is the brother of Gauri·munda, the king of the sorcerers who lives
on Mount Gauri. He is studying magic and practicing the 19.15
Ghost observance. It has many pitfalls, but if he completes it successfully our desires will come to nothing. When a woman shows respect to a man carrying out one of Gauri's observances, the great goddess grants her a wish; otherwise she bestows a curse. Let me explain it in brief: of obstacles to the attainment of success, there is none greater than anger. His powerful observance had almost succeeded when, by interrupting it, I had the pleasure of pleasing Gauri and I irritated you. When he became angry with you for being angry, Gauri destroyed his great magical wisdom as if it were
the wisdom of an idiot. It was for you alone that I did this 19.20
important deed, so please forgive me for angering you."

Invoking a lover's magical charms, she slowly drove the fearsome demon anger from my heart. My resolve was thus restored by her spells, and one day when I was relaxing Sanu·dasa said to me,

"There was a king here in Champa who adored his wife. When she was pregnant, he asked her about her cravings and she replied shyly, 'I want to play with you in the water of the ocean, where dolphins, crocodiles, crabs, fish and turtles play.'

19.25 rājñ" âpi Magadhaiḥ s'|Âṅgair
bandhayitv" āśu nimnagām
saraḥ sāgara|vistāram
a|vandhy'|ājñena khānitam.
tatra nakr'|ādi|saṃsthāna|dāru|yantra|nirantare
vimān'|ākāra|pota|sthau tau rājānau viceratuḥ.

ārabhya ca tataḥ kālāt tatra yātrā pravartitā
ādṛṣṭa|parapuṣṭeṣu divaseṣu mahī|bhujā.
te c' âite divasāḥ prāptāḥ paṭu|kokila|kūjitāḥ
sā ca yātr" êyam āyātā ramy" â|mṛta|bhujām api.
iṣyate yadi ca draṣṭuṃ saha Gandharvadattayā
asmad|ādi|parīvārais tataḥ sā dṛśyatām!› iti.

19.30 abhinīya tataḥ rātriṃ prātaḥ pravahaṇ'|āśritaḥ
nirgacchāmi sma Campāyāḥ paura|netr'|ôtpal'|ârcitaḥ.
cakṣur|mano|har'|ārāma|cchāyām adhyāsitaṃ tataḥ
pakkaṇaṃ dṛṣṭavān asmi Rāja|rāja|pur'|ôjjvalam.
tasya madhye ca mātaṅgaṃ gandha|mātaṅga|dhīratam
kālam apy ujjval'|āyāmaṃ ghan'|â|ghanam iv' âmbu|dam.
Kālindī|nīla|kālīṃ ca vṛddhāṃ piṅga|śiro|ruhām
dīpta|saudāmanī|cakrāṃ prāvṛṣeṇyām iva kṣapām.
dolā|līlā|vilolā ca tatr' âdṛśyata kanyakā
nīla|nīraja|māl" êva komal'|ânila|lāsitā.
19.35 cintitaṃ ca mayā kāntā yadi me kālikā bhavet
iyam eva tatas tanvī kṣipta|kuṅkuma|gauratā.

sthānāc c' âcalit" âiv' âsau dṛṣṭyā māṃ dūram anvagāt
mālay" êva palāśānām aṃśumantaṃ suvarcalā.
tāṃ c' āliṅgitavān asmi dṛṣṭyā dūrī|bhavann api
nitānta|snigdhayā prācīṃ prabhay" êva divākaraḥ.

The king, whose orders never came to naught, immediately had the people of Mágadha and Anga dam a river and dig a lake as wide as the ocean. It was filled with wooden devices shaped like crocodiles and other creatures, and the royal couple floated about on it in a boat resembling an aerial chariot. 19.25

The king inaugurated a festival that has been held since then in the season when the koyals appear. The days filled with the shrill calls of koyals have arrived, and so has the festival that delights even the gods. If you and Gandhárva·datta want to visit it with me and your other companions, then let's go!"

The next morning, I climbed aboard a chariot and went 19.30
out of Champa worshipped by the lotus-eyes of the citizens. Then, nestled in the shade of beautiful woodland groves, I saw a forest settlement that was as splendid as the city of Kubéra. In the middle of it was a forest-dweller as proud as a rutting elephant. He was black but tall, like a storm cloud. There was an old woman, too: jet black like the Yámuna and with golden hair, she was like a monsoon night ringed with flashing lightning. I noticed a young girl there playfully swinging on a swing, like a garland of blue lotuses
fluttering in a gentle breeze. I thought that were I to have 19.35
a black sweetheart then it would be this slip of a girl, who put the saffron hue of the crocus to shame.

Without moving from where she was, she followed me with her gaze, like a *suvárchala* flower following the sun with its garland of petals. Though keeping my distance, I embraced her with my gaze, like the sun embracing the east with its affectionate glow. The fond looks we cast were a

snigdhe dṛṣṭīr visarjy' êti dūtikā|pratidūtike
tayā mama mayā tasyā nītāḥ prāṇā vidheyatām.
ath' ārāmān abhikrudhyann āvayor vyavadhāyakān
mātaṅgīṃ manas" âgacchaṃ śarīreṇa mahā|saraḥ.
19.40 sa ca yātr"|ôtsavaś citro may" âny'|āhita|cetasā
tatra|sthen' âiva no dṛṣṭaḥ saṃsāra iva yoginā.
atha yātr"|ôtsave tatra pītv" êva madhu bhāskaraḥ
manda|manda|parispandas tāmra|maṇḍalatām ayāt.

mama tv āsīd «yathā devaḥ prācīṃ kamalinī|priyaḥ
a|prasādy' âiva tāṃ bhānuḥ pratīcim upasarpati.
tathā Gandharvadattāyāḥ pura ev' ânuvarṇya tām
mātaṅgīm anusarpāmi yathā rājā tathā prajāḥ!
atha vā mānuṣair eva yaḥ panthāḥ kāmibhir gataḥ
tam ev' ânugamiṣyāmi na deva|caritaṃ caret!»
19.45 Sānudāsam ath' âvocaṃ «Bharadvāj'|ātma|jā tvayā
pūrvam eva sa|yānena nagarīm abhinīyatām.
paścāj jana|samūhasya gacchantyāḥ pathi pāṃsavaḥ
parādhūsarayanty asyāḥ s'|ôtpal'|āmalak'|āvalīm.
śobhāṃ yātrika|lokasya paśyan praviśataḥ puram
purastād aham āyāmi saha nāgarakair» iti.

atha Gandharvadattāyāṃ pravṛttāyāṃ puraṃ prati
dārike dve parāvṛtya vanditvā mām avocatām.
«āvām ājñāpite devyā ‹svāminaṃ nirvinodanam
vinodayatam ālāpair yuvām a|paruṣair› iti.»
19.50 tatas te madayitv" âhaṃ toṣayitvā ca bhūṣaṇaiḥ
paṭu|vegena yānena pakkaṇ'|ântikam āgamam.

pair of messengers going back and forth: she enslaved my heart and I enslaved hers. Angry with the woodland groves for coming between us, I went to the forest girl with my mind, but with my body I went to the lake. Even though 19.40
I was there, my mind was elsewhere, and, like a yogin who does not notice the phenomenal world, I did not notice the wonderful festival celebrations. As if it had been drinking wine at the festival, the sun moved slowly and its orb took on a coppery hue.

I said to myself, "Just as the lotus's favorite god, the sun, goes over to the west without even taking leave of the east, so shall I, in front of Gandhárva·datta, praise the forest girl and go to her. As the sovereign, so the subjects! On the other hand, perhaps I will follow the way of human lovers: one shouldn't behave like a god!"

I said to Sanu·dasa, "Drive Bharad·vaja's daughter back 19.45
to the city early. If she goes on the road after the crowds, the dust will sully her garland of lotuses and mango flowers. I shall take up the rear with the gentlemen, and watch the festival-goers enter the city in their finery."

When Gandhárva·datta was on her way to the city, two courtesans came back. They greeted me and said, "Her ladyship has told us that you have nothing to amuse you, and instructed us to entertain you with charming conversation."
I got them drunk, made them happy with some jewelry, and 19.50
headed for the forest settlement in a speeding chariot.

s" âpi tatr' âiva dolāyāṃ sthitā mātaṅga|sundarī
gacchantam iva nirvyājam āgacchantaṃ samaikṣata.
viśrabdham atha tāṃ draṣṭuṃ śanair yānam acodayam
tatas tad api saṃprāptaṃ javena kulaṭā|dvayam.
āsīc ca mama «yad loke prasiddham abhidhīyate
‹śreyāṃsi bahu|vighnāni bhavant' îti tath" âiva tat.›

duḥkhena ca gṛhaṃ gatvā śūnyaḥ saṃmānya ca priyām
nidrām abhilaṣāmi sma mātaṅgī|saṃgam'|āśayā.
19.55 ardha|rātre tu sahasā pratibuddhā muneḥ sutā
prayukte mayi ye dāsyau te pānīyam ayācata.
dhauta|pramṛṣṭa|vadanā sv|āhit'|ānana|bhūṣaṇā
upaveśya puro 'kleśair apṛcchad bandhakī|dvayam.
«arya|putreṇa mātaṅgī tayā vā lola|netrayā
dṛṣṭo 'yaṃ taralen' êti?»

tatas tābhyāṃ niveditam.
«na tathā s" ârya|putreṇa prekṣitā jīrṇa|kanyakā
netrābhyām a|nimeṣābhyām arya|putras tayā yathā.»

tataḥ prāk pratibuddhaṃ mām apṛcchat Suprabhā|sutā
«jāgratha svapith' êty» uccair «jāgram' îti» may" ôditam.
19.60 tay" ôktam «ayam ārambho yuṣmākaṃ dṛśyate yathā
tathā Nalinikāṃ nūnaṃ kartum icchasi mām» iti.

«kv' âsau Nalinikā? kā vā? kasya v" êti» may" ôdite
Bharadvāja|sut" ākhyātum upākrāmata vṛttakam.

The beautiful forest girl was still there, sitting on the swing. She watched me on my way back with the same innocence that she had watched me on my way out. I calmly slowed down the chariot so that I could look at her. Then the two courtesans suddenly arrived there too. I said to myself, "The well-known saying that the way to the finest things is blocked by many obstacles is indeed true."

I went home in sadness, and, after going through the motions of paying my respects to my wife, I longed for sleep, in the hope of being united with the forest girl.

In the middle of the night, the sage's daughter suddenly 19.55
woke up. She asked the two servants that she had sent after
me to give her some water. She washed and wiped her face
and put on her makeup. Then she had the two courtesans sit
comfortably in front of her and inquired, "Did my lecherous
husband and that girl with the wandering eyes look at one
another?"

They replied, "Your husband did not look at the old man's daughter in the same way that she, with her unblinking eyes, looked at him."

I had woken up. Gandhárva·datta asked me whether I
was awake or sleeping, and in a loud voice I told her that I
was awake. She said, "It seems from your actions as though 19.60
you want to make a Nalínika of me."

When I asked her where this Nalínika was, who she was, and whose wife she was, Bharad·vaja's daughter began telling me a story.

«asti paścāt samudr'|ânte sv|ācāra|dhanavat|prajam
nagaraṃ Kānanadvīpaṃ Mahendra|nagar'|ôpamam.
a|Mahendra|guṇas tatra manu|j'|êndraḥ prajā|priyaḥ
putro mano|haras tasya saṃjñay" âpi Manoharaḥ.
vidit'|â|śeṣa|vedyo 'pi gandha|śāstra|priyo 'dhikam
nānā|ruciṣu sattveṣu kasya cit kiṃ cid īpsitam.
19.65 suhṛdau Bakul'|Âśokau Vasantasy' êva tasya yau
vasantam iva taṃ premṇā na kadā cid amuñcatām.

kadā cid dvāra|pālena vanditvā rāja|sūnave
kumār'|âvasatha|sthāya sa|mitrāya niveditam.
‹yuṣmān Sumaṅgalo nāma buddha|gandh'|ânuśāsanaḥ
a|grāmyo dhīra|vacanaḥ kasmād api didṛkṣate.›

‹gaccha praveśay' êty› uktvā dvāra|pālaṃ Manoharaḥ
vilepanam upādatta dhūpaṃ ca tvarito 'dahat.

Sumaṅgalo 'py anujñātaḥ praviśya dvāra|deśataḥ
śiro nipīḍya pāṇibhyāṃ saṃkocy' âṅgam apāsarat.
19.70 ‹anena mama dhūpena gandha|mālya|vivādinā
āghrātena śiraḥ|śūlam utpannam› iti c' âvadat.
ākṛṣṭe sthagikāyāś ca svasyāḥ phalaka|saṃpuṭe
Manoharaṃ muhuḥ paśyan svayaṃ dhūpam ayojayat.
tataḥ kṛta|namas|kāraḥ sa Manoharam abravīt
‹su|mano|gandha|saṃvādī dhūpo 'yaṃ dāhyatām› iti.

"On the shores of the western ocean is the city of Kánana·dvipa, whose people are virtuous and rich and which is the equal of the city of lord Indra. The king there did not have lord Indra's qualities but was devoted to his subjects. His son was charming even in name, being called Mano·hara.* Although he knew everything there was to be known, he was particularly fond of the science of perfumery. People have many different interests; everyone likes something!
Like Vasánta, he had two friends, Bákula and Ashóka, who 19.65
were so affectionate that they were inseparable from him, just as the *bákula* and *ashóka* flowers are inseparable from spring.*

One day when the prince was in his quarters with his friends, a doorkeeper greeted him and said, 'A man called Sumángala, who is learned in the science of perfumery, is sophisticated, and talks wisely, wants to see you for some reason.'

Mano·hara told the doorkeeper to go and show him in. He then hurriedly smeared himself with perfumed oil and lit some incense.

As soon as Sumángala had been introduced and came in through the door, he pressed his head with his hands,
hunched himself up and backed away. He said, 'This incense 19.70
clashes with your scent and that of the garland. Smelling it has given me a headache.' He removed a wooden writing tablet from his case and mixed up some incense, looking at Mano·hara all the while. After greeting Mano·hara respectfully, he said to him, 'Please burn this incense: it complements your scent and the flowers.'

tataḥ sa|Bakul'|Âśokas tasmin gandhe Manoharaḥ
pratīto gandha|śāstra|jñaṃ Sumaṅgalam apūjayat.
evaṃ ca kṛta|sat|kāraḥ rāja|putraṃ Sumaṅgalaḥ
dinais tri|caturair eva caturaḥ paryatoṣayat.
19.75 ekadā Bakul'|Âśoka|Sumaṅgala|puraḥ|saraḥ
manoharām agād draṣṭuṃ yakṣa|sattrāṃ Manoharaḥ.
tatra tatra tatas tena paśyatā tat tad adbhutam
yakṣī|pratikṛtir dṛṣṭā vinyastā citra|karmaṇi.
nir|jīv" âpi sphurant" îva mūk" âpi mṛdu|vāg iva
citre nyast" âpi sā tena citte nyast" âti|rāgiṇā.
draṣṭavyaṃ c' ânyad ujjhitvā ramaṇaṃ citta|cakṣuṣām
su|mano|gandha|dhūp'|ādyais tām ev' âikām asevata.
balavan|manmath'|âpāsta|bhogy'|â|bhogya|vicāraṇaḥ
nitambād ambaraṃ tasyāḥ sa kil' ākraṣṭum aihata.
19.80 citra|bhittim atha tyaktvā s" âpi Padm" êva padminīm
Viṣṇor vakṣa iva śyāmam asevata nabhas|talam.

uvāca rāja|putraṃ ca ‹nāmn" âhaṃ Sukumārikā
yakṣī yakṣa|pateḥ śāpāt prāpt" ālekhya|śarīratām.
tena kṣaṇika|roṣeṇa nārīṣu ca dayālunā
śāp'|ântam arthiten' âham iti nidhyāya dhīritā.
«citra|nyasta|tanuṃ yas tvāṃ manuṣyo 'bhibhaviṣyati
sa eva kṛta|śāp'|ântas tava bhartā bhaviṣyati.»

iti tvaṃ Rājarājena bhartā me pratipāditaḥ
sadṛśo vara|dānena śāpo 'pi hi mah"|ātmanām!
19.85 yadi te 'sti mayi prītis tataḥ krīḍat|sur'|âsuram
śailaṃ Śrīkuñja|nāmānaṃ yakṣ'|āvāsaṃ vrajer› iti.

Mano·hara, Bákula and Ashóka were won over by the fragrance and held Sumángala in high esteem as a connoisseur of perfumery. Sumángala was thus well received and the cunning fellow then spent three or four days ingratiating himself with the prince.

One day, Mano·hara went to visit the delightful festival 19.75
of the yakshas with Bákula, Ashóka and Sumángala. As he was looking around at the wonders there, he noticed a painted image of a *yakshi*. Although lifeless, she seemed to quiver; although dumb, she seemed to speak softly; although she was painted in a picture, the prince was smitten and placed her in his heart. Forgetting all the other charming and beautiful sights, he devoted himself to her and her alone, offering her gifts like flowers, perfumes and incense. His strong desire removed his sense of what was or was not to be enjoyed, and he even tried to take off her robe from
around her hips. Like Lakshmi abandoning her lotus and 19.80
resorting to Vishnu's dark chest, she left the wall painting and rose into the deep blue sky.

She said to the prince, 'I am a *yakshi* called Sukumárika. Because of a curse from the king of the yakshas, I was trapped in the painting. His anger is fleeting and he takes kindly to women, so, when I asked him how the curse would end, after reflecting for a while he consoled me by saying, "The man that disgraces you while you are trapped in the painting will end the curse and become your husband."

Thus Kubéra has given you to me as my husband. Even
the curse of a great man is like a blessing! If you love me, 19.85
then go to the place where the gods and demons play, the mountain called Shri·kuñja, home of the yakshas.'

ath' ântar|dhiṃ gatā yakṣī mahā|mohaṃ Manoharaḥ
taṃ c' ālokya tath"|âvasthaṃ viṣādaṃ Bakul'|ādayaḥ.
labdha|saṃjñaś ca tair uktaḥ śrutvā yakṣī|kathām asau
‹alam ākulatāṃ gatvā su|labhā Sukumārikā.
yady asau dur|gamaḥ śailas tatas taṃ Sukumārikā
yuṣmat saṃbhogam icchantī na tathā kathayed› iti.
ekadā pitaraṃ draṣṭuṃ sa gataḥ sa|suhṛd|gaṇaḥ
siddha|yātraṃ parāvṛttam apaśyat pota|vāṇijam.
19.90 rājño datta|mahā|ratnaḥ saḥ rājñā kṛta|sat|kriyaḥ
pṛṣṭas tena ‹bhavān kiṃ kim āścaryaṃ dṛṣṭavān?› iti.
ten' ôktam ‹ambu|dhes tīre devena vasatā satā
dṛṣṭaṃ kiṃ nāma n' āścaryam? āścarya|nidhir ambu|dhiḥ!
kiṃ tv ekad" âham adrākṣaṃ hṛta|poto nabhasvatā
sāndra|hema|prabhā|piṅgaṃ tuṅga|śṛṅga|srajaṃ nagam.
«kim etad?» iti pṛṣṭaś ca mayā niryāmako 'vadat
«vṛddhair eṣa samākhyātaḥ Śrīkuñjaḥ śṛṅgavān» iti.›
evam|ādi nivedy' âsau vāṇijaḥ sva|gṛhān agāt
rāja|putro 'pi rājānaṃ natvā vāṇijam anvagāt.
19.95 pradadāv atha sarva|svaṃ tasmai trāsena vāṇijaḥ
rāja|putrād gṛha|prāptād āḍhyaḥ ko nāma na traset?
ten' âpi su|mano|mālā|mātram ālabhya bhāṣitam
‹na sat|kāra|khalī|kāram arhanti śiśavo guroḥ.
kiṃ tu yas tāta|pādebhyaḥ Śrīkuñjaḥ kathitas tvayā
sa kutūhaline mahyaṃ spaṣṭam ākhyāyatām› iti.

Then the *yakshi* disappeared. Mano·hara was overcome and, seeing him like this, Bákula and the others grew despondent. After he had come to his senses and told them the *yakshi*'s story, they said to him, 'Do not worry. Sukumárika will be easy to find. She wants to be your lover. If the mountain were hard to reach, then she would not have spoken thus.'

One day, he went with his friends to visit his father and met a seafaring merchant who had returned from a successful journey. The merchant gave the king a large jewel, and 19.90
the king, after receiving him hospitably, asked him what wonders he had seen.

He replied, 'Your Majesty lives on the ocean shore: what wonders has he not seen? The ocean is a treasure trove of wonders! Nevertheless, one day, when my ship had been blown off course, I did see, surrounded by tall peaks, a mountain on which there was so much gold that it was yellow. When I asked the captain about it he said, "The elders call that mountain Shri·kunja."'

After telling this and other stories, the merchant went home. The prince bowed to the king and went after the merchant. In fear, the merchant offered him all his wealth— 19.95
what rich man is not frightened when a prince comes to his house? But he took only a garland of flowers, and said, 'Pupils should not abuse the hospitality of a teacher. However, I am interested in this Shri·kuñja that you mentioned to my revered father. Tell me more about it.'

pratyāśvastas tatas tasya vacobhir madhurair asau
Śrīkuñjaṃ sahitaṃ cihnair ity ākhyātuṃ pracakrame.
‹ath' âikadā maden' êva mahā|vyālo mataṅga|jaḥ
marutā tyājita|sthairyo yātaḥ potaḥ sva|tantratām.
19.100 praśānt'|ôtpāta|vātatvāt sāgare c' âmbara|sthire
citr'|ākārān apaśyāma prāṇino jala|cāriṇaḥ.
kva cit kesari|śārdūla|dvīpi|khaḍga'|rkṣa|śambarān
yūthaśaḥ prastuta|krīḍān unmajjana|nimajjanaiḥ.
anyatr' āviddha|karṇānāṃ strī|puṃsānām a|vāsasām
dhvani|mātraka|bhāṣāṇāṃ dvaṃdvāni paśu|dharmaṇām.
kva cid utpatatas tuṅgān nāgān āyata|pakṣatīn
pakṣa|cheda|bhay'|ālīnān nagān iva mah'|ârṇave.
avāc ca sahasā modaḥ kauveryāḥ pavan'|āhṛtaḥ
yasy' āghrāṇāya saṃpannaṃ manye ghrāṇa|mayaṃ jagat!
19.105 drakṣyantaḥ saṃbhavaṃ tasya sa|kutūhala|dṛṣṭayaḥ
dūrād girim apaśyāma ratna|kūṭa|stha|kiṃnaram.
«kim etad» iti pṛṣṭaś ca mayā niryāmako 'bravīt
«vṛddhair eṣa samākhyātaḥ Śrīkuñjaḥ śṛṅgavān» iti.›
ity|ādi kathitaṃ tena yad yat tat tan Manoharaḥ
saha|sāgara|dig|deśaṃ spaṣṭaṃ saṃpuṭake 'likhat.
āgamayya tataḥ potam āpta|niryāmak'|āsthitam
Bakul'|ādi|sahāyo 'sāv agāhata mah"|ârṇavam.
anukūla|mahā|vega|samīra|preritena saḥ
āsīdad a|cireṇ' âiva potena diśam īpsitām.
19.110 sadṛśaiḥ sphalaka|sthānāṃ cihnair janita|niścayaḥ
manaś|cakṣuḥ|śarīraiḥ sa Śrīkuñjaṃ yugapad gataḥ.
ambhodhi|jala|kallola|dhauta|nīl'|ôpalaṃ tataḥ

Relieved by his friendly words, the merchant started to describe Shri·kuñja in detail. 'Well, one day, like rut upsetting a wild elephant, the wind made the boat unstable and
it took on a mind of its own. After the storm had abated, 19.100
the sea became as calm as the sky, and we saw strangely shaped aquatic animals. In one place there were groups of lions, tigers, elephants, rhinoceroses, bears and deer playing openly, diving in and out of the water. Elsewhere there were pairs of naked men and women with pierced ears who behaved like animals, speaking gibberish. In another place there were huge flying elephants with long wings. It was as though the mountains were living at sea for fear of having their wings cut.*

Suddenly a scent blew in on the north wind that was such that I think mankind was endowed with its sense of
smell in order to smell it! We wanted to find out where it 19.105
came from, and, looking keenly into the distance, we saw a mountain with strange man-like creatures on its bejeweled peaks. When I asked the captain what it was he said, "The elders call it Mount Shri·kuñja."'

Mano·hara wrote down in detail on a writing tablet this and everything else that the merchant said, and made a chart. He then procured a boat with a reliable captain and set sail for the ocean with Bákula and the others.

Driven by a wind both favorable and strong, the boat
soon took him where he wanted to go. The similarity of 19.110
the landmarks to those on the writing tablet convinced him that he was in the right place, and he reached Shri·kuñja with his mind, eyes and body all at once. The boat put in at a sapphire stairway that was washed by the rolling waters

ākāś'|āśa|viśāl'|ôccaṃ potaḥ sopānam āsadat.
tatr' âiva suhṛdas tyaktvā yad utkaṇṭho 'noharaḥ
tena śail'|âgram ārohad dharmeṇ' êva tripiṣṭapam.
yakṣa|strī|puṃsa|vṛndaiś ca prekṣyamāṇaḥ sa|saṃmadaiḥ
saṃkalpa|cakṣuṣā paśyann agacchat Sukumārikām.
tatra kāś cid abhāṣanta ‹kṛt'|ârthā Sukumārikā
yay" âsminn āhitaṃ prema nar'|âmara|kumārake.
19.115 sur'|âsura|narāṇāṃ hi kasy' âyaṃ na manoharaḥ
yo vṛtaḥ saha|j'|â|hāryaiḥ śarīr'|ādi|guṇair?› iti.

prakrīḍantīm ath' âpaśyad viśāle mandir'|âjire
sve saṃkalpa|maye yakṣīṃ vakṣas' îva Manoharaḥ.
pratyudgamya tayā c' âsau rūp'|âjīvā|pragalbhayā
svinna|kaṇṭakite pāṇau gṛhītv" ântaḥ praveśitaḥ.
tasyāḥ pitaram adrākṣīt tatr' ārabdha|durodaram
rakt'|âkṣaṃ śātakaumbh'|âbhaṃ sa|madaṃ medur'|ôdaram.
upaveśya ca ten' âṅke ghrātvā mūrdhni Manoharaḥ
‹śvaśrūḥ paśy' êty› anujñātaḥ praviveś' âvarodhanam.

19.120 yatra saṃpūrṇa|tāruṇyāḥ karṇikāra|srag|ujjvalāḥ
śvaśrū|śvaśurayos tasya pitāmahyo 'pi yoṣitaḥ.
abhivādya ca tās tatra saḥ tābhir abhinanditaḥ
anujñātaś ca sa|snehaṃ prāviśat kanyakā|gṛham.
divyasya madhunaḥ pānaṃ divya|tantrī|ruti|śrutiḥ
divya|strī|saṃprayogāś ca Manohara|mano 'haran.

of the ocean and was as high and wide as the sky. The excited Mano·hara left his friends there and climbed to the top of the mountain by way of it, like a man ascending to heaven by way of his merit. Watched by delighted crowds of yakshas and *yakshis*, he looked about for Sukumárika with an amorous eye. A few among them said, 'Sukumárika has done well to inspire love in this princely demigod! For 19.115
who among the gods, demons and men would not find him charming, endowed as he is with handsomeness and other good qualities, both innate and acquired?'

Then Mano·hara saw his *yakshi* frolicking in the huge courtyard of a palace, just as she was frolicking in his lovelorn heart. She came to meet him with the brazenness of a courtesan, took hold of his sweating, goose-pimpled hand and led him inside, where he found her father playing dice. He had a fat stomach and was red-eyed, rosy-cheeked and drunk. He put his arm around Mano·hara, kissed him on the head and sent him to the harem, saying, 'Go and meet your mothers-in-law!'

The women there looked radiant in garlands of *karni·* 19.120
kara flowers and were in the full flush of youth, even the grandmothers of his parents-in-law. He greeted them and they welcomed him. With their leave he entered the girl's chamber, in the mood for love. Drinking divine wine, listening to divine lute music and making love to a divine woman transported Mano·hara's mind.

ity asau kṣaṇam āsīnaḥ Sukumārikay" ôditaḥ
‹atītā divasāḥ pañca kumāra pratigamyatām.
deva|lok'|âika|deśo 'yaṃ yat tato 'smin na labhyate
sthātuṃ mānuṣa|mātreṇa pañcamād divasāt param.
19.125 bhavantaṃ ca parityajya gaccheyuḥ pota|vāhakāḥ
vahana|svāminaṃ pañca pratīkṣante dināni te.›
śrutv" êdaṃ rāja|putrasya deva|putrasya yādṛśī
svargataś cyavamānasya dhyāma|dhyām" âbhavat prabhā.
taṃ dṛṣṭvā tādṛś'|ākāram avocat Sukumārikā
‹ady' ārabhya gamiṣyāmi tav' âiv' âhaṃ gṛhān› iti.
sa tayā dhīrito gatvā potam udvigna|vāhakam
tatr' âiva suhṛdo 'paśyad divya|ratn'|âmbara|srajaḥ.
‹sthitāḥ stha divasān etān kva kathaṃ v" êti› coditāḥ
tena te kathayanti sma ‹yathā yūyaṃ tathā vayam.›
19.130 Sukumārikay" ādiṣṭāḥ prahṛṣṭā guhyak'|âṅganāḥ
asmān upacaranti sma surān iva sur'|âṅganāḥ.
Mahā|devam upāsīnā mṛtā gacchanti mānuṣāḥ
sevamānā vayaṃ devaṃ devatām a|mṛtā gatāḥ!›
iti yakṣī|kathā|raktā mah"|âdhvānaṃ mahā|bhayam
tāsām ev' ânubhāvena saṃterus te mah"|ôdadhim.
vyāpārair ujjhitaṃ sarvais tri|varga|prāpti|hetubhiḥ
prāviśaṃs tad|viyog'|ārtaṃ śūnya|rāja|pathaṃ puram.
ath' âikā brāhmaṇī vṛddhā kim|artham api nirgatā
avaguṇṭhita|mūrdhānaṃ paśyati sma Manoharam.
19.135 tam asau pratyabhijñāya paritoṣa|skhalad|gatiḥ
gatvā dhyāna|par'|āsthānaṃ mahī|pālam atoṣayat.
mantri|prabhṛtayas tena vāritāḥ pura|vāsinaḥ
mā vocad dārakaṃ «kaś cit kva gato 'bhūd bhavān» iti.

When he had been there for what seemed like a moment, Sukumárika said to him, 'Five days have passed, o prince. You must return. The rule of the world of the gods is that a mere mortal may not stay here for more than five days.
The crew of the boat might abandon you and go: they wait 19.125
for a boat's patron for five days.'

On hearing this, the prince's countenance grew darker and darker, like that of a child of the gods being cast out of heaven. When Sukumárika saw him like this, she said, 'From now on I shall come to visit you at your house.'

Consoled by her, he returned to the boat and its anxious crew. He found his friends there wearing divine jewels, clothes and garlands. He asked them where and how they had spent the last few days and they replied, 'Just as you
have. Sukumárika sent some *yakshis* and they gladly looked 19.130
after us like goddesses looking after gods! Men who worship Shiva go to him when they die; serving you, we have become divine while alive!'

They were so absorbed in tales of the *yakshis* that they were aware of nothing else as they crossed the great expanse of the terrifying ocean.

When they entered the city, they found it stricken by its separation from the prince: the streets were empty and all activities in pursuit of the three aims of life had ceased. Then an old brahmin lady who had gone out for some reason or other saw Mano·hara, who had covered his head.
She recognized him and, stumbling with joy, she went to 19.135
the assembly, where everyone was deep in contemplation. She cheered up the king, and he told the ministers and other citizens that nobody was to ask his son where he had been.

rāja|putro 'pi rājānam avandata vilakṣakaḥ
so 'pi tasy' âṅkam āropya harati sma vilakṣatām.

svaṃ ca mandiram āgatya sa Sumaṅgalam uktavān
‹gandha|śāstra|phalaṃ sāraṃ dhūpam āyojyatām! iti.
ady' āgacchati yuṣmākaṃ sakhībhiḥ sahitā sakhī
su|gandhit'|â|pradhānaṃ ca ratam āhur a|ninditam.
19.140 gandha|rājaś ca yo 'smākaṃ ghuṣyate yakṣa|kardamaḥ
sa kardama|samas tāsām ato 'sau yakṣa|kardamaḥ.
tasmād ādaram āsthāya śāstram adya prakāśyatām
dhanur|vedasya kṛtsnasya viddha|sāraṃ hi sauṣṭhavam.›

iti protsāhitas tena sv'|ârthena ca Sumaṅgalaḥ
dhūpa|snānīya|gandh'|ādi yath"|ādeśam ayojayat.
Manoharas tu sa|suhṛt kṛta|kāmuka|ḍambaraḥ
āsanna|dayitā|śūnyāṃ duḥkha|śayyām asevata.

tataḥ sa tādṛśo gandhas tathā|yatnena sādhitaḥ
preritaḥ paṭun" ânyena samīreṇ' êva toya|daḥ.
19.145 bhāsā vicchāyayant" îva candra|kānt'|ādi|candrikām
praviśya sahas" âdhyāsta paryaṅkaṃ Sukumārikā.
tataḥ sa|smitam ālokya Bakul'|ādīn uvāca sā
‹sa|sahāy" âham āyātā yāta viśramyatām!› iti.

praṇamya teṣu yāteṣu kumāra|Sukumārike
yathā tathā|vidh"|ôtkaṇṭhe tath" âgamayatāṃ niśām.

The prince greeted the king bashfully, but the king put his arm around him and removed his bashfulness. When he reached his house, he said to Sumángala, 'Create an incense that is a distillation of all you have learned from your study of perfumery! My girlfriend is coming today and she will be bringing friends for you. They say that for perfect lovemaking there is nothing more important than fine fragrance. Our best fragrance is called "yaksha mud," 19.140
and to these ladies it will be as good as mud, so it deserves the name. Therefore today you must rise to the challenge and show off your learning. Excellence in archery is all about hitting the target!'

Urged on by the prince in this way—and by his own intentions—Sumángala obeyed and mixed up incense, bathing oils, scents and so forth. Meanwhile, in the melodramatic way of lovers, Mano·hara and his friends took to their beds, which, as yet empty of their approaching sweethearts, were beds of nails.

Then the scent that had been so carefully created was driven away by another more intense one, like a cloud being driven away by the wind. Seeming to eclipse the silvery light 19.145
of the moonstones and other gems with her radiance, Sukumárika suddenly entered and sat on a sofa. She smiled at Bákula and the others and said, 'I have brought my friends. Go and get comfortable!'

After they had bowed and left, the prince and Sukumárika passed the night as they had longed to.

saṃbhoga|ramaṇīyaiś ca śarīrair Bakul'|ādayaḥ
prabhāte rāja|putrāya rātri|vṛttaṃ nyavedayan.
rātrau rātrau sametānāṃ viyuktānāṃ divā divā
iti saṃvatsaro yātas tābhis teṣām a|cetitaḥ.

19.150 ekadā syandamān'|âśruḥ s'|ākrandā sā tam abravīt
‹sv'|âdhīnānāṃ par'|âdhīnaiḥ saha saṃgatir īdṛśī.
ady' ārabhya mayā devaḥ sevitavyo Dhan'|ēśvaraḥ
sakhī|sahitayā varṣaṃ gṛhīta|brahma|caryayā.
pitarau vandituṃ c' âham aṣṭamy|ādiṣu parvasu
sva|gṛhāya gamiṣyāmi tatra gacched bhavān iti.
tvat|saṅga|subhagā yā dik tām api prekṣya jīvyate
nindit'|âmṛta|pānena kiṃ punar darśanena te!›

tasyām uktv" êti yātāyām āyātā Bakul'|ādayaḥ
khaṃ paśyantam apaśyaṃs tam ‹iyaṃ yāt" êti› vādinam.

19.155 tataḥ sa|Bakul'|Âśoke sa|śoke pārthiv'|ātma|je
toṣa|gadgada|vāg uccair abhāṣata Sumaṅgalaḥ.
‹kim a|sthāne viṣādena! potam āruhya māmakam
dṛṣṭa|mārgā muhūrtena yāmas taṃ guhyak'|â|calam.
dhyāyantas tatra tāḥ kāntāḥ paśyantaś c' ântar" ântarā
saṃgam'|āśā|dhana|prāṇā yāpayāma samām› iti.

In the morning, the bodies of Bákula and the others looked beautiful from their lovemaking and told the prince what had happened in the night. Together during the nights and apart during the days, the ladies made a year go by for the men without them noticing.

One night, with tears streaming down her face, Suku- 19.150
márika sobbed to Mano·hara, 'This union is such that it is between those who are free and those who are beholden to others. Starting from today, I and my friends have to observe a vow of chastity and serve our lord, Kubéra, for a year. On the eighth day of each fortnight and other festival days, I shall go home to honor my parents. You must come there, too. Even the sight of somewhere that has been blessed by your presence makes my life worth living; how much more so a vision of you, which puts drinking the nectar of immortality to shame!'

After saying this, she left and Bákula and the others arrived. They found the prince looking at the sky, saying, 'She is gone!'

While the prince was grieving with Bákula and Ashó- 19.155
ka, Sumángala exclaimed in a voice choked with happiness, 'This is not the time for despair! Let's board my boat. We know the way, so we'll reach the yaksha's mountain in no time! Let's spend the year there dreaming of our sweethearts and seeing them from time to time; our lives will be a wealth of expectation and consummation!'

tataḥ sa tena potena prasthitaś ca mah"|ârṇavam
sa ca potaḥ samīreṇa dūraṃ hṛtvā vipāditaḥ.
rāja|putras tu dayitāṃ siddhāṃ vidyām iva smaran
tāṃ na cetitavān eva vipattiṃ māra|dāruṇām.
19.160 uttīrṇasy' âiva jala|dher velā|rodhasi sarpataḥ
caura|sainyena saṃyamya tasy' âlaṃ|karaṇaṃ hṛtam.
tatas taskara|sainyaṃ tad vāji|sainyena sarvataḥ
veṣṭitaṃ kuṭṭitaṃ baddham udbaddhaṃ pāda|peṣu ca.

ekaś cārutar'|ākāraḥ puruṣaḥ praṇipatya tam
kariṇī|pṛṣṭham āropya sa|sainyaḥ prasthitaḥ puraḥ.
a|dūraṃ c' ântaraṃ gatvā bandi|stuti|guṇ'|ânvayaḥ
Manoharaḥ puraṃ prāpat kuṅkum'|ālipta|catvaram.
ratna|vandana|mālānāṃ sa śṛṇvan paṭu|śiñjitam
āgacchat kala|rāsānāṃ nānā|pattri|srajām iva.
19.165 pur'|ânurūpa|śobhaṃ ca prāviśat sa nṛ|p'|ālayam
viśāla|maṇḍap'|āsīnaṃ Śakr'|ākāraṃ nar'|âdhipam.

avatīrya ca hastinyāḥ sa rājānam avandata
gāḍham āliṅgya ten' âpi ciraṃ prītyā nirūpitaḥ.
śarīr'|âvayavān dṛṣṭvā muhus tasy' âvadat tataḥ
‹kutaḥ Sumaṅgalād anyaś cakṣuṣmān?› iti bhū|patiḥ.

āsīc ca rāja|putrasya ‹sa ev' âyaṃ Sumaṅgalaḥ
bhaved aham iva bhraṣṭaḥ pota|bhaṅga|bhayād?› iti.

‹gaccha viśramya tāt' êti› rājñ" ôktaḥ prāviśat puram
apaśyan nata|mūrdhānaṃ sa tam eva Sumaṅgalam.

The prince set sail across the ocean in Sumángala's boat. The wind blew the boat far off course and it sank. The prince, however, had been thinking of his sweetheart; she was like a powerful magical spell and he was completely unaware of the disaster and the mortal danger it posed.

No sooner had he escaped from the ocean and was crawl- 19.160
ing along the shore than he was captured by a band of thieves
who stole his jewelry. Then a troop of horsemen surrounded
the band of robbers, beat them, bound them and hanged
them from the trees.

A particularly handsome man bowed to the prince and
had him sit on an elephant before setting off at the head
of the troop. They had not gone far when Mano·hara was
joined by bards singing his praises and he arrived at a city
whose squares were strewn with saffron. Continuing on his
way, he heard the shrill tinkling sound of bejeweled welcome
banners; they were like rows of multicolored songbirds. He 19.165
entered the king's palace, which was as beautiful as the city.
The king, sitting in a huge pavilion, looked like Indra.

Mano·hara dismounted from the elephant and greeted the king, who hugged him and stared at him lovingly for a long time. The king looked Mano·hara's body up and down and said, 'Nobody has eyes like Sumángala!'

The prince said to himself, 'It must be the same Sumángala! Could he, like me, have escaped from the calamitous shipwreck?'

The king told him to go and rest. He went into the palace, where he saw that very same Sumángala standing with his head bowed.

19.170 pṛcchati sma ca taṃ ‹bhadra mitre prāṇa|same tava
bhujau me Bakul'|Âśokau kaccit kuśalināv?› iti.
ten' ôktaṃ ‹Bakul'|Âśokau gṛhān kuśalinau gatau
yathā c' âham ih' āyātas tath" āśrotuṃ prasīdata.
punar|ukta|guṇ'|ākhyānam etat Nāgapuraṃ puram
dṛṣṭam eva hi yuṣmābhir nṛ|paś c' âiṣaḥ Puraṃdaraḥ.
Jayanta iti putro 'sya śūraś cāruḥ kaviḥ paṭuḥ
sa yena yūyam ānītāḥ sāgar'|ôpānta|kānanāt.
sutā Nalinikā nāma nṛ|pates tasya tādṛśī
yasyā na pramadā loke na c' âsti sadṛśo varaḥ.
19.175 varaṃ varayatā tasyāḥ pitrā dvīp'|ântarāṇy api
guṇa|rūp'|ântara|jñāna|śālinaḥ prahitā hatāḥ.
anena ca prapañcena yadā kālo bahur gataḥ
tadā mām ayam āhūya sa|dainya|smitam uktavān.
«tvaṃ na kevalam asmākaṃ sarv'|âdhyakṣa|gaṇ'|âgra|ṇīḥ
nātho 'pi bhava nas tāta saṃkaṭād uddharann itaḥ.
kula|śīla|vayo|rūpair yaḥ syād asyāḥ samo varaḥ
ādareṇa tam anviṣyes tyaja śrī|madirā|rujam.
bhūri|sāra|dhan'|āḍhyo 'pi guṇa|draviṇa|dur|gataḥ
dur|gatebhyaḥ su|dūreṇa śocanīyaḥ satām» iti.
19.180 tato Nalinikā|rūpam ālikhya phalake mayā
mahī s'|âṣṭādaśa|dvīpā parikrāntā var'|ârthinā.
yadā tu paṭu|yatno 'pi n' ālabhe varam īpsitam
tadā tyaktu|manaḥ prāṇāt prāvivikṣaṃ mah"|ôdadhim.

The prince asked him, 'Dear fellow, your friends Bákula 19.170
and Ashóka, who are as dear to you as life and like my arms to me, are they all right?'

He replied, 'Bákula and Ashóka are well and have gone home. Please be so kind as to listen to how I came to be here. This city is Naga·pura. Tales of its virtues are often told, and now you have seen it for yourself. The king is Puran·dara. His son is called Jayánta, a handsome warrior and a fine poet. It was he who brought you here from the forest on the seashore. The king's daughter is called Nalínika. There is not a girl like her in the world, nor is there a
groom worthy of her. In his hunt for a groom for the girl, 19.175
the king dispatched expert judges of character and looks, even as far as foreign shores. They have perished.

After a lot of time had been wasted in this way, the king summoned me and said with a sad smile, "Dear fellow, not only are you the head of all our administrators, but you shall have to become our savior, too, and rescue us from this difficult situation. You must diligently search for a groom who is a match for the girl in birth, character, age and looks. Ignore anyone intoxicated by wealth. To good people, a man who is poor in virtue, even if he is rich in wealth and property, is far more deplorable than a poor man."

I drew a picture of Nalínika on my writing tablet and 19.180
traveled around the earth's eighteen continents in search of a groom. When, despite my best efforts, I failed to find a suitable groom, I decided to kill myself and set sail across the ocean.

gataś ca Kānanadvīpaṃ dṛṣṭavān asmi saṃcaran
yuṣmad|guṇa|kath"|āsaktāḥ saṃtatāḥ sādhu|saṃpadaḥ.
tataḥ sa me sthir'|â|dhairyas tādṛṅ maraṇa|niścayaḥ
jyotsnay" êva tamo|rāśir yuṣmat|kīrtyā nirākṛtaḥ.
gandha|śāstra|vyasanino yuṣmān buddhvā ca lokataḥ
ātm" âpi gandha|śāstra|jñas tadā vaḥ śrāvito mayā.
19.185 tulya|jñāna|sva|bhāvā hi bhartṝṇām anujīvinaḥ
rañjayanti manaḥ kṣipraṃ guṇair api nirākṛtāḥ.
gandha|mālya|visaṃvādī dhūpo yac c' âpi dāhitaḥ
suhṛdbhiḥ saha yuṣmābhir ahaṃ jijñāsitas tadā.
yac ca yojitavān asmi gandha|māly'|ânuvādinam
dhūpaṃ tat phalake nyastām apaśyaṃ bhartṛ|dārikām.
tām ālokya tato yuṣmān manye 'haṃ dhanya|janmanām
ātmanaḥ rāja|putryāś ca vidhātuś ca kṛt'|ârthatām.
so 'haṃ sv'|ârtha|paro yuṣmān apahartum ito gataḥ
yāvad yuṣmad|guṇair eva hṛtaḥ sādhu|mano|haraiḥ.
19.190 tath" âpi sat|kṛto yuṣmān hartum ev' âham udyataḥ
pāpam adhyācaranty eva bhṛtyā bhartṛ|priy'|ēpsavaḥ.
puṇyair Nalinikāyāś ca yuṣmat|saṃgama|hetubhiḥ
sev"|ācār'|âpadeśena gat" âiva Sukumārikā.
idaṃ c' ântaram āsādya mayā yūyaṃ tvarāvatā
saṃnidhāpita|potena samudram avatāritāḥ.
pradeśe yatra c' âmbhodhir vipannaṃ vahanaṃ vahet
vipanna|vahanas tatra na ca kaś cana vidyate!
tena tau Bakul'|Âśokāv a|vipannau gṛhān gatau

I arrived at Kánana·dvipa. As I wandered about, I kept coming across groups of good people keenly talking of your qualities, whereupon my decision to kill myself, which had proved my lack of fortitude, was dispelled by your renown like darkness being dispelled by light.

When people told me of your passion for perfumery, I had you hear that I, too, was expert in it. If they have the 19.185
same interests and dispositions as their masters, servants quickly ingratiate themselves with them, even if they are bereft of virtue themselves. You and your friends tested me by burning incense that clashed with the smell of your garland. While I made up an incense that complemented the fragrance of your garland, I looked at the picture of my master's daughter on the writing tablet. When I looked at her, and then at you, I thought that the blessed lives of myself, the princess and the creator had achieved their aims. I had gone from here with the selfish intention of taking you away, meanwhile it was I who was taken, by your fine and charming virtues!

But even though you treated me well, I wanted nothing 19.190
other than to take you away. Servants who want the best for their masters will not stop at committing a sin. The merits acquired by Nalínika through her good deeds brought about her union with you, and they made Sukumárika leave under the pretext of having to work as a servant. Having got my chance, I lost no time in using my specially fitted boat to have you fall into the sea. Shipwrecks do not happen in an area where the sea is deep enough to support a strickenvessel! Bákula and Ashóka did not perish, and went home on the

idaṃ ca puram āyātā yathā yūyaṃ tathā vayam.
19.195 tasmān Nalinik" âdy' âiva yuṣmābhir anugamyatām
na hi Śrīḥ svayam āyāntī kāl'|âtikramam arhati!›
Manoharas tu tāṃ prāpya sarv'|ākāra|mano|harām
yathā|kāmam upābhuṅkta karī kamālinīm iva.
Sumaṅgalena sā c' ôktā ‹mā sma śethāḥ pṛthaṅ niśi
patyus te dayitā yakṣī m" âivaṃ naiṣīd asāv iti.
kupitā rāja|putrāya rāja|putrī kadā cana
un|nidr" âiva sa|nidr" êva suptā kila pṛthak kṣaṇam.
atha sev'|âvadhau pūrṇe varṣ'|ânte Sukumārikā
śayitaṃ pṛthag āsādya Manoharam apāharat.
19.200 yathā Nalinikā|bhartā Sukumārikayā hṛtaḥ
yuṣmān api hared eṣā tathā mātaṅga|kanyakā.
manyadhve yādṛśīm enāṃ kanyakā n' êyam īdṛśī
na hi caṇḍāla|kanyāsu rajyante deva|sūnavaḥ.
idaṃ Nalinikā|vṛttaṃ smṛtvā yūyaṃ may" ôditāḥ
na me Nalinikā|vārttā viras'|ântā bhaved» iti.
«an|anya|gata|saṃkalpam evaṃ māṃ mā sma kalpayaḥ!»
iti jihmaṃ puras tasyāḥ kāmuk'|ācāram ācaram.
Gandharvadattā|vacanāt priyatvaṃ
mātaṅga|kanyā sutarām agān me
madaṃ vidhatte madirā prakṛtyā
kim aṅga kānt'|ānana|saṅga|ramyā!

iti Bṛhatkathāyāṃ Ślokasaṃgrahe
Ajinavatī|lābhe Nalinik"|ākhyānam.

boat. I reached this city in the same way that you did. So, 19.195
you must go after Nalínika immediately, for when Lakshmi herself is coming, she should not have to wait!'

The girl's beauty was altogether ravishing, and when Mano·hara won her he enjoyed her to the full, like an elephant enjoying a lotus pond. Sumángala said to her, 'Do not sleep apart from your husband at night, lest his *yakshi* girlfriend should take him away.'

One night the princess was angry with the prince and, although she was awake, she pretended to be asleep. It seems she lay down apart from him for a while. A year had passed and Sukumárika's period of service was over. She found Mano·hara sleeping alone and abducted him.

Just as Nalínika's husband was abducted by Sukumárika, 19.200
so might this forest girl abduct you. This girl is not like you imagine her to be. The sons of gods do not fall in love with outcaste girls. I remembered this story of Nalínika and told it to you so that what happened to Nalínika, with its unpleasant outcome, might not happen to me." "You must not think of me like that—my love has but one object!" With these ambiguous words, I played the part of a lover to her.

Gandhárva·datta's speech had made me more in love with the forest girl. Wine is naturally intoxicating; how much more so when embellished by the touch of a sweetheart's mouth!

The story of Nalínika in the Winning of Ajínavati
in the Abridgement into Sanskrit Verse of the Long Story.

CANTO 20
AJÍNAVATI

20.1 ITI ŚEṢAṂ vasantasya
tanu|pāṭala|kuḍmalam
divasāṃś ca nayāmi sma
su|bhag'|ânila|candanān.
ekadā Dattaken' âham āgatya hasat" ôditaḥ
«ārya|putra vicitraṃ vaḥ krīḍā|sthānam upāgatam.
rāja|mārge mayā dṛṣṭā vṛddhā strī bhāsvara|prabhā
nāgarair ‹devi! dev' îti› vandyamānā var'|ârthibhiḥ.
sā c' āha prabhavant" îva ‹dāraka, pratigṛhyatām
tava bhartre mayā dattā kany" Âjinavat" îti› mām.
20.5 uktā sā ca mayā ‹devi bhṛtyatvāt paravān aham
dṛṣṭvā svāminam āyāmi tat kṣaṇaṃ kṣamyatām› iti.»
sa may" ôktas «tayā sākaṃ hasantaḥ sukham āsmahe
ten' āgacchatu s" âtr' âiva mad|vacaś c' êdam ucyatām.
‹bahūn saṃpṛcchya kanyāyāḥ kāryau dāna|pratigrahau
praṣṭavyāḥ santi c' âsmākaṃ tāvat pṛcchāmi tān aham.
anyac c' āgamyatām etad gṛhaṃ yadi na duṣyati
tvādṛś'|âtithi|sat|kāraḥ kāraṇaṃ śreyasām› iti.»
tataḥ prasthāpito gatvā pratyāgatya ca Dattakaḥ
mām abhāṣata bhāratyā gambhīra|bhaya|garbhayā.
20.10 «yuṣmat saṃdeśam ākarṇya tay" ôktaṃ bhīma|hāsayā
‹aho mahā|kulīnānām ācāraḥ sādhu|sevinām.
kim atr' Ôdayanaḥ rājā praṣṭavyaḥ suhṛdā tava
devī Vāsavadattā vā kiṃ vā Magadha|vaṃśa|jā.
Rumaṇvad|ādayaḥ kiṃ vā kiṃ vā Hariśikh'|ādayaḥ
āha yat «santi me ke cit tāvat pṛcchāmi tān» iti?

So it was the end of spring, with a smattering of buds 20.1
on the *pátala* trees, and the days I passed had lovely scents of sandal on the breeze.

One day Dáttaka came to me and said with a laugh, "Your Highness, an opportunity has arisen for you to have some sport. I saw an old woman in the main road. She shone brilliantly and the citizens were hailing her with calls of 'O goddess! O goddess!' in the hope of receiving her blessings. Somewhat condescendingly, she said to me, 'My boy, take my daughter Ajínavati. I have given her to your master.'

I said to her, 'Madam, as a servant, I answer to someone 20.5
else. I shall see my master and come back. Wait a moment.'"

I said to Dáttaka, "We can have some fun making a fool of this woman, so have her come here. Pass on the following message from me: 'Many people are to be consulted before a bride is offered and accepted, and there are those that I must consult—let me just go and ask them. One more thing: if you don't mind, please come to my house. Showing hospitality to someone such as you is a way to better oneself.'"

Dáttaka went as instructed. On his return, he said to
me in a voice filled with profound fear, "When she heard 20.10
your message she replied with a terrifying laugh, 'Oh the behaviour of noblemen when serving the virtuous! Is it King Udáyana, or Queen Vásava·datta, or Padmávati, the queen from the dynasty of Mágadha, or Rumánvan and the other ministers, or Hari·shikha and his other friends whom your friend has to consult on this matter when he says there are some people that he is just going to go and ask?

ājñāpayati yac c' âiṣa mām «ih' āgamyatām» iti
kim evam apamānyante guravo guru|sevibhiḥ.
atha vā kim ahaṃ tasya samīpaṃ kim asau mama?
a|cirād yāsyat' îty etat sa ev' ânubhaviṣyati.›
20.15 ity uktvā niścarantībhir jvālā|mālābhir ānanāt
dagdhvā Camp"|âika|deśaṃ sā mah"|ôlk" êva tirohitā.»

mama tv āsīd «vidagdh" êyaṃ
vṛddhā vipraśnikā dhruvam
indra|jāl'|âbhiyuktā vā
māyā|kārī bhaved» iti.

Bharadvāja|sutāyās tu tīvraḥ saṃtrāsa|kāraṇaḥ
asmad|hṛdaya|saṃtāpī paritāpa|jvaro 'bhavat.
mṛṇāl'|ânila|mukt"|ālī|jal'|ārdra|paṭa|candanaiḥ
asmad|aṅga|pariśvaṅgair n' âsyās tāpo nyavartata.
tataḥ śakra|dhanuḥ|sampā|balākā|cakra|lāñchanaiḥ
nir|ambu|d'|âmbara|chāyaiś channam ambaram ambu|daiḥ.
20.20 saṃtāpam apanetuṃ ca s'|āsāraiḥ paścim'|ânilaiḥ
samārohāma harmyasya sāndra|śubhra|sudhaṃ śiraḥ.
tatr' āruddha|praṇāl'|ādi|dāsī|dās'|ôttar'|âmbaraiḥ
pāścātya|marud|ādy'|ōti|jaḍaṃ jalam adhārayam.
tatr' ânyeṣām uro|mātre majjantaḥ kubja|vāmanāḥ
śanakaiḥ śānta|saṃtāpāṃ Bhāradvājīm ahāsayan.
iti naḥ krīḍato dṛṣṭvā prāsād'|âgra|mahā|hrade
jale rantum iv' ôṣṇ'|âṃśuḥ prāviśat paścim'|ârṇavam.

He instructs me to go to his house. Do people who honor their elders insult them like this? Am I to go to him or is he to come to me? He will come before long and see for himself what this is about!'

After saying this, she razed part of Champa with jets of 20.15
flame that came from her mouth. Then, like a comet, she
vanished."

I said to myself, "This crafty old woman must be a wise woman or an illusionist versed in magic."

Gandhárva·datta, however, was seized by an intense burning fever brought on by her anxiety, and it burned my heart
too. Neither lotus stems, nor cool breezes, nor strings of
pearls, nor cloths soaked in water, nor sandalwood paste,
nor my embraces could remove her fever. The sky became
covered with clouds the color of a cloudless sky, marked
with rainbows, lightning and flocks of cranes. So that we 20.20
might soothe her fever with the rain-bearing westerly winds,
we climbed onto the thickly whitewashed palace roof. Using the upper garments of the servant men and women to
block the gutters and channels, I dammed the water, which,
having come in on the west wind, was refreshingly cool.
Dwarves and hunchbacks made Gandhárva·datta laugh by
plunging into the water—which was only chest-high for
everyone else—and her fever slowly subsided. When it saw
us playing like this in the pool on top of the palace, the sun
entered the western sea as if to sport in the water.

Bharadvāja|tanū|jā tu niṣevya śiśiraṃ ciram
praśānt'|āgantu|saṃtāpā śīta|pīḍ'|ātur" âbhavat.
20.25 tām uro|bāhu|vāsobhiḥ samācchādya nirantaram
vi|śītāṃ kṛtavān asmi tāpa|śīt'|âpahāribhiḥ.
apanīta|pidhānaiś ca praṇālair makar'|ānanaiḥ
prāsādāt prāsravat toyaṃ Sumeror iva nirjharaiḥ.
prakīrṇa|salila|krīḍā|pīḍana|chinna|bhūṣaṇam
muni|pīt'|âmbudhi|chāyaṃ harmy'|âgraṃ tad adṛśyata.
tasminn abhinav'|âmbhoda|kumbh'|âmbhaḥ|kṣālan'|â|male
dānaiḥ paricarāmi sma samānaiḥ paricārakān.

iti kānte tri|yām'|ādau gamite mānita|priyaḥ
upāyi prabalāṃ nidrāṃ sukha|duḥkh'|âbhibhāvinīm.
20.30 yāte ca kṣaṇa|dā|pāde kaṭhora|sparśa|bodhitaḥ
gambhīr'|ēkṣaṇam adrākṣaṃ naraṃ vyātt'|āsya|kandaram.
anumāya ca taṃ pretaṃ mantra|garbham upāgatam
kv' âpi māṃ netum icchantaṃ netum aicchaṃ Yam'|ālayam.

Bharadvāj'|ātma|jā trastā mā sma nidrāṃ jahād iti
na taṃ tatra nihanmi sma bhīṣaṇ'|ārati|śaṅkitaḥ.
tuṣāra|jaḍam āropya sva|pṛṣṭaṃ kāṣṭha|niṣṭhuram
sa māṃ sopāna|mārgeṇa prāsād'|âgrād avātarat.
tat|prabhāvāc ca nidr"|ândhāḥ suptā jāgarikāḥ kṣitau
kakṣ"|ārakṣās tam adrākṣur na niryāntam a|cetanāḥ.

After Gandhárva·datta had spent a long time enjoying
the coolness, her impromptu fever abated and she started
to suffer from the cold. I warmed her up by tightly wrapping 20.25
my chest, arms and clothes around her, for they are effective
at removing both heat and cold. When the stoppers were
removed from the alligator-mouthed gutters, water flowed
down them from the roof terrace like water flowing down
the streams of Mount Suméru. Scattered with ornaments
that had been torn off during the playful fighting in the
water, the palace roof looked like the ocean floor after the
sage had drunk it dry.* When it had been washed clean
with pots of fresh rainwater, I went around to the servants,
giving them all presents.

After the first part of the night had thus passed agreeably, I
said goodnight to my sweetheart and fell into the deep sleep
that overcomes both happiness and sorrow. When another 20.30
quarter of the night had gone by, I was awakened by the
touch of something rough, and saw a man with sunken eyes
and a gaping, cavernous mouth. I surmised that he was a
ghost that had been conjured up by a spell, and that he
wanted to take me somewhere. I wanted to send him to the
land of the dead.

So that the already anxious Gandhárva·datta might not wake up, I did not kill him there and then for fear of his terrible screams. He put me on his back, which was as cold as ice and as hard as wood, and took me downstairs from the roof terrace. His powers had made the usually vigilant guards at the outer walls senseless with sleep and they were slumbering on the ground. Unconscious, they did not see

20.35 niṣkrāntaś ca parāvṛtya kakṣā|dvāraṃ yad aikṣata
kavāṭa|saṃpuṭas tatra śanair aghaṭayat svayam.
gṛhād dūram atītaś ca jānubhyāṃ tam atāḍayam
prahāraḥ sa tu me jāto jānu|pīḍā|prayojanaḥ.
yac ca kiṃ cid ahaṃ draṣṭum aicchaṃ paṭu|kutūhalaḥ
kula|putraḥ sa tatra sma kiṃ cit kālaṃ na gacchati.
āś"|ākāśa|viśālāsu viśikhāsu prasāritāḥ
apaśyaṃ dvīpināṃ kṛttīs tath" êdam abhavan mama.
«etāvanti kutaḥ santi dvīpi|carmāṇi kānane
āstīrṇāni kim arthaṃ vā ken' âpi viśikhāsv?» iti.
20.40 yāvat prāsāda|mālābhyo jāla|vāt'|āyana|cyutaiḥ
saṃtatair vitatā rathyā pradīp'|ârciṣ|kadambakaiḥ.
apanīta|vitarkaś ca tair.
gataḥ stokam antaram
prāsāde kva cid aśrauṣaṃ vacaḥ kasy' âpi kāminaḥ:
«ayi Candraka! kiṃ śeṣe? nanu bhrāto vibudhyatām!
n' ākarṇayasi kūjantam ulūkaṃ su|bhaga|dhvanim?
asmai daśa|sahasrāṇi dīyantāṃ bhūṣaṇāni ca
ayaṃ naḥ sukha|hetūnām agra|ṇīḥ suhṛdām» iti.
an|antaraṃ ca sāraṅga|dardūr'|âmbhoda|bandhunā
utkaṇṭhā|garbha|kaṇṭhena nīla|kaṇṭhena kūjitam.
20.45 tataḥ kāmī jvalat|krodhaḥ Candrakaṃ caṇḍam abravīt
«duṣṭasya caṭakasy' âsya mastakaś chidyatām!» iti.
mayā tarkayatā c' êdaṃ viruddham iti niścitam
ājñātam anayor nyāyye saṃmānana|vimānane.
bhāryā nāgarakasy' âsya para|saṃkrānta|mānasā
eka|paryaṅka|supt" âpi suptā bhartuḥ parāṅ|mukhī.
tay" ôlūka|dhvaniṃ śrutvā bhīru|nārī|vibhīṣaṇam
trastay" âtaḥ parāvṛtya gāḍham āliṅgitaḥ patiḥ.

him leaving. On his way out, he turned around and looked 20.35
at the gateway. The gates slowly closed themselves.

After we had gone some distance from the house, I kneed
him, but the attack resulted only in pain in my knees. I was
very inquisitive and whenever I wanted to look at something the gentlemanly ghost would stop there for a moment.
Spread out on highways that were as wide as the sky, I saw
leopard skins and wondered how there could be so many
leopard skins in the forest and why someone had scattered
them on the highways. But then I realized that all along the 20.40
road there were clusters of spots of light coming from the
latticed windows of rows of houses and my confusion was
thus removed.

After going a little further I heard the voice of some suitor
on a terrace somewhere: "Hey, Chándraka! Are you asleep?
Wake up, brother! Do you not hear the lovely sound of
the owl hooting? Give him ten thousand coins and some
jewelry. Of my friends that make me happy, he is the best!"

Soon after, the peacock, the friend of deer, frogs and
clouds, called out in a voice full of longing. At this the 20.45
suitor, burning with rage, spoke harshly to Chándraka: "Cut
off the head of that wicked sparrow!" I thought about this
and decided that it made no sense. Then I realized that
the praise and abuse being shown to these two could be
explained. The wife of this gentleman loved another man
and although they slept in the same bed she lay with her head
turned away from her husband. When she heard the noise
of the owl, which is terrifying to a timid lady, she became
scared. She turned over and held her husband in a tight
embrace. He loves his unloving wife and was pleased by his

tato virakta|bhāryeṇa bhāryā|raktena c' âmunā
ulūka|bhaya|pūrvo 'pi kānt"|āśleṣo 'bhinanditaḥ.
20.50 tena pūjām ulūkasya suhṛdaḥ kṛtavān ayam
yen' âsya vimukhī kāntā trāsād abhimukhī kṛtā.
śrutvā ca śikhinaḥ kekāḥ kānt'|ôtkaṇṭhā|vidhāyinīḥ
patyuḥ kaṇṭhaṃ parityajya sthitā bhūyaḥ parāṅ|mukhī ten'
ânena mayūrasya mastakaś cheditaḥ ruṣā
yen' âsy' âbhimukhī kāntā kūjatā vimukhī kṛtā.
ath' âtītya tam uddeśam aśrauṣaṃ mada|viddhayoḥ
kṛta|nigrahayor vācaṃ kulaṭā|viṭayor yathā.
«mano|ghrāṇa|harā gandhā yayā pratanu|tuṅgayā
āghrātā mama sā nāsā tvat|kṛte vikṛtā kṛtā!
20.55 kartarī|pāśa|saṃkāśau purā maṇḍita|kuṇḍalau
karṇau mama tathā bhūtau bhavatāṃ bhavato yathā!
s" âham evaṃ|vidhā jātā vipralabdhā khalu tvayā!
kṛta|ghna! tvam ap' îdānīm avajānāsi mām?» iti.
ath' âvocat patis tasyāḥ «kiṃ māṃ nindasi nandini
may" âpi nanu yat prāptaṃ tvad|arthaṃ tan na dṛśyate?
devāḥ kusuma|dhūp'|ādyaiḥ pitaraḥ piṇḍa|vāribhiḥ
samastās tarpitā yena dakṣiṇābhir dvi|jātayaḥ,
śūr'|âdhiṣṭhita|pṛṣṭhānāṃ cūrṇita|pratidantinām
yena c' âsi|sa|nāthena nikṛttāḥ kariṇāṃ karāḥ,
20.60 pṛthulāḥ komalās tuṅgāḥ pīnāḥ sat|kṛta|candanāḥ
ātma|śeṣa|para|strīṇāṃ yena bhuktāḥ payodharāḥ.
sa me vām'|êtaraḥ pāṇiḥ phulla|tāmaras'|âruṇaḥ
kṛttaḥ śastreṇa saṃdhānād bandhanād iva pallavaḥ,

sweetheart's embrace, which was precipitated by her fear of
the owl. So he praised his friend the owl, who had scared his 20.50
sweetheart into turning her averted face toward him. When she heard the cries of the peacock, they made her long for her sweetheart. She abandoned her husband's embrace and averted her face once more. Enraged, he wanted to have the peacock's head cut off, because with its call it had made his sweetheart turn her head away from him.

After leaving that place behind, I heard the voices of two drunken prisoners, a hussy and a rake: "This nose of mine was long and slender and I used to use it to sniff scents that captivated the mind and the sense of smell. Because of you,
it is now deformed! My ears used to look like scissor handles 20.55
and were adorned with earrings. May your ears become like mine have become! And now that I have become like this, you mock me! You ingrate! Are you now going to treat me with contempt?"

Then her husband said, "Why are you scolding me, my dear? Do you not realize that it is for your sake that I got what I got? That which offered flowers, incense and so forth to all the gods, rice balls and water to all the ancestors, and sacrificial fees to all the brahmins, which, holding a sword, chopped off the trunks of elephants on whose backs were sitting brave warriors who had destroyed their enemy's elephants, and which enjoyed the breasts—large, soft, pert, 20.60
full, and adorned with sandal paste—of my wife, others' wives and unmarried women, that right hand of mine, which was as pink as a blossoming lotus, has been cut off at the wrist by a blade, like a blossom from its stem.

adhunā vāma|pādasya śṛṇu caṇḍi parākramam
yena krāntā samudr'|ântā tīrtha|snānāya medinī,
yena c' ântaḥ|pur'|ārakṣa|parikṣiptena līlayā
vapra|prākāra|parikhāḥ śata|kṛtvo vilaṅghitāḥ,
so 'yaṃ māruta|saṃcāras tāmras tuṅga|nakh'|âṅguliḥ
pādo me yādṛśo jātas tādṛśaḥ kasya kathyatām.
20.65 atha vā yaḥ samudrasya tulayā tulayej jalam
sa guṇān pāṇi|pādasya gaṇayen manda|dhīr girā.
sarvathā dhig a|dhīraṃ māṃ yas tvādṛśyāḥ striyaḥ puraḥ
ātmanaḥ pāṇi|pādasya praśaṃsāmi guṇān!» iti.

ath' ânyatra śṛṇomi sma «pādaḥ ślokasya śobhanaḥ
āgatas taṃ likhāmy āśu datta me vartikām» iti.

evaṃ c' ân|anta|vṛtt'|ântāṃ Campāṃ paśyan kutūhalī
āgacchaṃ nagarī|dvāram uttaraṃ preta|vāhanaḥ.
mama tv āsīn «na mām eṣa gata|prāṇo jighāṃsati
uttareṇa hi nīyante na dvāreṇa jighāṃsitum.»
20.70 cintayann iti niryātaḥ prākāraṃ samayā vrajan
kṣīṇa|māṃsakam adrākṣaṃ bālakaṃ gata|jīvakam.
ath' âcintayam «ālokya kṣaṇaṃ bāla|cikitsitam
śoṣitaḥ śuṣka|Raivatyā varāko 'yaṃ mṛtaḥ śiśuḥ.
yadi jīvantam adrakṣyaṃ likhitvā maṇḍalaṃ tataḥ
atrāsye maraṇād enam iṣṭvā krūra|grahān» iti.

Now, cruel lady, listen to the exploits of my left leg, which
crossed the earth as far as the ocean to bathe in the sacred
sites. A hundred times it jumped with ease across ramparts,
walls and ditches after being surrounded by harem guards.
Tell me, who has a leg like mine used to be—as swift as the
wind, copper-colored, and with long nails and toes? Only 20.65
someone stupid enough to weigh the water of the ocean
with a pair of scales would measure with words the good
qualities of my hand and foot. Shame on me for singing the
praises of my hand and foot in front of a woman like you!"

In another place I heard someone say "I have thought of a beautiful quarter-verse. I shall write it down. Quickly, give me a pen!"

Looking on in fascination on Champa and its endless
scenes like these, I arrived at the northern gate of the city
on the back of the ghost. I said to myself, "This ghost does
not want to kill me, for people are not taken through the
northern gate to be killed."* While I was thinking this, 20.70
we passed beyond the city walls. As we walked alongside
them I noticed the emaciated corpse of a boy. I recalled for
a moment the science of pediatrics and realized that the
poor child had died of consumption at the hands of the
consumptive demoness Révati. If I had seen him while he
was still alive, I could have saved him from death by drawing
a magic diagram and making offerings to the planets arrayed
against him.

dṛṣṭavān asmi c' ânyatra citra|vastra|vibhūṣaṇam
puruṣaṃ proṣita|prāṇam ath' êdam abhavan mama.
«rajju|śastr'|âgni|pānīya|jarā|jvara|gara|kṣudhām
n' âyam anyatamen' âpi kena nāma mṛto bhavet.
20.75 aye! nūnam ayaṃ kāmī kāmayitv" ânya|kāminīm
nidrā|sukham upāsīnaḥ pratibuddhaḥ pipāsitaḥ.
‹sukha|supt" êti› c' ânena na sā strī pratibodhitā
gav'|âkṣa|sth'|ôda|pātra|stham udakaṃ pītam ātmanā.
apanīta|pidhānaṃ ca dṛṣṭvā taj jala|bhājanam
sva|viṣ'|ânala|dāh'|ārtaḥ praviṣṭaḥ prāg bhujaṃ|gamaḥ.
tena tad viṣam udgīrṇaṃ tena tad dūṣitaṃ jalam
tena pītena mūḍho 'yaṃ sadyaḥ prāṇair viyojitaḥ.
tasyāś ca para|kāminyā dārikābhiḥ sa|saṃbhramam
prākāra|śṛṅga|randhreṇa nikṣiptaḥ parikhā|taṭe.
20.80 a|mṛto yadi dṛṣṭaḥ syāj jīvitaḥ syād ayaṃ mayā
mantra|maṇḍala|mudrāṇām upāṃśu|smaraṇād iti.»

ath' ânyatr' âham adrākṣaṃ nindit'|âsura|kanyakām
aśoka|śākhi|śākhāyām udbaddhāṃ kām api striyam.
aṅgaiḥ kusuma|sindūra|kuṅkum'|âlaktak'|ôjjvalaiḥ
nīl'|ârdh'|ōruka|saṃvīta|viśāla|jaghana|sthalām.
nikṣiptaṃ ca tay" â|dūraṃ kara|churita|candrikam
cīna|paṭṭ'|âṃśuka|nyastam an|arghyaṃ ratna|maṇḍanam.

«kim artham anayā straiṇaṃ kṛtaṃ sāhasam» ity aham
parāmṛśya bahūn pakṣān idaṃ niścitavān dhiyā.
20.85 iyaṃ pati|vratā yoṣin nūnaṃ bhartuś ca vallabhā
na vimānitavān etāṃ patiḥ parihasann api.
tena suptena mattena jijñāsā|kupitena vā
gṛhītaṃ nāma kasyāś cit pramadāyāḥ pramādinā.

In another place I saw a corpse in fancy clothes and jewelry, and I thought, "How can this man have died? It can't have been from a rope, a weapon, fire, drink, old age, fever,
poison or hunger. Ah! Surely he must be a lover who had 20.75
been making love to another man's girlfriend. After enjoying a blissful sleep, he woke up thirsty. Thinking that the woman was fast asleep he did not wake her and drank some water from a jug by the window. A snake had earlier seen that the jug's lid was off and, suffering from the burning heat of its own poison, had gone inside. It disgorged its venom, which poisoned the water. When the foolish fellow drank it, it killed him instantly. The adulteress's maidservants hastily threw him from a gap in the battlements onto
the side of the moat. If I had seen him while he was not 20.80
yet dead, I could have saved his life by secretly invoking magical charms, diagrams and gestures."

Then, in another place, I saw a woman who put *ásura* maidens to shame hanging from the branch of an *ashóka* tree. Her body, adorned with flowers, vermilion, saffron and lac, looked lovely, and her wide hips were covered by a short blue petticoat. She had cast off her priceless jewelry nearby. Wrapped in a piece of silk, it gave off rays that eclipsed the moonlight.

I considered several hypotheses as to why she had committed this rash, womanly action before deciding upon the
following. She was a devoted wife and her husband loved 20.85
her. He did not treat her with disrespect, even in jest. When he was either asleep, drunk or angry with her questioning, he carelessly mentioned the name of some young lady. That name, which she had not heard before, hit her as hard as a

tena c' â|śruta|pūrveṇa vajra|pāta|pramāthinā
gāḍhaṃ tāḍitayā krūraṃ kṛtaṃ karm' êdam etayā.
sarvathā putra|dārāṇāṃ pitā|bhartṛ|samaḥ ripuḥ
n' âsti yas tān ati|snehād lālayaty eva kevalam.
varaṃ c' âti|tiras|kāro bālānāṃ n' âti|lālanā
dṛśyante hy avasīdanto dhīmanto 'py ati|lālitāḥ.
20.90 vasan'|ābharaṇaṃ yac ca bhū|tale svayam ujjhitam
tat taskara|kara|sparśa|parihār'|ârtham etayā.
niś|caurā c' ēdṛśī Campā yan Meru|gurur apy ayam
alaṃ|kāro 'py a|sat|kāraḥ saṃkāra iva dṛśyate.

etāni c' ânyāni ca nāgarāṇāṃ
paśyan vicitrāṇi viceṣṭitāni
cit'|ânal'|āloka|hṛt'|ândha|kāram
agaccham ujjīva|jan'|âdhivāsam.

ath' âpaśyaṃ śivās tatra trāsitāḥ piśit'|âśinīḥ
dīna|bhīṣaṇa|phet|kārāḥ kukkuraiḥ khara|bukkitaiḥ.
ujjhit'|âmbaram ud|bāhu prakīrṇa|kaca|saṃcayam
paritaḥ kuṇapaṃ nṛtyad ḍākinī|maṇḍalaṃ kva cit.
20.95 kva cit puruṣam ut|khaḍgam upātta|ghaṭa|karparam
«mahā|māṃsaṃ mahā|sattvāḥ krīyatām!» iti vādinam.
sa|śastra|puruṣa|vrāta|rakṣit'|āśā|catuṣṭayam
sādhakaṃ siddhi|nistriṃśam utpatantaṃ nabhaḥ kva cit.

ity|ādi|bahu|vṛtt'|ântaṃ paśyatā preta|ketakam
yātrāṃ yā gacchatā dṛṣṭā sā dṛṣṭā sthavirā mayā.
vaṭa|mūle citā|vahnau vāma|hast'|ârpita|sruvā
haṃ|kār'|ântena mantreṇa juhvatī nara|śoṇitam.
taṃ ca pretam asau dṛṣṭvā sādhit'|ādeśam āgatam
guru|harṣa|viśāl'|âkṣī karma|śeṣaṃ samāpayat.

violent thunderbolt, and she carried out this terrible act. For sons and wives there is no enemy like their fathers and husbands, whose excessive affection serves only to spoil them. It is better to treat young people with great contempt than to indulge them excessively, for even the wise are seen to falter when they have been excessively indulged. She delib- 20.90
erately abandoned her clothes and jewelry on the ground to avoid being touched by the hand of a thief. But there are no thieves in Champa: even this jewelry, which is as valuable as Mount Meru, has been ignored as if it were rubbish.

As I looked at these and other bizarre examples of the citizens' behavior, I arrived at the abode of the dead, where the darkness was dispelled by the light from funeral pyres.

I saw flesh-eating jackals there. Terrified by the harsh barking of the dogs, they were giving out wretched howls of anguish. In one place I saw a circle of witches with upraised arms and flowing hair dancing naked around a corpse. In 20.95
another place I saw a man brandishing a sword and holding a skull that he was using as a bowl. He was saying, "Mighty ones, buy some human flesh!" Then, guarded in each of the cardinal directions by a troop of armed men, there was an accomplished magician with a magical sword who was floating up into the sky.

As I surveyed the cremation-ground where this and several other similar scenes were taking place, I saw the old lady that I had seen on my way to the festival. From a ladle held in her left hand she was offering human blood into a funeral pyre at the foot of a banyan tree, using a spell that ended with the syllable "*ham*." When she saw that the ghost had returned having carried out her instructions, a

20.100 taṃ ca datt'|ârgha|sat|kāram avocat kṛta|karmaṇe
«sv|āgataṃ candra|vaktrāya! kumāro mucyatām!» iti.

mama tv āsīd «aho kaṣṭā candramasy' āpad āgatā
yena kāka|mukhasy' âsya mukham etena tulyate!»

sa tu māṃ śanakair muktvā bāhu|jaṅghaṃ prasārya ca
dakṣiṇ'|âbhimukhas tāram āraṭy" āpatitaḥ kṣitau.

atha mātaṅga|vṛddhā mām avocad datta|viṣṭarā
«śmaśānam āgato 'sm' îti khedaṃ mā manaso gamaḥ.
śmaśāne Bhagavān Rudraḥ sa|Rudrāṇī|Vināyakaḥ
sa|Mātṛ|pramath'|ânīkas tri|saṃdhyaṃ saṃnidhīyate.
20.105 yatra Rudraḥ surās tatra sarve Hari|puraḥ|sarāḥ
na hy anyatra tuṣār'|âṃśur anyatr' âsya marīcayaḥ.
mokṣa|svarg'|ârtha|kāmāś ca śrūyante bahavo dvi|jāḥ
prāptāḥ preta|vane siddhiṃ tasmān n' êdam a|maṅgalam.
yad|arthaṃ tvaṃ mam' ānītas tad etat saṃniśāmyatām
na hi niṣ|kāraṇaḥ khedas tvādṛśām upapadyate.

āsīn mātaṅga|nāth'|êndraḥ kṣuṇṇa|śatrur mataṅga|jaḥ
śarīr" îva Mahad|bāhor Mahāsiṃhaḥ patir mama.
ahaṃ Dhanamatī nāma mantra|śaktiś ca yā mama
sā dineṣu gamiṣyatsu vijñātā bhavatā svayam.
20.110 Caṇḍasiṃhaṃ Mahāsiṃhaḥ putram utpādya niṣṭhitaḥ
phala|bhāram iv' ân|antaṃ ghanaḥ kusuma|saṃcayaḥ.
sut" Âjinavatī nāma Caṇḍasiṃhasya kanyakā
rātriṃ divam asūyanti yasyai Tridaśa|kanyakāḥ.

profound joy widened her eyes as she finished off the rest of the ritual. After welcoming him with an offering of water, 20.100
she said to her dutiful servant, "Welcome, moon-face! Let go of the prince!"

I said to myself, "Oh dear, a terrible calamity has befallen the moon for its face to be compared to this crow-faced fellow!"

He released me gently, spread out his arms and legs, and, facing south, disappeared into the ground with a loud shout.

The old forest woman offered me a seat and said, "Don't be worried about being in the cremation-ground. Lord Rudra, his consort, Ganésha, the mother goddesses and his host of attendants gather in the cremation-ground at the three daily junctures. Indra and all the other gods are 20.105
wherever Rudra is, for the moon and its rays cannot be in different places. One hears of many brahmins seeking liberation, heaven or wealth who have found success in the cremation-ground, so it is not inauspicious. Listen to why I have brought you here—people like you are not made to suffer without reason.

There was a chief of the forest-dwellers who laid waste to his enemies as if he were Indra's elephant in human form. He was Maha·simha, my husband. I am called Dhana·mati, and in the coming days you will discover for yourself the power of my magic. Maha·simha fathered a son, Chanda· 20.110
simha, and then died, like a plant closely covered in flowers dying after producing a boundless bounty of fruits. Chanda·simha had a daughter called Ajínavati, who is the constant envy of the daughters of the gods. When she went with us

tayā mahā|saroyātrām asmābhiḥ saha yātayā
Bhāradvājī|dvitīyas tvaṃ dṛṣṭaḥ pravahaṇ'|āśritaḥ.
ath' âvasth" âbhavat tasyāḥ k" âpi dur|jñāna|kāraṇā
dur|labhe bhavati strīṇāṃ dṛṣṭe tvādṛśi yādṛśī.
sakhībhir anuyukt" âsau bahuśaḥ kleśa|kāraṇam
yadā n' âkathayaj jñātā mantra|śaktyā mayā tadā.
20.115 prārthanā|bhaṅga|jaṃ duḥkham a|saṃcintya svayaṃ mayā
pautryāḥ prāṇa|paritrāṇaṃ kariṣyantyā bhavān vṛtaḥ.
dīrgh'|āyuṣā yadā c' âhaṃ paribhūtā tathā tvayā
sādhayitvā tathā pretaṃ tvam ih' ānāyito mayā.
ten' Âjinavatīṃ tubhyaṃ prayacchāmi balād api
mālām a|dhārayanto 'pi labhante hi div'|âukasaḥ.»

s" âtha paścān|mukhī sthitvā pautrīm «eh' îty» abhāṣata
ath' âdṛśyata tatr' âiva s" âpy an|āgatam āgatā.
«Cedi|Vats'|ēśa|dāyādaṃ mayā mantrair vaśī|kṛtam
varaṃ pāṇau gṛhāṇ' êti» tām avocat pitā|mahī.
20.120 madīyaṃ ca tadīyena svinnaṃ svinnena pāṇinā
sphurantaṃ sphurat" âgṛhṇād dakṣiṇaṃ dakṣiṇena sā.
tasyāḥ kara|rucā tāmre dṛṣṭi|pātaiḥ sit'|â|sitaiḥ
apaśyaṃ kuṅkum'|ābhe 'pi sva|kare varṇa|saṃkaram.
atha mām avadad vṛddhā «śvaśuro dṛśyatām» iti
tatas tām avadaṃ «devi jano 'yaṃ paravān» iti.
tataḥ puruṣam adrākṣam arka|maṇḍala|bhāsuram
āvartayantam utkāntiṃ candra|kānt'|âkṣa|maṇḍalam.

to the festival at the great lake, she saw you and Gandhárva·datta sitting in the carriage. Then she fell into a state whose cause was unfathomable, such as befalls women when they see an unattainable man like you. Her friends repeatedly asked her the reason for her distress. When she did not answer, I used my magic power to find out. I wanted to 20.115
save my granddaughter's life, and without considering the anguish that would result from my request being turned down, I asked you to marry her myself. When Your Reverence treated me with contempt, I conjured up the ghost and had you brought here. So I am forcing Ajínavati on you. The gods get garlands even if they won't wear them."

She looked behind her and told her granddaughter to come. The girl appeared there and then, as if she had been present all along. Her grandmother said to her, "This is the heir to the throne of Chedi and Vatsa, and I have used magic spells to bring him under my control. Take your bridegroom by the hand."

With her right hand, which was clammy and shaking, she 20.120
took hold of my right hand, which was clammy and shaking. As my gaze took in both black and white, I saw the commingling of the castes in my own hand: even though it was saffron-hued, the light from her hand made it look ruddy. Then the old woman said to me, "You must meet your father-in-law," and I replied, "Whatever you say, madam." I saw a man as brilliant as the sun, casting light upon his moonstone-eyed retinue.

Dhanamatyā mam' ākhyātam «ayaṃ vidyā|dhar'|ēśvaraḥ
Gaurimuṇḍo mahā|Gaurīm ārādhayitum icchati.
20.125 Vyālak'|Âṅgārakau c' âsya bhrātārau paricārakau
yāv etau pārśvayor asya bhujāv iva mahā|balau.
yen' Âmitagatir baddhaḥ kadambe mocitas tvayā
so 'yam Aṅgārako yo 'sau jahāra Kusumālikām.
ārabhya ca tataḥ kālād Gaurimuṇḍaḥ sah'|ânujaḥ
dviṣantam antaraṃ prāpya bhavantaṃ hantum icchati.
tena Mānasavegaś ca Gaurimuṇḍ'|ādayaś ca te
an|antāś ca mahāntaś ca bhaviṣyantaś ca śatravaḥ.
pramattam a|sahāyaṃ ca divya|sāmarthya|dur|gatam
tvām etad|viparīt'|ârim pāntu deva|guru|dvijāḥ.
20.130 tan n' âyaṃ tava saṃbandhaḥ kanyā|mātra|prayojanaḥ
Caṇḍasiṃha|sahāyo 'pi mahad asya prayojanam.»

mama tv abhūd «abhūn mitram ekaḥ Amitagatir mama
idānīṃ Caṇḍasiṃho 'pi su|mahā|bala|mātṛkaḥ.»
iti saṃkalpayann eva chāyā|churita|candrikam
vimānam aham adrākṣam avarūḍhaṃ vihāyasaḥ.
gacchat" âpi sthireṇ' êva tena mānasa|raṃhasā
kham agacchann iv' âgacchaṃ vahanen' êva sāgaram.

ath' âpaśyaṃ vimānasya dūrād avani|maṇḍalam
lok'|â|lok'|ādi|paryantam ādarśa|parimaṇḍalam.
20.135 idam īdṛśam ākāśam an|āvaraṇam īkṣyate
sa tu n' âsti pradeśo 'sya yo vimānair an|āvṛtaḥ.
apsaraḥ|śata|saṃbādhaṃ sa|krīḍā|giri|niṣkuṭam
nikṛṣṭasy' âpi devasya vimānaṃ yojan'|āyatam.

Dhánamati said to me, "This is Gauri·munda, the king of the sorcerers. He is seeking to propitiate the great goddess Gauri. At his sides, like two mighty arms, are his servants, 20.125
the brothers Vyálaka and Angáraka. This is the same Angáraka as the one that impaled Ámita·gati on a *kadámba* tree—later to be freed by you—and who abducted Kusumálika. Since then, Gauri·munda and his *protégés* have taken you for an enemy and plan to kill you when they get the chance. So now you have Mánasa·vega and Gauri·munda and his followers as formidable foes and in the future you will get countless more. You are foolish, alone, and have no supernatural powers. Against enemies like these, only the gods, your parents and the brahmins can protect you. So 20.130
this union is not just about you getting the girl, it also has the important purpose of making Chanda·simha your ally."

I said to myself, "Ámita·gati was my only friend. Now there is Chanda·simha too, with his mighty mother." As I was thinking this, I saw an aerial chariot descend from the sky, its light eclipsing that of the moon. It was as fast as thought but seemed stationary even when it was moving, and as I went up into the sky in it I felt as if I was going nowhere, like in a ship going across the ocean.

From the great height of the chariot I saw the disk of the earth. It looked like a round map, showing everything as far as the mountains at the end of the world. The sky 20.135
looks empty but there is no part of it that is not full of aerial chariots. Even a lowly god's aerial chariot is one *yójana* long, crowded with hundreds of heavenly damsels, and has pleasure groves and mountains in which to sport. Along

so 'ham evam an|antāni kāntimanti mahānti ca
gacchāmi sma vimānāni paśyann āyānti yānti ca.
kasminn api tato deśe kasy' âpi śikhare gireḥ
kasyām api diśi sphītam adṛśyata puraḥ puram.
tasmāc c' ôdapatad bhāsvad vimānaṃ vyāpnuvan nabhaḥ
śṛṅgāt prāg|a|calasy' êva sahasra|kara|maṇḍalam.
20.140 māmakena vimānena saha tat samagacchata
śarīram iva mātaṅgyāḥ śarīreṇa nir|antaram.
kṛṣṇ'|âṅga|śyāma|tuṅg'|âṅgas tāmr'|âpāṅg'|āyat'|ēkṣaṇaḥ
āgamat puruṣas tasmāt prabhāva iva dehavān.
tatas taṃ pratyabhijñāya dṛṣṭaṃ yātrā|mah"|ôtsave
kathitaṃ Dhanamaty" âhaṃ Caṇḍasiṃham avandiṣi.
asau c' ānanda|ja|sveda|stimitair ut|tanū|ruhaiḥ
aṅgair aṅgaṃ samāliṅgya sneh'|ārdraiḥ karkaśair api.
apasṛtya tato dūraṃ namayitv" ônnataṃ śiraḥ
«jyog|bharto jaya dev' êti» sa māṃ uktv" êdam abravīt.
20.145 «asmābhiḥ sevakaiḥ kāryam idaṃ yuṣmāsu bhartṛṣu
āliṅganaṃ tu bhartṝṇāṃ bhṛtyaiḥ paribhavo mahān.
bālo 'pi n' âvamantavyo jāmāt" êti bhavādṛśaḥ
mahatī devatā hy eṣā tvādṛg|rūpeṇa tiṣṭhati.»
ity|ādi bahu tat tan māṃ yāvad eva vadaty asau
Caṇḍasiṃha|puraṃ tāvat tumul'|ôtsavam āsadam.
tasya kiṃ varṇyate yatra viśālaṃ viśikhā|talam
citraṃ citrair mahā|ratnair Indrāṇī|jaghan'|ôcitaiḥ?
etena parikhā|śāla|prāsāda|sura|sadmanām
avaśy'|ādheya|śobhānām ākhyātaṃ rāmaṇīyakam.

the way I saw countless similarly beautiful and enormous aerial chariots coming and going.

Then, in an unknown country on top of an unknown hill in an unknown region, I saw before me a sumptuous city. A dazzling chariot took off from it and flew up into the sky, like the sun with its thousand rays rising up above the peak
of the eastern mountain. It came alongside my chariot, in 20.140
the same way that the body of the forest girl was right next to mine. A man emerged from it. With his tall body as black as a crow's and wide eyes that were red around the edges, he was like majesty incarnate. I recognized him as the man I had seen at the festival celebrations and whom Dhana·mati had told me about. I greeted Chanda·simha. He embraced me with a body wet with the sweat of bliss and tingling all over; though rough, tenderness had made it soft.

Then he moved back some distance, bowed his noble head and after addressing me with "May you long be my
master! Victory to you, o king!" he said the following: "I am 20.145
a servant and you are my master, but I must do this despite it being a great insult for servants to embrace their masters. Even if he is young, a man like you is not to be treated with disrespect because he is one's son-in-law, for a great divinity resides in men of your beauty."

He continued to talk to me like this until I reached his city, where a festival was in full swing. How might one describe that place, where the wide avenues were paved with wonderful precious gems worthy of Indráni's hips? The beauty of the ramparts, houses, palaces and temples, and the splendor that they must have contained, was pro-

20.150 tasya kiṃ varṇyate yasya māṇavāḥ smiti|mānasāḥ
na stanyam api yācante jananīr api bālakāḥ?
tasya kiṃ varṇyate yatra paśu|pāla|sutair api
sakalāḥ sakalā vidyā mātṛk" êv' ânuśīlitāḥ?
tasya kiṃ varṇyate yatra yoginām eva kevalam
prakṣayo na ca jāyante rathyāḥ prāsāda|saṃkaṭāḥ?
yena doṣeṇa saṃsārāt paritrasyanti mokṣavaḥ
sa tasmin mokṣa|śāstreṣu śrūyate Kapil'|ādibhiḥ.
yac ca dūṣita|saṃsārair vastu|doṣair a|dūṣitam
a|kalmaṣa|guṇāt tasmād ramaṇīyatamaṃ kutaḥ.
20.155 na c' êdaṃ Caṇḍasiṃhasya puram ekaṃ praśasyate
anyeṣām api siddhānām īdṛśāny adhikāny api!

avaruhya ca bhūmi|ṣṭhāt tasmād ambara|mandirāt
prāviśaṃ kanyak"|āgāraṃ hasit'|âmbara|mandiram.
tasmin parijano divyaiḥ prakārair mām upācarat
kim artham api c' āhutā mātr" Âjinavatī gatā.
sā yadā tan niśā|śeṣam uttaraṃ ca divā|niśam
n' āgat" âiva tad" āsīn me tvar'|ātura|mater matiḥ.
«darśana|smita|saṃbhāṣā|sparśan'|āliṅgan'|ādibhiḥ
samastair a|samastaiś ca ramayanti priyāḥ priyān.
20.160 kiraṇair indu|lekh" êva gat" âiva saha tair asau
aham apy eṣa tiṣṭhāmi duḥkha|saṃtapta|mānasaḥ.
tat kim etat? kathaṃ nv etad?» ity|ādi bahu cintayan
vivāha|vighna|saṃbhrāntam aikṣe s'|ântaḥ|puraṃ puram.

claimed by the city itself. How might one describe that 20.150
place where the children have a happy disposition and do not pester their mothers, even for their breasts? How might one describe that place where even the cowherds' sons have studied all the sciences and arts, as if they were the alphabet? How might one describe that place where only yogins cast off their bodies and the roads are not hemmed in by the mansions? The vices that usually inspire fear in those who want to be liberated from the wheel of rebirth are prescribed there by Kápila and others in treatises on liberation! Where could be more delightful than that stainless place which is
unsullied by the material faults that blight the world? And 20.155
this city of Chanda·simha is not the only one that is to be praised—other perfected masters have cities like it, and better ones too!

When the flying palace landed, I alighted from it and entered the girl's house, which put the flying palace to shame. The servants there attended to me in a heavenly fashion. Ajínavati's mother called her for some reason and she left. When she did not return at the end of the night, nor the next day, nor the following night, I became impatient and thought, "Sweethearts delight their lovers with glances, smiles, sweet talk, caresses, embraces and so forth, all at once
or one by one. But she has gone away and taken them with 20.160
her, like the crescent moon leaving with its rays, and I am waiting here with my heart burned up by anxiety. What is going on? Why has this happened?" While thinking a host of thoughts like these I noticed that the city and the inner apartments were in a state of confusion about the delay to the wedding.

āsīc ca mama «Campāyāḥ preto mām anayan niśi
Jyeṣṭha|kṛṣṇa|catur|daśyām Ārdra|sthe tārakā|patau.
nūnam Āṣāḍha|śukl'|ādau pañcamyām uttarāsu ca
Phalguṇīṣu vivāho 'yaṃ rājñā kārayit" āvayoḥ.
ayaṃ māhā|kulaḥ rājā Śruti|Smṛti|viśāradaḥ
tad Brāhmeṇa vivāhena sūnoḥ saṃskāram icchati.»

20.165 upāsya caturaḥ kaṣṭān pāvakān iva vāsarān
tāṃ prāpaṃ kanyakām ante tapaḥ|siddhim iv' ēpsitām.»

ghan'|â|ghan'|âmbhodhara|jāla|kālīm
a|dṛṣṭa|tārā|gaṇa|rāja|bimbām
tayā saha prāvṛṣam āsi ramyām
a|śukla|pakṣ'|ânta|niśām iv' âikām.

s" âikadā sa|parīvārā nibhṛta|krandita|dhvaniḥ
anuyuktā mayā «kaccin nṛpaḥ kuśalavān?» iti.
tayā tu pratiṣiddh" âpi dārikā Megharājikā
nivedayitum ārabdhā «śrūyatāṃ bhartṛ|dāraka.
pūrvaṃ Vikaciko nāma sva|chandaḥ khe|car'|âdhamaḥ
svais tyaktaḥ s'|âparādhatvāt kiṃ cit kālam ih' āsthitaḥ.

20.170 kanyā sarvasya dṛśy" êti ten' âsau bhartṛ|dārikām
āsīnāṃ pitur utsaṅge dṛṣṭvā rājānam uktavān.
‹duhitā tava yady eṣā tato mahyaṃ pradīyatām
madīya|guṇa|saṃkhyā ca buddh" âiva bhavatām› iti.

ten' ôktaṃ ‹kena na jñātāḥ? prasiddhā hi guṇās tava!
kiṃ tu komala|janm" êyaṃ prauḍhā tāvad bhavatv› iti.
ten' âpy āmantrya rājānaṃ sva|deśāya gamiṣyatā
ā|yoṣid|bāla|go|pālam ālāpaḥ śrāvitaḥ pure:

I thought to myself, "The ghost brought me here from Champa on the fourteenth night of the dark fortnight of Jyeshtha, when the moon was in the constellation of Ardra. I expect the king will have arranged for our marriage to be held on the fifth day of the bright fortnight of Ashádha, with the moon in the second Phálguni constellation. The king is from a noble family and is well versed in the scriptures, so he wants to have his daughter married according to the sacred
rites." After waiting for four torturous days that were like 20.165
fires of purification, I married the girl on the last; it was as though she was the desired reward of an ascetic observance.

In her company I spent a delightful rainy season, during which the many heavy storm clouds made it so dark that the orb of the moon was not to be seen, and it passed as though it were but one night of the new moon.

One day the girl and her retinue were sobbing gently. I inquired after the health of the king. Despite being forbidden to do so by Ajínavati, her servant Megha·rájika went ahead and said to me: "Listen, my lord. There was an impetuous wretch of a sky-ranger called Vikáchika, who had been cast out by his own people because of his wickedness and spent
some time here. A young girl can be looked at by anyone, 20.170
and when he saw the princess sitting on her father's lap he said to the king, 'If this girl is your daughter, then give her to me. You know very well how many good qualities I have.'

He replied, 'Who does not know? Your qualities are renowned! But the girl is still young. Let her grow up first.' He took his leave of the king and just before he left for his own country he let everyone in the city, from the women and children to the cowherds, hear about the conversation:

‹rājñā mahyaṃ sa|sat|kāraṃ datt" Âjinavatī sutā
diṣṭyā vṛddhir bhavaty adya mam' êva bhavatām!› iti.
20.175 sa bhartṛ|dārikāṃ śrutvā bhartṛ|dāraka|bhartṛkām
vismṛt'|ôpakṛtaḥ krodhād āha rājānam a|trapaḥ:
‹bhavataḥ ko 'yam ācāraḥ sad" ācār'|âbhimāninaḥ?
yad dattvā tanayāṃ mahyam anyasmai dattavān! iti.
atha v" âlam upālabhya bhavantam a|bhaya|trapam!
sutā vā vyavahāro vā yuddhaṃ vā dīyatām› iti.
ath' āha vihasan rājā ‹na yuddhaṃ na mam' ātma|jām
labdhum arhati dīrgh'|āyur vyavahāras tu dīyate.›
ity uktvā taṃ mahī|pālaḥ sa|mantri|gaṇa|mātṛkaḥ
Vāyumukta|mah"|âdhyakṣaṃ Saptaparṇapuraṃ gataḥ.
20.180 yuvām api rucau satyāṃ śobhit'|āśā|vihāyasau
tatr' âiva sahitau yātaṃ Rohiṇī|Śaśināv iva.»
may" ôktaṃ «bhīru mā bhaiṣīḥ! kiṃ|narī|kaṇṭhi mā rudaḥ!
Megharājyā yath" ākhyātaṃ jitaḥ sa capalas tathā.»
iti tasyāḥ paritrāsa|tuṣāra|mlāpitaṃ mayā
sāntva|bāl'|ātapa|sparśān mukh'|âmbhojaṃ vikāśitam.
mām ādāya tataḥ pāṇau sā gatv" âmbara|vartmanā
sapta|parṇa|pur'|ôdyāne Saptaparṇapure sthitā.
abravīc ca «nir|utkaṇṭhaiḥ kṣaṇam ekam ih' āsyatām
yāvad emi sakhīṃ dṛṣṭvā vanditvā ca gurūn» iti.

'With due ceremony, the king has promised me his daughter Ajínavati. Both I and you are to be congratulated today!'

When he heard that you had married the princess and the 20.175
promise to him had been forgotten, he was furious and dared to say to the king, 'How can you behave like this, you who are always proud of your good conduct? After betrothing your daughter to me, you have given her to someone else! But there is no point in scolding you: you have neither fear nor shame! Give me either your daughter, or a court hearing, or a fight!'

The king said with a laugh, 'Venerable sir, you are worthy of neither a fight nor my daughter, so I shall grant you a court hearing.'

After telling him this, the king went with his cabinet and his mother to Sapta·parna·pura, where Vayu·mukta is the
senior judge. If you so wish, both of you should go there 20.180
together, beautifying the sky like Róhini and Shashi."*

I said, "Sweet lady, do not be afraid! Divine songstress, do not cry! According to what Megha·rájika has said, that rash fellow will be defeated."

The warm touch of my comforting words was like the rising sun, and I made her lotus-face, which had withered with the frost of fear, burst into bloom. She took me by the hand and flew to Sapta·parna·pura, landing in the city's *sapta·parna* flower garden. She said, "Be patient and wait here for a moment, while I go and see a friend of mine and pay my respects to my elders."

20.185 tasyām utpatya yātāyām udyāne saṃcarann aham
sthūla|mauktika|varṇāni sapta|parṇāni dṛṣṭavān.
taiś ca grathitavān asmi kadalī|paṭu|tantubhiḥ
bandhūka|taralaṃ hāram utpalaiś churit'|ôdaram.
padma|rāg'|êndra|nīl'|ādi|nānā|ratn'|ôpala|prabhaiḥ
kusumaiḥ kalpayāmi sma kambū|nūpura|mekhalāḥ.

avatīrya tato vyomnaḥ sā priyā priya|vādinī
«nirjitaḥ sa dur|ātm' êti» hṛṣṭā mām apy aharṣayat.
«katham» ity anuyuktā ca mayā s'|ādaram abravīt
«anuyogam upekṣante vivakṣanto 'pi vācakāḥ.
20.190 vāyumuktān mayā gatvā vandit'|ântaḥ|pura|striyā
Vāyumuktā sakhī dṛṣṭā kany" ântaḥ|pura|vartinī.
tatr' âhaṃ kṣaṇam āsīnā jita|jīmūta|garjitām
pradhvanantīṃ śṛṇomi sma bherīṃ bhairava|garjitām.
‹kim etad?› iti pṛṣṭā sā saṃbhram'|ôt|karṇayā mayā
sakhī svāṃ dārikām āha yāhi vijñāyatām» iti.

sā muhūrtād iv' āgatya śvasit'|ôtkampita|stanī
‹vardhase devi diṣṭy" êti› mām uktv" ôktavatī punaḥ.
‹bherīṃ tāḍitavān eṣa gatvā Vikacikaḥ sabhām
Vāyumukt'|âkṣa|darśāś ca samāyātāḥ sabhā|sadaḥ.
20.195 te tam āhur «bhavān kasmād bherīṃ tāḍitavān?» iti
ārya|veṣaḥ sa tān āha puraḥ sthitvā nir|āsanaḥ:
«Caṇḍasiṃhaḥ sutāṃ dattvā mahyaṃ nagara|saṃnidhau
anyasmin dattavān yatra nagaraṃ pṛcchyatām!» iti.

After she had flown off, I wandered about in the garden 20.185
and noticed some *sapta·parna* flowers that were the color of rough pearls. Using strong banana fibers, I tied them into a garland, with waving *bandhúka* flowers and blue lotuses woven into the middle. I made bracelets, anklets and belts from flowers that resembled rubies, sapphires and various other gemstones.

Then my sweet-talking sweetheart came down from the sky. She was overjoyed and made me overjoyed, too, by telling me that the scoundrel had been defeated. When I asked her how, she said respectfully, "Even when they want
to speak, speakers wait to be asked! After I had seen Vayu· 20.190
mukta, I paid my respects to the ladies of the harem and saw my friend Vayu·muktá, a girl who lives in the inner apartments. I had sat there for a while when I heard kettle-drums resounding, their fearsome rumble louder than that of thunder. Pricking up my ears, I asked my friend what was going on, and she told a maid to go and find out.

She returned almost immediately, her chest heaving. She said to me, 'Congratulations, Your Majesty!' and continued, 'Vikáchika went to the assembly and sounded the kettle-drum and then Vayu·mukta, the judges and the members of
the assembly arrived. They asked him why he had sounded 20.195
the kettledrum. Wearing the dress of a nobleman, he stood in front of them and said, without sitting down, "Chanda·simha betrothed his daughter to me in the presence of the whole city and then he gave her to someone else. Ask the citizens about it!"

«ucyatām» iti c' ôktena tātena kila saṃsadā
Megharājyā yad ākhyātaṃ tad ev' ākhyātam āha ca.
«madīya|pura|vāstavyān sākṣiṇaś c' âyam āha yān
pṛcchyantāṃ te 'pi teṣāṃ ced a|viruddhā pramāṇatā.»
ath' ôktaṃ Vāyumuktena saṃbhāṣita|sabhā|sadā
«nṛ|pater Manu|kalpasya kim etasya parīkṣayā?
20.200 na hi prāmāṇya|rājasya jijñāsā|saṃśaya|chidaḥ
pratyakṣasy' ânumānena pramāṇatvaṃ pramīyate.
tasmāt pratyarthinā rājñā vyavahāre parājitaḥ
arthī Vikacikaḥ kanyām anyāṃ mṛgayatām» iti.
tataḥ Vikacikaḥ kruddhaḥ sphaṭity utthāya saṃsadaḥ
utpatya nabhasā gacchann uccair āha sabhā|sadaḥ.
«dhik khalān khalu caṇḍālān! pakṣa|pāta|hatāñ jaḍān
aham eva hi kartavye kartavye buddhivān!»» iti.»
āsīc ca mama yat satyam āśaṅkā|kaluṣaṃ manaḥ
«kasmin punar asau kārye kartavye buddhimān?» iti.
20.205 tatas tais tām alaṃ|kṛtya śarat|kusuma|bhūṣaṇaiḥ
śarīra|śarad|ākāra|taskarām idam abravam.
«priy'|ākhyāna|prahṛṣṭena vibhram'|ābharaṇaṃ mayā
tav' āropitam aṅgeṣu su|bhag'|âṅgi virājate!»
sā tatas tān alaṃ|kārān dviṣatī kaṇṭakān iva
mām avocad vidhūy' âṅgam asūyā|manthara|smitā.
«aparāsv api bhāryāsu yuṣmābhir idam āhitam
na hi dṛṣṭaṃ vin" âbhyāsāt kriyā|kauśalam īdṛśam.
tasmān nir|mālya|tulyena na kāryam amunā mama
kā hi dur|labham ātmānaṃ kitavaiḥ paribhāvayet?»

The assembly told your father to speak and apparently he said exactly what Megha·rájika said. Then he said that if there were no objection to their testimony, the residents of his city mentioned by Vikáchika should be called as witnesses.

Vayu·mukta consulted the assembly and said, "This king is like Manu; what is the point of cross-examining him? The authoritativeness of direct perception, which is the best 20.200
means of acquiring knowledge and cuts through doubt, cannot be established by inference. Thus the plaintiff, Vikáchika, has been defeated in the case by the defendant, the king, and should look for another girl."

At this, the enraged Vikáchika stormed out of the assembly, flew up into the air and screamed at the assembly: "Shame on you vile outcastes—prejudiced idiots! When I have something to do, I know how to do it!" ' "

My mind was clouded with anxiety and I asked myself what the deed might be that he knew how to do. Then I 20.205
adorned Ajínavati with the ornaments I had made from the autumn flowers; she stole the beauty from autumn itself and I said to her, "Overjoyed by your delightful words, I have put these alluring ornaments on your body. You are beautiful and they look lovely!"

Spurning the ornaments as if they were thorns, she brushed them off her body and said to me with a jealous smirk, "You have done this for your other wives as well: skill such as this doesn't come about without practice. As a result, these are no better than discarded offerings and you are not to adorn me with them. What woman would have her precious person insulted by a cheat?"

20.210 mama tv āsīd «a|pūrv" êyam asyā viṣama|śīlatā
upāyair dur|nivarty" âiva praṇāma|śapath'|ādibhiḥ.
nārī ca laghu|sāratvāt taraṃga|śreṇi|cañcalā
nauk" êva pratikūl" âśu kuśalaiḥ parivartyate.
bhāryā|jñāti|gṛhe vāsaś ciraṃ daurbhāgya|kāraṇam
yadi vipratyayaḥ kaś cid bhartāraṃ kiṃ na paśyasi.
bhartrā te cāṭu|kāreṇa bhāryāṃ toṣayatā kila
tat kṛtaṃ dur|vidagdhena yena bhāry" âiva roṣitā.
su|bhagaṃ karaṇaṃ yad yat samācarati dur|bhagaḥ
su|tarāṃ tena ten' âsya daurbhāgyam upacīyate!
20.215 sarvathā vārayiṣyāmi putrān api bhaviṣyataḥ
‹mā ciraṃ putrakāḥ sthāta bhāryā|jñāti|gṛheṣv› iti.»
tayā tu man|mukhaṃ dṛṣṭvā hrīta|trasta|vilakṣayā
a|snigdha|smitayā «hā hā kim etad?» iti bhāṣitam.

ataḥ param «a|yukto 'yaṃ prapañca» iti tām aham
anayaṃ vepamān'|âṅgīm āliṅgy' ôtsaṅgam aṅganām.
sā tu labdha|samāśvāsā dīrghikā|tīrtha|vartinī
«arya|putra prasīd' êti» vyāharat tāram āturā.

paśyāmi sma tataḥ kha|sthaṃ taṃ vidyā|dhara|pāṃsanam
paritaḥ sphurita|sphīta|maṇḍal'|âgr'|âṃśu|maṇḍalam.
20.220 roṣa|bhīṣaṇa|ghoṣeṇa ten' ôktaṃ «dharaṇī|cara
te paśyat' êyaṃ kāntā hriyate! dhriyatām!» iti.

krodh'|âpahata|dhairyatvād vācy'|â|vācy'|â|vivecinā
saṃbhāvita|sva|sāreṇa may" âsāv iti bhartsitaḥ.
«ākāśa|gaś|caro 'sm' îti kiṃ tvaṃ nīca vikatthase
kāko 'pi hi nabhaś|cārī na ca muñcati nīcatām!
yaḥ siṃha|śirasi nyasya kākaś caraṇam utpatet
na tena paribhūtaḥ syāt kesarī dharaṇī|caraḥ.»

I said to myself, "This difficult behavior of hers is un- 20.210
precedented and hard to counter with entreaties, promises or other such means. But because she lacks substance, a woman is like a small boat at the whim of the waves, and, when going the wrong way, can be quickly turned around by a skilful man. A lengthy stay at the house of one's wife's relatives brings about marital discord. If you don't believe me, why don't you take a look at your husband?* In trying to please his wife, your flatterer of a husband has foolishly made her angry. When a lover is out of favor, his amorous
acts only add to his unpopularity! I shall certainly deter my 20.215
future sons from staying for long in the houses of their wives' relatives." She looked at my face and, embarrassed, frightened and uncomfortable, said with an unfriendly smile, "Oh! What is the matter?"

Then, thinking it improper to expand on the matter, I took the trembling lady in my arms and sat her on my lap. She was consoled, but then, by the steps to the rectangular bathing tank, she screamed in distress, "My lord, help!"

I saw in the sky that disgrace of a sorcerer, ringed by
rays of light from the tips of his dazzling swords. In a voice 20.220
made terrifying by his rage he said, "Earth-rover, look! Your sweetheart is being abducted! Save her!"

My patience dispelled by anger, I did not consider what I should or shouldn't say. Confident of my strength, I berated him: "Lowlife! Why are you boasting about being a sky-rover? A crow moves through the sky but that doesn't stop it being a lowlife! When a crow flies off after putting its foot on the head of a lion, it has not humilated the golden-maned earth-rover."

evam uttejyamāno 'pi n' âvatīrṇaḥ sa bhū|talam
paritaś cakitaḥ paśyan s'|âvajñānam iv' âbravīt.
20.225 «sthala|kacchapa|kalpāya vainateya|parākramaḥ
tvādṛśe mādṛśaḥ krudhyan kena pāpān na śocyatām.»
ity uktvā karuṇ'|ākrandāṃ tām asau khe|car'|âdhamaḥ
bhuvaḥ śyena iva śyāmām ādāy' ôdapatad divam.
ath' âpaśyaṃ mahā|jvālā|jvāla|saṃkucit'|âmbarām
āpatantīṃ divaṃ devīm utpāt'|ôlkām iv' â|śivām.
caṇḍa|vidyā|dhar'|ânīka|parivāraṃ ca bhū|patim
Mahākālam iva kruddhaṃ gaṇ'|âmara|gaṇ'|ânugam.
uttāna|vadanaś c' âhaṃ Caṇḍasiṃham anuvrajan
anyatr' âiva gataḥ kv' âpi diṅ|moha|muṣita|smṛtiḥ.
20.230 bhrāmyatā śrāmyatā rūkṣa|vṛkṣeṣ' ûpavane ghane
cirād ākarṇito dhīrād uccakair uccaran dhvaniḥ.
«he! he! Kālākṣi! Kālākṣi! Gaṅge! Gaṅge! Mah" îti» ca
vatsalānāṃ vivatsānāṃ rambhaś ca su|bhago gavām.
gatvā ca tvaray" âpaśyaṃ yāṣṭīkaṃ pālam agrataḥ
Kulattha|sthūla|pulakam uru|jaṅgh'|ōru|vistṛtam.
pratimalla|bhuj'|ānāma|bandhura|skandha|kaṃdharam
vegavac|carpaṭ'|ātāḍa|kiṇa|karkaśa|karṇakam.
tatas tam abravaṃ sāmnā satataṃ mahitaṃ gavām
«bhraṣṭaḥ panthā mam' âṭavyāṃ tam ākhyātu bhavān» iti.

Despite being provoked like this, he did not come down to earth. Looking around in surprise, he said somewhat disdainfully, "By getting angry with someone like you, who 20.225
is no better than a stranded tortoise, someone like me, who is as brave as Gáruda, will certainly be made to regret his sins." Then, like an eagle taking a koyal, the despicable sky-rover took the girl, who was crying out in distress, and flew up into the sky. I saw my queen flying through the sky consuming the firmament with the flames of a blazing inferno, as if she were an ill-omened shooting star. And I saw the king, surrounded by an army of fearsome sorcerers, like an angry Maha·kala followed by his troop of demigods and immortals. Looking upward and following Chanda·simha, I lost my sense of direction and ended up somewhere altogether different.

After wandering wearily for ages among scrawny trees, 20.230
I heard shouting from the depths of a dense thicket: "Hey! Hey! Kalákshi! Kalákshi! Ganga! Ganga! Mahi!" and then I heard the sweet lowing of cows separated from their beloved calves. I hurried over and saw before me a cowherd carrying a staff. He had the thick bristly hair of a Kuláttha and broad calves and thighs. His neck and shoulders were hunched from being pressed down by the arms of his opponents in battle and his ears had rough calluses from being violently slapped. The cows were all the while honoring him with their lowing as I said to him, "Sir, I am lost in the forest. Please tell me the way."

20.235 ten' ôktaṃ «gokule rātriṃ gamayitvā gata|śramaḥ
prage draṣṭā sva|panthānaṃ tad" êta sva|gṛhān» iti.

gatvā tena sah' âpaśyaṃ ghoṣam āsanna|gokulam
mandra|mantha|dhvani|kṣipta|Mandar'|āsphālit'|ârṇavam!
a|kuṭṭima|samā yatra s'|âṅgaṇ'|ôṭaja|bhūmayaḥ
harid|gomaya|saṃmārga|saṃprasārita|Mānasāḥ.
bandhūka|cūtakā|stambaiḥ parikṣipt'|ôṭaj'|âṅgaṇaiḥ
yatra n' ābhīra|nārīṇāṃ paribhūtaṃ kar'|âdharam.
yatra tumbī|latā|jālaiḥ kuṭī|paṭala|rodhibhiḥ
lajjitāḥ paṅkajinyo 'pi kalik"|âṅguli|tārjitāḥ.
20.240 yasminn a|dṛṣṭa|dur|darśa|pāṃsu|saṃkāra|saṃkaṭāḥ
nir|a|vācya|talā rathyāḥ kūrdad|uddāma|tarṇakāḥ.
karṇikār'|â|malair aṅgaiḥ pṛthulair jaghana|sthalaiḥ
sa tādṛṅ|malinaḥ strīṇāṃ yatra veṣo vibhūṣitaḥ.
vana|gokula|vṛddhatvād yatra go|pā gav|ārjavāḥ
gopyas tu catur'|ācārā naṭīr apy atiśerate!

evam|ādi|prakāreṇa ghoṣeṇa hṛta|mānasam
māṃ go|paḥ sva|gṛhaṃ nītvā gṛhiṇīm āhvayan mudā.
«Sudeva|duhitaḥ kv' âsi nanu go|pāla|dārike?
devas te gṛham āyātaḥ sa bhakty" ārādhyatām!» iti.

He replied, "Spend the night in the cowherds' village; in the morning, when you are rested, you will find your way home." 20.235

I went with him and saw the cowherds' village with their cattle nearby. The sound of the ocean being churned by Mount Mándara was nothing compared with the rumbling sound of the milk being churned there! The surfaces of the huts and yards there were not as flat as inlaid floors but, smeared all over with reddish cow dung, they looked like Lake Mánasa. The courtyards of the huts there, strewn with *bandhúka* flowers and mango blossoms, failed to overshadow the hands and lips of the cowherd ladies. The abundant gourd creepers covering the huts' roofs put even the lotus flowers to shame, scolding them with their finger-like
buds. No unsightly dust or rubbish or obstructions were to 20.240
be seen in the pothole-free streets, where frisky calves were gambolling. The women's bodies, which were as spotless as *karni·kara* flowers, and their voluptuous hips made their clothes, as filthy as they were, look beautiful. Having grown up in a graziers' settlement in the forest, the cowherds were as straightforward as cows, but the cowgirls were even more cunning than showgirls!

That is what the graziers' settlement was like, and I was charmed by it. The cowherd took me to his house and joyfully called his wife: "Sudéva's daughter, where are you, young cowgirl? A god has come to your house; you must serve him with devotion!"

20.245 tataḥ payoda|śakalāt sā kal" êva kalāvataḥ
gṛhān niragamad gaurī prakīrṇa|tanu|candrikā.
dāru|danta|śilā|mayyaḥ pratimās tāvad āsatām
na tāṃ vedhāḥ kṣamaḥ sraṣṭuṃ madh'|ûcchiṣṭa|mayīm api.
bhāvabhir vartamānaiś ca kavibhiḥ kim udāhṛtaiḥ
na tāṃ varṇayituṃ śaktau Vyāsa|Vālmīkināv api.
sā māṃ gomaya|pīṭha|sthaṃ svas" êva svaccha|mānasā
ā|śiras|pādam a|śrāntā saṃvāhitavatī ciram.
yaṃ yam ev' ôpasāraṃ sā tuccham apy ācaren mayi
sarvam anv asahe taṃ taṃ dākṣiṇya|kṣaya|śaṅkayā.
20.250 salilaiḥ kāṃsya|pātra|sthair adhāvac caraṇau mama
s'|ôttam'|âṅgeṣu c' âṅgeṣu nava|nītam adān mudā.
ucchādya kaṇa|kalkena tatra stīmita|mastakaḥ
lodhra|karbūra|mustābhir ghṛṣṭo 'haṃ snapitas tayā.
aśitvā c' âśanaṃ medhyam alp'|ânnaṃ bahu|go|rasam
vi|pāpmānam iv' ātmānam amanye madya|pāyinam!
kalpayitvā tu me go|paḥ śayyāṃ valkala|pallavaiḥ
«etat te gṛham» ity uktv" âṃsa|bhāro vrajam avrajat.
mama tv āsīd «ayaṃ manye vīta|rāg'|ādi|bandhanaḥ
sa|kleśaḥ ko nu viśvasyād dāreṣu ca pareṣu ca?
20.255 s'|ādhāraṇa|kalatrāṇām īrṣyā|kṣobhita|cetasām
tiraścām api dṛśyante prakāśa|maraṇā raṇāḥ.
ayaṃ tu dayitān dārān muni|mānasa|hāriṇaḥ
mayi nikṣipya yāt' îti vyakta eṣa sa puṃgavaḥ.
atha vā niṣ|pravīṇeṣu bahir|vṛtti|kuṭumbiṣu
nārī|tantreṣu tantreṣu kim ācāra|parīkṣayā.
rajaka|dhvaja|go|pāla|mālā|kāra|naṭa|striyaḥ

Like a digit of the moon emerging from behind a cloud, 20.245
a pale lady emerged from the house, casting a delicate lunar light. Forget statues of wood, ivory or stone: the creator could not have made her, even from wax! There is no point in talking of present or future poets: even Vyasa and Valmíki would not have been able to describe her! I sat on a cow dung seat and, as pure in heart as a sister, she tirelessly massaged me for an age from head to toe.

I went along with everything that she did to me, however
unnecessary, lest she stop the expert massage. She washed 20.250
my feet with water from brass pots. She joyfully put fresh butter on my head and body. She scrubbed me with a paste made from seeds and rubbed my wet head with *lodhra* flowers, *karbúra* root and *musta* grass before washing me. I ate pure food without much grain but lots of milk, and considered myself—a wine drinker—free from sin! The cowherd made me a bed from bark and twigs and, saying, "This is your house," he shouldered his load and went to the cowshed.

I said to myself, "This fellow must be free of the emotional bonds of passion and so forth: who with such afflictions would be so trusting of his wife and strangers?
Even animals, whose wives are common property, are well 20.255
known for fighting to the death when their minds are enraged by jealousy. But this fellow has entrusted to me his wife, who could captivate the mind of a saint, and is leaving. He is clearly a remarkable man. Anyway, there is no point in scrutinizing the conduct of unrefined households, where the men of the household work outside and the women are in charge. When well-behaved women are found among

dṛśyante yāḥ sad|ācārāḥ sā tāsāṃ bāla|śīlatā.
eṣā tu go|pa|yoṣ" âpi rūpiṇy api taruṇy api
evaṃ gambhīra|dhairy" êti dur|bodhāḥ para|buddhayaḥ!»

20.260 cintām etāṃ kurvataḥ kārya|vandhyām
āsīt sā me s'|ôpakār" âiva rātrīḥ
sadyaḥ kāntā|kaṇṭha|viśleṣa|duḥkham
ārāt sahyaṃ cetasā yan na soḍham.

tataḥ prātaḥ sa māṃ go|paḥ kṛpālur iva tattva|vit
ghorāt kāntāra|saṃsārād a|cirād udatārayat.
«eṣa te Saṃbhava|grāmaḥ prāṃśu|prāg|vaṃśa|kānanaḥ
dṛśyante yasya sīmāntāḥ sīramantaḥ sa|saṃkaṭāḥ.
deś'|ântaram abhipretam atra viśramya gamyatām»
iti māṃ idam uktv" âsau nivṛttaḥ kṛta|bandhanaḥ.

ath' êkṣu|gahana|chāyāḥ kṣipta|śāradik'|ātapāḥ
sevamānaḥ prayāmi sma saṃtapto bhānu|bhānubhiḥ.

20.265 vikāśi|kumud'|ārāmāḥ praśaṃsan sarasīḥ kva|cit
sthalīr iva nidāgh'|ânte phull'|â|virala|kandarāḥ.
kva cid garbhita|śālīni śāleyāni kutūhalī
sa|gundrā|gahanān' îva palvalāni vilokayan.
kva cid utkūla|Kālindī|sar'|âmbhaḥ|pūritair iva
kṛta|haṃsa|dvi|jātīyaiḥ sarobhiḥ prīṇit'|ēkṣaṇaḥ.
sattv'|ākāra|satī|kāra|komal'|āpāṇḍu|pāṃsubhiḥ
kṛṣṭair ākṛṣṭa|dṛṣṭiś ca jāhnavī|pulinair iva.
evam|ādi|śarat|kāla|kānti|vismārita|priyaḥ

washermen, liquor distillers, cowherds, garland makers and showgirls, it is because they have a childish disposition. But this cowherd's wife, despite being beautiful and young, is so profoundly composed. . . the minds of others are hard to fathom!"

For me, reflecting like this on something I could do noth- 20.260
ing about, the night was beneficial: the previously insufferable torment of being separated from the embrace of my beloved was suddenly bearable.

In the morning, the cowherd quickly led me across the fearsome forest, like a kindly sage delivering me from the horror of transmigration. "Before you is the village of Sámbhava, in which there is a grove of tall bamboos toward the east. Its boundaries are where you can see the closely plowed fields. Rest there before going to your destination." After saying this to me, he turned back, and I was grateful to him.

I went on my way, resorting to the shade of the sugarcane thickets that tempered the autumnal heat: the sun's
rays were scorching me. In places I marveled at pools with 20.265
groves of blossoming lotuses; they were like valleys full of flowers at the end of summer. Elsewhere I looked on with curiosity at paddy fields ready for harvest; they resembled ponds full of *gundra* thickets. In other places I feasted my eyes on lakes that seemed like they were filled with overflowing water from the Yámuna; the brahmins had become swans. My gaze was drawn by plowed fields where, like the sandy banks of the Ganga, the pure appearance of the soft pale soil made one think of a virtuous woman. These and other lovely autumnal sights made me forget my beloved. As I was walking along I saw a man coming toward me

gacchan puruṣam adrākṣaṃ grāmād āyāntam antike.
20.270 sa tu māṃ ciram īkṣitvā bravīti sma sa|vismayaḥ
«citram! ārya|kaniṣṭhasya yūyaṃ su|sadṛśā» iti.
mama tv āsīd «a|saṃdigdhaṃ dṛṣṭavān eṣa Gomukham
na hi tasmād ṛte kaś cid asti mat sadṛśaḥ kṣitau.»
pṛcchāmi sma ca taṃ «bhadra saḥ kaniṣṭhaḥ kva tiṣṭhati?
kīdṛśā vā vinodena gamayed divasān?» iti.
tatas ten' ôktam «atr' âiva grāme gṛha|patir dvi|jaḥ
asti sādhāraṇ'|ârth'|ârthaḥ priya|vādī Prasannakaḥ.
ekadā brāhmaṇaḥ pṛṣṭas tena brahma|sabhāṃ gataḥ
‹āgataḥ katamād deśāt kim arthaṃ vā bhavān› iti.
20.275 ten' ôktam ‹āgatāv āvām Avanti|viṣayād dvi|jau
bhrātarau sa ca me jyeṣṭho yātrāyām anyato gataḥ.
tad gaveṣayamāṇo 'ham etaṃ grāmam upāgataḥ
chāttrāṇām atra sarveṣām upapannaḥ samāgamaḥ.›
ity ukte tena ten' ôktam ‹idaṃ vaḥ sa|dhanaṃ gṛham
yena yen' âtra vaḥ kāryaṃ tat tad ādīyatām› iti.
gṛhe gṛha|pates tasya kṣamāvān api śīlataḥ
trasta|bhṛtya|kṛt'|ārādhaḥ Durvāsovad vasaty asau.
hālikatvān na jānāmi jñātā kiṃ kim asāv iti
yan|mātraṃ tu vijānāmi tan|mātraṃ kathayāmi vaḥ.
20.280 chāttrais tāvat kim uddiṣṭair a|prāpta|sakal'|āgamaiḥ
ācāryā api vidyāsu tasy' âiva chāttratāṃ gatāḥ.
iti c' āhuḥ ‹kim asmābhir vṛth" âiv' ātm'|âvasādibhiḥ?
Viśvakarm" âtha vā Brahmā kasmān n' âyam upāsitaḥ?›

from the village. He looked at me for a long time before 20.270
saying with surprise, "How strange! You look very like the
young master."

I said to myself, "Surely this man must have seen Go·mukha, for other than him there's no one in the world who looks like me." I asked him, "Good sir, where is this youngster? In what diversions does he pass his days?"

He replied, "Here in this very village there is a silver-tongued brahmin householder called Prasánnaka, who uses his wealth for the common good. One day a brahmin came to the brahmins' assembly and was asked by him, 'From what country and for what reason have you come, sir?'

He replied, 'I and my brahmin brother came here from 20.275
the country of Avánti. During the journey my elder brother
took a different path. In my search for him I have come
to this village. All the students are supposed to be meeting here.'

The brahmin replied, 'This house and its contents are at your disposal. Take whatever you need.'

Even though he is forgiving in nature, the servants in
his host's house wait upon him in fear, and he lives like
the sage Durvásas.* I am a plowman, so I do not know
all the things that he knows, but I'll tell you as much as
I can. I won't bother talking of students who are yet to 20.280
master all their schoolwork—even the teachers are learning
the sciences from him! They have said, 'There's no point in
depriving ourselves. This man is Vishva·karman or Brahma:
why shouldn't we serve him?'

evam|ādi|vinodo 'sāv ārya|jyeṣṭhaṃ pratīkṣate
utkaṇṭhaḥ sarvataḥ paśyañ jīmūtam iva cātakaḥ.
ārya|jyeṣṭho bhavān eva yadi tad laghu kathyatām
a|kāla|kaumudī grāme sahasā jṛmbhatām» iti.

«āma saumya sa ev' âham» iti saṃvādito mayā
ūrdhva|cūḍaḥ sa vegena prati grāmam adhāvata.
20.285 sahasā tena c' ôtkṣipto grāme trāsita|kātaraḥ
utthitas toṣa|nirghoṣas tāla|saṃpāta|saṃkulaḥ.
viniḥsṛtya tato grāmād Gomukho vikasan|mukhaḥ
dūrād eva yathā|dīrgham apatan mama pādayoḥ.
bālair āliṅgitaiḥ putrair dāraiś ca na tathā priyaiḥ
janyate janitā prītis tena me suhṛdā yathā.
prasanna|vadanaṃ c' ārāt tad ākhyātaṃ Prasannakam
āliṅgya sahitas tena Saṃbhava|grāmam āsadam.
ubheṭī|kūṭa|paṭala|prāsād'|ādi|gatā ca mām
grāmīṇā janatā yāntam aṅgulībhir adarśayat.
20.290 prīt'|ânucara|vargeṇa Prasannaka|niveśane
kṛt'|âsu|kara|sat|kāraḥ prerayaṃ divasaṃ kṣaṇam.

śayanīya|gṛha|sthaṃ ca mām abhāṣata Gomukhaḥ
«nītavantaḥ kathaṃ yūyam iyato divasān?» iti.

ghoṣa|vās'|âvasāne ca sva|vṛtte kathite mayā
pṛṣṭaḥ sva|vṛtt' ācaṣṭa Gomukhaḥ priya|vistaraḥ.
«asty ahaṃ sva|gṛhāt prātar yuṣmān sevitum āgataḥ
pratibuddhān na c' âpaśyaṃ pāṇḍāv api divā|kare.
saṃbhrāntamat|prayuktā ca praviśya paricārikā
‹hā! śūnyam!› iti s'|ākrandā nirgatā vāsa|mandirāt.
20.295 tataḥ sa|Vatsa|Kauśāmbī|krandita|hrāda|pūritāḥ

Passing his time like this, he waits for his elder brother, eagerly looking all around like a *chátaka* bird watching for a raincloud.* If you, sir, are his elder brother, then say so straightaway, and we can hold an impromptu festival in the village."

When I said, "Yes, kind sir, I am he," the fellow sprinted
toward the village, topknot flying. No sooner had he got to 20.285
the village than the sounds of cheering and clapping broke
out, striking fear in the fainthearted. Go·mukha, his face
beaming, came out of the village and from a distance he used
his full height to fall at my feet. The affection produced by
the embrace of young sons or a dear wife is nothing to
that which was produced in me by my friend. A man with a
happy expression standing nearby was introduced as Prasánnaka. I embraced him and accompanied him to the village of
Sámbhava. The villagers, standing on raised ground, roofs,
terraces and so forth, pointed me out as I passed.* The 20.290
delighted servants in Prasánnaka's house revived me with
their hospitable welcome and I passed the day in an instant.

When I was in the bedroom, Go·mukha said to me, "What have you been doing all these days?"

After telling him my story, up to my stay at the cowherds'
village, I asked what had happened to him, and Go·mukha,
who loves a long story, said, "I came from my house to serve
you one morning and I saw that you were not up, even
though the sun had just risen. Concerned, I told a servant
girl to go in. She came out of the bedroom screaming, 'Oh!
It is empty!' Then the Vindhya hills, the sky, and the four 20.295
directions were filled with the cries of the people of Vatsa and
Kaushámbi and seemed to scream out in pain. Clapping his

Vindhy'|ākāśa|diśaś caṇḍam āraṭann iva pīḍitāḥ.
atha tāḍita|hastena ‹mā mā bhaiṣṭ' êti› vādinā
Ādityaśarmaṇā lokaḥ siddh'|ādeśena vāritaḥ.
sa c' âvocan mahī|pālam ‹alaṃ gatvā viṣaṇṇatām
na hy a|darśana|mātreṇa bhānoḥ saṃbhāvyate cyutiḥ!
yasya Vegavatī rakṣā kṣamā saṃrakṣaṇa|kṣamā
Brahma|jātir iv' â|vadhyā sa kasmād duḥ|sthatām iyāt?
atha v" ôttiṣṭhata! snāta! juhat' âśnīta! gāyata!
paścād vārtt'|ôpalambhāya viyad ālocyatām!› iti.
20.300 idaṃ śrutv" âpi n' âiv' āsīt kasmai cid aśane ruciḥ
utkaṇṭhā|viṣayād anyat kiṃ s'|ôtkaṇṭhāya rocate.
ath' ôttāna|mukhāḥ paurāḥ khaṃ paśyantaḥ samantataḥ
vicchinn'|âbhra|lav'|ākāraṃ kim apy aikṣanta pūrvataḥ.
‹kim etad?› iti paurāṇāṃ yāvad vākyaṃ samāpyate
tāvad āsannam adrākṣaṃ puraḥ Amitagatiṃ divaḥ.
śara|pāt'|ântare c' âsya vadhū|veṣa|vibhūṣaṇām
Vegavat|tanayāṃ devīṃ yāntīm antaḥ|puraṃ prati.
atha vyajñāpayaṃ devaṃ ‹deva Prājñaptikauśikiḥ
diṣṭy" Âmitagatiḥ prāptaḥ prītyā saṃbhāvyatām› iti.
20.305 sa tu māṃ abravīt karṇe ‹kathaṃ katham ayaṃ mayā
vidyā|dharo manuṣyeṇa satā saṃmānyatām?› iti.
tatas tam uktavān asmi ‹yayā Hariśikh'|ādayaḥ
tay" Âmitagatir dṛṣṭyā viśrabdhaṃ dṛśyatām› iti.
‹āgacch' āgaccha tāt' êti› sa tam āhūtam āgatam
prasārita|bhujaḥ prahvam āmṛśat pṛṣṭha|mūrdhani.
so 'pi nyubjikayā dūram apasṛtya praṇamya ca
āhūtaḥ punar ādiṣṭam adhyāst' ân|uccam āsanam.

hands, the soothsayer Adítya·sharman, whose predictions are known to come true, made everyone stop, telling them not to be frightened. He said to the king, 'Do not be sad. Just because one can't see the sun, one doesn't suppose that it has fallen down! He has Végavati to look after him. She is capable of protecting the earth and is as invincible as one born from Brahma—how could he be in difficulty? So get up! Bathe! Offer sacrifices! Eat! Sing! Then look to the sky for news!'

Even after hearing this, no one had any interest in eating: 20.300
for one who longs for something, nothing holds any interest other than the object of his longing. Their faces raised, the citizens looked all around the sky and noticed something in the east that looked like a piece of broken cloud. No sooner had the citizens asked what it was than I saw Ámita·gati before me in the sky. An arrowshot away from him I saw princess Végavati dressed up like a bride and heading for the inner apartments. I requested the king, 'Your Highness, we have been lucky enough to receive a visit from Ámita·gati, the son of Prajñápti·káushika. You should greet him favourably.'

He whispered in my ear, 'How on earth am I, a man, to 20.305
show due respect to this sorcerer?'

I replied, 'Look confidently upon him, in the same way that you would look at Hari·shikha and the others.'

The king summoned him, saying, 'Come, come, my son.' He came and bowed, and the king held forth his arm and touched him on the top of his back. Still bowing, Ámita·gati retired some distance and prostrated himself. Called over once again, he sat on a low seat that was offered to him. It

taṃ rājā kṣaṇam āsīnam a|khedam idam uktavān
‹bhrātuḥ kathaya vṛtt'|ântam› iti.
ten' ôditaṃ tataḥ:
20.310 ‹rājñā Mānasavegena cakravartī nabhas|talāt
pātito 'ndhatame kūpe sva|vīryāc c' ôtthitas tataḥ.
Vegavaty api sa|krodhā jitvā bhrātaram ambare
iyaṃ mat|sahit" āgatya gatā rāj'|âvarodhanam.
yuva|rājo 'pi Campāyāṃ Vīṇādattaka|veśmani
sukhaṃ tiṣṭhati mā bhūt tad|viśaṅkā bhavatām› iti.
‹mātarau putra paśy' êti› samādiṣṭo mahī|bhujā
sa mayā sahito gatvā devyau dūrād avandata.
kṣaṇaṃ c' ântaḥ|pure sthitvā niryātaḥ sa may" ôditaḥ
‹vistareṇa sakhe mahyaṃ bhartur vṛttaṃ nivedyatām.
20.315 bhidyante na rahasyāni gurūṇāṃ saṃnidhau tathā
yathā bhinna|rahasyānām a|śaṅkaiḥ suhṛdām› iti.
ath' ôktaṃ tena ‹yady evaṃ vivikte kva cid āsyatām
na h' îdaṃ śakyam ākhyātuṃ na śrotuṃ prasthitair› iti.
ath' ântaḥ|pura|niryūhe nirākṛta|mahā|jane
āsīnāya sa me vṛttaṃ yuṣmad|vṛttam avartayat.
‹asty ahaṃ yuva|rājena mocitaḥ śaṅku|bandhanāt
ten' âiva ca kṛt'|ânujñaḥ prāyām Aṅgārakaṃ prati.
cakra|varti|bhayāc c' âsau tyaktavān Kusumālikām
balavat|saṃśrayāt kena dur|balena na bhīyate?
20.320 so 'ham ādāya viśrabdhaṃ tvat sakhīm āśrame pituḥ
avasaṃ divasān etān kadā cit Kāśyapa|sthale.
adya c' ânugṛhīto 'smi smaratā cakra|vartinā
sa ca gatvā mayā dṛṣṭas tiṣṭhann avaṭa|saṃkaṭe.

took a moment for him to sit down and get comfortable, and then the king said, 'Tell us the news of your brother.'

He replied:* 'King Mánasa·vega dropped the emperor 20.310
from the sky into a pitch-black well from which, using his own strength, he escaped. Végavati was furious and defeated her brother in the sky. She came here with me, and has gone to the king's harem. The prince is living comfortably in the house of Vina·dáttaka in Champa—do not worry about him.'

The king told him to go and see his two mothers. I accompanied him and he greeted the two queens from afar. After spending a short while in the inner apartments, he came out and I said to him, 'Friend, tell me in detail the news of our master. Secrets are not divulged in the presence 20.315
of elders in the same way that they are freely divulged before trusted friends.'

He said, 'In that case, let's sit somewhere in solitude: this story is not to be told nor listened to while out and about.'

Then, in a tower in the inner apartments where members of the public are excluded, I sat down and he started to tell me your story. 'The prince freed me from being impaled and, at his request, I went after Angáraka. In fear of the emperor, Angáraka released Kusumálika: what weak man does not fear a man who has recourse to the strong? I took 20.320
the girl—your friend—to my father's hermitage, and spent the last few days in peace there and at Káshyapa·sthala. Today the emperor graced me by thinking of me. I went and found him in dire straits in the well. When he was standing on the rim of the well, he kindly ordered me to protect Végavati in her fight with her brother. I flew off

sa c' âvaṭa|taṭa|stho mām ājñay" ânugṛhītavān
«yudhyāmānāṃ saha bhrātrā rakṣa Vegavatīm» iti.
utpatya ca mayā dṛṣṭā nirjitā bhrātṛ|śātravā
utkhāta|nija|rāg" êva yoginī|cakra|vartinī.
sā tu māṃ praṇataṃ dūrād ājñāpitavatī laghu
«bhrātaḥ prajñaptim āvartya svāmī vijñāyatām» iti.
tāṃ vijñāpitavān asmi «devi Campā|nivāsinaḥ
bhavane Dattakasy' āste tatra saṃbhāvyatām» iti.
atha dūreṇa māṃ jitvā vegād Vegavatī gatā
prāvṛḍ|jaḍam iv' âmbhodaṃ samīraṇa|paraṃ|parā.
prāpya c' âti|cirāc Campām ahaṃ Dattaka|veśmani
dṛṣṭavān mānuṣ'|â|dṛśyāṃ devīṃ devasya saṃnidhau.
nāga|bhog'|âṅka|paryaṅke niṣaṇṇaṃ ca nabhaḥ|patim
jagat|patim iv' Ânanta|bhujaṅg'|ôtsaṅga|śāyinam.
pṛṣṭaś ca yuva|rājena s'|ādareṇ' âiva Dattakaḥ
«rūpaṃ Gandharvadattāyāḥ kīdṛg ity ucyatām» iti.
Vegavatyā tataḥ krodha|dainya|vailakṣya|dhūmrayā
«paśy' Âmitagate bhartur ācāram» iti bhāṣitam!
varṇitaṃ Dattaken' âpi rūpaṃ tasyās tathā yathā
sadyo vikasitaṃ bhartur devyās tu mlānam ānanam.
ath' ôktaṃ śanakair bhartrā «Dattakaḥ kūpa|kacchapaḥ
yena Gandharvadattāyā rūpam eṣa praśaṃsati.
yadi paśyed ayaṃ mugdhaḥ priyāṃ Madanamañjukām
dūre Gandharvadatt" āstāṃ Rambhām api na varṇayet!»
uktaś c' ârya|duhitr" âhaṃ kampayitvā śanaiḥ śiraḥ
«bahu śrotavyam atr' âsti nipuṇaṃ śrūyatām!» iti.
punar apy uktavān svāmī «sā tath" âpi priyā priyā
priyāṃ Vegavatīṃ prāpya yat satyaṃ vismṛt" âiva me.»

and found her defeated, her brother her enemy. With her passion apparently destroyed, she was like an empress of the *yóginis*. But when I bowed from afar she quickly gave me an order: "Brother, use your magic to find out about our master."

I said to her, "Princess, he is in the house of Dáttaka, a resident of Champa. Meet him there." 20.325

Leaving me far behind, Végavati sped off, like a gale leaving behind a cloud heavy with rain. After a long while I arrived in Champa and saw the princess in Dáttaka's house, invisible to human eyes and close to His Highness. The lord of the air, Nara·váhana·datta, was sitting on a sofa curved like a sea serpent, as if he were the lord of the universe, Vishnu, reclining on the serpent Anánta. The prince respectfully asked Dáttaka, "Tell me about Gandhárva·datta's beauty."
Ashen with anger, sadness and disappointment, Végavati 20.330
said, "Ámita·gati, behold our master's behavior!"

Dáttaka described Gandhárva·datta's beauty in such a way that our lord's face beamed, but the princess's fell. Our lord made an aside: "It is because Dáttaka is a tortoise in a well that he praises Gandhárva·datta's beauty. Were this simple fellow to see my beloved Mádana·máñjuka, then forget Gandhárva·datta—he would not even have words for Rambha!"

Gently shaking her head, her ladyship said to me, "There's a lot to be heard in this matter. Listen closely!"

Our master continued, "That lovely lady was indeed dear 20.335
to me, but the truth is, when I won my beloved Végavati I completely forgot her."

tataḥ sadyas tad|aṅgāni lajjā|mukulitāny api
adrākṣaṃ vikasant' îva tuṅgī|bhūtais tanū|ruhaiḥ.
uktaś c' âsmi tayā smitvā «bhrāto gacchāva saṃprati
yāvan n' â|param etena kiṃ cid dur|vaca ucyate.
ekena paṭun" ân|ekaṃ dūṣyate madhuraṃ vacaḥ
viṣa|toya|laven' êva dugdha|kuṇḍam ur'|ûdaram.»
yāvatyā velayā devyā vākyam ity|ādi kalpitam
devaḥ saṃcintya tāvatyā paścād ūhitavān idam.
20.340 «yathā prāpya dvitīyāṃ me vismṛtā prathamā priyā
tṛtīyāyās tathā prāptyā dvitīyā vismariṣyate.
kāvya|strī|vastra|candreṣu prāyeṇa viguṇeṣv api
a|purāṇeṣu rajyante sva|bhāvād eva jantavaḥ.
tena Gandharvadattāyāḥ śulkaṃ saṃpādyatām aham
prasahya svī|kariṣyāmi Kṛṣṇām iva Dhanaṃjayaḥ.»
iti dāruṇayā patyur iyaṃ vācā vimohitā
dṛṣṭyā dṛṣṭi|viṣasy' êva niś|ceṣṭā vasudhām agāt.
tataḥ kiṃ|kārya|mūḍhena mayā katham api prabhuḥ
pratīkāra|śat'|â|vadhyaṃ vṛtt'|ântaṃ taṃ na bodhitaḥ.
20.345 utthāya ca sa|saṃjñ" êyaṃ divam utpatya bhāṣate
«vandamānā guroḥ pādān kṣapayāmi śarīrakam.
atha vā kuru bandhutvaṃ bhrātaḥ kāṣṭhāni saṃhara
rāja|dvāre śmaśāne vā yas tiṣṭhati sa bāndhavaḥ.
duḥkhāni hy anubhūyante sa|śarīraiḥ śarīribhiḥ
duḥkh'|âdhikaraṇaṃ tan me śarīraṃ dahyatām!» iti.

At that moment I saw her body, which had looked like a bud shrunken with disappointment, appear to blossom as she tingled all over. With a smile, she said to me, "Brother, let's go now, before he says another unkind word. A single harsh word destroys a host of kind ones, just as a drop of poisoned water spoils a huge vat of milk."

While the princess was talking like this, the prince was
thinking. Then he said, "As soon as I got a second lover, 20.340
I forgot the first, and by getting a third, the second will be forgotten. As a rule, when it comes to poetry, women, clothes and the moon, people are by nature attracted to them when they are new, even if they have no good qualities. So, let a bride-price be fixed for Gandhárva·datta; I shall win her in the competition, just as Árjuna won Dráupadi!"

Like a look from a snake with a venomous glance, these harsh words from her husband made her faint and she fell to the floor unconscious. I was at a loss as to what to do; somehow I managed to prevent our master from finding out what had happened—a hundred remedies could not
have cured it. When she came to, she stood up and rose 20.345
up into the sky, saying, "While worshipping the feet of my father I shall cast off this worthless body. Brother, be a good friend and fetch some wood. A friend is one who is there both at the palace gates and the cremation-ground. People experience sorrows because they have bodies. This body is the repository of my sorrows. Let it burn!"

may" ôkt" «êyaṃ kva devasya devī Vegavataḥ sutā
kva c' â|sadṛśam etat te vadanān nirgataṃ vacaḥ.
yadi tyakta|śarīrāṇāṃ śarīraṃ na punar bhavet
tato n' âiva virudhyeran n' ātma|nairātmya|vādibhiḥ.
citta|vṛtti|nirodhena yat khinnair mokṣubhiś ciram
mustā|granthi|pramāṇena tad viṣeṇ' âiva labhyate.
tasmān nāstikyam ujjhitvā sarva|sarva|jña|ninditam
dharm'|âdhikaraṇaṃ devi śarīraṃ pālyatām!» iti.
tayā tu sarvam ev' êdam a|śrutvā śūnya|cetasā
«nanu saṃhara dārūṇi kiṃ cireṇ' êti» bhāṣitam.
may" ôktaṃ «yadi yuṣmākam ayaṃ cetasi niścayaḥ
aham eva tataḥ pūrvaṃ praviśāmi citām» iti.
ath' âhaṃ paruṣ'|ālāpam uktaḥ kupitayā tayā
«mām anumriyamāṇas tvam ucyase kiṃ janair?» iti.
ath' âinām uktavān asmi «satyam etad virudhyate
jīvitaṃ tu mahā|doṣaṃ tathā ca śrūyatāṃ kathā.»
asyās tv ākāś'|āsāno duḥ|śliṣṭ'|ālāpa|karpaṭām
cittam ākṣiptavān asmi kathā|kanthāṃ prasārayan.
«asti Bhāgīrathī|kacchaḥ prāṃśu|kāśa|śar'|ākaraḥ
badarī|khadira|prāya|kāntāra|taru|dur|gamaḥ.
sphīta|sīm'|ânta|luṇṭhāka|khaḍgi|śabara|taskarāḥ
durga|rājaṃ yam āśritya rājabhyo 'pi na bibhyati.
prabhāvād yasya śārdūlair viralī|kṛta|gokulaiḥ
goṣṭha|śvā iva gāyante mattā mṛgayu|dantinaḥ.
yac ca gharm'|ânta|vād'|âgni|jvālā|janita|vedanam

I said, "Here you are, the wife of the prince and the daughter of Végavan, and words as unbecoming as these have come out of your mouth! If those who abandon their bodies did not get a new one, then there would be no dispute between those who argue for the soul's existence and those
who argue for its nonexistence. The end achieved by wearied 20.350
seekers of liberation through suppressing the activities of the mind would be attained with a pea-size drop of poison. So, good lady, give up your nihilism, a position rejected by all philosophers. The body is the repository of religious merit—look after it!"

But she hadn't heard any of this, and said vacantly, "Just gather some wood. Why are you taking so long?"

I said, "If this is your decision, then I shall enter the pyre first."

She became angry and said to me harshly, "What will people say about you if you follow me to your death?"

I replied, "It's true, it would be wrong, but to stay alive 20.355
would be a grave sin. Listen to a story in this connection."

Remaining in the sky, I held her attention by telling a patchwork of a tale made of scraps of incoherent chatter. "There is a region on the banks of the Bhagírathi which is thick with tall grasses and reeds and rendered impenetrable by a forest full of jujube and acacia trees. It is bursting with bandits, armed tribals and thieves. Staying in that formidable fortress, they have no fear even of kings. Because of the jungle, tigers decimate the cattle population, making the hunting elephants in rut howl like the guard dogs at
the cowsheds. The milk-white waters of the Ganga soothe 20.360
the distress brought on at the end of the hot season by the

payaḥ|śveta|payaḥ|pūrair nirvāpayati Jāhnavī.
tatr' ânyatra śara|stambe badarī|jhāṭa|veṣṭite
bilaṃ kṛtvā śata|dvāram uvāsa kila mūṣika.
vāneyaiḥ pāvanair annair Jāhnavīyaiś ca vāribhiḥ
sa bhṛtyān bibharām āsa vaikhānasa iv' āśrame.

kadā cit proṣite tasminn āhār'|āhāra|kāṅkṣiṇi
gṛham asy' āgaman mitram ākhur nagara|gaś|caraḥ.
āsīnaś c' ârghya|pādyābhyām asau mūṣikay" ârcitaḥ
tām apṛcchat ‹kva yāto naḥ sakhā sakhi bhaved?› iti.

20.365 tay" ‹āhār'|ârtham› ity ukte prasthitaṃ tam uvāca sā
‹ayam āyāti te bhrātā su|muhūrtam udīkṣyatām.
a|sat|kāre gṛhād yāte kṛta|ghne 'pi sa te sakhā
nidr"|āhār'|âbhilāṣābhyāṃ sapta|rātraṃ viyujyate.
tvaṃ punas tasya mitraṃ ca cirāc ca gṛham āgataḥ
nir|ātithyaś ca yām' îti vṛṣas tvam a|viṣāṇakaḥ!›

yāvac c' êyaṃ kathā tāvan nirgranth'|âṅga|malīmasaiḥ
dhūmair dhūsarito bhānuḥ svar|bhānu|timirair iva.
an|antaraṃ ca s'|âṅgāra|bhasma|saṃtāna|hāriṇaḥ
apavanta nabhasvantaḥ Gaṅgā|tāṇḍava|hetavaḥ.
20.370 tataḥ pṛṣata|gokarṇa|paraṃ|para|paraṃ|parāḥ
laṅghit'|ôdbhrānta|śārdūlāḥ prādhāvann abhi Jāhnavīm.
ath' âsau mūṣikaḥ pāpas tām āmantrya sa|saṃbhramaḥ
apagantum upakrāntas tayā saṃbhrāntay" ôditaḥ.
‹aho nagara|vāsitvaṃ devareṇa prakāśitam
mahā|sāhasam ārabdham ātmānaṃ yena rakṣatā!

flames of fires started by lightning. There, it is said, in a clump of reeds surrounded by a thicket of jujube bushes, a rat made a burrow with a hundred entrances. He sustained his dependents on pure forest food and Ganga water, like a sage in a hermitage.

One day when he had gone out in the hope of fetching something to eat, a friend of his, a town rat, arrived at his house. He sat down and was welcomed by the lady rat with an offering of water for washing his feet. He asked her, 'Dear lady, where might my friend have gone?'

When she told him that he had gone to get food, he set off, 20.365
but she said to him, 'Your brother is on his way back. Wait for a while. If someone, even an ingrate, leaves the house without being properly looked after, your friend won't eat or sleep for a week. You are his friend and have come to the house after a long time, yet you say you are leaving without accepting our hospitality. You are as paradoxical as a bull without horns!'

While they were having this conversation, the sun became veiled in a murk as dirty as a naked hermit's body, like the shadow of the demon of the eclipse. Soon a gale blew up, raising a constant stream of embers and ash, and
making the Ganga do a dance of destruction. A succession 20.370
of antelopes and deer ran one after the other to the Ganga, leaping over terrified tigers. That wretched rat quickly said goodbye to his hostess and started to leave. She was scared and said, 'Brother-in-law, by putting such energy into saving yourself you have shown what it is to be a city-dweller! I've heard that city-dwellers versed in books on religious and material matters say that for the sake of himself a wise

nāgarāḥ kila bhāṣante dharm'|ârtha|grantha|kovidāḥ
ātm'|ârthe sakalāṃ jahyāt paṇḍitaḥ pṛthivīm iti.
tvadīyena tu mitreṇa mitr'|â|mitrā vipad|gatāḥ
śarīra|nir|apekṣeṇa sva|guṇā iva rakṣitāḥ.
20.375 atha vā kṛtam ālāpair a|kālo 'yam udāsitum!
dāva|dāha|bhayād bālān paritrāyasva putrakān!
bahūn etān ahaṃ mugdhān an|unmīlita|locanān
pañca|rātra|prasūtatvāt saṃcārayitum a|kṣamā.
tvaṃ punaḥ puruṣaḥ śaktaḥ priy'|āpatyaś ca yatnataḥ
tuṅga|Gaṅgā|taṭīṃ yena saṃcāraya sutān› iti.

sa tu pāp'|ākhur ālambya saṃbhrānta|vyāghra|vāladhim
muṣikām avakarṇy' âiva Gaṅgā|rodhaḥ parāgamat.
tataḥ pāṣāṇa|varṣasya patataḥ kuṭṭimeṣv iva
utthitaḥ paritaḥ kacchaṃ paṭuḥ paṭa|paṭā|dhvaniḥ.
20.380 ath' ālocya bubhukṣos taṃ kakṣaṃ kakṣaṃ vibhāvasoḥ
sarvaṃ jvālā|chalen' âṅgaṃ jihvā|mayam iv' âbhavat.
dāva|kāl'|ânalaḥ stamba|kakṣa|saṃsāram āyatam
dagdhvā nir|indhanaḥ śāntaḥ prāpya Gaṅgā|taṭ'|âmbaram.
tataḥ paṭu|marud|vyasta|bhasma|skandha|vasuṃdharaḥ
kṣaṇena dadṛśe kacchaḥ prāṃśu|valmīka|saṃkulaḥ.

etasminn īdṛśe kāle śaṅkā|grastaḥ sa mūṣikaḥ
anumāya cirāc cihnair ājagāma svam ālayam.
tatr' âpaśyat tataḥ kāntām antar|gṛham a|cetanām
jvālā|vyatikar'|ôṣṇābhir utsvinnāṃ dhūma|vartibhiḥ.
20.385 sarvān āliṅgya sarv'|âṅgaiḥ śāvakān gata|jīvakān
dīrgha|nidrām upāsīnām a|saṃmīlita|locanān.

man should abandon the whole world. Whereas, when his friends or enemies have been in trouble, your friend has guarded them as though they were his own virtues, with no regard for his person. But enough talk—this is not the time 20.375
for standing by! Save my young children from the terrifying forest fire! See how many innocent babies there are, their eyes still unopened. Having given birth five nights ago, I am unable to carry them. You, however, are an able man and fond of children. Do your best to take them to the Ganga's lofty bank.'

But even after listening to the lady, that vile rat clung to the tail of a terrified tiger and escaped to the bank of the Ganga. Then a loud crackling sound started up all around the marsh, like a rain of stones on a tiled floor. Looking 20.380
at the different bushes where the voracious blaze had taken hold, it seemed as if its body were made of tongues in the guise of flames. Like the fire of doomsday destroying the world, the forest fire quickly burned up the scrubland and then, its fuel spent, it went out when it reached the bank of the Ganga. The strong wind had driven the ash into heaps, making the land around the river suddenly seem to be covered in towering termite mounds.

Thus things stood when the rat, consumed by anxiety, eventually managed to reach his house, using landmarks to work out the way. Inside the house he found his beloved insensible, charred by plumes of smoke hot from the fire. She was lying in eternal sleep, her body wrapped around her 20.385
lifeless litter. They had never opened their eyes. He stood stupefied for an age. When he came to he started to wail,

atha mūḍhaś ciraṃ sthitvā prabuddho vilalāpa saḥ
vilāp'|âika|vinodā hi bandhu|vyasana|pīḍitāḥ.
‹mahā|bhūtāni bhūtāni bhūtānāṃ bhūtaye kila
mahā|bhūtena bhūt'|âṅge bhavatā kim idaṃ kṛtam?
varaṃ brahma|vadh'|ādīni pātakāni mahānty api
na punar yat tvayā pāpa duṣ|karaṃ duṣ|kṛtaṃ kṛtam.
nanu brahma|vadh'|ādīni yānti niṣkṛtibhiḥ kṣayam
śaraṇ'|āgata|bāla|strī|kṛta|hatyās tu duṣ|kṣayāḥ.
20.390 yasmān niṣ|karuṇen' êdaṃ dagdham ākhu|kulaṃ tvayā
daśa|janma|sahasrāṇi tasmād ākhur bhaviṣyasi!
atha vā nirdahatv eṣa dīpta|śāpa|hut'|āśanaḥ
tam eva capalaṃ yena sarva|bhakṣaḥ kṛto bhavān!›
ity|ādi vilapantaṃ taṃ sametya sa suhṛd dhruvaḥ
mūṣikair aparaiḥ sārdham alīkam avadad vacaḥ.
‹svayam eva sakhe sakhyā strītvād vāma|sva|bhāvayā
mayi prārthayamāne 'pi kuṭumbam avasāditam.
daśa|kṛtvo may" ôkt" êyaṃ «bhavatī sahitā mayā
Gaṅgā|kūlaṃ tribhir vāraiḥ śāvakān nayatām» iti.
20.395 a|saṃbhrāntā ca mām āha «kātarāṇāṃ bhavādṛśām
apāya|śata|darśinyaḥ svaccha|vṛtte 'pi buddhayaḥ.
vetasvan|naḍval'|ôpāntam antare palvalaṃ mahat
nīl'|â|virala|parṇāś ca jambū|vañjula|rājayaḥ.
na c' âgner asti sāmarthyam a|dāhyaṃ dagdhum īdṛśam
so 'ti|dūreṇa vicchinnaḥ katham asmān dahed? iti.›
sa tu mitrīyamāṇas taṃ ciram ālokya pṛṣṭavān
‹evam uktaḥ prajāvatyā bhavān kiṃ kṛtavān?› iti.

for wailing is the only pastime for those pained by the loss of their kin.

'The elements are said to have come into being for the benefit of living beings. Why, element, have you done this to the body of a living being?* Crimes like the murder of a brahmin, though great, are preferable to this heinous misdeed of yours, you sinner! Crimes like the murder of a brahmin can be atoned for with penances, but for murdering women and children who seek protection there is no atonement. Because you have cruelly burned this family of 20.390
rats, you shall be born as a rat ten thousand times! Moreover, may this raging fire of a curse consume the restless one that made you so voracious!'*

As he sobbed thus, his old friend arrived with some other rats. He lied to him, saying, 'Friend, my friend your wife, with her contrary womanly nature, brought about the demise of her family herself, despite my protestations. Ten times I told her, "Madam, you and I must take the infants to the bank of the Ganga in three journeys."

Unruffled, she said to me, "Even in a safe situation the 20.395
minds of cowards like you find a hundred dangers. Between us and the fire there is a large pond surrounded by canes and reeds, and rows of rose apple and *vánjula* trees with abundant dark leaves. The fire cannot burn a fireproof place like that. Cut off at such a distance, how is it going to burn us?"'

The other rat, still treating him like a friend, looked at him for a long time before saying, 'When my wife said that to you, what did you do?'

ten' ôktaṃ ‹vāma|śīlatvād yad" êyaṃ pratyavasthitā
niṣ|pratyāśas tadā prāṇān ahaṃ rakṣitavān› iti.

20.400 lajjamāne nate tasmin sthite '|sādhāv adhomukhe
ākhur anyatamas teṣāṃ tam a|sādhum abhāṣata.
‹tuṣān gopayatā tyaktāḥ prājñena kalamās tvayā
rakṣatā su|tyajān prāṇāṃs tyaktā yad dus|tyajā guṇāḥ.
prāṇānāṃ ca guṇānāṃ ca viśeṣaḥ syāt kiyān iti
mīmāṃsitvā ciraṃ devāḥ sāmyam eṣām akalpayan.
tān Prajāpatir āh' âitya «mā kṛdhvaṃ viṣamaṃ samam
taraṃga|taralāḥ prāṇā guṇā Meru|sthirā» iti.
atha vā mṛta eva tvam! utkrāntaṃ paśya te yaśaḥ!
a|yaśo|maraṇāt trastā yaśo|jīvā hi sādhavaḥ.
20.405 «sakhe dāv'|âgninā dagdhaṃ tvat|kuṭumbaṃ mam' âgrataḥ
ahaṃ jīvita» ity etat ko brūyān mūṣikād ṛte?›

iti te tam upālabhya parisaṃsthāpya c' êtaram
kuṭumbaṃ c' âsya saṃskṛtya pratijagmur yath"|āgatam.
sa c' ākhur mūṣika|śreṇyā tasmād ārabhya vāsarāt
āsana|sthāna|saṃbhāṣā|saṃbhogair varjitaḥ kṛtaḥ.

ahaṃ tu svāminīṃ dṛṣṭvā pavitrita|cit'|ânalām
a|kṣat'|âṅgaḥ svayaṃ mandaḥ kiṃ vakṣyāmi puraḥ prabhoḥ.
catur|vargasya dharm'|āder hetuḥ sādhu|samāgamaḥ
sādhubhir varjyamānasya naṣṭam etac catuṣṭayam.
20.410 tad gariṣṭhād ato doṣād laghiṣṭhaṃ maraṇaṃ mayā
aṅgī|kṛtam alaṃ prāṇair a|kīrti|malinair!» iti.

He replied, 'When, because of her contrary nature, she decided to stay put, I became desperate and saved my life.'

As that wicked rat stood there hanging his head in shame, 20.400
another of the rats there said to the wretch, 'You clever fellow! By protecting the chaff you have thrown away the rice: in looking after your worthless life you have thrown away your precious virtue. The gods spent an age debating the difference between life and virtue before deciding that they were equal. Then Praja·pati came and said, "Do not make unequal things equal: life is as fleeting as a wave while virtue is as constant as Mount Meru." You are as good as dead! See, your reputation is finished! Good men fear dishonor
like death; they live for glory. Who other than a rat could 20.405
say, "Friend, your family was burned in front of me by a forest fire. I survived"?'

They poured scorn upon that rat and comforted the other. After carrying out funeral rites for his family, they went back the way they had come. From that day forth the rat was barred from sitting, staying, speaking or enjoying himself with his peers.

But after seeing my mistress sanctify the funeral pyre, what am I, my body unharmed, to say to my master, foolish as I am? The company of virtuous men brings about religious merit and the other three aims of man. If a man
is shunned by the virtuous all four are lost. Death is easier 20.410
for me to accept than this terrible crime. I don't want a life stained by ignominy!"

yāvac ca samayaṃ baddhvā kathā parisamāpyate
tāvad āvām anuprāptāv āsthānaṃ bhavatām› iti.

tataḥ sa sat|kṛtaḥ rājñā vasan'|ābharaṇ'|ādibhiḥ
prītaḥ prītaṃ mahī|pālaṃ praṇipatya tiro 'bhavat.

tatr' â|cira|gate devaṃ senā|patir abhāṣata
‹tantreṇa saha gacchantu Campāṃ Hariśikh'|ādayaḥ.
rāja|putrasya n' āgantuṃ na sthātuṃ tatra yujyate
pānthasy' êv' â|sahāyasya pur'|âdhiṣṭhāna|vāsinaḥ.
20.415 śatāni pañca nāgānām abhyast'|âstra|niṣādinām
tāvanty eva sahasrāṇi tādṛśām eva vājinām.
pattayaś ca pratiṣṭhantāṃ vāji|saṃkhyā|catur|guṇāḥ
patti|rakṣyā hi mātaṅgāḥ karmaṇyāḥ samareṣv› iti.

prāpta|kālam idaṃ stutvā rājā senā|pater vacaḥ
tantreṇa sahitān asmān prāhiṇod yuṣmad|antikam.
atha Vindhy'|â|cala|chāyāṃ guñjad|vānara|kuñjarām
ākrāmantaḥ prayāmaḥ sma svaccha|śaila|sarij|jalām.
saṃniviṣṭaṃ ca tat tantram anyasmin Vindhya|sānuṣu
dhvanat|paṭaha|śṛṅgaṃ ca caura|cakram upāgatam.
20.420 a|dṛṣṭa|taru|pāṣāṇa|śakunta|mṛga|cāraṇaḥ
dṛṣṭaḥ pulīndra|bhāvena Vindhyaḥ pariṇamann iva.
tataḥ pulindra|kodaṇḍa|ṣaṇḍa|muktaiḥ śilī|mukhaiḥ
saṃtatair vayam ākrāntāḥ śalabhair iva śālayaḥ.
atha nāg'|âdhirūḍhena sainā|patyena tat kṛtam
praty|akṣam api yad dṛṣṭaṃ na kaś cit samabhāvayat.
tat|kara|bhramita|prāsa|cakra|prānta|parāgatāḥ

Just as the story was about to reach its conclusion with the pact being seen through, we arrived at your assembly.'

Ámita·gati was welcomed hospitably by the king with clothes, jewelry and so forth. Happy, he bowed down before the delighted sovereign and disappeared.

No sooner had he gone than the commander of the armies said to the king, 'Hari·shikha and the others should go to Champa with an army. It is not right for the prince, a resident of the citadel, to return here or remain there
with no escort, like a wayfarer. Five hundred elephants 20.415
with trained archers for riders and five thousand similarly equipped horses must set forth with four times as many infantry—elephants are useful in battle but have to be protected by infantry.'

The king approved of the general's timely advice and sent us to you with an army. As we marched we reached the shade of the Vindhya mountains, with its huge chattering monkeys and pure mountain streams. When the army was camped on one of the Vindhya plateaus, a band of robbers
fell upon them, drums and horns sounding. The trees, rocks, 20.420
birds, deer and travelers vanished and Vindhya looked as though it was turning into bandits. Next, we were assailed by a rain of arrows from the bandits' myriad bows, like a paddy field being attacked by locusts! Then the general's son, seated on an elephant, did something that no one could believe, even having seen it with their own eyes.* With his hand he spun his spear so that when the enemies' arrows struck the edge of the circle they turned back and killed the enemies themselves! Obscured by the spinning spear, his body could not be seen, but from the result of its actions one

parāvṛtya parān eva parāghnat para|mārgaṇāḥ.
bhrānta|kunta|parikṣiptaṃ na śarīram adṛśyata
tasya bāhu|sahasraṃ tu phalena samabhāvyata.
20.425 ākrānta|catur|āśeṣu Vindhya|kāntāra|vāsiṣu
tad|visṛṣṭān apaśyāma yugapat patataḥ śarān.
sphurat|kiraṇa|nistriṃśa|pāṇir Yaugandharāyaṇiḥ
dṛṣṭaḥ sarveṇa sarveṣāṃ pulīndrāṇāṃ puraḥ sthitaḥ.
sarvath" ânena saṃdṛṣṭaṃ para|cakram ud|āyudham
tad|āsanna|vimāna|sthair dṛṣṭam apsarasāṃ gaṇaiḥ.
pratipakṣa|kṣayaṃ ghoram akarot taṃ Tapantakaḥ
kṛta|Brahm'|âstra|mokṣeṇa Droṇen' âpi na yaḥ kṛtaḥ.
may" âpi sa|turaṃgeṇa tatra tatr' âbhidhāvatā
niṣ|prayojana|yatnena sve pare c' ôpahāsitāḥ.
20.430 tatas taskara|cakreṇa vyatibhinnaṃ bhavad|balam
nīhāra|nikareṇ' êva bhāsvat|kara|kadambakam.
etasminn ākule kāle śāla|skandh'|āvṛtaḥ paraḥ
dṛḍhaṃ marmaṇi bāṇena mat|turaṃgam atāḍayat.
turaṃgas tu tathā pāda|tāḍanāny a|vicintayan
sthāṇu|pāṣāṇa|gartāṃś ca yathā|vegam adhāvata.
din'|ântena ca nirgatya gahanād Vindhya|kānanāt
sthit' âiv' âmucat prāṇān paścāt kāyam apātayat.
tataḥ saṃhṛtya dārūṇi gurūṇi ca bahūni ca
tasy' ânuṣṭhitavān asmi saṃskāraṃ s'|ôdaka|kriyam.
20.435 diṅ|moha|bhrānta|cetāś ca prāṃśum āruhya śākhinam
etaṃ grāmakam adrākṣam ārād ākula|gokulam.
āgataś c' âham etena sādhun" ārādhitas tathā
yathā gurur yathā devo yathā rājā yathāv varaḥ.
taṃ ca taskara|sen"|ânyam aghnan Hariśikh'|ādayaḥ
iti mahyam iyaṃ vārttā kathitā pathikair iti.»

could have believed it had a thousand arms. The inhabitants 20.425
of the Vindhya forests had attacked from the four directions
and we could see that the arrows repelled by him were falling
on them all at the same time! Everyone saw Yaugan·dhará-
yana's son, glittering sword in hand, facing up to all the
bandits.* Using every means available, he made the enemy
army surrender their weapons in full view, and they were
watched by bands of *apsárases* that had approached them in
their aerial chariots. Tapántaka did terrible damage to the
enemy, the like of which was not done even by Drona when
he fired Brahma's missile.

As for me, dashing hither and thither on my horse without rhyme or reason, I amused both our men and those
of the enemy. Then the bandits' army pressed against your 20.430
troops, like a bank of fog obscuring the rays of the sun.

At that chaotic moment, one of the enemy, hidden behind the trunk of a *shala* tree, dealt my horse a heavy blow
with an arrow in a vital organ. The horse, paying no attention to being kicked, nor to tree stumps, rocks and holes,
galloped away. At the end of the day, he emerged from the
dense Vindhya forest. Still standing, he breathed his last
and finally collapsed. I gathered several heavy logs and performed his cremation, together with a water offering.

I had no idea of where I was and climbed a tall tree. In 20.435
the distance I saw this village and its many herds of cows.
When I arrived, this good man showed me the respect due
to a teacher, a god, a king or a bridegroom. Travelers told
me the news that Hari·shikha and the others had killed the
leader of the bandits' army."

kāntā|suhṛd|guṇa|kathā|śravaṇ'|ôtsukasya
ramyā vi|nidra|nayanasya gatā mam' âsau
sarv'|êndriy'|ârtha|janitāni hi sevyamānā
dīrgh'|â|sva|vṛttir iva hanti sukhāni nidrā.

ity Ajinavatī|lābhaḥ.

Eager to hear favorable tales of my sweetheart and my friends, I passed that night without getting a wink of sleep. Sleep, like a long period of not living one's usual life, destroys the pleasures brought about by all the objects of the senses.

Thus ends the Winning of Ajínavati.

CANTO 21
DESTINY

21.1 TATRA MITRA|prakāṇḍena
Gomukhena vinoditaḥ
māsam āsiṣi vipraiś ca
prasannaiḥ sa|Prasannakaiḥ.
ekadā Gomukhen' ôktaṃ «yojane grāmakād itaḥ
Avimukt'|â|vimuktatvāt puṇyā Vārāṇasī purī.
ā|Prāgjyotiṣa|Kaśmīra|Dvārakā|Tāmraparṇi yat
tat sarvaṃ su|labhaṃ tasyāṃ mano|hāri vinodanam.
kadā cic c' ôpalabhyeta tatra pānthāt kutaś cana
vārttā Hariśikh'|ādīnām ataḥ s" āgamyatām!» iti.
21.5 tam uktvā «yuktam ātth' êti»
taṃ c' āmantrya Prasannakam
s'|ākrandāt Saṃbhava|grāmāt
prati Vārāṇasīm agām.
atha stok'|ântar'|ātītaṃ mām abhāṣata Gomukhaḥ
«vahāni kim ahaṃ yuṣmān yūyaṃ vahata mām?» iti.
cintitaṃ ca mayā «hanta! vinaṣṭaḥ khalu Gomukhaḥ
‹yūyaṃ māṃ vahat' êty› eṣa no brūyāt katham anyathā.
āsanasy' âpi yaś chāyāṃ madīyasya namasyati
ariṣṭ'|āviṣṭatāṃ muktvā katham itthaṃ sa vakṣyati?»
sa may" ôktaḥ sa|dainyena «bhavān guru|pada|śramaḥ
tan madīyam a|śaṅkena pṛṣṭham āruhyatām» iti.
21.10 tena c' ôktaṃ vilakṣeṇa «mā grahīta yathā śrutam
n' êyaṃ saṃbhāvyate cintā jāt'|âriṣṭe 'pi mādṛśi.
kiṃ tu yaḥ kiṃ cid ācaṣṭe pānthasya pathikaḥ pathi
voḍhā bhavati tasy' âsau kheda|vismaraṇād» iti.
sa may" ôkto «bhavān eva sarva|vṛtt'|ânta|peśalaḥ
ākhyātuṃ ca vijānāti yat tataḥ kathayatv!» iti.

I SPENT A MONTH there being entertained by my fine friend Go·mukha, as well as by Prasánnaka and the other happy brahmins. 21.1

One day Go·mukha said, "A *yójana* from this village is the city of Varánasi, which is holy on account of its inseparability from Avimúkta* and where all the enticing amusements found from Prag·jyótisha to Kashmir and from Dvarka to Tamra·parni are easily available.* Perhaps we might get news of Hari·shikha and the others from some traveler there, so let's go!"

I told him that what he said was right and bade goodbye to Prasánnaka before leaving the weeping village of Sámbhava for Varánasi. 21.5

We had gone a short distance when Go·mukha said to me, "Am I to carry you or will you carry me?"

I thought, "Oh dear! Go·mukha must be on his last legs. Why else would he have asked me to carry him? He bows before the shadow of my throne; how could he speak like this unless he is nearing death?"

I said to him sadly, "Tiredness is weighing down your feet. Don't hesitate to climb on my back."

Abashed, he replied, "Don't take what you hear at face value. A man like me couldn't think of such a thing even if he were nearing death. On a journey the traveler who tells a story to another traveler becomes his carrier, because he makes him forget his fatigue." 21.10

I said to him, "You have all sorts of stories up your sleeve and know how to tell them, so speak on!"

ten' ôktaṃ «pañca kathyante kathā|vastūni kovidaiḥ
dharm'|ârtha|sukha|nirvāṇa|cikitsāḥ saha|vistarāḥ.
tatra sattv'|ôpakār'|ârthā kāya|vāṅ|mānasa|kriyā
prabhavaḥ sarva|dharmāṇāṃ jagatī jagatām iva.
21.15 yen' ôpāyena mitratvaṃ yānti madhya|stha|śatravaḥ
sarv'|ârthānām asau hetur guṇānām iva saj|janaḥ.
para|strī|gaṇikā|tyāgaḥ saṃtoṣo manda|roṣatā
n' âti|saktiś ca dāreṣu sukhaṃ duḥkhaṃ viparyayaḥ.
s'|âṅgasya sukha|rāg'|āder an|aṅgasya ca dehinaḥ
saṃbandh'|â|bhāvam aty|antaṃ nirvāṇaṃ vidur īśvarāḥ.
ardha|rātre 'pi bhuñjānaḥ param'|ârtha|bubhukṣitaḥ
kūṭa|vaidya|parityāgī rogair dūreṇa varjyate.
dṛṣṭa|saṃsāra|sārāṇām ṛṣīṇāṃ ko hi mādṛśaḥ
a|sāro guru|sārāṇi darśanāni viḍambayet?
21.20 tena yat kiṃ cid uc|chāstraṃ bāla|bhāvād udāhṛtam
śuka|vāśita|niḥ|sāram idaṃ me mṛṣyatām» iti.

idam|ādīḥ kathāḥ śṛṇvan nir|antara|sur'|ālayām
Gaṅg"|ābharaṇam ākhyātāṃ prāpaṃ Vārāṇasīṃ tataḥ.
tatra bāhya|niviṣṭasya śūnyasya pura|sadmanaḥ
jarad|dāru|sudhā|citram adhyatiṣṭhāma maṇḍapam.

He said, "The experts speak of five subjects for stories: religious merit, wealth, happiness, liberation and healing, together with all the details that go with them. Physical, vocal and mental actions serve to benefit living beings and are the birthplace of all religious merit, just as the earth is the
birthplace of all creatures. The means by which those who 21.15
are indifferent or hostile become friends is the cause of all wealth, just as good people are the cause of virtues. Giving up courtesans and other mens' wives, being content, being slow to get angry and not being excessively attached to one's wife: that is happiness. Unhappiness comes from doing the opposite. The masters say that ultimate liberation consists in the soul's having no attachment to pleasures, passions and so forth, whether physical or otherwise. If a man eats when truly hungry—even in the middle of the night—and shuns quack doctors, diseases will steer clear of him. But what man as worthless as me could imitate the precious observations of sages who have discovered the essence of the phenomenal
world? The words contravening the scriptures that I have 21.20
naively spoken are as worthless as the chattering of a parrot. Forgive me for them."

Listening to speeches such as this, I reached the city that, with its unbroken succession of temples, is called the jewel of the Ganga: Varánasi. Outside the city was a deserted house. We stayed in the pavilion, with its decrepit beams and cracked plaster.

Gomukhas tu kṣaṇaṃ sthitvā mām avocad gata|śramam
«muhūrtakam an|utkaṇṭhair iha yuṣmābhir āsyatām.
yatra sthātavyam asmābhir upalabhya tam āśrayam
āgacchām' îti» mām uktvā calair uccalitaḥ padaiḥ.
21.25 gatvā ṣoḍaśa|viṃśāni padāni sahasā sthitaḥ
tataḥ kim api niścitya nivṛtto mām abhāṣata.
«yad idaṃ yuṣmad|aṅgeṣu divyaṃ bhūṣaṇam āhitam
idam ādāya gacchāmi sthātuṃ n' âsy' êha yujyate.
tri|daṇḍi|pāṇḍar'|âṅg'|ādi|pāṣaṇḍaiś chadma|kaṅkaṭaiḥ
Vārāṇasī mahā|caurais tīrtha|dhvāṅkṣair adhiṣṭhitā.
yuṣmān ekākino dṛṣṭvā s'|âlaṅkārān nir|āyudhān
teṣāṃ sāhasikaḥ kaś cid an|arthaṃ cintayed» iti.
«evaṃ bhavatu nām' êti» may" âsāv anumoditaḥ
tad" ābharaṇam ādāya prāviśat tvaritaḥ puram.
21.30 ath' â|cira|gate tasmin parivrāḍ|brahma|cāriṇau
paricaṅkramaṇa|śrāntau tasminn eva nyasīdatām.
āsīc ca mama «tāv etau nūnaṃ pāṣaṇḍi|taskarau
nir|āyudh'|â|sahāyaṃ māṃ muṣituṃ kila vāñchataḥ.
tad eteṣāṃ sahasreṣu sa|kṛpāṇa|kareṣv api
gavām iv' ôdviṣāṇānāṃ matir me manthar'|ādarā.
ūru|mūla|stha|śāstreṣu pravrajyā|kaṅkaṭeṣu yaḥ
prayuṅkte nirghṛṇaḥ śastraṃ ko 'nyaḥ klībatamas tataḥ?»
evam|ādi|vikalpaṃ mām asāv ālokya maskarī
nir|āśa iva vidrāṇo brahma|cāriṇam uktavān.
21.35 «jalpāka|grathitair granthaiḥ Sāṃkhya|Yog'|ādibhir vayam
vipralabdhāḥ sukhaṃ tyaktvā mokṣa|mārge kila sthitāḥ.
yathā tṛṇam upādātum ambar'|âmbhojam eva vā

After we had been there for a while and I was rested, Go·
mukha said to me, “Be patient and wait here for a moment.
I shall find us a place to stay and come back.” He hurried
off. When he had gone sixteen or twenty paces he suddenly 21.25
stopped. Making his mind up about something, he came
back and said to me, “I shall take with me the beautiful
jewelry that you are wearing. It should not stay here. Varánasi is infested with brahmins carrying triple staves, ash-
smeared ascetics and other heretics, who, protected by their
disguises, are thieves, carrion crows at a place of pilgrimage.
Seeing you alone and carrying jewelry but not weapons, a
rash man among them might contemplate an evil deed.”

I agreed, saying to him, “So be it!” and he took my jewelry
and hurried off into the city. He had not been gone long 21.30
when a wandering ascetic and a student who were tired
from walking around the city came and sat down in that
very place.

I said to myself, “These two have got to be impostors
and thieves. I am unarmed and alone; surely they want to
rob me. But even if there were thousands of them, daggers
in hand, I would have little regard for them: they would be
like cows with raised horns! Who is more cowardly than the
man shameless enough to use his blade on those who have
asceticism as their armor and books in their belts?” While
I was vacillating thus, the ascetic looked me over, and, like
a man who has lost hope suddenly having a revelation, he
said to the student, “The books on systems such as Samkhya 21.35
and Yoga have been put together by sophists! Deceived by
them, we abandoned pleasure and set forth on the road to
liberation. Our efforts toward liberation are like someone

kaś cin mahat tapaḥ kuryān mokṣ'|ârtho nas tathā śramaḥ.
tṛṇavat su|labho mokṣo yadi khedo '|phalas tataḥ
atha kh'|âmboja|duṣ|prāpas tato naṣṭā mumukṣavaḥ.
para|lokasya sad|bhāve hetuḥ sarva|jña|bhāṣitaḥ
sarva|jñasy' âpi sad|bhāvaḥ pañca|divya|pramāṇakaḥ.
yo 'py upādīyate hetuḥ sarva|jñ'|âstitva|siddhaye
so 'py a|siddha|viruddh'|ādi|doṣ'|āśīviṣa|dūṣitaḥ.
21.40 tad alaṃ viṭa|vācāṭa|ghaṭitaiḥ kāvya|karpaṭaiḥ
sevamānā yathā|chandam āsmahe viṣayān!» iti.

brahma|cārī tu s'|āvegaḥ parivrājakam uktavān
«prasāritas tvayā kasmād a|sāro malla|daṇḍakaḥ?
pratijñā|hetu|dṛṣṭ'|ântāḥ sādhavas tāvad āsatām
sarva|tantr'|â|viruddhena siddh'|ânten' âiva bādhyase.
a|sattāṃ para|lokasya śuṣka|tarkeṇa sādhayan
vitaṇḍā|vāda|vārtt'|ārtaḥ sādhu śocyo bhaviṣyasi.
atha v" āstām idaṃ tāvad idaṃ tāvan nigadyatām
Smṛtīnāṃ viṭa|kāvyatvaṃ kathaṃ veda bhavān» iti.

21.45 ten' ôktaṃ «mānuṣāṇāṃ ca prāyaḥ sarva|śarīriṇām
Nandīśa|pramukhair uktam ahaṃ jānāmi lakṣaṇam.
yaś c' âiṣaḥ puruṣaḥ ko 'pi pānthaḥ pāṃsula|pādakaḥ
eṣa vidyā|dhar'|êndrāṇām indraḥ kila bhaviṣyati.
enaṃ dṛṣṭv" âdhitiṣṭhantam etaṃ jarjara|maṇḍapam
malla|daṇḍaka|niḥ|sārān utprekṣe sakal'|āgamān.
a|dṛṣṭ'|ârthāḥ kila granthā dṛṣṭ'|ârthair Gāruḍ'|ādibhiḥ

undergoing extreme austerities in order to obtain a blade of grass or a sky-lotus. If liberation is as easy to find as a blade of grass, then exerting oneself is pointless; if it is as hard to find as a sky-lotus, then all those who seek it are done for! The proof of the existence of the next world is the word of the omniscient being, but the existence of the omniscient being has as its proof the five divine attributes. Therefore the very basis of the proof of the existence of the omniscient being is marred by internal faults such as inconclusiveness and contradiction. So let's be done with patchwork poetry 21.40
pieced together by libertines and lecturers and indulge our senses in whatever way we wish!"

But the student was put out and said to the ascetic, "Why are you taking up the cudgel? It won't get you anywhere. Forget whether the thesis, basis and example of the syllogism are right; you are wrong because the doctrine is accepted by all philosophical systems. If you use dry logic to prove the nonexistence of the next world, you will suffer a round of pointless arguments and rightly end up miserable. But let's leave that aside for the moment; first tell me how you know that the scriptures are the poetry of libertines."

He replied, "I know the characteristic marks of men and 21.45
almost all other living beings as described by Shiva and the rest. You see this man, a traveler with dusty feet? He, apparently, is to become the emperor of the sorcerers! Seeing him staying here in this ruined hall makes me think that all the scriptures are as pointless as sophistic wrangling. From the existence of books whose application is obvious, such as that by Gáruda, we can infer that books whose applications are not obvious do in fact have a purpose, just as we can infer

arthavanto 'numīyante yācakair iva dāyakāḥ.
yathā ca viṭa|kāvyatvān mṛṣā puruṣa|lakṣaṇam
Śruti|Smṛti|Purāṇ'|ādi tathā saṃbhāvyatām iti.»
21.50 itaras tam ath' âvocad «atīta|bhava|saṃcitam
iṣṭ'|ân|iṣṭa|phalaṃ karma daivam āhur vicakṣaṇāḥ.
yac c' êdaṃ lakṣaṇaṃ nāma śarīreṣu śarīriṇām
etad daiv'|âbhidhānasya lakṣaṇaṃ pūrva|karmaṇaḥ.
na c' â|puruṣa|kārasya daivaṃ phalati kasya cit
kāla|kāraṇa|sāmagrīm Īśvaro 'pi hy apekṣate.
ayaṃ tu taruṇaḥ kalyaḥ kānti|kṣipta|sur'|âsuraḥ
kuṇṭhayā gaṇḍa|maṇḍānāṃ manda|ceṣṭatayā samaḥ.
yathā dhanur a|dhānuṣkaṃ yathā bījam a|vāpakam
sattā|mātra|phalaṃ puṃsas tathā daivam a|pauruṣam.»
21.55 parivrāḍ abravīd «daivaṃ pauruṣād balavattaram
jñāpakaṃ c' âsya pakṣasya śrūyatāṃ yan mayā śrutam.
asti Sindhu|taṭe grāmaḥ Brahmasthalaka|nāmakaḥ
tatr' āsīd Vedaśarm" êti catur|vedo dvi|j'|ôttamaḥ.
tasya yo 'nyatamaḥ śiṣyaḥ pāṭhaṃ prati dṛḍh'|ôdyamaḥ
tasmād eva ca sa chātrair āhūyata Dṛḍhodyamaḥ.
Tamobhedaka|nāmnaś ca gṛha|sthasya gṛhe sadā
dāpitaṃ bhojanaṃ tasy' ācchādanaṃ Vedaśarmaṇā.
tatra Bhinnatamā nāma parivrāṭ Pāñcarātrikaḥ
vāsam āvasathe tasya karoti sma Dṛḍhodyamaḥ.
21.60 anena ca prakāreṇa paṭu|śraddhāna|medhasā
adhītaṃ daśabhir varṣais tena Veda|catuṣṭayam.

the existence of donors from beggars. And since the science of characteristic marks, being the poetry of libertines, is pointless, we must come to the same conclusion about revelatory, reflective, historical and other such scriptures."

The student replied, "Actions accumulated during past 21.50
lives, with their desirable and undesirable results, are called destiny by the wise. And the characteristic marks on the bodies of embodied beings are in fact the marks of that which is called destiny, namely past actions. But if a man makes no effort himself, destiny bears no fruit for him. The supreme being takes note of all circumstances and conditions. As for this young and healthy fellow whose beauty surpasses that of the gods and demons, his lazy, torpid demeanor has made him no better than a rhinoceros or a frog. Without human effort, destiny merely exists, producing nothing, like a bow without an archer or a seed without a sower."

The ascetic replied, "Destiny is more powerful than hu- 21.55
man effort. I have heard a story that proves my point—listen.

On the banks of the Sindhu there is a village called Brahma·sthálaka. An eminent brahmin called Veda·sharman, who knew the four Vedas, lived there. One of his pupils tried very hard at his lessons and as a result was called Dridhódyama by the other students.* Veda·sharman made an arrangement for him regularly to receive food and clothes in the house of a householder called Tamo·bhédaka. A Pañcha·rátrika ascetic called Bhinna·tamas lived in the village
and Dridhódyama lodged in his house. In this way, with his 21.60
strong faith and sharp intellect he learned the four Vedas in ten years.

atha Bhinnatamāḥ kṛtvā varṇ'|āśrama|kathāṃ ciram
praśānta|jana|saṃpāte pradoṣe tam abhāṣata.
‹bahu|go|mahiṣī|bhūmi|dāsī|dāsam idaṃ mayā
tantra|sthānaṃ upāntaṃ ca cāṭ'|ādibhyaś ca rakṣitam.
dhyān'|ādhyāya|pradhānaṃ ca vihitaṃ bhikṣu|karma yat
vaiśya|karm'|âbhiyuktasya tasya nām' âpi n' âsti me.
adhunā tu vacaḥ|kāya|parispand'|âpahāriṇī
para|loka|samāsannā jarā|tandrīr iv' āgatā.
21.65 gṛha|medhi|vrata|sthānām alasānāṃ sva|karmasu
dharma|sādhanam uddiṣṭam ṛṣibhis tīrtha|sevanam.
āha Ved'|ânta|vādaś ca tārakaṃ Brahma tantrayet
etasmān na vimuñceyur Avimuktaṃ mumukṣavaḥ.
śvaḥ prasthāt" āsmahe tasmāt prātaḥ Vārāṇasīṃ prati
Buddha|dharme praśastā hi dharmasya tvaritā gatiḥ.
bhavat" âpi Śruti|Smṛtyoḥ prāmāṇyam anujānatā
niyogen' âiva kartavyaḥ patnī|putra|parigrahaḥ.
gṛha|sth'|āśrama|dharmaś ca gav|ādi|dhana|sādhanaḥ
na ca pratigrahād anyad viprasya dhana|sādhanam.
21.70 tat sukh'|ôpanataṃ c' âitad a|nindyam ati|bhūri ca
sa|dāsī|dāsam asmākaṃ dhanam ādīyatām› iti.

ten' ôktaṃ ‹yuṣmad|ādiṣṭam a|kāryam api mādṛśaḥ
na vikalpayituṃ śaktaḥ kiṃ punar nyāyyam īdṛśam.
kiṃ tv āmantrya pitṛ|sthānau vidyā|jīvita|dāyinau
kart" âsmi bhavad|ādeśam ativāhya niśām› iti.

One evening, after Bhinna·tamas had finished a lengthy
discourse on the classes and stages of life and people had
stopped dropping by, he said to Dridhódyama, 'I protect
this homestead, with its many cows, buffaloes, fields and
female and male servants, from criminals and so forth. The
chief duties of a monk are meditation and study. I am busy
with my work as a farmer and do not do them even in name.
But now it seems that the weariness of age has arrived, slack-
ening the pulse in my voice and body—the next world is
at hand! When those who have taken the vow of a domes- 21.65
tic sacrificer are sluggish in carrying out their activities, the
sages prescribe a pilgrimage as the means of fulfilling their
duty. The doctrine of Vedánta says Brahman is the guide
to liberation, so those seeking liberation should not fail to
visit Avimúkta. Thus I shall set out for Varánasi tomorrow
morning—in the religion of the Buddha the swift pursuit of
righteousness is praised. And you, accepting the authority
of the traditional scriptures, will be obliged to take a wife
and have children. Wealth such as cows and so forth is necessary for fulfilling the duties of the householder's stage of
life, and there is no way besides receiving gifts for a brahmin
to get wealth. So take this fortune of mine, complete with 21.70
my male and female servants: it has come to you easily, there
is nothing at fault with it and it is vast.'

He replied, 'If you ordered it, a man like me could have no qualms about doing something wrong, let alone something right! But let me take my leave of the two men who took the place of my father in giving me knowledge and life and do what you have instructed me once the night has passed.'

yātāyāṃ tu tri|yāmāyāṃ tam āmantrayituṃ gatam
saṃpratiṣṭhāsamāno 'pi ciraṃ bhikṣur udaikṣata.
yadā tu divas'|ârdhe 'pi gate chāttraḥ sa n' āgataḥ
taṃ gaveṣayituṃ bhikṣuḥ svayam eva tadā gataḥ.

21.75 sa tu ten' âṅgaṇe dṛṣṭo Tamobhedaka|veśmanaḥ
śanaiś caṅkramaṇaṃ kurvan nīcaiś c' āmnāya|mānasam.
uktaṃ ca ‹bhavatā kasmād iyac ciram iha sthitam?
ath' ârthen' âiva ten' ârthas tathā naḥ kathyatām!› iti.

tatas ten' ôktam ‹etasmin gṛhe ken' âpi hetunā
vyagraḥ parijanaḥ sarvas tatra tatr' âbhidhāvati.
yāṃ yām eva ca pṛcchāmi «kim etad?» iti dārikām
sā sā mām āha saṃrabdhā «śivaṃ dhyātu bhavān» iti.
taṃ c' âdy' âpi na pṛcchāmi Tamobhedakam ākulam
ten' âhaṃ n' āgataḥ kṣipraṃ sakāśaṃ bhavatām› iti.

21.80 atha Bhinnatamāḥ smitvā Dṛḍhodyamam abhāṣata
‹yen' âyam ākulo lokas tad ahaṃ kathayāmi te.
Tamobhedaka|bhāryāyāḥ prasūtiḥ pratyupasthitā
ayaṃ parijanas tatra tatra tatr' ākul'|ākulaḥ.
dārikā jāyate c' âsya tāṃ ca tvaṃ pariṇeṣyasi
sā ca rāga|grah'|āviṣṭā duṣṭa|ceṣṭā bhaviṣyati.›

iti tasmin kṛt'|ādeśe gate sva|vivadhaṃ prati
itaraś cintayām āsa śaṅkā|kampita|mānasaḥ.
‹brāhmaṇī brāhmaṇasy' âsya yadi kanyāṃ vijāyate
tataḥ Bhinnatamo|vākyam a|bhūt'|ârthaṃ na jāyate.

21.85 stobh'|āveśa|viṣ'|āccheda|kriyāsu vyakta|śaktibhiḥ
śeṣāṇām api mantrāṇāṃ sāmarthyam anumīyate.›

When the night was over, he went to say his goodbyes, and the monk, keen to get going, waited a long time for him. But when half the day had gone and the pupil still had not returned, the monk went to look for him himself.
He found him in the courtyard of Tamo·bhédaka's house, 21.75
slowly walking about and softly reciting scriptures from memory. He said, 'Why have you stayed here for so long? Tell me the reason—it had better be good!'

He replied, 'For some reason, all the staff in the house are preoccupied and running about the place. Every maid that I ask what is going on excitedly tells me to think auspicious thoughts. I have not yet been able to consult Tamo·bhédaka, who is in a frenzy. That is why I have not hurried back to you.'

Then Bhinna·tamas smiled and said to Dridhódyama, 'I 21.80
shall tell you why everyone here is in a frenzy. Tamo·bhédaka's wife is about to give birth, so the servants are running all over the place in a panic. A daughter is going to be born to him and you shall marry her. She will be influenced by a malign planet, which will make her impassioned and badly behaved.'

After making this prediction, he went on his way. Anxiety unsettled Dridhódyama's mind and he said to himself, 'If the brahmin's wife has a daughter, then the words of Bhin-
na·tamas will come true. When one sees that rites that use 21.85
a chanted interjection to remove poison are effective, one infers the efficacy of all the other formulas.'

iti cintayatas tasya dīno gṛha|patir gṛhāt
‹hā daivaṃ khalam!› ity|ādi lapan nīcair vinirgataḥ.
kṣaṇāc ca śva|gṛhītasya mārjārasy' êva kūjataḥ
antar|bhavanam udbhūtaḥ śv'|āgāra|paruṣa|śrutiḥ.
tataḥ prasādhitā nāryo lajjā|prāvṛta|mastakāḥ
pakṣa|dvāreṇa nirjagmur nairāśy'|ôttāna|pāṇayaḥ.
paricāraka|vargaś ca śocad|bandhu|kadambakam
amantrayata ‹vāmasya vidheḥ kiṃ kriyatām?› iti.

21.90 evaṃ|prāya|prapañce tu gṛhe tasmin Dṛḍhodyamaḥ
siddha|pravrajit'|ādeśa|jāta|bhītir acintayat.
‹parivrājaka|vākyena tathā|bhūtena sādhitam
daivaṃ puruṣa|kāreṇa janāḥ paśyantu bādhitam.
Sindhu|deśaṃ parityajya deśād deśaṃ parivrajan
ayaṃ pariharāmy enāṃ dūrataḥ kardamām› iti.

evam|ādi vimṛśy' âsāv a|saṃmantry' âiva saṃskṛtān
daśa|yojanam adhvānam ekāhena palāyitaḥ.
sa|dvīpāṃ ca parikramya varṣair dvādaśabhir mahīm
Gaṅgā|taṭam upāgacchat tīrth'|ôpāsana|kāmyayā.
21.95 ath' ātapa|pipās'|ārtaś chāyā|salila|vāñchayā
kasmiṃś cid brāhmaṇa|grāme kaṃ cana prāviśad gṛham.
tatra c' ālindak'|āsīnām arka|tūl'|ābha|mūrdha|jām
yayāce brāhmaṇīm ‹amba pānīyaṃ dāpyatām!› iti.

sā tv abhāṣata saṃbhrāntā ‹hale! putri Tamālike
āsan'|ôdakam ādāya laghu nirgamyatām› iti.

While he was thinking this, the master of the house emerged. He was downcast and muttering things like 'Oh, accursed destiny!' Immediately afterward, a shrill sound arose in the house, like that of a kennel where a squealing cat has been caught by the dogs. Well-dressed ladies, their heads covered in shame, went out by a side door, waving their hands in despair. The servants and the grieving relatives said, 'When fate is unfavorable, what can be done?'

With the events in the house turning out like this, Dri- 21.90
dhódyama became terrified of the ascetic's prediction coming true and said to himself, 'The power of destiny may have been demonstrated by the ascetic's words coming to pass, but now let everyone see it thwarted by human effort! I shall leave Sindh and, wandering from country to country, steer well clear of this tainted girl.'

After thinking through all this without even consulting the brahmins, he fled, covering ten *yójana*s in a single day. He circumambulated the earth and its continents in twelve years and then arrived at the banks of the Ganga in the
desire of worshipping at a sacred site. Stricken by heat and 21.95
thirst and longing for shade and water, he entered a house in a village of brahmins. A brahmin lady was sitting on a veranda, her hair resembling the rays of the sun. He asked her, 'Mother, please give me some water!'

Flustered, she said, 'Hey! Tamálika, my girl, come quickly, and bring a chair and some water.'

tataḥ pīṭh'|ālukā|hastā vasit'|âsita|kañcukā
āpiṅg'|âpānta|keś'|ântā kanyakā niragād gṛhāt.
diśas taralayā dṛṣṭyā paśyantī saṃtata|smitā
paṅgu|bhaṅgura|saṃcārā cirāt prāpad Dṛḍhodyamam.
21.100 ‹āsyatām atra mitr' êti› vadantyā śūnyayā tayā
pīṭha|buddhyā puras tasya nikṣiptaṃ jala|bhājanam.

atha tām abravīd vṛddhā ‹muktv" âitām a|vinītatām
apareṇ' ôda|pātreṇa jalam āvarjyatām!› iti.

sā tu kṛtrima|saṃtrāsa|janit'|ôtkaṭa|vepathuḥ
antar|hasita|bhugn'|âuṣṭhī vṛddh"|ājñāṃ samapādayat.

tato gata|śramaṃ vṛddhā pṛcchati sma Dṛḍhodyamam
‹āgacchati kuto deśāt kaṃ vā yāti bhavān?› iti.
ten' ôktaṃ ‹na sa deśo 'sti n' āgacchāmi yataḥ kṣitau
yac ca brūtha «kva yās' îti» tatra viñjāpayāmi vaḥ.
21.105 kasmiṃś cid brāhmaṇa|grāme kurvan baṭuka|pāṭhanām
saṃtuṣṭo grāma|vāsobhir ninīṣe divasān› iti.

tatas tam abravīd vṛddhā ‹nīti|jñaiḥ satyam ucyate
na hy a|taptena lohena taptaṃ saṃdhīyate kva cit.
mama dvau putra|naptārāv adhun" âiv' ôpanītakau
tau ca saṃyojitau puṇyair arthināv arthinā tvayā.
bhavān adhyāpanen' ârthī tau c' âdhyayana|kāṅkṣiṇau
naṣṭ'|âśva|dagdha|ratha|vad yogo 'stu bhavatām!› iti.

tatas tasyai pratijñāya tau baṭū pāṭhayann asau
antevāsi|gaṇaṃ c' ânyam asthāt saṃvatsara|dvayam.

Carrying a stool and a gourd, and wearing a black robe,
a girl with long auburn hair came out of the house. Her
eyes darted about the place and she smiled constantly. She
slowly hobbled over to Dridhódyama and, absent-mindedly 21.100
saying 'Sit on this, my friend,' she threw the water pot down
in front of him, thinking it was the stool.

The old lady said to her, 'Stop being so ill-mannered and fetch some water in another pot!'

Feigning fear, she trembled violently, her lips askew with a suppressed smile, and did as the old lady had asked.

When Dridhódyama was rested, the old lady asked him
what country he had come from and where he was going.
He replied, 'There isn't a country on earth which I have not
been through on my way here. And you ask where I am
going; let me tell you the answer to that. I am going to pass 21.105
my days teaching the boys in a village of brahmins, content
in the company of the villagers.'

The old lady said to him, 'The moral philosophers were right when they said that hot iron can never be joined with cold. I have two grandsons who have just become ready to be educated. They need you, you need them, and your merits have brought you together. You want to teach, they want to learn. May you come together like a man who has lost his horses and a man whose chariot has been reduced to ashes!'

He gave her his consent and spent two years teaching the two boys and another group of pupils who lived nearby.

21.110 ekadā tām abhāṣanta vṛddhām āgatya bāndhavāḥ
‹kasmād Dṛḍhodyamāy' êyaṃ dīyate na Tamālikā?
ye jāmātṛ|guṇās teṣāṃ kaś cid asti kva cid vare
Dṛḍhodyame punaḥ paśya yadi kaṃ cin na paśyasi.
dur|labhaḥ su|labhī|bhūtas tasmāt svī|kriyatām ayam
kena vanyaḥ karī vārīm āgataḥ svayam ujjhitaḥ?›
iti tair bodhitā vṛddhā pratītā tān ayācata
‹yady evaṃ svayam ev' âyaṃ pūjyair abhyarthyatām› iti.
te tatas tam abhāṣanta ‹bhautika brahma|cāriṇā
āmnātāś c' âvabuddhāś ca Vedāḥ sa|smṛtayas tvayā.
21.115 a|vaśyaṃ c' âdhunā kāryaḥ śuddha|patnī|parigrahaḥ
uraḥ|kaṇṭh'|âuṣṭha|śoṣasya mā bhūd vaiphalyam anyathā.
ataḥ pratīṣyatām eṣā sarva|śuddhā Tamālikā
jyeṣṭhaṃ jyeṣṭh'|āśramasy' âṅgaṃ trayī Vidy" êva dehinī.›
evam|ādi sa tair uktaḥ kṣaṇam etad acintayat
‹yuktaṃ yad brāhmaṇair uktam atra tāvat kim ucyate.
yaś c' âsau Sindhu|viṣaye dūṣitaḥ kṛtyayā tayā
pāre|sāgaravat so 'pi dūratvāt su|dur|āgamaḥ.
atha daivena s" âiv' êyam ānītā Sindhu|deśataḥ
sūcī|sūtra|gate daivāt tataḥ kaḥ kutra mokṣyate?›
21.120 evam|ādi sa niścitya pratiśrutya ‹tath" êti› ca
pariṇīya ca tāṃ kanyāṃ saṃvatsaram ayāpayat.
atha yāta|tri|yāmāyāṃ tri|yāmāyāṃ Dṛḍhodyamaḥ
jṛmbhā|vedita|nidr"|ântāṃ pṛcchati sma Tamālikām.
‹brūhi sundari paśyāma kuṭumbasy' âsya kaḥ prabhuḥ?
k" êyaṃ bhavati te vṛddhā? kāv etau baṭukāv iti.›

One day some relatives of the old lady came and said to her, 'Why don't you have Tamálika marry Dridhódyama? Every suitor has one or other of the virtues of a son-in-law, but looking at Dridhódyama you can see that he lacks none of them. A rarity is in your grasp—you must make him yours. Who would free a wild elephant that has come of his own accord to the restraining post?' 21.110

When they told her this, the old lady was convinced and asked them, 'If it is to be so, worthy kinfolk, then please ask him yourselves.'

They said to him, 'Your Reverence, as a student you memorized and understood the Vedas and the traditional
scriptures. Now you must marry a pure wife so that the 21.115
breath in your chest, throat and lips does not go to waste. Therefore take this girl, the perfectly pure Tamálika, and, as if she were an incarnation of the three Vedas, take the best part of the best stage of life!'

He thought for a moment about everything they had said to him: 'The brahmins are right—what more is there to say on the matter? The man in Sindh sullied by that demoness is as far away as the far shore of the ocean and extremely unlikely to come here.* And if destiny has in fact brought the girl here from Sindh it could make a thread fall through the eye of a needle: no one could escape from it anywhere!'

Having made up his mind like this, he gave his consent 21.120
and married the girl. A year went by. Once, near the end of the night, when Tamálika's yawns revealed that she had woken up, Dridhódyama asked her, 'Tell me, beautiful girl, who is the head of your family? What relation is the old lady to you? Who are those two boys?'

tayā tv āyata|niśvāsa|kathit'|āyata|duḥkhayā
srut'|âśru|kaṇikā|śreṇyā kathitaṃ skhalad|akṣaram.
‹asyā brāhmaṇa|vṛddhāyāḥ priyaḥ sādhur abhūt patiḥ
yasya vidyā|dhanais tṛptāḥ śiṣya|yājaka|yācakāḥ.
21.125 tena c' â|śeṣa|Vedāya kṣam"|ādi|guṇa|śāline
duhitā gṛha|jāmātre chāttrāya pratipāditā.
tāḍitaś caraṇen' âpi yaḥ kṣamāvān abhūt purā
sa jāmātṛtayā krodhād gamitaḥ kṛṣṇa|sarpatām.
mahāntam api saṃmānaṃ manyamāno vimānatām
śvaśrū|śvaśurayoḥ khedam ātmanaś c' âkarod vṛthā.
ekadā parihāsena syālakas tam abhāṣata
«Durvāsaḥ|sadṛśas tāta dur|ārādho bhavān» iti.
«yady evaṃ dur|dur|ūḍhena kiṃ may" ārādhitena vaḥ»
ity uktvā manthar'|ālāpaḥ sa|dāro gata eva saḥ.
21.130 śvaśrū|śvaśura|mitrāṇām avakarṇya kadarthanām
nirapekṣaṃ sva|deśāya Sindhu|deśāya yātavān.
tatra ca grāmam adhyāsya Brahmasthalaka|nāmakam
a|cirān nitya|kāmyāni karmāṇi niravartayat.
tasya tasyāṃ ca bhāryāyāṃ Kāla|rātri|samā sutā
yamau ca tanayau jātau Yama|Kālau kulasya yau.
aham eva ca sā kanyā tau c' âitau kāka|tālukau
yair mātā|pitarāv eva bālair eva samāhitau.
Sindhu|deś'|âika|deśaś ca Sindhunā caṇḍa|raṃhasā
dur|vāra|guru|pūreṇa sahas" ākṛṣya nīyate.
21.135 atha mātā|pitṛbhyāṃ nas tad|bhayād avadhāritam
mātā|maha|gṛhaṃ yāntu bālā me niviśantv› iti.

A long sigh told of her deep sadness, and with teardrops
streaming forth she stuttered, 'The old brahmin lady had
a beloved husband, a good man who made pupils, patrons
and beggars happy with his knowledge and riches. He be- 21.125
trothed his daughter to a pupil who knew the entire Veda
and abounded in patience and other virtues; he became his
son-in-law. Previously the pupil would have even forgiven
being kicked; as a son-in-law he was as irascible as a black
snake. He would regard even great courtesy as an insult,
and needlessly caused trouble for his parents-in-law and for
himself.

One day his brother-in-law said to him as a joke, "You,
my boy, are as hard to please as Durvásas." "If I'm so ill-
bred," he boomed, "then why do you try to please me?"
At this, he left with his wife. He paid no heed to the re- 21.130
proaches of his in-laws and friends and without a thought
for his homeland he went to Sindh. He settled in a village
there called Brahma·sthálaka and before long he had completed the duties expected of him. He and his wife had a
daughter who was like the black night of doomsday, and
twin sons, who were the death and destruction of his family. The girl is me and these two poor lads are the two
boys. We were only with our parents as children. Part of
Sindh was suddenly swept away by the impetuous Sindhu,
its powerful flood impossible to stem. In fear of it, our par- 21.135
ents decided that their children should go and stay at their
maternal grandparents' house...'

tataḥ śaṅk"|êṣu|bhinnas tām abhāṣata Dṛḍhodyamaḥ
‹śeṣaṃ su|jñānam ev' âsyāḥ kathāyāḥ sthīyatām› iti.
āsīc c' âsya ‹saḥ sarva|jñaḥ parivrājaka|bhāskaraḥ
sphuṭaṃ Bhinnatamā eva bhinn'|â|jñāna|tamā yataḥ.
anubhūtau tathā|bhūtau tad|ādeśau may" âdhunā
tṛtīya|parihārāya tyajāmi pṛthivīm› iti.

atha dvā|daśa|varṣāni bhrāṃtvā dvīp'|ântarāṇi saḥ
nirviṇṇaś cintayām āsa kiṃ cid dhavala|mūrdha|jaḥ.
21.140 ‹ādiṣṭaṃ yat parivrājā tat tay" ônmāda|mattayā
kālen' âitāvatā nūnam a|kṛtyaṃ kṛtyayā kṛtam.
asmābhiś ca na Ved'|ôktaṃ na Ved'|ânt'|ôktam īhitam
vraṇair iva visarpadbhiḥ kv' âp' îtaṃ puruṣ'|āyuṣam.
tena Vārāṇasīṃ gatvā tīrth'|ôpāsana|hetukam
puṇyaṃ svarga|phalaṃ kurvann ayāmi divasān› iti.

tataḥ sāgaram uttīrya Gaṅgāsāgaram āgamat
tataḥ Vārāṇasīṃ prāpad a|muñcann eva Jāhnavīm.
prāviśann eva c' âpaśyan nara|dhātu|paricchadam
skhalad|ālāpa|saṃcāraṃ mahā|Pāśupataṃ puraḥ.
21.145 taṃ c' ânu sphaṭika|prāya|karṇa|kaṇṭha|vibhūṣaṇām
madirā|tāmra|jihm'|âkṣāṃ vicitra|gala|kaṇṭhikām.
dvi|guṇī|kurvatīṃ mārgaṃ vaṅkair gati|nivartanaiḥ
a|mukta|nija|nirmokāṃ bhujaṃgīm iva yoṣitam.

Pierced by the arrow of anxiety, Dridhódyama said to her, 'Stop! The rest of the story is all too clear.' To himself he said, 'Bhinna·tamas, that shining light of an ascetic, was omniscient! He clearly lived up to his name—he had cast asunder the darkness of ignorance!* I have now seen two of his predictions come true. To avoid the third I shall leave this land.'

He wandered across other continents for twelve years. Then, depressed, with his hair starting to go gray, he thought
to himself, 'After all this time, surely that crazy witch has 21.140
done the terrible deed that the ascetic foretold. I have never striven after the teachings of the Veda or Vedánta; my life as a man has disappeared as if through weeping sores. Therefore I shall go to Varánasi to worship at the sacred sites and spend my days doing good deeds that have heaven as their reward.'

So he crossed the ocean and arrived at Ganga·ságara. Then, without leaving the Ganga, he made his way to Varánasi. Just as he was entering the city, he saw a Páshupata ascetic wearing ornaments made from human bone. His
speech was slurred and his gait unsteady. Following him 21.145
was a woman wearing earrings and necklaces of crystal. Wine had made her eyes bloodshot and crossed, and there was a strange pendant on her throat. Like a she-snake in the process of shedding its slough, she made the road twice as long with her zigzagged staggering.

sā tu Kāpāliken' ôktā ‹drutam ehi Kapālini
na yāvad Avimuktasya dhūpa|vel" âtivartate.
huṃ|huṃ|kār'|ādibhiḥ stutvā saṃsthā|traya|paraṃ dhruvam
tataḥ śuṇḍika|śāleṣu mārgayāmi surām!› iti.
evaṃ|prāye ca vṛtt'|ânte ciraṃ dṛṣṭvā Dṛḍhodyamam
papāta pādayos tasya tār'|ākrandā Kapālinī.
21.150 punaḥ Kāpāliken' ôktaṃ ‹muñca brāhmaṇam adhva|gam!
parihāsaś ciraṃ caṇḍi viruddhas tyajyatām!› iti.
s" âbravīd ‹eṣa me bhartā! daivataiḥ pratipāditaḥ!
tvaṃ tu dhṛṣṭa viṭo bhūtvā kiṃ vyāharasi mām?› iti.
taṃ ca prapañcam ālokya sa pradeśaḥ sa|kautukaiḥ
janair a|gaṇitair vyāptaḥ Śramaṇa|brāhmaṇ'|ādibhiḥ.
sā c' âvocac ‹catur|Veda rikta|Vedo 'si sarvathā!
sa|Vedaḥ ko hi nir|vedaṃ Ved'|ôktaiḥ karmabhir vrajet?
na tvay" ôtpāditāḥ putrā n' âgni|hotram upāsitam
n' ârcitāḥ pitaraḥ piṇḍair vāyu|bhūtena hiṇḍitam!
21.155 tvayā Dṛḍhodyama tyaktā s" âhaṃ mandā Tamālikā
kulāt kulam aṭant" îdaṃ carāmi kulaṭā|vratam.
a|vṛddha|kula|vāsinyas taruṇyaḥ pati|varjitāḥ
yair a|duṣṭāḥ striyo dṛṣṭās te dṛṣṭāḥ kena cit kva cit.
tena tyaktavatā dārān yat tvayā pāpam arjitam
tān eva bharamāṇena tat samucchidyatām!› iti.
atha lajjā|viṣād'|ândham ūcur viprā Dṛḍhodyamam
‹bhagavatyā yad uktaṃ tat tattvataḥ kathyatām!› iti.

The Kapálika said to her, 'Come quickly, Kapálini, the hour of the incense ceremony at Avimúkta has not yet passed! I'll use mantras like *"hum hum"* to worship the best god of the trinity, and then I'll look for something to drink in the taverns!'

At this point in the story, the Kapálini stared at Dridhódyama before falling shrieking at his feet. The Kapálika said, 21.150
'Leave the brahmin traveler alone! This is a bad joke and it has gone on long enough, crazy lady. Stop it!'

She said, 'He is my husband! The gods have brought him back! But you, you traitor, why did you turn into a scoundrel and desert me?'

As they caught sight of this to-do, countless curious people filled the area, Buddhists and brahmins among them.

She continued, 'You know the four Vedas but you completely abandoned them! What man who knows the Vedas could lose his faith by acting in accordance with them? You didn't have sons, you didn't perform the fire sacrifice, you didn't worship your ancestors with funeral offerings, you just
vanished like the wind! Dridhódyama, you abandoned me, 21.155
and now I, poor Tamálika, wander from house to house, observing the vows of a nun. Has anyone ever met anyone who has seen young women living in their new homes remain chaste after being abandoned by their husbands? Atone for the sin you committed in abandoning your wife by taking her back!'

Dridhódyama was stunned by shame and despair. The brahmins said to him, 'Tell us the truth about what this nun has said!'

ten' ātmanaś ca tasyāś ca dvi|j'|ādi|jana|saṃnidhau
Brahmasthalaka|vās'|ādi yad vṛttaṃ tan niveditam.

21.160 ath' ôktaṃ brāhmaṇair ‹brahman
brāhmaṇī parigṛhyatām
rakta|dāra|parityāgam
ācaranti na sādhavaḥ.
yac ca kiṃ cid a|kartavyam a|nāthyād anayā kṛtam
tasya kṛcchratamaiḥ kṛcchrair viśuddhiḥ kriyatām› iti.

ten' ôktaṃ ‹yādṛśaṃ pāpaṃ prāyaścittair apohyate
pūjyānām eva tad buddham idaṃ budhyata yādṛśam.
hīna|varṇ'|âbhigāminyaḥ pātakinyaḥ kila striyaḥ
iyaṃ tv a|śubha|sāvarṇaṃ yam upāste sa dṛśyatām.
tad upāstām iyaṃ bhadrā yam upāsac chivaṃ dhruvam
sukhānāṃ c' ôpahartāraṃ mahā|Pāśupataṃ patim.›

21.165 ity uktavati sā tasminn uvāc' ôpacita|trapā
‹ā mṛtyos tvat|samīpa|sthā nayāmi divasān› iti.

ath' âiko brāhmaṇas teṣu Dṛḍhodyamam abhāṣata
‹madīyā duhitā brahman rūpiṇī pariṇīyatām.
dhanaṃ me Dhana|dasy' êva s" âiva c' âikā sutā yataḥ
tatas tasya ca tasyāś ca bhaved bhartā bhavān!› iti.

āsīc c' âsya ‹kim ady' âpi syān na syād iti cintayā
parivrājaka|vākyaṃ hi kṛt'|ârthī|kṛtam etayā.›
pratijñāya ca tāṃ kanyāṃ dadānād brāhmaṇāt svayam
sa|mahā|draviṇa|skandhām upayeme Dṛḍhodyamaḥ.

21.170 Tamālik" âpi saṃhārya keśān kāṣāya|cīvarā
Dṛḍhodyama|gṛh'|āsannā vasatī kālam akṣipat.
Dṛḍhodyamo 'pi saṃtataṃ dvi|jāti|karma sādhayan
Har'|ôttam'|âṅga|lālitām upāsta Jahnu|kanyakām.

In the midst of the crowd of brahmins and others he related what had happened to both himself and the woman since they lived in Brahma·sthálaka.

The brahmins said, 'Brahmin, take back the brahmin 21.160
lady. Good men do not abandon loving wives. Whatever crimes she has committed because of having no protector must be atoned for with the severest of penances.'

He replied, 'Your Reverences know what kind of sins are atoned for by ritual expiations. You must realize what kind this is. Women who fornicate with low-class men are indeed sinners, but look at the man this woman is devoted to: he may be distasteful, but he is of her caste. So let the good lady serve as her husband the lucky fellow whom she already serves: that provider of pleasures, the Páshupata.'

When she was told this, she was most indignant and said, 21.165
'I shall spend my days with you until I die!'

Then one of the brahmins said to Dridhódyama, 'Brahmin, I have a daughter and she is beautiful: marry her. I have wealth like Kubéra's and the girl is my only child. You must become master of them both!'

He said to himself, 'There's no need now to worry about what might or might not happen because this woman has fulfilled the ascetic's prediction.' Dridhódyama agreed to wed the girl that the brahmin had spontaneously offered and received both her hand in marriage and a great fortune.
As for Tamálika, she shaved her hair, put on the saffron 21.170
robes of an ascetic and passed her time living near Dridhódyama's house. Dridhódyama, meanwhile, constantly carried out the duties of the twice-born and served Ganga as she caressed Shiva's head. So, despite his considerable

tat tena yena kṛta|duṣ|kara|pauruṣeṇa
  vākyaṃ na Bhinnatamasaḥ kṛtam a|pramāṇam
śūreṇa daiva|hariṇā prabhuṇā prasahya
  tasmāj jitaḥ puruṣa|kāra|gaj'|âdhirājaḥ.»

iti Priyadarśanā|lābhe Daiv'|ākhyānam.

exertions, he did not disprove Bhinna·tamas's prediction. The king of the elephants, human effort, was conquered in battle by its master, the valiant lion of destiny."

Thus ends the Story of Destiny
in the Winning of Priya·darshaná.

CANTO 22
HUMAN EFFORT

22.1 Tataḥ kiṃ cid vihasy' ôktaḥ
parivrāḍ brahma|cāriṇā
"yathā puruṣa|kārasya
prādhānyaṃ tan niśāmyatām.
āsīd Ujjayanī|vāsī sārthak'|ârtha|parigrahaḥ
vaṇik Sāgaradatt'|ākhyaḥ sāgar'|â|gādha|mānasaḥ.
sāgaraṃ tena yātena mukta|potena gacchatā
aparaḥ prekṣitaḥ potas tarala|dhvaja|lakṣaṇaḥ.
‹aṅg' ā|potam amuṃ yena potaṃ prerayat' êti› saḥ
yāvan niryāmakān āha tāvat potau samīyatuḥ.
22.5 tataḥ Sāgaradattas taṃ pota|svāminam uktavān
‹yūyaṃ ye vā yatastyā vā tan naḥ pratyucyatām› iti.
ten' ôktaṃ ‹Buddhavarm" âhaṃ vaṇig Rājagṛh'|ālayaḥ›
‹bhavantaḥ ke kuto v" êti› tataḥ so 'pi nyavedayat. atha
kāvya|kathā|pāna|tantrī|gīta|durodaraiḥ
sa|vinodau jagāhāte tau dur|gādhaṃ mah"|ôdadhim.
gatvā ca Kāñcana|dvīpam upānt'|ân|anta|kāñcanau
prāptavantau parāvṛtya samudra|taṭa|pattanam.
atha Sāgaradattena Buddhavarm" êti bhāṣitaḥ
‹prītir naḥ sthiratāṃ yāyād yathā saṃpādyatāṃ tathā.
22.10 bhāryāyāṃ guru|garbhāyāṃ niragaccham ahaṃ gṛhāt
tasyāś ca divasair ebhir jātam anyatarad dvayoḥ.
duhitā cet tato dattā bhavat|putrāya sā mayā
putraś cet tvaṃ tatas tasmai dadyāḥ sva|tanayām› iti.
ten' ôktaṃ ‹mahad āścaryam! iyam eva hi no matiḥ!
atha vā kim ih' āścaryam ekam ev' âvayor vapuḥ.›

THE STUDENT chuckled and said to the ascetic, "Now 22.1
listen to how human effort is more powerful than
destiny.

There lived in Ujjáyani a merchant called Ságara·datta, who had a considerable fortune and a mind as unfathomable as the ocean. Once when he was sailing across the ocean at full speed he saw another boat, its ensign fluttering. No sooner had he told his crew to hurry up and bring the boat
alongside it than the two craft came together. Ságara·dat- 22.5
ta said to its captain, 'Tell us who you are and where you are from.'

He replied, 'I am Buddha·varman, a merchant from Raja·griha,' and asked, 'Who are you, sir, and where are you from?' Ságara·datta told him and then, amusing themselves with poems, stories, drinking, music, song and games of dice, the two of them explored the unfathomable ocean. They went to the Golden Isle, where they acquired a vast amount of gold before returning to a town on the coast. Then Ságara·datta said to Buddha·varman, 'In order to so-
lidify our friendship, let's do the following. When I left 22.10
home, my wife was pregnant. After all this time, she will have given birth to a boy or a girl. If it's a girl, I shall betroth her to your son; if it's a boy, you should betroth your daughter to him.'

He replied, 'That's quite amazing! I had the very same idea! But, then again, there's nothing amazing about it—you and I are one and the same.'

iti tau kṛta|saṃbandhau pariṣvajya parasparam
mahā|mahiṣa|sārthābhyāṃ yathā|sthānam agacchatām.
praṇipatya ca rājānāv Avanti|Magadh'|âdhipau
tat|prayukt'|âti|sat|kārau yayatuḥ sva|gṛhān prati.
22.15 tatra sat|kriyamāṇau ca sat|kurvāṇau ca saṃtatam
bandhubhir brāhmaṇ'|ādīṃś ca gamayām āsatur dinam.
tataḥ Sāgaradattasya paryaṅkam adhitiṣṭhataḥ
utsaṅge dārikā nyastā virājat|kunda|mālikā.
‹kasy' êyaṃ kunda|māl" êti› sa bhāryām anuyuktavān
s" âpi ‹kasy' âparasy' êti› śanair ācaṣṭa lajjitā.
tena c' ôktam idaṃ ‹yādṛg bālikā kunda|mālikā
yayoḥ syād īdṛśaḥ putraḥ pitarau tau sa|putrakau!
tasmād duhitṛ|māt" êti mā gās tvaṃ bhīru bhīrutām
22.20 na Kīrti|jananī Vidyā nindyā bhavitum arhati!› tām ity|ādi
samāśvasya payo|nidhi|samāgamam
Buddhavarma|sakhitvaṃ ca tasyai kathitavān asau.
‹kasy' êyaṃ kunda|māl" êti› tām apṛcchad yataḥ pitā
prasiddhā tasya nāmn" âpi sā tataḥ Kundamālikā.
Buddhavarm" âpi papraccha nir|ālāpāṃ kuṭumbinīm
‹tasmin garbhe tav' ôtpannaṃ yat tan naḥ kathyatām› iti.
atha vāmanam ek'|âkṣaṃ rūkṣaṃ tundila|danturam
lamb'|âuṣṭhaṃ bhugna|pṛṣṭhaṃ ca sā taṃ putraṃ samarpaya
so 'bravīt ‹kiṃ vṛth" âiv' âyaṃ dhṛtaḥ kurubhakas tvayā?
kasmād īkṣaṇikāṃ pṛṣṭvā garbha eva na pātitaḥ?
22.25 yaḥ sa Sāgaradattena saha saṃbandhakaḥ kṛtaḥ
vikṛt'|ākṛtin" ânena sa pretena nirākṛtaḥ.
saṃdiśed yadi nām' âsāv ahaṃ duhitṛvān iti
tadā kiṃ pratisaṃdeśyaṃ may" âhaṃ putravān?› iti

Having thus made a pact, they embraced one another and left for their respective countries with huge caravans of buffalo. They paid their respects to their kings, the rulers of Avánti and Mágadha, and showered them with gifts before going to their homes. Each of them spent the day at 22.15
home receiving hospitality from his family and giving it to brahmins and others.

When Ságara·datta was sitting on his sofa, a baby girl with a magnificent garland of jasmine flowers was put in his lap. He asked his wife, 'Who is the father of this girl garlanded in jasmine?' Embarrassed, she whispered back, 'Who else but you?' He said, 'Lucky the parents who have a son like this little jasmine-garlanded girl! Darling, don't be upset because you are the mother of a daughter. Knowledge is the mother
of Lady Fortune and is not to be scorned!' After reassuring 22.20
her like this, he told her about his meeting on the ocean and his friendship with Buddha·varman. Because her father had asked, 'Who is the father of this girl garlanded in jasmine?' the girl was known by the name Kunda·málika.*

Meanwhile, Buddha·varman had asked his silent wife to tell him what had been produced from her womb. She showed him a stunted, one-eyed, hideous, buck-toothed, droopy-lipped hunchback—their son. He said, 'Why have you needlessly given birth to this freak? Why didn't you
consult a fortune-teller and have an abortion?* The pact 22.25
made with Ságara·datta has been nullified by this deformed ghoul. If he sends a message that he has a daughter, then how can I reply that I have a son?'

bhāryāṃ c' âvocad ‹āgacched dūtaḥ Mālavakād yadi
enaṃ kurubhakaṃ tasmai na kaś cit kathayed› iti.
‹ayaṃ kurubhakaḥ kasmād?› iti yat taṃ pit" âbravīt
vyāharanti sma taṃ paurās tataḥ Kurubhak'|ākhyayā.

ath' âtīte kva cit kāle Buddhavarmā rahaḥ sthitaḥ
lekhaṃ Sāgaradattena prasthāpitam avācayat.
22.30 ‹svasti Rājagṛhe pūjyaṃ Buddhavarmāṇam! ūrjitam
Ujjayanyāḥ pariṣvajya vijñāpayati Sāgaraḥ.
sakhyās te duhitā jātā śreyo|lakṣaṇa|bhūṣaṇā
rūpeṇa sa|dṛśī yasyāḥ pramadā na bhaviṣyati.
tav' âpi yadi bhāryāyāḥ putro jātaḥ śivaṃ tataḥ
kanyā ced vāma|śīlena devena muṣitā vayam.
nir|nimitt" âpi hi prītir yā na saṃbandha|bṛṃhitā
Śrīr utsāha|sa|nāth" êva prayāti sthiratām iti.›

tataḥ sat|kṛtya taṃ dūtam apṛcchad gṛhiṇīṃ vaṇik
‹tasminn evaṃ gate kārye brūhi kiṃ kriyatām?› iti.
22.35 tay" ôktaṃ ‹dvy|aṅgula|prajñā jānīyur vā striyaḥ kiyat
kiṃ tu pṛṣṭ" êti vakṣyāmi pṛṣṭa|dhṛṣṭā hi mādṛśī.
saty'|ân|ṛtaṃ vaṇig|vṛttaṃ parityājyaṃ na vāṇijaiḥ
saha|jaṃ hi tyajan vṛttaṃ dur|vṛtta iti nindyate.
putras tāvat tav' ôtpannas tatra k" ân|ṛta|vāditā
ye punas tasya doṣās tān mithyā bhaṇa guṇā iti.
ākhyāyante hi sarv'|ârthāḥ kṛtrimair eva nāmabhiḥ
āhur «madhurakaṃ» ke cit taṃ tādṛṅ mārakaṃ viṣam.
kārye hi guruṇi prāpte mithyā satyam ap' îṣyate
«Aśvatthāmā hataḥ Drauṇir» ity ūce kiṃ na Pāṇḍavaḥ.

He told his wife, 'If an envoy arrives from Málava, no
one is to mention this freak to him.' Because his father had
said, 'Why did you give birth to this freak?' the townspeople
called the child by the name Freak.

After some time had passed, Buddha·varman, in private,
read a letter from Ságara·datta. 'Hail to the honorable Bud- 22.30
dha·varman in Raja·griha! Ságara of Ujjáyani warmly embraces you and informs you that a daughter has been born
to your friend's wife. She is adorned with most auspicious
markings, and no woman will match her beauty. If your wife
has had a son then we are lucky. If she has had a daughter
then fate has been contrary and robbed us. For a friendship
is groundless if not confirmed by an alliance, just as majesty
protected by power becomes enduring.'

The merchant welcomed the envoy hospitably and then
asked his wife, 'Tell me, what is to be done now that the
matter has come to this?'

She replied, 'Women have tiny brains: what are they to 22.35
know? But you have asked me, so I shall answer; a woman
like me is emboldened by being questioned. A merchant's
vocation involves truth and untruth, and is not to be given
up by him: a man who gives up his birth-given vocation is
reviled as a rogue. You have in fact had a son, so there is no
lie in saying so, but you must falsely describe his faults as
virtues. All things are described by contrived names: there
is that lethal poison which people call "sweetie"! When an
important matter is at stake, it can be wrong to want to be
truthful; did not the Pándavas say that Drona's son Ashvat-
tháman had been killed?* Driven by greed for wealth, men 22.40
like you go to the salty sea—so terrifying with its deathly

22.40 dhana|gardha|parādhīnāḥ kāla|huṃ|kāra|dāruṇe
krīḍā|kamalinīṃ yānti tvad|vidhāḥ kṣāra|sāgare.
sāṃyātrika|pates tasya duhitā bhavato gṛhe
na vin" âmbhodhi|sāreṇa praveṣṭā dhana|rāśinā.
tasmān mā sm' âvamanyadhvam a|dhanyair dur|labhāṃ śriya
kṛcchr'|āyāsa|śata|prāpyāṃ na kṛcchr'|âdhigatām› iti.

ity|ādi|vacanaṃ tasyāḥ ‹s'|ûktam!› ity abhinandya saḥ
dadau Sāgaradattāya saṃdeśaṃ dūta|saṃnidhau.
‹vaktavyaḥ suhṛd asmākam asmākam api dārakaḥ
utpannas tādṛśo yasya kathitā katham ākṛtiḥ.
22.45 atha vā ye guṇāḥ ke 'pi tasya śārīra|mānasāḥ
svayam ev' âsi tān dṛṣṭā kiṃ nas taiḥ kathitair?› iti.
ity|ādi bahu saṃkīrṇam asau saṃdiśya sādaram
dūtaṃ prasthāpayām āsa sa|pātheya|pradeśanam.

evam aṣṭāv atikrāntāḥ samā dūta|samāgamaiḥ
atha dūtaḥ sphuṭ'|ālāpaḥ Buddhavarmāṇam uktavān.
‹ahaṃ Sāgaradattena sa|kalatreṇa bhāṣitaḥ
«jāmātaram an|ālokya mā sm' āgacchad bhavān» iti.
tan mām Ujjayanīṃ yūyaṃ yadi gacchantam icchatha
taṃ me dārakam ākhyāta tadīyāṃś ca guṇān› iti.
22.50 tena tu kṣaṇam utprekṣya samagra|smṛtin" ôditam
‹āste mātula|śāle 'sau Tāmraliptyāṃ paṭhann› iti.

anen' âpi prapañcena catuṣ|pañca samā yayuḥ
atha tri|caturāḥ prāpur dūtāś catura|bhāṣiṇaḥ.
te c' ādṛtam an|ādṛtya Buddhavarmāṇam abruvan
‹āha saṃbandhinī yat tvāṃ sadāraṃ tan niśāmyatām:

roar—as if it were a lotus play-pond! The daughter of that lordly sea trader will not enter your house without bringing a pile of riches from the ocean. So don't spurn a fortune beyond the reach of the poor; it would take a hundred terrible penances to win it, but you've won it with none!'

Praising her words, he said 'Well spoken!' and gave the envoy a message for Ságara·datta. 'Tell my friend that we have had a boy whose appearance can hardly be described.
As for his physical and mental qualities, well, say to him 22.45
that he will see them for himself—there is no point in my telling him them.' After giving him this very ambiguous message, he sent the envoy on his way with money for the journey.

Eight years went by with messengers going back and forth like this. Then an envoy said plainly to Buddha·varman, 'Ságara·datta and his wife have told me that I am not to return without seeing their prospective son-in-law, so if you want me to return to Ujjáyani, show me the boy and these virtues of his.'

Buddha·varman looked at him for a moment and with 22.50
complete composure replied, 'He is staying at his uncle's house in Tamra·lipti, studying.'

Four or five years went by like this. Then three or four voluble envoys arrived. Showing no respect to the respected Buddha·varman, they said, 'Listen to what your friend's wife has to say to you and your wife:

«amī saṃvatsarā yātās trayo|daśa|catur|daśāḥ
ady' âpi ca na paśyāmo vayaṃ jāmātur ākṛtim.
‹dṛṣṭasya kila paṇyasya bhavataḥ kraya|vikrayau
iti loka|pravādo 'yaṃ bhavat" âpi na kiṃ śrutaḥ?
22.55 tvaṃ yac c' āttha ‹paṭhann āste Tāmraliptyām asāv iti›
idam apy ati|dur|baddhaṃ sa|vyājam iva vācakam.
yeṣāṃ karma ca vṛttiś ca vihite pāṭha|pāṭhane
teṣām api paricchinnaḥ pāṭha|kālaḥ kiyān api.
tvadīyena tu putreṇa tyakta|sarv'|ânya|karmaṇā
paṭhatā sakalaṃ janma neyam ity a|samañjasam.
tasmāt krīḍām imāṃ tyaktvā Yama|hāsa|vibhīṣaṇām
atra vā Tāmraliptyāṃ vā dārako darśyatām» iti.›
iti ‹yāvad asau tāvat pūjyair viśramyatām› iti
tān uktvā gṛhiṇīm ūce Buddhavarmā sa|saṃbhramaḥ.
22.60 ‹an|utprekṣy' âiva mandena doṣam āgāminaṃ mayā
dur|āśā|grasta|cittena pramadā|vacanaṃ kṛtam.
tvat|putrasya hi ye doṣāḥ kāṇa|danturat"|ādayaḥ
kālen' âitāvatā teṣāṃ katamaḥ prakṣayaṃ gataḥ?
vardhamāne śarīre hi nijā doṣāḥ śarīriṇām
sutarām upacīyante śarīr'|âvayavā iva.
tasmād darśaya dūtebhyaḥ putraṃ Hara|gaṇ'|ākṛtim
atha vā paṇḍiten' âivam upāyaś cintyatām!› iti.
tayā c' ôktaṃ ‹may" ôpāyaḥ kīdṛśo 'py atra cintitaḥ
yady asau rocate tubhyaṃ tataḥ prastūyatām!› iti.
22.65 ‹ucyatām› iti ten' ôktā karṇe kim api s" âbravīt
so 'pi ‹śobhanam!› ity uktvā tam upāyaṃ prayuktavān.
vivikte brāhmaṇaṃ mitraṃ tat|pratigraha|jīvinam
priy'|ālāpa|śata|prītam ayācata sa|dīnataḥ.
‹Śvetakāka|prasiddhasya mama putrasya ye guṇāḥ
ākāraś ca prakāraś ca yādṛk kiṃ tasya kathyate.

"Thirteen or fourteen years have now gone by and still we have not seen what our prospective son-in-law looks like. Have you not heard the saying that a commodity is
bought or sold only when it has been seen? When you 22.55
announce that he is studying in Tamra·lipti, it seems like a most unlikely and deceitful thing to say. Those whose work and way of life are devoted to learning the Vedas have only a certain amount of time set aside for their studies. That your son could have given up all other activities to spend his entire life studying is unbelievable, so stop playing this game, which is as terrifying as Yama's laugh, and produce the boy, either here or in Tamra·lipti."'

Buddha·varman replied, 'Please rest, gentlemen, until he
arrives,' and then said to his wife in a panic, 'I foolishly did 22.60
not even consider the difficulties that would result when, my mind consumed by despair, I did the bidding of a woman. It's not as if any of your son's faults, such as his being one-eyed or buck-toothed, will have disappeared after all this time: as a body grows, its innate physical flaws, like its limbs, grow even faster. So show the envoys our son, who looks like one of Shiva's troop, or think of a plan, wise one!'

She replied, 'I have thought of a plan of sorts to get us out
of this: if you approve of it, let's carry it out.' He told her to 22.65
tell him and she whispered something in his ear. 'Brilliant!' he said, and put the plan into action.

In an isolated spot he made a request to a brahmin friend of his who lived off his charity and had been won over with a hundred kind words. He said sadly, 'There is no point in describing the qualities, looks and manner of my son, the notorious Shveta·kaka. You know all about my corre-

yac ca Sāgaradattena mayā ca paribhāṣitam
buddhaṃ tad bhavataḥ sarvaṃ saha|dūta|samāgamam.
tena naṣṭena sauhārdaṃ suhṛdā sthiratāṃ naya
atha vā sv'|ârtha ev' âyaṃ tava dhiṅ māṃ mudh"|ākulam!
22.70 ya eṣa bhavataḥ putro Yajñaguptaḥ su|rūpavān
Śruti|Smṛty|ādi|tattva|jñaḥ kalāsu ca viśāradaḥ.
eṣa Sāgaradattasya tanayām upayacchatām
tādṛśīm eva c' ānīya mat|putrāya prayacchatu.
yac ca ratna|suvarṇ'|ādi lapsyate draviṇaṃ tataḥ
tasy' âṃśas tava bhāv" îti› lajjate kathay" ânayā.
evam|ādi sa ten' ôktaḥ s'|ôtsāhaṃ sv'|ârtha|tṛṣṇayā
abravīt ‹tvad|vidheyaiḥ kiṃ mad|vidhaiḥ prārthitair?› iti.
Yajñaguptam ath' āhūya saṃnidhau Buddhavarmaṇaḥ
pitā śrāvitavān etaṃ vṛtt'|ântaṃ pūrva|mantritam.
22.75 ten' ôktaṃ ‹guru|vākyāni yuktimant' îtarāṇi vā
śiśubhir na vicāryāṇi tasmād evaṃ bhavatv!› iti.
tataḥ kati cid āsitvā divasān Buddhavarmaṇā
Yajñaguptaḥ sv|alaṃ|kāraḥ saṃbandhibhyaḥ pradarśitaḥ.
abravīc c' âyam ‹āyātaḥ Tāmraliptyāḥ sa dārakaḥ
ākāraś ca guṇāś c' âsya dṛśyantāṃ yādṛśā› iti.
tatas tair vismitair uktam ‹a|nindyā Kundamālikā
saha bāla|vasantena yad anena sameṣyati.
guṇānāṃ tv etadīyānām anveṣaṇam an|arthakam
dṛśyate nir|guṇānāṃ hi n' ēdṛś" ākāra|dhīratā.
22.80 kiṃ tu nām' âsya duḥ|śliṣṭam ayaṃ Kurubhakaḥ kila
na hi kubja|palāś'|ākhyā pārijātasya yujyate.
atha vā duḥ|śravaṃ nāma śrūyate mahatām api
«kledur» ity ucyate candro «mātari|śv" êti» mārutaḥ!

spondence with Ságara·datta and the arrival of the envoys. Your friend is in trouble: affirm your friendship with him. Anyway, it is in your own self-interest—shame on me for worrying needlessly! Your son Yajña·gupta is handsome, has 22.70
a good knowledge of the scriptures and is skilled in the arts. Let him marry Ságara·datta's daughter, bring her here untouched, and give her to my son. A share of the jewels, gold and other goods that are received will go to you...' His words were making him embarrassed.

On hearing all this, out of self-interest the brahmin said eagerly, 'There's no need for men like you to make entreaties to men like me!' He summoned Yajña·gupta and, in the presence of Buddha·varman, he told him the plan they had discussed. The boy said, 'Children should not question the 22.75
orders of their parents, whether reasonable or not, so I shall do as you say.'

After a few days Buddha·varman produced Yajña·gupta, in his finery, before the prospective in-laws' envoys. He said, 'Here's the boy, back from Tamra·lipti. See how handsome and virtuous he is!'

They were amazed and said, 'Kunda·málika will be perfect when she is united with this youthful personification of spring! There is no need to check his virtues, for looks and composure like his are not seen in people without them. But his name is inappropriate—apparently he is known as 22.80
Freak. It is not right for the tree of paradise to be called the twisted *palásha!* Mind you, even great things can have unpleasant names. The moon is called "tumor" and the wind "mother's dog"! And one cannot take issue with a name

na c' âpi guṇavad|vācya|vācakaṃ paribhūyate
āśrayasya hi daurbalyād āśritaḥ paribhūyate.
sarvathā s'|ârtha|vāhasya prasūt" âdya kuṭumbinī!
yuvayor adya sauhārdaṃ gataṃ kūṭa|stha|nityatām!
tasmād āśutaraṃ gatvā tyakta|nidr"|āśan'|ādikām
vardhayāmo vayaṃ diṣṭyā s'|ârtha|vāha|kuṭumbinīm.
22.85 bhavadbhir api puṇy'|āhe vara|yātrā pravartyatām
na h'|ādānīṃ vivāhasya kaś cid asti vighātakaḥ!›

ity uktvā teṣu yāteṣu sāravat|prābhṛteṣu saḥ
Yajñaguptaṃ varī|kṛtya vara|yātrāṃ vyasarjayat.
yo 'sau Kurubhakas taṃ ca Yajñaguptaṃ cakāra saḥ
saṃjñayā Yajñaguptaṃ tu varaṃ Kurubhakaṃ vaṇik.
kalpita|brāhmaṇ'|ākalpas tula|hem'|âṅgulīyakaḥ
śreṣṭhi|putro 'pi jāmātur āsīt tatra vayasyakaḥ.
vara|yātrā cirāt prāpad Avanti|nagarīṃ tataḥ
utkānti|kānta|vṛtt'|ântāṃ yakṣa|sen" Âlakām iva.
22.90 Siprā|taṭe niviṣṭaṃ ca jany'|āvāsakam āvasat
vasant'|ôpahṛta|śrīka|pur'|ôdyāna|manoharam
tṛṇī|kṛta|Mahākālās tad ahaḥ sa|kutūhalāḥ
a|tṛpta|dṛṣṭayo 'paśyan varaṃ paura|paraṃ|parāḥ.

sa c' âujjayanakair dhūrtair vaṅka|vācaka|paṇḍitaiḥ
veṇu|vīṇā|pravīṇaiś ca kāṃ cid velām ayāpayat.
ath' âsau syālaken' ôktaḥ kalpit'|āhāra|bhūṣiṇā
‹sajjaṃ vaḥ pānam annaṃ ca kim ādhve? bhujyatām› iti.

when it designates something virtuous—only when something is wanting does one take issue with its attributes. The wife of the caravan-leader has acquired another child this very day! Today your friendship with him has been affirmed forever! The caravan-leader's wife has been unable to sleep
or eat: let us quickly go and congratulate her. As for you, sir, 22.85
you must set out with the groom's party on an auspicious day, for now there is no obstacle to the marriage!'

So saying they left with expensive presents, and Buddha·varman sent forth the groom's party, with Yajña·gupta as the groom. The merchant had Freak be Yajña·gupta and the boy called Yajña·gupta be the groom, Freak. Dressed up as a brahmin wearing heavy rings of gold, the merchant's son became the prospective son-in-law's trusty friend. The groom's party eventually arrived in Ujjáini, which was so splendidly decorated and festive that it was like the yakshas' army arriving at Álaka.* They stayed in a house for 22.90
grooms' parties on the banks of the Sipra. It had delightful public gardens to which spring had brought its beauty. Ignoring Maha·kala's temple, that day crowds of curious citizens queued to see the groom, and they could not get their fill of looking at him.

Meanwhile, Yajña·gupta spent some time with inhabitants of Ujjáyani: rogues, vagabonds, preachers, priests and skilled flute and lute players. Then his prospective brother-in-law arranged a feast and said to him, 'Your food and drink are ready. What are you waiting for? Please eat.'

sa c' ân|ek'|āsanām ekām ālokya manu|bhūmikām
‹kena ken' âtra bhoktavyam?› iti syālakam uktavān.
22.95 ten' ôktaṃ ‹jāta|rūp'|âṅgaṃ tuṅga|vidruma|pādakam
yūyaṃ madhyamam adhyādhvam āsanaṃ paṭu|vāsanam.
ye c' âite datta|vetr'|âṅge yuṣmān ubhayataḥ same
ete jyeṣṭha|kaniṣṭhau te syālakāv adhitiṣṭhataḥ.
pārśvayor ubhayor dīrghā yā c' āsana|paraṃ|parā
tav' âsyām upaveṣṭavyaṃ śeṣayā syāla|mālayā.›
varas tu kṣaṇam a|vyūhya syālam etad abhāṣata
‹asmābhiḥ saha yuṣmābhir na kāryaṃ pāna|bhojanam.
gotr'|ācāro 'yam asmākaṃ tāvat pānaṃ na sevyate
bhujyate v" â|paraiḥ sārdhaṃ yāvan na pariṇīyate.
22.100 pariṇīya nivṛttena labdh'|ājñena satā pituḥ
kāryam etan na vā kāryaṃ vin" ādeśād guror› iti.
‹evaṃ nām' êty› anujñātaḥ śvaśureṇa varaḥ pṛthak
durmanāyita|saṃbandhī pūtam āhāram āharat.
yāte yāme ca yāminyā garjad|vāditra|maṇḍalaḥ
gṛhaṃ Sāgaradattasya pariṇetum agād asau.
tatr' ālambitavān vadhvāḥ sphurac|cāmīkaraṃ karam
smaran guru|vaco dhairyān nir|vikāra|karo varaḥ.
sa c' âtr' âgniṃ parikramya caṇḍa|śūl'|ākulaḥ kila
pāṇibhyām udaraṃ dhṛtvā mumoha ca papāta ca.
22.105 praśānt'|ôcchvāsa|niḥ|śvāse tasmin saṃmīlit'|ēkṣaṇe
mūkit'|ôddāma|dhūryeṇa kranditena vijṛmbhitam.

However when he saw but one dining room and several seats, he asked his prospective brother-in-law, 'Who is going to be eating here?'

He replied, 'You are to sit in the middle on the golden 22.95
chair with the long coral legs and bright covering. Your eldest and youngest prospective brothers-in-law will be sitting on those cane chairs set up on either side of yours. The rest of your garland of brothers-in-law will sit on that long line of chairs to both sides.'

Without pausing to think, the groom, however, said to his prospective brother-in-law, 'I cannot eat or drink with you. Our family's custom is that we cannot eat or drink
with others until we are married. After I am married and 22.100
have returned with my father's permission I will be able to do so; I cannot do it without the consent of my parents.'

His father-in-law consented, saying, 'So be it,' and the groom, to the chagrin of his bride's family, ate his pure food apart from them.

When the night was over, he went with an entourage of noisy musicians to Ságara·datta's house to be married. Once there, the groom took the bride's hand, which was glittering with gold. Sticking to his father's instructions, he had not adorned his hand. After ritually circumambulating the fire he seemed to be overcome by an acute pain: he held
his stomach with his hands, passed out and collapsed. His 22.105
breathing stopped, his eyes closed and he gave forth a cry that would have silenced an untamed bull.

śvaśrūr jāmātaraṃ dṛṣṭvā tāḍit'|ôraḥ|śirās tataḥ
uccair bhartṛ|sam'|âvasthām ākrośat Kundamālikām.
‹hā! hat" âsi! vinaṣṭ" âsi! dhik tvāṃ pracchanna|rākṣasīm
jita|Pradyumna|rūpo 'yaṃ patir utsādito yayā!
tvam eva na mṛtā kasmād ahaṃ vā duḥkha|bhāginī
yayā tvaṃ sakalaṃ janma draṣṭavy" â|mṛtayā mṛtā.
kathaṃ jīvati sā yā strī bāl" âiva mṛta|bhartṛkā?
dūr'|ântara|gariṣṭho hi nārīṇāṃ jīvitāt patiḥ!
22.110 yā ca mātā sutām iṣṭāṃ cārutā|śīla|śālinīm
śaktā vidhavikāṃ draṣṭuṃ jyeṣṭhā Kālasya sā svasā!›
ity|ādi vilapanty eva sā ca niś|ceṣṭan" âbhavat
hṛday'|ôdara|saṃdhiś ca jāmātuḥ spanditaḥ śanaiḥ.
tataḥ paura|samūhasya jāmātari tathā|vidhe
harṣa|hās'|âṭṭa|hāsānām āsīn n' ântaram ambare.
śanakaiś ca sa niḥ|śvasya jihma|sphurita|pakṣmaṇī
udamīlayad ā|tāmre locane guru|tārake.
tataḥ Sāgaradattena kṛtas tādṛṅ mah"|ôtsavaḥ
vṛddhatā|labdha|putreṇa yo nṛpeṇ' âpi duṣ|karaḥ.
22.115 ‹kim etad?› iti pṛṣṭaś ca sa vaidyaiḥ pratyuvāca tān
‹āmāśaya|gataṃ śūlaṃ bādhate guru mām› iti.
atha vāsa|gṛha|sthasya vaidyā jāmātur ādṛtāḥ
śūlasy' āma|nidānasya kṛtavantaś cikitsitam.
śūlair āyāsyamānasya labdha|nidrasya c' ântare
tasya jāgrad|vadhūkasya katham apy agaman niśā.

When she saw her son-in-law, his mother-in-law beat her chest and head, and screamed at Kunda·málika, who was in the same state as her husband, 'Aah! You are done for! You are finished! Shame on you, you demoness in disguise: your husband is more handsome than the god of love and you have done him in! Why aren't you dead? And why not me, too? I shall have to share in this suffering and see you for the rest of my life, me alive and you dead! When a woman's husband dies while she is still just a girl, how can she live? For women, a husband is far more important than life! A 22.110
mother who can bear to see her dear daughter, a beautiful and virtuous girl, as a widow, is Death's elder sister!'

As she was ranting like this, she, too, fell unconscious. At the same moment her son-in-law's chest throbbed gently and as a result joyous laughs and cheers from the assembled townspeople filled the air. He slowly started to breathe and, squinting, he opened his torpid bloodshot eyes. Then Sá-gara·datta held a celebration so great that it would have been hard even for a king who had obtained a son in his dotage to have matched it. When the doctors asked the 22.115
groom what was the matter, he replied, 'I had a severe attack of indigestion.' He went to his bedroom and the attentive doctors made him a cure for the indigestion. Suffering from stabbing pains and occasionally getting some sleep while his bride kept vigil over him, he somehow got through the night.

nāgar"|âti|viṣā|mustā|kvatha|pān'|âvatarpitaḥ
a|sneh'|âlpatar'|āhāraḥ so 'bhavat praty|ahaḥ kṛśaḥ.
svayaṃ bheṣaja|peṣ'|ādi|vyāpṛtā Kundamālikā
vismṛt" êva vadhū|lajjāṃ bhartṛ|māndya|bhay'|āturā.
22.120 tataḥ patim upāsīnāṃ sa kubjaḥ Kundamālikām
aṅgeṣu bhaya|sann'|âṅgīṃ kurvan kelīṃ kil' âspṛśat.
abravīc ca ‹vimuñc' âinaṃ kirāṭam a|paṭuṃ viṭam
devatā|gurubhir dattaṃ kāntaṃ toṣaya mām› iti.
ath' ôtthāya tataḥ sthānād bhartṛ|śayyā|tiras|kṛtā
‹k" êyaṃ kelir an|āry" êti› vadhūr bhartāram abravīt.
sa tāṃ sa|smitam āha sma ‹mā sma grāmeyikā bhava!
kā hi nāgarikaṃ|manyā hāsyāt naṭa|baṭos traset?
dhaninām īdṛśāḥ kṣudrāḥ prāyo vācālatā|phalāḥ
na hi mūkaṃ śukaṃ kaś cic ciraṃ dharati pañjare.
22.125 tasmāt krīḍanakād asmād a|baddha|bhāṣamāṇakāt
hasataḥ spṛśataś c' âṅgaṃ bhīru mā vitrasīr› iti.
tena sā bodhit" âpy evaṃ sad|ācāra|kul'|ôdbhavā
caṇḍābhir ghaṭa|dāsībhis taṃ bhuktaṃ nirabhartsayat.
āsīc ca Yajñaguptasya ‹yāvad ev' âiṣas mūḍhakaḥ
rahasyaṃ na bhinatty etat tāvan nyāyyam ito gatam.›
taṃ kadā cid abhāṣanta bhiṣajo niṣ|phala|kriyāḥ
‹pān'|āhāra|vihāreṣu kim icchati bhavān?› iti.
tataḥ kṣāmatar'|ālāpas tān avocac cirād asau
‹pitarau draṣṭum icchāmi priya|putrau priyāv iti.›

Drinking decoctions of *nágara*, *atívisha* and *musta*, and eating small amounts of plain food, he grew thinner every day. Kunda·málika was herself involved in preparing the medicines, and she was so overcome with worry for her husband's debilitated condition that she seemed to forget her bridal bashfulness.

While Kunda·málika was tending to her husband, the 22.120
hunchback playfully touched her body, which had grown weak with worry. He said, 'Leave this merchant—he's boorish and dissolute—and make me happy. I am your beloved and have been betrothed by the gods and my parents.'

Getting up from her seat and concealing herself behind her husband's bed, the bride said to her husband, 'What is this unseemly joke?'

With a smile he said to her, 'Don't be so provincial! What woman who considers herself sophisticated would be worried by the pranks of a fool? Rich people often keep wretches like him for their chatter: no one keeps a dumb parrot in a cage for long. So, my darling, don't be frightened of this 22.125
babbling buffoon when he jokes and touches your body.'

Despite being given this advice, the girl was from a respectable family and harangued the hunchback as a man who frequented sluttish strumpets.

Yajña·gupta said to himself, 'We should leave here before this idiot gives away our secret.'

When the doctors, whose remedies had had no effect, asked him what he wanted in the way of food, drink and entertainment, after a long pause, he said to them in a very faint voice 'I want to see my parents. They love me and I love them.'

22.130 atha Sāgaradattāya vaidyair evaṃ niveditam
‹evaṃ vadati jāmātā tac ca pratividhīyatām.
yad yad vaidyena kartavyam āmāśaya|cikitsitam
kṛtam apy a|kṛtaṃ tat tad etasmiñ jātam āture.
sva|deśāya tu yāto 'yaṃ bhaved api nir|āmayaḥ
jagat|prasiddhi|siddhaṃ hi suhṛd|darśanam auṣadham.›
dhātrī|pradhāna|parivāra|camū|sa|nāthām
ambhodhi|sāra|dhana|hāra|mah"|ôṣṭra|yūthām
śyāmāṃ niśām iva kṛśena tuṣāra|bhāsā
prāsthāpayat saha vareṇa vaṇik tanūjām.
prayāṇakaiś ca yāvadbhir agād Rājagṛhaṃ varaḥ
śreṣṭhī ca dvi|guṇān prītān prāhiṇot paricārakān.
22.135 ‹anya|jāmātṛ|vārttābhyāṃ dvābhyāṃ dvābhyāṃ prayāṇakāt
nivartitavyaṃ yuṣmābhir› iti c' âsāv uvāca tān.
prathamād vāsakād yau ca nivṛttau paricārakau
śreṣṭhine kathitaṃ tābhyāṃ ‹varaḥ sva|stho manāg› iti.
yathā yathā ca yāti sma vāsakān uttar'|ôttarān
śanakaiḥ śanakair māndyam atyajat sa tathā tathā.
anyāt tu vāsakād anyau nivṛtta|paricārakau
varaṃ Sāgaradattāya hṛṣṭa|puṣṭ'|âṅgam ākhyatām.
ath' âsāv iti harṣ'|ândhas tyakta|pātra|parīkṣaṇaḥ
ā|catur|veda|caṇḍālaṃ vitatāra nidhīn api.
22.140 kṛtrimas tu varaḥ prātas tyakta|jāmātṛ|ḍambaraḥ
gṛhīta|brāhmaṇ'|ākalpaḥ prasthitaḥ pada|gaḥ pathi.
veṣeṇ' āgantunā muktaḥ sa reje nijayā śriyā
s'|êndra|cāpa|taḍid|dāmnā ghanen' êva niśā|karaḥ.

Then the doctors informed Ságara·datta of his son-in-law's request and said to him, 'You must make arrangements for this to happen. Even though everything that can be done by a doctor to cure indigestion has been done, it has had no effect on his illness. But he might recover if he goes to his own country—the sight of one's friends is renowned throughout the world as a medicine.' 22.130

In the care of an army of servants headed by a nurse, and with a train of huge camels bearing the wealth of the ocean, the merchant sent forth his daughter with the groom and they looked like a dark night with a thin sliver of a moon.

The merchant sent twice as many trusty servants as there were stages on the groom's journey to Raja·griha. He told 22.135
them, 'At each stage two of you are to return with the latest news of my son-in-law.'

The two servants that returned from the first halt told the merchant that the groom was a little better. With each subsequent halt that he reached, he slowly shook off more of his debility. When the last two servants returned from the last halt, they told Ságara·datta that the groom was hale and hearty. At this, he was blinded by joy, and with no regard for the worthiness of the recipients he distributed his riches to everyone from learned brahmins to outcastes.

In the morning, however, the fake groom gave up his pretense of being a son-in-law, put on the clothes of a brahmin and set off along the road on foot. Once out of his uncustomary costume, he shone with his own innate splendor, like the moon emerging from a cloud wreathed in rainbows and lightning. 22.140

vara|pravahaṇaṃ tac ca Kundamālikay" āsthitam
āruroha var'|ākāraḥ prītaḥ Kurubhakaḥ khalaḥ.
taṃ dṛṣṭvā vikṛt'|ākāraṃ jita|Śaṃkara|kiṃkaram
pravidhūya vadhūr aṅgaṃ locane samamīlayat.

vadhū|varam atha draṣṭuṃ sakalā sa|kutūhalā
niragāt tyakta|kartavyā javanā janatā purāt.
22.145 tau ca dur|baddha|sambandhau muktā|loha|guḍāv iva
dṛṣṭvā dhūta|karaiḥ paurair adhikṣiptaḥ Prajāpatiḥ.
‹kāma|cāreṇa Kāmo 'pi tāvan n' âiva praśasyate
kiṃ punar yaḥ sad|ācāraḥ sarga|hetur bhavādṛśaḥ?
sarvathā vāma|śīlānāṃ tvam eva param'|ēśvaraḥ
yen' âitāv apsaraḥ|pretau dur|yojyau yojitāv iti.›

Buddhavarm" âpi niryāya sarva|śreṇi|puraḥ|saraḥ
vadhūm abhyanayat kāntyā jita|rāja|gṛhaṃ gṛham.
aṅka|stha|vadhukas tatra sa c' âvocat kuṭumbinīm
‹iyam ev' âstu te putras tanayā ca vadhūr!› iti.
22.150 manyamāneṣu māneṣu vandamāneṣu bandiṣu
naṭ'|ādiṣu ca nṛtyatsu s'|ârkaṃ tad agamad dinam.

atha cakṣur|manaḥ|kāntam āvāsaṃ Kundamālikā
Yajñagupta|vayasyena kubjakena sah' āviśat.
tatra śayyā|samīpa|stham āsthitā citram āsanam
vadhūr vara|vayasyo 'pi tad|an|antaram unnatam.
cintayantas tatas tatra sarve moh'|ândha|mānasāḥ
a|mūl'|âgrāṇi pattrāṇi lilikhur namit'|ānanāḥ.

Dressed as a groom and delighted, the vile Freak climbed aboard the groom's carriage, where Kunda·málika was sitting. When the bride saw him looking worse than one of Shiva's troop with his deformed appearance, she shuddered and shut her eyes.

Everyone had abandoned their work and hurried out of the town, curious to see the married couple. When they saw 22.145
the ill-matched pair, who were like a pearl and a lump of iron, the townspeople wrung their hands and denounced the creator. 'Not even the god of love, who behaves as he wishes, could be praised for this; how much less someone like you, the source of creation, who is meant to be well behaved? You really are the patron deity of the contrary—these two, a heavenly damsel and a ghoul, are unjoinable but you have joined them!'

Buddha·varman himself had come out, escorted by all the members of his guild. He led the bride to his house, which surpassed a king's palace in beauty. Once there, while embracing the bride, he said to his wife, 'May this girl be both
a son and a daughter to you!' With rites of honor being cel- 22.150
ebrated, bards singing, and actors and dancers performing, the day went with the sun.

Then Kunda·málika entered a beautiful and enchanting bedroom with the hunchback and his friend Yajña·gupta. The bride sat on a brightly coloured chair next to the bed, and the groom and his friend sat on a high seat next to it. Lost in thought, their minds numbed with confusion, they all lowered their heads and doodled on the floor. In this delicate situation Kunda·málika said to herself, 'Why won't

asminn acintayat kaṣṭe vṛtt'|ânte Kundamālikā
‹api nām' âiṣa māṃ muktvā brāhmaṇo na vrajed?› iti.
22.155 āsīt Kurubhakasy' âpi vivikte rantum icchataḥ
‹api nām' âiṣa niryāyād bahir vāsa|gṛhād?› iti.

Yajñaguptas tayor buddhvā tat|kāl'|ôcitam iṅgitam
gamanaṃ c' ātmanaḥ śreyas tato nirgantum aihata.

sā tam ucchalitaṃ dṛṣṭvā sa|viṣādam abhāṣata
‹dārān āpad|gatān muktvā prasthitaḥ kva bhavān?› iti.

ten' ôktaṃ ‹yasya dārās tvaṃ vidhātrā parikalpitā
«āpann" âsm' îti» mā vocas tiṣṭhantī tasya saṃnidhau.
tat samālabhatām eṣa tvad|āliṅgana|cumbanam
vayaṃ tu khara|dharmāṇo bhāra|mātrasya bhāginaḥ.›
22.160 ittham uktvā sa c' ânyābhiḥ preṣyābhiḥ saha niryayau
an|icchām aicchad ākraṣṭuṃ grāmyaḥ Kurubhakaś ca tām.
tatas tāratar'|ārāvaiḥ śroṇī|caraṇa|bhūṣaṇaiḥ
vyāharant" îva taṃ vipraṃ nirjagāma javena sā.
matta|pramatta|paure ca nṛtyad|bhṛtya|nir|antare
Yajñaguptas tayā n' âiva dṛṣṭas tatra gṛh'|âṅgaṇe.
‹eṣo yāty! eṣa yāt' îti› sādṛśya|bhrānti|vañcitā
yaṃ kaṃ cid api sā yāntam anvayāsīt tad|āśayā.
rabhasena ca niryāya rathyā|patham avātarat
Hiṇḍī|vāditra|bhītā ca kumbha|kāra|kuṭī|gamāt.
22.165 tatra Kāpālikaṃ dṛṣṭvā suṣuptaṃ mada|mūrchayā
‹su|śliṣṭā hanta rakṣ" êyam› ity adhyavasitaṃ tayā.
ath' ābharaṇam unmucya mahā|sāraṃ śarīrataḥ

this brahmin leave me and go away?' Freak was also wanting 22.155
to have some fun in private and said to himself, 'Why won't this fellow get out of the bedroom?'

Yajña·gupta had noticed their subtle and timely hints, and, deciding that it would be best for him to go, he tried to leave.

When she saw him jump up, the girl said anxiously, 'Where are you going, leaving your wife in this terrible situation?'

He replied, 'You mustn't say that you are in a terrible situation when you are sitting next to the man whose wife fate has destined you to be! Let him receive your embraces and kisses; as for me, I am subject to a cruel law and my lot is but a burden.'

After saying this, he left with the rest of the servant girls. 22.160
The brutish Freak tried to grab the unwilling girl. Seeming to call after the brahmin with the shrill cries of the ornaments on her hips and ankles, she ran out. The courtyard was full of excited drunken townspeople and dancing servants, and she could not find Yajña·gupta there. Thinking, 'There he goes! There he goes!' she was caught out by someone who looked like him, and went after whoever it was in the hope that it was him. Frightened by the hymns to Durga coming from a potter's hut, she rushed out onto
the street. Seeing a Kapálika ascetic there, fast asleep in a 22.165
drunken stupor, she decided, 'Ah! That's the perfect way to protect myself!' Then she took off her expensive jewelry and, behaving like a true merchant, tied it securely in her robe. She appropriated the Kapálika's accoutrements—his

abhyasta|vaṇig|ācārā babandha dṛḍham ambare.
khaṭv'|âṅg'|ādikam ādāya Kāpālika|paricchadam
ghūrṇamānā madād grāmaṃ bāhyaṃ niragamat purāt.
tatra ca brāhmaṇī kā cit tayā śveta|śiro|ruhā
sva|gṛh'|âlindak'|āsīnā dṛṣṭā karpāsa|karttrikā.
ekākiny eva sā daivaṃ ninditvā karuṇa|svanā
‹dhik kṣudraṃ Buddhavarmāṇam!› iti sa|krodham abravīt.
22.170 tām apṛcchad asāv ‹ārye nirvyāja|guṇa|śālinaḥ
sādhoḥ kiṃ duṣ|kṛtaṃ tasya nindyate yad asāv› iti.
tay" ôktam ‹ati|mugdho vā dhūrto vā Bhagavann asi
tadīyaṃ duṣ|kṛtaṃ yena prakāśam api na śrutam.
atha vā śroṣyati bhavān anyatas tat su|duḥ|śravam
mādṛśī tu na śakt" âiva vaktuṃ prakṛti|kātarā.›
yāvac c' êdam asāv āha tāvad uccaistarāṃ pure
ḍiṇḍima|dhvani|saṃbhinnā paribabhrāma ghoṣaṇā.
‹aho rāja|samādeśo yo vadhūṃ Buddhavarmaṇaḥ
nāgaraḥ kaś cid ācaṣṭe sa dāridryeṇa mucyate.
22.175 yaḥ punaḥ sva|gṛhe mohāt pracchādayati taṃ nṛpaḥ
pāṭayaty a|dhanaṃ kṛtvā dāruṇaiḥ krakacair› iti.
ath' êdaṃ brāhmaṇī śrutvā netr'|âmbu|plāvit'|ānanā
paritoṣa|parādhīnā jahāsa ca ruroda ca.
abravīc ca ‹kim āścaryaṃ yad Ujjayaniko janaḥ
n' âtisaṃdhīyate dhūrtair Mūladeva|samair iti.
sādhu sādhu mahā|prājñe su|jāte Kundamālike
yayā sa|kubjakaḥ pāpaḥ Buddhavarm" âtisaṃdhitaḥ!
yathā Rājagṛhaṃ putri tvay" êdaṃ sukham āsitam
Yajñaguptena saṃgamya tvay" âpi sthīyatāṃ tathā.›

skull-staff and so forth—and, with a drunken stagger, went to a village outside the town.*

She saw a white-haired brahmin lady there sitting on the veranda of her house spinning cotton. She was completely alone and cursing fate in a sad voice. Then she said angrily, 'Shame on that wretch Buddha·varman!'

Kunda·málika asked her, 'Madam, he is a fine man, hon- 22.170
est and virtuous. What wrong has he done that he is to be cursed like this?'

She replied, 'Your Holiness must either be very stupid or an impostor not to have heard about his wrongdoing—everyone knows about it. But you will have to hear it from someone else. A naturally timid lady like me cannot bear to tell such a terrible tale.'

No sooner had she said this than a proclamation noisily rang out around the town to the sound of drums: 'Hear ye! The king decrees that any citizen reporting the whereabouts of Buddha·varman's daughter-in-law will be freed
from poverty. But if anyone is foolish enough to hide her 22.175
in their house, the king will confiscate their property and have them chopped up with sharp saws!'

When she heard this, the brahmin lady was overcome with joy; her face bathed in tears, she both laughed and cried. She said, 'It's not surprising that the people of Ujjáyani won't let themselves be cheated by these villains—they are as bad as Mula·deva. Well done, Kunda·málika! Well done, you noble and clever girl, for having tricked the wicked Buddha·varman and his hunchback! You must stay, my girl, so that you can live happily in Raja·griha together with Yajña·gupta.'

22.180 ity|ādi bruvatīṃ śrutvā cintayām āsa tām asau
‹niṣ|kāraṇa|janany eṣā gopāyiṣyati mām› iti.
śanaiś c' âkathayat tasyai vṛttaṃ vṛtt'|ântam ātmanaḥ
gāḍham āliṅgya sā c' âināṃ prītā prāveśayad gṛham.
avatārya ca tatr' âsyās tāṃ Kāpālika|taṇḍikām
tad|bhāra|parikhinnāni gātrāṇi paryavāhayat.
abhyajya snapayitvā ca sukh'|ôṣṇaiḥ salilair asau
sthūla|cela|dal'|āstīrṇe śayane samaveśayat.
paridhāya ca tām eva bībhatsām asthi|śṛṅkhalām
bhrāmyat saṃbhrānta|pauraṃ tat sā prātaḥ prāviśat puram.
22.185 ‹kiṃ|nimittam ayaṃ lokaḥ saṃcaraty ākul'|ākulaḥ?›
iti pṛṣṭavatī kaṃ cid asau pura|nivāsinam.
ten' ôktam ‹iha ca sthāne śreṣṭhinaḥ Buddhavarmaṇaḥ
putraḥ Kurubhako nāma sva|nāma|vikṛt'|ākṛtiḥ.
tasmai c' ânyena ṣaṇḍhena pariṇīya dvi|janmanā
śailūṣeṇ' êva lubdhena sva|bhāryā pratipāditā.
sā taṃ Kurubhakaṃ tyaktvā mārgayantī ca taṃ dvi|jam
pradoṣe kv' âpy apakrāntā lokas ten' âyam ākulaḥ.›
tatas tatas tayā śrutvā s'|ântaḥ|smitam udāhṛtam
‹bhadra ṣaṇḍhasya tasy' āśu gṛhaṃ nayata mām› iti.
22.190 tatas tan|madhur'|ālāpa|rakta|paura|puraḥ|sarā
Yajñagupta|gṛhaṃ prāpad brahma|nirghoṣa|bhūṣaṇam.
tatra c' âgni|gṛha|dvāri vyākhyāna|karaṇ'|ākulam
s'|ântevāsinam āsīnaṃ Yajñaguptaṃ dadarśa sā.
tato nidhāya khaṭv'|âṅgaṃ racita|svastik'|āsanā
‹ko 'yaṃ vyākhyāyate grantha?› ity apṛcchat sa|matsarā.

When she heard her say all this, Kunda·málika thought, 22.180
'This selfless lady will hide me.'

She quietly told her what had happened to her and the delighted lady gave her a hug and ushered her into her house. Once inside, she had her take off her Kapálika garb. Her limbs were weary from wearing it and she massaged them. Then she rubbed her with oil, washed it off with pleasantly warm water and made her lie down on a bed covered with a thick quilt.

The next morning, Kunda·málika put on the hideous bone necklace and went into the town, where the people
were running about excitedly. She asked one of the towns- 22.185
people why everyone was going around in such a frenzy. He replied, 'The head of the merchants here, Buddha·varman, has a son called Freak who is as disfigured as his name suggests. Some impotent brahmin got married and then, as if he were an actor, the greedy fellow gave his own wife to Freak. Yesterday evening she left Freak and went off somewhere to look for the brahmin. That is why everyone is so excited.'

When she heard this she smiled inwardly and said, 'Good man, quickly, take me to the impotent brahmin's house.'
The citizen was charmed by her courteous words and he 22.190
accompanied her to Yajña·gupta's house, which was adorned with the sounds of Vedic chants. She saw Yajña·gupta sitting with his pupils at the door to the fire sanctuary, busy giving an explanation. She put down her skull-staff and sat down cross-legged in a yogic posture. Then she asked aggressively, 'What is the book that is being explained?'

so 'bravīd ‹Bhagavann eṣā Mānavī dharma|saṃhitā
etasyāṃ cāturāśramyaṃ cāturvarṇyaṃ ca varṇyate.›
tay" ôktaṃ ‹kim alīkena? na h' îyaṃ dharma|saṃhitā
lokāyatam idaṃ manye nir|maryāda|jana|priyam.
22.195 kva dharma|saṃhitā kv' êdam a|dharma|caritaṃ tava?
na hi vaidyaḥ sva|śāstra|jñaḥ kuṣṭhī māṃsaṃ niṣevate.
vyācakhyānena vipreṇa Mānavīṃ dharma|saṃhitām
vyatikrānta|sa|varṇena pariṇītā varā tvayā.
sā c' â|khaṇḍa|śarīreṇa su|rūpeṇa kalā|vidā
yūnā ca kāṇa|kuṇṭhāya matkuṇāya kil' ārpitā.
tan Māheśvara pṛcchāmi kim artham idam īdṛśam
tvayā kṛtam a|kartavyaṃ yuktaṃ cet kathyatām› iti.
so 'bravīd ‹Bhagavan yuktam a|yuktaṃ vā bhavatv idam
vidheyair a|vikāry'|ârthād guru|vākyād anuṣṭhitam.
22.200 tathā hi Jāmadagnyena dur|laṅghyād vacanāt pituḥ
mātuḥ kṛttaṃ śiras tatra kim āha Bhagavān?› iti.
tay" ôktaṃ ‹divya|vṛtt'|ântā n' â|divyasya nidarśanam
na hi «Rudreṇa pīt" êti» pibanti brāhmaṇāḥ surām.
na ca prājñena kartavyaṃ sarvam eva guror vacaḥ
guruḥ kiṃ nāma na brūyād duḥkha|krodh'|ādi|bādhitaḥ?
tīvra|śūl'|ātura|śirāḥ putraṃ brūyāt pitā yadi
«śiro me chinddhi putr' êti» kiṃ kāryaṃ tena tat tathā.
yac ca mātuḥ śiraḥ kṛttaṃ Rāmeṇa vacanāt pituḥ
tat tasy' âiva prabhāvena sadyaḥ saṃghaṭitaṃ punaḥ.
22.205 tvayā tu guru|vākyena kṛt'|â|kartavya|karmaṇā
divya|prabhāva|hīnena tat kathaṃ kāryam anyathā?

He replied, 'Your Holiness, this is Manu's treatise on law. The four life stages and four castes are being described in it.'

She said, 'Why are you lying? This is no treatise on law. I think it's about materialism, the favorite of people with no morals. How can this be a treatise on law when you behave 22.195
so lawlessly? A doctor who knows medicine would not eat meat if he had leprosy. You are a brahmin and have been explaining Manu's treatise on law, yet you committed a crime against your caste when you married your bride. Apparently she has been given by an able-bodied, handsome, talented and healthy man to a one-eyed, cretinous dwarf. So, follower of Shiva, I want to know why you committed such a crime. If there was a reason for it, then let it be told!'

He replied, 'Your Holiness, justified or not, let it be. Those who serve obey their masters' unchangeable orders. Did not Párashu·rama cut off his mother's head at the invi- 22.200
olable order of his father? What does Your Holiness say to that?'

She replied, 'Those who are not divine should not use the behavior of the divine as an example: the fact that Rudra drank alcohol is no reason for brahmins to drink it. And a wise man should not do everything his master tells him. A master troubled by sadness or anger could say anything. If a father with a splitting headache told his son to cut off his head, should the boy do just that? And when Párashu·rama cut off his mother's head at his father's command, he had the power to replace it immediately. At your master's command 22.205
you did something that should not have been done, but you do not have divine power, so how are you to undo it? Now you shall have to stay married to that lovely girl. You have

idānīm api tām eva bhavān vineṣyati priyām
guru|vākyaṃ kṛtaṃ pūrvaṃ yad gataṃ gatam eva tat!›

tasyām ity|ukta|vākyāyām asāv āsīn nir|uttaraḥ
vādi|vācye hi nir|doṣe kiṃ vācyaṃ prativādinaḥ?
evaṃ ca ciram āsitvā nabho|madhya|gate ravau
bhikṣā|vel"|âpadeśena tam āmantry' ôccacāla sā.

tena c' ôktā ‹svam ev' êdam ṛddhimac ca gṛhaṃ tava
ten' âtr' âiva sad" āhāraṃ karotu Bhagavān› iti.

22.210 tatas tayā vihasy' ôktaṃ ‹Nāstikasya bhavādṛśaḥ
a|saṃbhojyam a|bhojyatvād annaṃ Kāpālikair api.
kṛtv" âpi tu mahat pāpaṃ paścāt|tāpaṃ karoti yaḥ
punaḥ|saṃvaraṇaṃ c' âsau yāti bhojy'|ânnatām› iti.

evam|ādi tam uktv" âsau gatvā ca brāhmaṇī|gṛham
apanīya ca taṃ veṣam ācaran majjan'|ādikam.
taṃ ca Kāpālikaṃ kalpaṃ sāyam ādāya sā punaḥ
Yajñagupta|gṛhaṃ gatvā dina|śeṣam ayāpayat.
anna|kālaṃ ca rātriṃ ca nayantī brāhmaṇī|gṛhe
śeṣaṃ ca Yajñaguptasya s" ânayad divasān bahūn.

22.215 kadā cic c' âbhavat tasyās ‹tṛṣṇā|vaśa|ga|cetasā
a|kāryam idam etena kṛtaṃ karma dvi|janmanā.
tena śakyo may" ānetum ayaṃ darśita|tṛṣṇayā
kārye hi su|labh'|ôpāye na muhyanti su|medhasaḥ.›

atha muktā|latām ekām aruṇāṃ taral'|âṃśubhiḥ
asau vikrāpayām āsa tayā brāhmaṇa|vṛddhayā.
hema|rūpyaṃ ca tan|mūlyam āhat'|ân|āhataṃ śuci
tāmra|kumbha|yuga|nyastaṃ sīm'|ânte nihitaṃ tayā.
atha dhātu|kriyā|vāda|nidhi|vād'|āśrayair asau

already carried out your master's instructions; what's done is done!'

When she said this, he had no answer: when a disputant's argument is faultless, what is there for his opponent to say? She sat there for a long time, until the sun reached the middle of the sky, and then, under the pretext that it was time to go begging, she took her leave and stood up.

He said to her, 'These riches and this sumptuous house are yours: Your Holiness may eat here every day.'

She laughed and said, 'Even Kapálikas cannot eat food 22.210
from an atheist like you: it's forbidden. But if a man does penance after committing a heinous sin, he rehabilitates himself and his food becomes edible.'

After saying all this to him, she went to the brahmin lady's house, removed her disguise and took a bath. At dusk she dressed as a Kapálika again and went to Yajña·gupta's house, where she spent the rest of the evening. For several days she spent mealtimes and nights at the brahmin lady's house and the rest of the time at Yajña·gupta's.

One day she said to herself, 'It was because his mind 22.215
was swayed by greed that the brahmin did this evil deed. Therefore it should be possible for me to take him in by appealing to his greed. When there is an easy way to do something, clever people do not make mistakes.'

So she had the old brahmin lady sell a pearl necklace of hers that glowed red from the rays of the gems inlaid in it. She put the sparkling gold and silver that she got for it, both minted and unstruck, in a pair of copper pots and buried them at the village boundary. Then, after sitting with Yajña·gupta for a long time discussing the sciences of metallurgy

ālāpaiś ciram āsitvā Yajñaguptam abhāṣata:
22.220 ‹«eka|rātraṃ vased grāme pañca|rātraṃ muniḥ pure»
iti pravrajit'|ācāram etaṃ veda bhavān iti.
etāvantam ahaṃ kālaṃ vatsa Rāja|gṛhe sthitaḥ
tyakta|pravrajit'|ācāras tad bhavat|prīti|vañcitaḥ.
gṛhiṇo 'pi hi sīdanti sneha|śṛṅkhala|yantritāḥ
viraktāḥ sva|śarīre 'pi niḥ|saṅgāḥ kiṃ mumukṣavaḥ?
tena Vārāṇasīṃ gantum aham icchāmi saṃprati
tīrtha|darśana|tantrā hi Somasiddhānta|vādinaḥ.
anyac c' âhaṃ vijānāmi dāridrya|vyādhi|vaidyakam
Mahākāla|mataṃ nāma nidhān'|ôtpāṭan'|āgamam.
22.225 mayā ca dhyāna|khinnena van'|ânte parisarpatā
ujjvalair lakṣitaś cihnaiḥ ken' âpi nihito nidhiḥ.
yadi c' âsti mayi prītis tataḥ svīkriyatām asau
sa|phalāḥ khalu saṃparkāḥ sādhubhis tvādṛśair› iti.

Yajñaguptas tam utkhāya nidhiṃ tat sahitas tataḥ
sa|dhīr'|āptatara|chāttraḥ pracchannaṃ gṛham ānayat.
tatra pitre nidhānaṃ tat prītaḥ kathitavān asau
Mahākāla|mata|jñātvaṃ tasya Kāpālikasya ca.
tam uvāca pitā putraṃ ‹tyaktvā Vedān an|arthakān
mahā|bhiksoḥ mahā|jñānaṃ Mahākāla|mataṃ paṭha.
22.230 divyaṃ cakṣur idaṃ tāta Mahākāla|mataṃ matam
nidhi|garbhāṃ naro yena chidrāṃ paśyati medinīm.
mahā|Pāśupatas tasmān Mahākāla iva tvayā
Mahākāla|matasy' ârthe yatnād ārādhyatām› iti.

and finding buried treasure, she said to him, 'You know 22.220
the practice of traveling ascetics: the sage should spend one night in a village and five nights in a town. Having spent all this time in Raja·griha, my boy, I have neglected to behave as a wandering ascetic should because of my infatuation with you. Even householders get into trouble when chained by the fetters of love; how much more so liberation-seekers, who are free of attachments and have no love for even their own bodies? So I want to go to Varánasi now. Visiting holy places is a duty for those who follow the Soma·siddhánta.* And another thing: I know a way of curing the disease of poverty. It's called the Doctrine of Maha·kala and is a treatise
about finding buried treasure. Tired from meditating, I was 22.225
wandering at the edge of the forest when I realized that there were clear signs that someone had buried treasure there. If you are fond of me then please accept it. Contacts with good men such as yourself are sure to be fruitful.'

Accompanied by her and some of his more dependable and trustworthy pupils, Yajña·gupta dug up the treasure and took it to his house in secret. Once there, the delighted fellow told his father about the treasure and the Kapálika's knowledge of the Doctrine of Maha·kala. His father said to him, 'Give up the Vedas; they are pointless. Study from the great ascetic this great wisdom, the Doctrine of Maha·kala.
This Doctrine of Maha·kala is like divine sight: using it a 22.230
man can see through the earth to where treasure is buried. Therefore, so that you might learn the Doctrine of Maha·kala, you must strive to propitiate this Páshupata ascetic as if he were Maha·kala himself.'

iti protsāhitas tena Mahākāla|mat'|ârthinā
Yajñagupto bravīti sma prasthitāṃ Kundamālikām.
‹aham apy anugacchāmi bhavantaṃ tīrtham a|sthiram
dṛṣṭ'|â|dṛṣṭa|mahā|śreyaḥ|kāraṇaṃ mādṛśām› iti.

tayā tu vāryamāṇo 'pi vācā manda|prayatnayā
Mahākāla|mata|prepsur asau n' âiva nivṛttavān.

22.235 atha Vārāṇasīṃ gatvā Yajñaguptāya sā dadau
ratnaṃ n'|âti|mahā|mūlyam iti c' âinam abhāṣata.
‹asya ratnasya mūlyena yathā|sukham ih' āsyatām
na tu tāruṇya|mūḍhena saṃbhāṣyā gaṇikā tvayā.
tvādṛk nava|daśa|prāyaḥ śrotriyaḥ sa|kutūhalaḥ
veśyā|vaśyaḥ sva|dārāṇāṃ yāty a|vaśyam a|vaśyatām.
gaṇikā|ḍākinībhiś ca pīta|sarv'|âṅga|lohitaḥ
yaj jīvati tad āścaryaṃ kva dharmaḥ kva yaśaḥ|sukhe?›

ity|ādim ādeśam asau tadīyaṃ
‹tath" êty› anujñāya tathā cakāra
ārādhya|vākyāni hi bhūti|kāmāḥ
sevā|vidhi|jñā na vikalpayanti.

22.240 caturaḥ pañca vā māsān Vārāṇasyāṃ vihṛtya tau
Naimiṣaṃ jagmatus tasmād Gaṅgādvāraṃ tataḥ Kurūn.
Kurubhyaḥ Puṣkaraṃ tatra gamayitvā ghan'|āgamam
Kārttik'|ânte mahā|puṇyaṃ dṛṣṭavantau Mahālayam.

With his father covetous of the Doctrine of Maha·kala and thus spurring him on, Yajña·gupta said to Kunda·málika as she set forth, 'I shall accompany you to that perilous place of pilgrimage; for people like me it is a source of great fortune in this and future lives.'

Despite her halfhearted attempts to talk him out of it, he was eager for the Doctrine of Maha·kala and would not
turn back. When they reached Varánasi, she gave Yajña· 22.235
gupta a not very valuable jewel, saying to him, 'With the proceeds from this jewel you can live comfortably here. But don't be carried away by your youth and go cavorting with courtesans. When an inquisitive student of nearly nineteen like you falls under the spell of a prostitute, he inevitably becomes impotent with his own wife. Courtesans are witches—after they have drunk all your blood, it is a miracle if you survive. Where's the religious merit, where are the glory and pleasure in that?'

He accepted everything that she told him and did as she said. Men who are seeking their fortune and know how to cultivate people do not quibble with what those who are to be propitiated have to say.

After spending four or five months in Varánasi they went 22.240
to Náimisha. From there they went to Ganga·dvara and then to the country of the Kurus.* From there they went to Púshkara, where they spent the monsoon. At the end of the month of Kárttika they reached the very sacred site of Mahálaya.*

Yajñaguptam ath' âvocad ekadā Kundamālikā
‹bahu|draviṇam utpādya dadāmi bhavate nidhim.
tam ādāya gṛhān gaccha dṛṣṭ'|â|dṛṣṭ'|ârtha|sādhanam
tri|vargeṇa hi yujyante gṛhasthā gṛha|medhinaḥ.
a|śruta|śrutayo mūḍhā raṇḍā nir|vasavo 'pi vā
bhavanti khalu dharm'|ârthaṃ tīrtha|yātrā|parāyaṇāḥ.
22.245 aham apy adhunā gacchāmy Avanti|nagarīṃ prati
sā hi Kāpālik'|ālīnā gaṇikānām iv' ākaraḥ!
mahā|Pāśupatās tatra niśāta|śita|paṭṭiśāḥ
yātrāyāṃ kila yudhyante yuddha|mātra|prayojanāḥ.
tatra Kāpālikaḥ kaś cin nihanyād api māṃ balī
kāka|tālīya|mokṣā hi śastra|pañjara|cāriṇaḥ.
Ujjayanyāṃ ca yat pāpaṃ duṣ|kṛtaṃ kṛtavān asi
svargavad brahma|ghātena tena sā dur|gamā tvayā.
ten' āyāsa|phalaṃ tatra viśaṅke gamanaṃ tava
prāvṛtya ca tataḥ paśya sa|nidhiḥ pitarāv› iti.
22.250 āsīc c' âsya ‹prasannau me pādāv asya mah"|ātmanaḥ
hanta saṃprati saṃprāptaṃ Mahākāla|mataṃ mayā!
loko hi prāṇa|saṃdehe prāṇa|dhāraṇa|kāraṇam
sarvam apy ujjhati sphītaṃ kim u grantham an|arthakam.
ciram ārādhitaś c' âyaṃ nirapekṣaḥ sva|jīvite
Mahākāla|mataṃ tan me kathaṃ nāma na dāsyati.
yaṃ ca doṣam ahaṃ tatra kṛtavān guru|śāsanāt
tasya pracchādan'|ôpāyo yat kiṃ cid iva tucchakaḥ.
māṃ deva|kula|koṇeṣu līnaṃ kāla|paṭac|caram
paruṣ'|ākula|keśaṃ ca na kaś cid lakṣayiṣyati.›

One day Kunda·málika said to Yajña·gupta, 'I have unearthed a very valuable treasure, which I am going to give to you. You must take it home; it will make your fortune in this and future lives. Householders who make sacrifices to the domestic fire should aim for all three goals of life. Only those who do not know the scriptures, fools, cripples and the destitute should wholly devote themselves to visiting pilgrimage places in order to gain religious merit. As 22.245
for me, I shall now go to Ujjáyani, for that city is as full of Kapálikas as it is of courtesans! The Páshupata ascetics supposedly there on pilgrimage fight one another with their sharp-pointed tridents—fighting is all they are interested in. Some strong Kapálika there might even kill me: for those who live by the sword, liberation can come at any time. The terrible crime that you committed in Ujjáyani makes it as hard for you to go there as it would be for a brahmin-killer to go to heaven. I'm afraid that going there will only bring you trouble, so take the treasure and go back to see your parents.'

Yajña·gupta said to himself, 'Aha! The great saint is pleased 22.250
with me. The Doctrine of Maha·kala is now within my grasp! When people are in fear of their lives, they will even give up their entire fortunes to save themselves, to say nothing of a worthless book! I have spent a long time ingratiating myself with this man and he has no regard for his own life, so why on earth would he not give me the Doctrine of Maha·kala? And it is as easy as anything to cover up the sin I committed there at my father's behest. If I secrete myself in the corners of the temples in black ragged clothes, my hair filthy and unkempt, no one will pay me any attention.'

22.255 yuktam ity|ādi nirdhārya so 'bravīt Kundamālikām
‹kiṃ c' ântevāsināṃ yuktaṃ moktum ācāryam āpadi?
yā gatir bhavataḥ s" âiva mam' âpi saha|cāriṇaḥ
na hi gacchati pūrṇ'|êndau kalaṅko 'sya na gacchati.›
ity|ādi vadato valgu jāta|saṃmada|mānasā
anujñātavatī tasya gamanaṃ Kundamālikā.

ath' Âvanti|purīṃ gatvā Yajñaguptam uvāca sā
‹iha Bhadravaṭe bhadra vinayasva pathi|śramam.
āgacchāmi nidhiṃ dṛṣṭvā nihitaṃ kena cit kva cit
yāvat tāvat tvay" ôtkaṇṭhā na kāryā mām a|paśyatā.
22.260 Ujjayanyāṃ nidhānāni dur|labhāni yatas tataḥ
āśaṅke ciram ātmānaṃ paribhrāntam itas tataḥ.
āyuṣmantaḥ prajāvanto '|pitṛvanto 'pi vā samāḥ
na hy Aujjayanakāḥ paurāḥ sthirān nidadhate nidhīn.›

evam|ādi tam uktv" âsau gatvā Siprā|sarit|taṭam
muktvā Kāpālik'|ākalpam a|malām akarot tanum.
kunda|śubhra|parīdhānā śaṅkha|sphaṭika|maṇḍanā
śarad|dyaur iva s" âbhāsīj jyotsnā|tārā|kul'|ākulā.
bhinna|varṇāṃ ca bhindantī stanābhyāṃ kaṇṭha|kaṇṭhikām
jāla|śikya|sthit'|âlābūḥ sā pratasthe sa|piṇḍikā.
22.265 tataḥ Kāpālikā mattāḥ pibanto baddha|maṇḍalāḥ
vyāharanti sma tām uccaiḥ kuñcit'|âṅguli|pāṇayaḥ.
‹ehy ehi taral'|âpāṅgi yas te Kāpālikaḥ priyaḥ
tena sārdhaṃ yathā|śraddhaṃ pānam āsevyatām!› iti.

tatas tatr' âpi sā tebhyaḥ prakṛtyā pratibhāvatī
tān ati|drutayā gatyā jagāma ca jagāda ca.
‹paśyantīṃ ca ramaṇīyāṃ spṛśyamānāṃ ca bhīṣaṇām
alaṃ Bhagavatāṃ dṛṣṭvā māṃ dṛṣṭi|viṣa|kanyakām!
patir mama hi gandharvaḥ krūratā|jita|rākṣasaḥ

Deciding that he was right, he said to Kunda·málika, 22.255
'Is it right for students to desert a teacher in a dangerous situation? I shall accompany you wherever you go: when the full moon moves on, so too do its blemishes.' When he said these charming words, Kunda·málika was overjoyed and gave him permission to come.

When they reached Ujjáyani, she said to Yajña·gupta, 'Shake off the fatigue of the journey here at Bhadra·vata. I shall return when I've found a treasure that someone has buried somewhere. Until then, don't be worried if you don't
see me. In Ujjáyani, buried treasures are hard to find, so 22.260
I'm afraid I may have to look around for a long time. Old people, family men, orphans—they're all the same. None of the citizens of Ujjáyani buries substantial treasures.'

After saying this, she went to the bank of the River Sipra, where she took off her Kapálika accoutrements and washed her body. Wearing a jasmine-white robe and ornaments of conch shell and crystal, she shone like an autumn sky filled with a host of brilliant stars. Her breasts breaking the line of her necklace and giving it a different color, she set off with a
gourd in a knapsack and a begging bowl in her hand.* Some 22.265
drunken Kapálikas drinking in a circle crooked their fingers and shouted at her, 'Come here, girl with the wandering eye! Come and drink your fill with the Kapálika of your choice!'

Even in these circumstances she was more quick-witted than them. She quickened her step and said, 'While looking, I'm lovely, but touched, I'm terrifying! That's enough looking at me, Your Reverences—I'm a girl to poison your eyes! My husband is a *gandhárva*, crueler than a demon,

īrṣyāvān a|pramattaś ca sadā rakṣati mām asau!
22.270 tena mām abhiyuñjānā Kandarpa|śara|tāḍitā
Yamen' êva kṣayaṃ nītā koṭir yuṣmādṛśām› iti.
tataḥ Kāpālikair uktam ‹uktaṃ yad anayā śriyā
tan na kevalam etasyām adhikaṃ c' ôpapadyate.
trailokye '|nidratā|hetor asyāḥ kānt'|ākṛteḥ kṛte
āścaryaṃ yan na yudhyante Brahma|Viṣṇu|Maheśvarāḥ.
tasmād gandharvam anyaṃ vā kaṃ cit trailokya|sundaram
anugṛhṇātu sa|snehair iyam ālokitair› iti.
tataḥ sā parikarṣantī sa|pāṣaṇḍi|gaṇā purīm
āśīḥ|kalakal'|ônnītam agacchad bhavanaṃ pituḥ.
22.275 hṛṣṭ" ârtha|varga|saṃbādhaṃ sapta|kakṣaṃ praviśya tat
mātur vāsa|gṛha|dvāri ‹bhikṣāṃ deh' îti› c' âbravīt.
gṛhād gṛhīta|bhikṣā ca niryāya paricārikā
ā|śiraś|caraṇ'|âṅguṣṭham apaśyat Kundamālikām.
cirāc ca pratyabhijñāya ghnatī sa|hṛdayaṃ śiraḥ
praviśya kathayām āsa svāminyai śanakair asau.
‹utsann" âsi! vinaṣṭ" âsi! yasyās te dharaṇī|dhṛtā
śirīṣā|mālikā|lolā duhitā Kundamālikā.
sā hi Kāpālik'|ākalpa|kalaṅkāṃ dadhatī tanum
iyaṃ tiṣṭhati te dvāri svayaṃ vā dṛśyatām!› iti.
22.280 idam ākarṇya niṣkrāntā sā tāṃ dṛṣṭvā tathā|vidhām
vācyatām an|apekṣy' âiva snehād etac cacāra sā.
bibheda lavaśaḥ picchaṃ kapālaṃ ca kapālaśaḥ
ciccheda guḍikāṃ śaśvat śaṅkha|sphaṭika|maṇḍanam.
pāṭayitvā ca tāṃ tasyās tantuśaḥ kaṇṭha|kaṇṭhikām
maṅgala|snāna|śuddh'|ântāṃ śuddh'|ântam anayat tataḥ.

jealous and always alert as he watches over me! Like the god 22.270
of death himself, he has killed millions of men like you, who, struck by the arrow of the god of love, have made a play for me.'

The Kapálikas said, 'What this goddess of beauty says is more than likely in her case. Her beauty has stopped the universe from sleeping and it is a miracle that Brahma, Vishnu and Shiva are not fighting one another. So let her favor her gandhárva or some other world-famous beau with her amorous glances.'

Dragging the city after her, she arrived with a troop of heretics at her father's house, from which emerged the murmur of prayers. The seven-floored house was filled with all 22.275
she could want, and she went inside, overjoyed. At the door to her mother's bedroom she asked for alms. A servant came out with an offering and looked Kunda·málika over from head to toe. After a long time she recognized her and went inside beating her chest and her head. She whispered to her mistress, 'You are ruined! You are lost! The girl that you held to your breast, the fluttering *shirísha* garland that was your daughter Kunda·málika, is standing at your door, her body sullied by the garb of a Kapálika! See for yourself!'

When she heard this, she went out and saw the girl look- 22.280
ing just as the servant had said. With no regard for impropriety, the mother's affection made her tear the girl's feathered headpiece into shreds, shatter the skull she was carrying and smash over and over again her begging bowl and ornaments of conch and crystal. Then she ripped off her necklace and pulled it apart, purified her with a ritual bath and led her to the inner apartments.

tatr' âinām abravīn mātā ‹mātar viśrabdham ucyatām
kim etad evam ev' êti›
sā tatas tām abhāṣata.
‹a|kasmād bhrāntir ambāyāḥ katham tava sutā satī
a|satībhir api kṣiptaṃ caret Kāpālika|vratam?
22.285 āstāṃ tāvat kathā c' êyaṃ tāta|pādān ih' āhvaya
asti me guru kartavyaṃ sādhyate tac ca tair› iti.
atha Sāgaradattas tām ālokya vyāhṛt'|āgataḥ
‹kiṃ? kim etat kathaṃ c' êti› śaśaṅke viṣasāda ca.
taṃ ca dṛṣṭvā tathā|bhūtam a|trastā Kundamālikā
āśvāsayitum āliṅgya vavande vijahāsa ca.
abravīc c' âinam āśvastam ‹āste Bhadravaṭ'|āśrame
jāmātā tava sa syālais tasmād ānāyyatām› iti.
tad|ādiṣṭaiś ca saṃrabdhair gṛhītaḥ syālakair asau
‹labdho 'si putra|caur' êti› mṛṣā paruṣa|bhāṣibhiḥ.
22.290 ‹kiṃ tiṣṭhasi śaṭh' ôttiṣṭha! pratiṣṭha sva|puraṃ prati
tvām āhūyati rāj" êti› sa|smitāś c' âinam abruvan.
tatas tān pratyabhijñāya saṃbhāvya vadha|bandhane
Mānastokam ṛcaṃ japtvā śikhā|bandhaṃ cakāra saḥ.
sa|sāntvaṃ c' âbravīd ‹aṅga kṣaṇam etad udīkṣyatām
mama Kāpāliko mitraṃ yāvad āyāty asāv iti.›
sa tais tāraṃ vihasy' ôktas ‹tvaṃ yan mitram udīkṣase
sa gataḥ prathamaṃ tatra ten' âiva grāhito bhavān.
niṣprayojana|sauhārdā vacaḥ|sadṛśa|cetasaḥ
suhṛdo 'pi virajyante khalānāṃ tvādṛśām› iti.

Once there, the girl's mother said to her, 'Young lady,
speak freely. What is all this about?'

She replied, 'Mother, you have no reason to be upset.
How could your virtuous daughter adopt the vow of a Kapálika, which even immoral women scorn? But that story must 22.285
wait for a while. Call my dear father. I have an important
job to do, and he can make it happen.'

Ságara·datta was summoned. When he saw her he asked
anxiously, 'What? What is going on? How can this be?' and
sank down in despair.

Seeing him like this, Kunda·málika was unruffled. She revived him with a hug, greeted him respectfully and laughed.
When he had recovered, she said to him, 'Your son-in-law
is staying at a hermitage in Bhadra·vata. Have his brothers-
in-law fetch him.'

At their father's command, the brothers-in-law seized
Yajña·gupta. 'You are caught, child-snatcher!' they taunted
him. Smiling, they continued, 'Why are you here, you 22.290
rogue? Get up! Go to your town. The king is summon-
ing you!'

Then he recognized them and, imagining execution or
imprisonment, he muttered a Vedic verse for protection
and tied up his topknot.* He pleaded with them, 'Please
just wait a moment until my Kapálika friend returns.'

They laughed loudly and told him, 'The friend you are
waiting for has gone ahead. It was him that had us seize you.
Even if they are friends, those for whom friendship has no
motive and who say what they think become disillusioned
with scoundrels like you.' He was sad and silent and they 22.295

22.295 taṃ viṣaṇṇaṃ prahṛṣṭās te mūkaṃ bahu|paṭu|svanāḥ
gṛhītvā gṛham ājagmuḥ prīta|bandhu|jan'|āvṛtam.

tatra Sāgaradattena prīti|kaṇṭakita|tvacā
pariṣvaktasya jāmātuḥ sa|prāṇam abhavad vapuḥ.
kṛt'|ârgh'|ādi|saparyaś ca sa nivartita|bhojanaḥ
adhyaśeta mahā|śayyāṃ ramya|maṇḍapa|saṃstṛtām.
tatr' âsya śvaśurau syālāḥ syāla|bhāryāś ca s'|ātma|jāḥ
āptāś ca śreṣṭhinaḥ paurāḥ paritaḥ samupāviśan.
s" âth' āgacchad vaṇik|kanyā madhur'|ābharaṇa|kvaṇā
vācāla|kala|haṃs" êva niṣkalaṅk'|âmbarā śarat.
22.300 guravaḥ sat|kṛtā mūrdhnā vācā sa|vayasas tayā
Yajñaguptaḥ punar dṛṣṭyā sa|rāg'|âñjana|garbhayā.
adhyāsya ca puraḥ pitror asau vāmanam āsanam
vivāh'|ādi|yathā|vṛttam ātma|vṛttaṃ nyavedayat.

āsīc ca Yajñaguptasya ‹dhig dhiṅ me vi|phalāḥ kalāḥ
dvy|aṅgula|prajñayā yo 'haṃ vañcitaḥ kula|kanyayā.
atha vā dvy|aṅgula|prajñāḥ puruṣā eva mādṛśāḥ
kuś'|âgrīya|dhiyo yoṣā yāsāṃ karm' êdam īdṛśam.
kim ataḥ param'|āścaryaṃ yan nāgarikay" ânayā
tiṣṭhatāṃ gati|saṃsthāne svaro 'pi parivartitaḥ.
22.305 «Virāṭa|nagare Pārthaiḥ kathaṃ mūḍh'|ātmabhiḥ sthitam»
iti ye vicikitseyus teṣām eṣā nidarśanam.
sarvathā guru|vākyena yan mayā caritaṃ mahat
tasmād asmy anay" âiv' âdya mocitaḥ pātakād› iti.

were overjoyed and uproarious as they took him to the house, which was teeming with delighted relatives.

There Ságara·datta, his skin tingling with excitement, embraced his son-in-law and the life came back to him. After he had been welcomed with offerings of water and so forth, he finished eating and lay down on a large bed that had been made in a beautiful pavilion. There his parents-in-law, his brothers-in-law with their wives and children, worthy guild-leaders and citizens sat around him. Then the merchant's daughter arrived to the sweet sound of her ornaments; she was like autumn with its sonorous swans
and spotless skies. She greeted her parents with her head, 22.300
her peers with her voice, and Yajña·gupta with a look full of passion and kohl. She sat on a low seat in front of her parents and told them everything that had happened to her after her wedding.

Yajña·gupta said to himself, 'Curse my useless talents—I have been tricked by a well-bred girl with a tiny brain. On the other hand, men like me have tiny brains, and women who can do things like this must have minds as sharp as blades of *kusha* grass. But what is most amazing is that this cunning girl, in front of everyone, changed her gait, her
appearance, even her voice! She is an example for those who 22.305
are uncertain as to how the dimwitted Pándavas could have stayed in the city of king Viráta.* Anyway, today she has freed me from the heinous sin I committed at my father's bidding.'

vṛtt'|ântaṃ c' âitad ākarṇya prahṛṣṭena mahī|bhṛtā
saha|jāmātṛk" ānītā sva|gṛhaṃ Kundamālikā.
tasmin bahu|mahā|grāmaṃ dānaṃ bahu|suvarṇakam
sa dattvā Yajñaguptāya sa|smitas tām abhāṣata.
‹yathā dvi|jāti|karmabhyo na hīyate patis tava
tvayā dhīratayā putri tathā saṃpādyatām› iti.

22.310 tay" âti|dhairy'|âṅkuśa|vārit'|ērṣyayā
dvi|jāti|kanyāṃ pariṇāyitaḥ patiḥ
na hi kṣit'|īśān a|vilaṅghya|śāsanān
vilaṅghayanti priya|jīvita|śriyaḥ.
dvi|jāti|kanyāṃ rati|putra|kāmyayā
sukhāya śuddhāya ca Kundamālikām
niṣevamānaḥ su|kṛtaṃ ca saṃtataṃ
nināya vipraḥ sa|phalaṃ samā|śatam.
paugaṇḍāya vitīrṇay" âpi vidhinā
yasmād vaṇik|kanyayā
citr'|ôpāya|paraṃparā|caturayā
prāptaḥ patir vāñchitaḥ
saṃtoṣa|kṣata|sattva|sattva|dayitaḥ
saṃsevitaḥ kātaraiḥ
tasmāt pauruṣa|mārutena balinā
daiv'|âdrir unmūlitaḥ.

iti Priyadarśanā|lābhe
Puruṣa|kāra|kathā.

When the king heard the story, he was overjoyed and had Kunda·málika and her husband come to his palace. He gave Yajña·gupta generous presents of land and gold, and said to Kunda·málika with a smile, 'Use your wits, my girl, to make sure that your husband does not neglect his duties as a brahmin.'

So, warding off her jealousy with the goad of her great 22.310
resolve, she had her husband marry a brahmin girl, for those who care for their lives and good fortune do not contravene the inviolable orders of a king. Devoting himself to the brahmin girl for purposes of passion and progeny, and to Kunda·málika for pure pleasure, the brahmin lived a hundred fruitful years, doing good deeds all the while.

Despite having been betrothed with due formality to a runt, the merchant's daughter won the husband she desired by craftily employing a succession of various ruses, and the mountain of destiny, dear to beings whose goodness has been worn down by complacency, and cherished by cowards, was uprooted by the hurricane of human effort."

Thus ends the story of Human Effort
in the Winning of Priya·darshaná.

CANTO 23
NANDA AND UPANÁNDA

ITY ĀKHYĀYA KATHITAU ca mithaḥ pravrajitau gatau
drutaǀpravahaṇ'ǀārūḍhaḥ Gomukhaś ca parāgataḥ.
mām avocat sa vanditvā «prītiǀdāsaḥ Punarvasuḥ
sarvaǀnāgarakaǀśreṇiǀgrāmaṇīr dṛśyatām» iti.

atha praṇatam adrākṣam anǀulbaṇaǀvibhūṣaṇam
yuvānam api vainītyād lajjitaǀsthaviraṃ naram.
Gomukh'ǀākhyātaǀmāhātmyaṃ taṃ c' āliṅgitavān aham
saṃbhāvitaǀguṇāḥ sadbhir arhanty eva ca satǀkriyām.
23.5 atha yānaṃ samāruhya tat Punarvasuǀvāhakam
sāṃyātrika iv' âmbhodhiṃ tadǀāvāsam avātaram.
sevit'ǀāhāraǀparyantaǀśarīraǀsthitiǀsādhanaḥ
dinaǀśeṣaṃ nayāmi sma gītiǀśrutiǀvinodanaḥ.
tataḥ suptaǀjane kāle pṛṣṭavān asmi Gomukham
«katham eṣa tvayā prāptaḥ suhṛd?» ity atha so 'bravīt.
«śrūyatām asmy ahaṃ yuṣmān vanditvā punar āgataḥ
na ca kaṃ cana paśyāmi yogyam āśrayaǀdāyinam.
tataś cintitavān asmi dhanaǀvidy"ǀādiǀdāyinām
saṃbhavaḥ sarvaǀsādhūnāṃ n' âsti rājaǀkulād ṛte.
23.10 yogaǀkṣemaǀprayuktā hi prāyaḥ sajǀjanaǀsaṃsadaḥ
rājaǀdvāraṃ vigāhante samudram iva sindhavaḥ.
rājaǀdvāraṃ tato gatvā yāciṣye kaṃ cid āśrayam
rājaǀdvāraṃ hi kāryāṇāṃ dvāram uktaṃ budhair iti.

nigrah'ǀânugrahaǀprāptaǀlokaǀkolāhal'ǀākulam
tad gatvā smṛtavān asmi pret'ǀâdhipaǀdhan'ǀâdhipau.
‹mahāǀmanuṣyaǀcaritaḥ puruṣo 'yaṃ vibhāvyate
āśrayaǀprārthanā tasmān n' âsmin saṃpadyate mṛṣā...
ayam anyaḥ suǀveṣo 'pi kīnāśaǀviras'ǀākṛtiḥ

HAVING THUS TOLD one another their stories, the two of them left together and Go·mukha returned on a fast carriage. He greeted me and said, "Meet Punar·vasu, a devoted servant, and leader of all the citizens' guilds."

I looked at the fellow as he bowed. He was a soberly dressed young man whose courtesy would have put our elders to shame. Go·mukha had spoken of his greatness and I embraced him. Those whose praises are sung by good men deserve to be treated well.

Then I boarded Punar·vasu's carriage and, like a seafaring 23.5
trader arriving at the sea, I arrived at his house. After having
my bodily requirements looked after in various ways that
culminated in a meal, I spent the rest of the day amusing
myself by listening to music. When everyone was asleep, I
asked Go·mukha how he had met this friend and he replied,
"Listen. After taking your leave I came to the city, but I did
not find anyone suitable for providing us with a place to stay,
and I thought that there was no possibility of finding good
men who would be generous with their wealth, learning and
so forth anywhere other than the palace. Decent wealthy 23.10
men generally flow toward the royal gate like rivers to the
ocean. So I went to the royal gate in search of someone to
take us in—the wise say that a royal gate is a gateway to
what one wants.

When I got there, the tumult and fervor of people being punished or rewarded made me think of the gods of death and wealth. 'This man appears to act like a man of rank: a request made to him for somewhere to stay will not be in vain. . . This other man, although well dressed, looks niggardly and unpleasant, so a request to him won't get a

tena saṃbhāvyate n' âsmāt prārthanā|phalam aṇv api. . . ›
23.15 puruṣaṃ puruṣaṃ tatra ciram itthaṃ vicārayan
abhyantarāt pratīhāraṃ dṛṣṭavān asmi nirgatam.
sv|asti|kāra|namas|kāra|jyot|kārān sa ca kāryiṇām
pratimānitavān sarvān sakṛn|namita|mastakaḥ.
atha vijñāpanā|mātraṃ paśyadbhiḥ kārya|sādhanam
kāryibhir yugapat tatra kārya|vijñāpanā kṛtā.

tebhyas ten' âpi sāmānyam ekam ev' ôttaraṃ kṛtam
‹bhavataḥ su|mukhaḥ rājā mā tvariṣṭa bhavān!› iti.

sa pratīhāra|veṣaṃ ca vāra|bāṇ'|ādim aṅgataḥ
avatārya samīpa|sthe nyastavān paricārake.
23.20 taṃ ca dṛṣṭvā samāpt" âiva samāśraya|gaveṣaṇā
na hi dṛṣṭa|suvarṇ'|âdris tāmraṃ dhamati vātikaḥ.
svasti|kṛtvā tatas tasmai sva|gṛhān pratigacchate
māṃ muhuḥ paśyatā prītyā ten' âiva sahito 'gamam.
gṛhe ca kṛta|satkāram asau māṃ anuyuktavān
‹āgacchati kutaḥ kiṃ vā mad icchati bhavān?› iti.

may" ôktaṃ ‹bhrātarāv āvāṃ dvijau dvāv āgam'|ârthinau
vidyā|sthānam idaṃ śrutv" Âvanti|deśāt samāgatau.
iha vāsitum icchāvo yuṣmat|kṛta|parigrahau
balavattara|gupto hi kṛśo 'pi balavān› iti.

23.25 ten' ôktaṃ ‹tvādṛśām etad guṇa|grahaṇa|kāṅkṣiṇām
a|grāmy'|ālāpa|rūpāṇāṃ sva|gṛhaṃ bhavatām!› iti.

jot. . .' I deliberated about each of the men there like this 23.15
for a long time. Then I saw the chamberlain emerge from inside. He acknowledged all the blessings, bows and cheers of the supplicants with a single bow of the head. The supplicants, supposing that the only way to have their wishes seen to was to make them known, made them known all at once.

The chamberlain gave them a single answer that applied to them all: 'The king is favorably inclined to you. Do not be impatient!'

He took off his chamberlain's dress—his armor, arrows and so forth—and gave them to a servant standing nearby.
On seeing him, I had realized that the search for somewhere 23.20
to stay was over. When he finds a mountain of gold, a smith stops smelting copper. I greeted him politely as he walked home. He gave me a friendly look for a moment and I fell in with him. He welcomed me into his home and asked, 'Where do you come from, sir, and what do you want from me?'

I replied, 'We are two brahmin brothers in search of education. We heard about this seat of learning and came here from the land of the Avántis. We would like to stay here under your protection. Protected by the mighty, even a weak man is strong.'

He said, 'People like you who strive after virtue and are 23.25
of cultured speech and appearance can treat this house as their own!'

muhūrtaṃ tatra c' āsīnaḥ śrutavān aham utthitam
kṣubhit'|âmbhodhi|kallola|kolāhalam iva kvaṇam.
māṃ tad|ākarṇan'|ôtkarṇam asau sa|smitam uktavān
‹kiṃ tvam etan na vetth' êti› ‹na ved' êti› may" ôditam.
‹ayaṃ Punarvasur nāma dātā vāṇija|dārakaḥ
vṛtaḥ kitava|saṃghena dīvyati dyūta|maṇḍape.
yadā vijayate dyūte sa sarvaṃ draviṇaṃ tadā
vitaraty arthi|vargāya tasy' âiṣas tumulo dhvaniḥ.
23.30 jīyamāne punas tasmiñ jānu|mūrdha|stha|mastakāḥ
viṣāda|muṣit'|ālāpā dhyāyanti êivam arthinaḥ.
yadi kautūhalaṃ tatra tato 'sau dṛśyatām› iti.

pratīhāreṇa kathite tataś cintitavān aham.
‹nīti|vidyā|vayo|vṛddhair amātyaiḥ kiṃ prayojanam
yeṣāṃ yantrita|vāk|kāyair agrato duḥkham āsyate.
yaḥ sa|māna|vayaḥ|śīlo mukta|hastaḥ sa|kiṃ|cana
vyasanī ca sva|tantraś ca so 'smākam adhunā suhṛt.
tasmād dyūta|sabhām eva yāmi draṣṭuṃ Punarvasum.›

nirdhāry' êti tam āmantrya dyūta|kāra|sabhām agām.
23.35 s" ākīrṇā devana|vyagraiḥ sabhā kitava|candrakaiḥ
saras' îv' āmiṣ'|āsvāda|gṛddhair baka|kadambakaiḥ.
tatr' ânyatamayor akṣān dīvyator akṣa|dhūrtayoḥ
akṣaḥ koṇena patitaḥ saṃdigdha|pada|pañcakaḥ.
‹pañcako 'yaṃ padaṃ n' êdaṃ› ‹padam etan na pañcakaḥ›
iti jātā tayoḥ spardhā paraspara|jay'|âiṣiṇoḥ.

After sitting there for a moment, I heard a sound rise up like the roar of a wave in a stormy sea. Seeing me prick up my ears, the chamberlain said with a smile, 'Do you not know what that is?' When I said that I didn't, he continued, 'It's Punar·vasu, a generous man, the son of a merchant. He's playing dice in the gaming hall, surrounded by a gang of gamblers. When he wins at dice, he distributes all his winnings among the beggars—that racket is coming from
them. But when he is beaten, sadness steals the beggars' 23.30
tongues, and with their heads on their knees they meditate on Shiva. If you're interested, go and meet him.'

When the chamberlain said this, I thought, 'What is to be gained from ministers advanced in morality, wisdom and years, before whom one has to sit uncomfortably, curbing one's tongue and actions? Now we have a friend of the same outlook, age and disposition as us, who is generous in every respect, knows how to enjoy himself and is his own master. Therefore I shall go straight to the gaming hall to meet Punar·vasu.'

Having made up my mind, I took my leave of the chamberlain and went to the gaming hall. It was packed with 23.35
high rollers intent on the dice, like a siege of herons at a lake, greedy to taste flesh. Two skilled players were rolling the dice when a die fell on its corner, leaving it unclear as to whether it was a four or a five. 'It's a five, not a four!' 'It's a four, not a five!' The two of them started to argue, each wanting to beat the other.

tayor ekatareṇ' ôktaṃ ‹madhya|sthaḥ pṛcchyatām› iti
pratyuktam itareṇ' âpi ‹yath" êcchasi tath" âstv› iti.
ath' âikaḥ puruṣaḥ prāṃśuḥ pṛṣṭas tābhyām a|nāgaraḥ
‹katarat paśyasi spaṣṭaṃ pada|pañcakayor?› iti.
23.40 tatra c' ânyatamen' ôccair uktam utkṣipta|pāṇinā
‹dīrghatvād eṣa nir|buddhir ato 'nyaḥ pṛcchyatām› iti.
tataḥ pṛṣṭo 'paro hrasvaḥ so 'pi tena nivāritaḥ
‹n' ēdṛśāḥ praśnam arhanti bahu|doṣā hi khaṭvakāḥ!›
atha māṃ dṛṣṭavantau tau pṛṣṭavantau ca s'|ādaram
‹sādho yadi na doṣo 'sti tato nau chinddhi saṃśayam.
tvaṃ na dīrgho na ca hrasvas tasmāt prājño na duṣṭa|dhīḥ
tena madhya|pramāṇatvād gaccha madhya|sthatām› iti.
cintitaṃ ca mayā ‹kaṣṭaḥ khala|saṃdigdha|nirṇayaḥ
pāra|draviṇa|gṛddheṣu kitaveṣu viśeṣataḥ.
23.45 avaśyaṃ tu kalā|jñānaṃ khyāpanīyaṃ kalā|vidā
a|prakāśaṃ hi vijñānaṃ kṛpaṇ'|ârtha|nir|arthakam.
na ca dyūta|kal" ânyatra kitavebhyaḥ prakāśyate
na hi prayuñjate prājñā veśād anyatra vaiśikam.
dyūte jeṣyati yaś c' âtra sa me mitraṃ bhaviṣyati
dhanavan|mitra|lābhaṃ hi nidhi|lābh'|ādikaṃ viduḥ.›
ity|ādi bahu niścitya puras teṣāṃ sa|vistaram
akṣ'|âṣṭā|pada|śārīṇām ākhyaṃ bhūmeś ca lakṣaṇam.
tataḥ saṃdigdha|pātasya tasy' âhaṃ koṇa|pātinaḥ
su|piṣṭam iṣṭakā|kṣodam akṣasy' ôpari dattavān.
23.50 ath' âsāv iṣṭakā|kṣodaḥ padasy' ôpari yo 'patat
so 'patat sakalo bhūmau pañcakasy' ôpari sthitaḥ.

One of them said, 'Let's ask someone impartial,' and the other agreed.

They asked a tall rustic fellow, 'Which do you see showing—the four or the five?'

Then the other man threw up his hands and cried, 'This 23.40
man is so tall he's stupid. Let's ask someone else.'

So he asked another man, a dwarf, but he, too, was rejected by the other gambler: 'Men like him aren't to be asked—midgets have too many faults!'

Then they noticed me and asked politely, 'Good sir, if you don't mind, please settle our dispute. You are neither tall nor short, so you are wise, not ill-intentioned. Therefore, with your medium stature, please be our mediator.'

I thought, 'It is difficult to make a decision about a dispute in a game, particularly between gamblers greedy for
each other's wealth. But those with a skill must show it: 23.45
knowledge kept secret is as useless as money among the miserly. And skill at dice is not to be shown off anywhere other than among gamblers: the wise do not use their knowledge of harlotry anywhere other than in a brothel. Whoever wins the game will be my friend, and they say that winning a rich friend is better than finding a buried treasure.'

After much such deliberation, I explained to them at length the characteristics of eight-faced dice and the playing area. Then I put some fine brick dust on top of the die that
had fallen on its corner and whose value was in doubt. The 23.50
brick dust that fell on the four all fell onto the ground; that on the five remained. As a result, I told them, 'The side marked with five has its face uppermost because the dust has remained on it. That is my judgment.' As I stood there

tatas tān uktavān asmi ‹yo bhāgaḥ pañcak'|âṅkitaḥ
tasy' ôttānatvam utkṛṣṭaṃ kṣodas tatra yataḥ sthitaḥ.
etāvan mama vijñānam› ity uktv" âvasthite mayi
‹aho sādhv!› iti nirghoṣaḥ samantāt sahas" ôtthitaḥ.

tatas tatr' ôditaṃ kaiś cid ‹ayam akṣa|viśāradau
dhruvaṃ vijayate dūrān Nala|Kuntī|sutāv iti.›
te 'paraiḥ kupitair uktā ‹jitau Nala|Yudhiṣṭhirau
ayaṃ jayati jetārāv api Puṣkara|Saubalau!›

23.55 iti praśasyamānaṃ māṃ tiryag dṛṣṭvā sa|matsaraḥ
pada|vādī jito yo 'sāv asau mantharam uktavān.
‹yeṣāṃ dyūta|paṇ'|â|bhāvas te kim artham ih' āsate?
dyūta|sthāne hi kiṃ kṛtyaṃ pravīṇaiḥ prāśnikair?› iti.

āsīc ca mama ‹kasmān māṃ kaulaṭeyaḥ kṣipaty ayam?
yo 'haṃ trailokya|sāreṇa paṇena paṇavān!› iti.
atha nikṣipya sa|krodhaṃ yauṣmākaṃ bhūṣaṇaṃ bhuvi
‹ehi dīvyāva mitr' êti› tam ahaṃ dhūrtam uktavān.
sa ca dhūrtair alaṃ|kāraḥ prasarpad|bahala|prabhaḥ
dṛṣṭas tṛṣṇā|viśāl'|âkṣaiḥ pataṃgair iva pāvakaḥ.
23.60 ath' âsau krodha|lobhābhyām akṣa|dhūrtaḥ pratāritaḥ
mayā saha sa|saṃrambham akṣān ārabdha devitum.
tena c' âhaṃ tribhiḥ pātair an|akṣa|kuśalaḥ kila
prabuddhair gardha|gṛddhena sahasra|tritayaṃ jitaḥ.
tatas tat sakṛd unmocya sahasra|tritayaṃ mayā
lakṣam ekena pātena jitaḥ saḥ kitav'|âdhamaḥ.
vijayāj jṛmbhit'|ôtsāhaḥ śaṅkitaś ca parājayāt
na virantuṃ na vā rantum asāv aśakad ākulaḥ.

‹dīvya vā dehi vā lakṣaṃ saumy' êti› ca may" ôditaḥ
vailakṣyād ghaṭṭayann akṣān na kiṃ cit pratipannavān.

after saying this, a cry of 'Bravo!' suddenly broke out all around.

Then some people there said, 'This man beats such skilled dice players as Nala and Yudhi·shthira hands down!' Others joined the fray, saying, 'Beat Nala and Yudhi·shthira? This man would beat even their vanquishers, Púshkara and Shákuni!'*

While they were singing my praises, the angry player who 23.55
had called four and been beaten looked askance at me and said slowly, 'Why should those who have no stake to bet have a place here? There's no need for expert judges in a gaming hall.'

I said to myself, 'Why is this whoreson having a go at me? I've got a stake as valuable as the three worlds!' Then I angrily threw your piece of jewelry onto the ground and said to the gambler, 'Come on, my friend, let's play dice!' The gamblers looked at the brilliant ornament with eyes
wide with desire, like moths looking at a fire. Egged on by 23.60
anger and greed, the dice player excitedly started to play dice with me. Pretending not to be a skilled player, I was beaten on three rolls by the greedy fellow and lost three thousand. Then the useless player bet the three thousand all at once, and, in one throw, I won a hundred thousand off him. He had been encouraged by his victory and was bewildered in defeat. In his confusion, he could neither stop nor play on.

When I said to him, 'Dear fellow, either play or hand over the hundred thousand,' he shook the dice with embarrassment, and did neither.

23.65 etasminn antare bhṛtyaṃ svam avocat Punarvasuḥ
‹kitavo 'yam idaṃ lakṣam a|calaṃ dāpyatām› iti.
māṃ c' âyaṃ svaṃ gṛhaṃ nītvā harṣād ṛju|tanū|ruhaḥ
tathā pūjitavān devaṃ Haraṃ datta|varaṃ yathā.
māṃ c' âvocad ‹dhanaṃ yat tad bhavadbhiḥ kitav'|ârjitam
tad udgrāhy' êdam ānītaṃ lakṣaṃ te gṛhyatām› iti.

may" âpy uktam ‹upānte yad draviṇaṃ tvat|parigrahāt
sādhitaṃ bhavatā yac ca tasya svāmī bhavān› iti.

uktaṃ c' ânena ‹yan nāma yuṣmābhiḥ svayam arjitam
svāmino yūyam ev' âsya dhanasy' êty atra kā kathā.
23.70 yad ap' îdaṃ may" âvāptaṃ yuṣmat svāmikam eva tat
adhigacchati yad dāso bhartur eva hi tad dhanam.

yac ca pṛcchāmi tan mahyaṃ prasāde sati kathyatām
bhū|talaṃ yūyam āyātāḥ kiṃ nimittaṃ tripiṣṭapāt?
manye saty api devatve bhavadbhiḥ krīḍay" āhṛtaiḥ
ākār'|ântara|nirmāṇaṃ n' âty|antam anuśīlitam.
tathā ca varṇa|saṃsthāna|kalā|vijñāna|saṃpadaḥ
dṛṣṭāḥ kena manuṣyeṣu yādṛśo bhavatām› iti.

tena yat satyam ity ukte duḥkham āśitavān aham
dūreṇa hy ati|nindāyā duḥkha|hetur ati|stutiḥ.
23.75 Vārāṇasī|praveśeṣu pratīhārāya pṛcchate
yan mayā kāryam ākhyātaṃ tad ev' âsmai niveditam.

ath' ânen' ôktam ‹āścaryaṃ jyeṣṭhasya jagatāṃ guṇaiḥ
tvādṛśasy' âpi yo jyeṣṭhaḥ kīdṛśaḥ sa bhaviṣyati.
kiṃ v" ânena vimarśena jyeṣṭhas tiṣṭhati yatra saḥ
sarva|tīrth'|âdhike deśe taṃ prāpayata mām!› iti.

In the meantime, Punar·vasu said to his servant, 'Have 23.65
this player hand over the hundred thousand as fixed,' and he took me to his home, his skin tingling with happiness. Then he worshiped Lord Shiva for giving him a boon and he said to me, 'I had the money that you won from the gambler paid up and brought here. Here it is, your hundred thousand—take it.'

I replied, 'It is as a gift from you that the money has come to me: you procured it, so you are its owner.'

He said, 'You won the money yourself: you and you alone are its owner. There's nothing more to be said on the matter.
You are the owner of what I procured. The money obtained 23.70
by the slave belongs to the master alone.

Please be so kind as to answer my question: for what reason have you come to earth from heaven? I think that you are divine and out of playfulness have not completely altered your form. Who has seen such a wealth of beauty, talent and knowledge among mortals?'

In truth, his words made me uncomfortable, for too much praise is a far greater cause for discomfort than too
much criticism. I gave him the same reason for our coming 23.75
to Váránasi as I had given the chamberlain when he asked.

Then he said, 'It's amazing: you surpass the whole world with your good qualities. What will someone with even greater qualities than you be like? But there's no point in talking about it. Take me to the place where your superior is; it must be better than all the sacred sites!'

ath' âinam aham ādāya gatavān bhavad|antikam
yac c' ôttaram atas tatra pratyakṣaṃ bhavatām api.
iti kṣipram ayaṃ labdho mayā vaḥ paricārakaḥ
na hiṃsanti na sarvatra śriyaḥ puṇyavatām!» iti.

23.80 tatas tam uktavān asmi «vipadas tena dur|labhāḥ
phalaṃ su|caritasy' êva hṛdayaṃ yasya Gomukhaḥ.
kiṃ tu saṃśraya|mātreṇa pīḍanīyaḥ Punarvasuḥ
par'|ânnaṃ hi vṛthā|bhuktaṃ duḥkhāy' âiva satām» iti.

evam|ādibhir ālāpair ardham ardhaṃ ca nidrayā
nītavān asmi yāminyāḥ prātaś c' āgāt Punarvasuḥ.
taṃ ca vandita|mat|pādam avocad iti Gomukhaḥ
«ballavaḥ kuśalaḥ kaś cit kutaś cana gaveṣyatām.
tvad|anyasya gṛhe n' ânnam arya|jyeṣṭhena sevitam
para|pāka|nivṛttā hi sādhu|vṛttā dvi|jātayaḥ.

23.85 ādar'|ārādhitaś c' âyaṃ tvadīyaṃ paribhuktavān
ārādhan'|ânurodho hi caritaṃ mahatām» iti.

pratyākhyāna|vicittas tu tam āha sma Punarvasuḥ
«yady evaṃ jagad|īśānāṃ kiṃ n' âsti bhavatām?» iti.

a|cirāc ca tad|ānītau saṃbhāvya|guṇa|saṃpadau
ākāra|kṣipta|Nāsatyāv apaśyaṃ puruṣau puraḥ.
tau ca māṃ ciram ālokya vadanaṃ ca parasparam
prasārya sa|bhujān pādāñ «jay' êty» uktvā bhuvaṃ gatau.
tau c' āhūya may" āyātau spṛṣṭa|pṛṣṭhau sabhājitau
vanditvā punar abrūtāṃ «brūta kiṃ kriyatām?» iti.

23.90 tatas tau Gomukhen' ôktau «bhavantau kila ballavau
satyaṃ ced idam āryasya pākaḥ saṃsādhyatām» iti.

So I took him to you. You were witness to what followed. That is how I quickly obtained him as a servant for you. The good fortunes of the virtuous are beneficial everywhere!”

I replied, “Go·mukha is like the reward of good deeds: 23.80
for the man who has him as a friend, calamities are far away. But Punar·vasu is only to be troubled for a place to stay. It pains good men to eat another's food unnecessarily.”

We spent the night half in conversation like this and half in sleep. Punar·vasu arrived in the morning. He touched my feet in salutation, and Go·mukha said to him, “Please find a good cook from somewhere. My noble master has not eaten food in any house other than yours, for good brahmins refuse the cooking of others. He ate yours after 23.85
being asked so politely. It is the way of great men to give in to requests.”

Put out by this rejection, Punar·vasu replied, “If that is what lords of the world do, then why shouldn't you behave thus?”

Not long afterward, he brought in two men with suitable talents. I saw them before me and they were more beautiful than the Ashvins. They looked at me for a long time and then at one another. Prostrating themselves at full length, they fell to the floor with cries of salutation. I called them over and honored them by touching them on the back. They saluted me again and asked what they could do for me. Go·mukha said to them, “Apparently you are cooks. If 23.90
that is true, then prepare some food for his lordship.”

tau ca prītau pratijñāya nikartya nakha|mūrdha|jān
snātau s'|ôṣṇīṣa|mūrdhānau mahānasam agacchatām.
atha vā tiṣṭhati vyāsaḥ samāsaḥ śrūyatām ayam
sarvā tābhyām a|pūrv" êva prakriyā saṃprasāritā.
yāvatyā c' âparaḥ sthālīm adhiśrayati ballavaḥ
tāvatyā velayā tābhyāṃ pāka eva samāpitaḥ.
tato nirvartita|snāna|devat"|ânala|tarpaṇaḥ
āhāra|sthānam adhyāsi vipra|paṅkti|nir|antaram.
23.95 «pañca tittirayaḥ pakvāś catvāraḥ kukkuṭā!» iti
āhāro yaiḥ praśastas tair aśitaṃ prākṛt'|âśanam.
āhāraṃ yadi severan sakṛt tam amṛt'|âśanam
samutsṛṣṭ'|âmṛt'|āhārā bhaveyur n' âmarās tadā!

tataḥ samāpit'|āhāraḥ karṇe Gomukham abravam
«sūdābhyāṃ bhukta|bhaktābhyām ayutaṃ dīyatām» iti.
sa gatvā sahitas tābhyāṃ cirāc c' āgatya kevalaḥ
smita|saṃsūcita|prītir upākramata bhāṣitum.

«mayā yāv uditāv etau ‹na yūvām etad arhatha
avasthā|sādṛśaṃ kiṃ tu yat kiṃ cid gṛhyatām› iti.
23.100 tayor ekatareṇ' âtha ‹bhartur dauḥ|sthitya|vartinaḥ
na yuktaṃ dhanam ādātum āvābhyām› iti bhāṣitam.

sa kruddhen' êtareṇ' ôkto ‹dhik tvāṃ dīnatar'|âśayam
jita|Trailokya|vitt'|ēśaṃ vitt'|ēśaṃ yo 'nukampase.
mahā|padma|sahasrāṇi yat|prasādād vimāninām
su|sthitāni bhaviṣyanti dauḥ|sthityaṃ tasya kīdṛśam?
prayacchaty ayutaṃ yaś ca pākasy' âikasya niṣkrayam
duḥ|sthitas tādṛśo yasya su|sthitas tasya kīdṛśaḥ?›

Delighted, they agreed. After cutting their nails and hair, taking a bath and putting on turbans, they went to the kitchen. To cut a long story short, everything that they produced was without equal. In the time that it would take another cook to get a pot on the fire, they had finished cooking. I took a bath, made offerings to the gods and the sacred fire, and sat down to eat in a room full of rows of
brahmins. Those who praise what they eat by saying "Five 23.95
partridges and four cocks!" have eaten only lowly food. If the immortal gods were to eat that ambrosial food just once, they would stop eating the nectar of immortality and be immortals no more!

When I finished eating I whispered to Go·mukha, "Give ten thousand to the cooks for preparing the meal." He went off with them and returned some time later, alone. His smile indicated that he was happy and he started to talk.

"When I said to them, 'You deserve better than this, however please accept this trifle, which befits our circumstances,' one of them replied, 'It is not right for us to accept 23.100
a gift from our master when he is in dire straits.'

The other became angry and said to him, 'Shame on you for being so weak-hearted that you take pity on this lord of wealth who is richer than Kubéra. How can a man be in reduced circumstances when by his grace millions of sky-rovers are going to be fabulously rich? And what is a man who offers ten thousand in return for one meal when he is in dire straits going to do when he is in luck?'

evam|ādi bruvann eva sa mālyam iva tad dhanam
dhārayitvā kṣaṇaṃ mūrdhnā prasthāya prāptavān gṛham.
23.105 ath' âinaṃ pṛṣṭavān asmi paṭu|kautūhal'|ākulaḥ
‹divyam aiśvaryam āgāmi kathaṃ veda bhavān?› iti.

tatas ten' ôktam «asy' âiva Brahmadattasya bhū|pateḥ
Śata|yajñ'|âdhika|śrīkaḥ pañca|yajñaḥ pit" âbhavat.
cikitsā|sūda|śāstra|jñaḥ śilpitve 'py a|śaṭho 'bhavat
dvitīya iva tasy' ātmā Devavān iti ballavaḥ.
«śarīram etad|āyattaṃ mam' êti» kṛta|buddhinā
rājñā tasmai sva|rājyasya daśamo 'ṃśaḥ prakalpitaḥ.
Nand'|Ôpananda|nāmānau tasya sūda|pateḥ sutau
tādṛś'|ākāra|vijñānāv āvām eva ca viddhitau.
23.110 bālābhyām eva c' āvābhyāṃ sūda|śāstra|cikitsite
saha|jñāna|prayogābhyāṃ kula|vidy" êti śikṣite.

ekadā nau pit" âvocat «putrakau śṛṇutaṃ hitam
śrotāraṃ guru|vākyānāṃ na spṛśanti vipattayaḥ.
pada|vākya|pramāṇāni kāvyāni vividhāni ca
bhavadbhyāṃ śikṣitavyāni citr'|ādiś ca kalā|gaṇaḥ.
kadā cid a|jitaṃ jetuṃ yāto yātavya|maṇḍalam
śāstra|kāvya|kath"|ālāpair vinodaṃ prabhur icchati.
vijñāya tu tad|āsthānam a|saṃnihita|paṇḍitam
vinodaṃ tasya kuryātaṃ śāstr'|ālāp'|ādibhir yuvām.
23.115 pragalbhāḥ pratibhāvanto bahu|vṛtt'|ânta|paṇḍitāḥ
prakāśita|mano|vṛttair bhṛtyāḥ krīḍanti bhartṛbhiḥ.
eka|vidyaḥ punas tatra pragalbho 'pi tapasvikaḥ
sva|vidy"|ālāpa|paryāya|khinnaś ciram udīkṣate.

While saying all this, he put the money on his head like a wreath and then straightaway set out for his house. Overcome by a keen curiosity, I asked him how he knew of 23.105
your future divine sovereignty.

He replied, 'The father of our present king Brahma·datta kept the five sacrifices and was even more illustrious than Indra. He had a cook, Dévavat, who was like a second self to him. He knew the medical and culinary sciences, and wasn't a bad craftsman, either. Realizing that his body depended on him, the king gave him a tenth of his kingdom. The master cook had two sons, Nanda and Upanánda, who were like him in looks and intelligence. We are those two sons. While still children, we learned cooking and medicine in 23.110
both theory and practice because they were our hereditary sciences.

One day our father said to us, "My boys, listen to some good advice. Those who listen to the words of their parents are not touched by misfortune. You must study grammar, logic and the various forms of poetry, as well as painting and all the other arts. One day the king might set off to conquer an unbeaten enemy army and want to be amused with learned discussions, poetry and stories. Seeing that there are no scholars in his assembly, it will be up to you two to amuse him with learned discussions and so forth. When 23.115
their masters reveal what takes their fancy, bold servants who have presence of mind and are versed in a range of subjects can have some fun. But the poor man who is expert in just one topic, even if he is bold, gets exhausted waiting an age for the conversation to turn to his field of expertise. The man who has a wide range of knowledge and whose

abhyasta|bahu|vidyaś ca nir|viparyāsa|mānasaḥ
gata|saṃśaya|duḥkhatvāt sukhinām param'|ēśvaraḥ.
utsāhena ca śikṣethām āyur|aiśvarya|lakṣaṇam
dīrgh'|āyur|vittavanto hi saṃsevyāḥ sevakair iti.»
tac ca pitr|ājñay" â|śeṣam āvābhyām anuśīlitam
ramy'|āsvādaṃ ca pathyaṃ ca ko 'vamanyeta bheṣajam?
23.120 tad «vidyā|dhara|cakrasya cakra|vartī bhaviṣyati
jyeṣṭhaś candra|sahasr'|âṃśu|dīrgh'|āyuś c' êti» nau matiḥ.
tena prasārit'|âṅgābhyām āvābhyām eṣa vanditaḥ
na hi vandana|sāmānyam arhanti bahu|vanditāḥ.
bahavo h' îha tiṣṭhanti brāhmaṇās tīrtha|kukkuṭāḥ
śiraḥ|spandana|mātreṇa tān āvāṃ pūjayāvahe.
tasmād yasmād a|saṅgena sarvatr' āgama|cakṣuṣā
jyeṣṭhasya dṛṣṭam aiśvaryam ataḥ śraddhīyatām› iti.»
prajñapti|Kauśika|suta|pramukhair uktaṃ
Nandasya niścitataraṃ vacanāt tad āsīt
bhāvaṃ hi saṃśaya|tamaḥ|paṭal'|âpinaddham
udbhāvayanty a|vitathā vacana|pradīpāḥ.

iti Bṛhatkathāyāṃ Ślokasaṃgrahe Priyadarśanā|lābhe
Nand'|Ôpananda|kathā.

mind is free from contradictions reigns supreme among those who are happy because he does not suffer from doubt. Study diligently the signs of health and sovereignty; servants should serve those who live long and have power."

So, at our father's instruction, we studied that science in its entirety: who would spurn a medicine that is both
delicious and wholesome? Our opinion is that your elder 23.120
brother will be the emperor of all the sorcerers and as long-lived as the sun and the moon. That is why we saluted him by prostrating ourselves; those who are saluted by many do not deserve an ordinary salutation. There are many brahmins here, hypocrites in a holy place, to whom we show respect simply by nodding our heads. It is with no prior attachment and with a trained eye that we have realized your elder brother's absolute sovereignty, so you should believe in it!'"

The words of the son of Káushika the magician and the others were confirmed by what Nanda said. The light of truth reveals the reality hidden behind the dark veil of doubt.

Thus ends the story of Nanda and Upanánda
in the Winning of Priya·dárshana
in the Compendium of Verses from the Great Story.

CANTO 24
PRIYA·DARSHANÁ

24.1 ATHA NAND’|Ôpanandābhyāṃ
sevyamānaḥ sva|karmaṇā
Punarvasu|gṛhe stokān
divasān avasaṃ sukhī.
kadā cin mandir’|âgra|sthaḥ kurvann āś”|âvalokanam
śramaṇāṃ dṛṣṭavān asmi śiṣyā|saṃgha|puraḥ|sarīm.
kavibhis tair an|ātma|jñair buddhir āyāsyate vṛthā
ye tasyā varṇa|saṃsthāne varṇayanti hata|trapāḥ.
sarvathā taṃ vidhātāraṃ dhig yat kiṃ|cana|kāriṇam
yen’ ākāra|viruddho ’syām ācāro dur|bhagaḥ kṛtaḥ.
24.5 sarvo hi viniyog’|ârtham arthaḥ sarveṇa sṛjyate
ghaṭayitvā ghaṭaḥ kena loṣṭena śakalī|kṛtaḥ.
dhātrā punar iyaṃ sṛṣṭā komal” êva mṛṇālinī
śoṣitā tuhinen’ êti dhik tasya khalatām iti.
tatas tāṃ ciram ālokya nir|nimiṣeṇa cakṣuṣā
Gomukhaḥ sphurit’|ôtsāhaḥ pṛcchati sma Punarvasum.
«alaṃ|kṛta|purī|mārgair ūru|gaurava|mantharaiḥ
eṣā pravrajitā bhadra kva gacchati gatair?» iti.
ten’ ôktam «Ṛṣidatt” êyam ārhataṃ dharmam āsthitā
vīta|rāgatayā siddhān atiśete Jinān api.
24.10 eṣā bāla|sakhīṃ dṛṣṭvā satataṃ rāja|dārikām
kanyak”|ântaḥ|purād eti yāti sva|śayan’|āsanam.»
ity|ādi kathayitv” âsāv Ṛṣidattām avandata
«ambike saha|śiṣyāyās te namo ’stu namo ’stv!» iti.
taṃ ca pravrajit” âvocad «a|saṃbhāṣyo bhavān» iti
«kim artham» iti ten’ ôkte tay” ôktam «avadhīyatām.
jñān’|âdhikṣipta|sarva|jñau rūpa|vismārita|Smarau
dvijau jyeṣṭha|kaniṣṭh’|âkhyau tvad|gṛhe kila tiṣṭhataḥ.
tat saṃdarśana|saṃbhāṣā|janitaṃ ca sukhaṃ tvayā
draviṇaṃ kṛpaṇen’ êva pracchannam upabhujyate.

I SPENT A FEW HAPPY days in Punar·vasu's house enjoying 24.1
the cooking of Nanda and Upanánda. Once, when I
was on the roof of the house taking in the view, I saw a nun
with a group of pupils. Any foolish poets shameless enough
to describe her looks and figure would be exerting their
intellects in vain. Shame on the fickle creator for making
her live that unfortunate life, which was inconsistent with
her appearance. People create things in order to use them. 24.5
Who makes a pot and then smashes it with a stone? But the
creator had made that girl like a slender lotus stem and she
had been withered by the frost—shame on him for being
so wicked!

Go·mukha stared unblinkingly at her for an age and then, quivering with excitement, he asked Punar·vasu, "Where, my friend, is this nun going, adorning the streets of the city with her stately, heavy-hipped gait?"

He replied, "She is Rishi·datta, a follower of the religion
of the arhats, and she surpasses even the perfected Jinas in
passionlessness. She regularly visits her childhood friend, 24.10
the king's daughter, and then leaves the girl's apartments to
go home."

After saying this, he greeted Rishi·datta: "Homage to you and your pupils, madam, homage to you!"

The nun replied, "You are not to be spoken to, sir." "Why?" asked Punar·vasu, and she said, "Pay attention. Apparently there are two brahmin brothers staying in your house, who put the omniscient to shame with their intelligence and make everyone forget the god of love with their looks. Like a miser enjoying his wealth, you have been pri-

24.15 suhṛt sādhāraṇaṃ yasya sukhaṃ sa paramaṃ sukhī
sukha|saṃvaraṇ'|āyāsād viparītas tu duḥkhitaḥ.
suhṛdbhiḥ kupitais tasmād a|saṃbhāṣyaḥ kṛto bhavān
teṣām atr' ānay'|ôpāyaḥ samarthaś cintyatām» iti.

ath' ôccair Gomukhen' ôktam «a|cireṇa Punarvasuḥ
[.....................................].»
[.......................................]
saha|Nand'|Ôpanandaś ca Jin'|āyatana|maṇḍapam.

arhatas tatra vanditvā saṃghaṃ cīvara|vāsasam
Ṛṣidattāṃ ca tad|datte viṣṭare samupāviśam.
24.20 avalambita|bāhus tu mukta|kakṣaś ca Gomukhaḥ
sthitvā deva|kula|dvāre Jina|stotram udāharat.
«namo 'stu sarva|siddhebhyaḥ sādhubhyaś ca namo 'stu vaḥ
Ṛṣabha|pramukhebhyaś ca sarva|jñebhyo namo 'stv!» iti.

«sādhu śrāvaka! dhanyo 'si yaḥ sarva|jñaṃ namasyasi»
ity|ādi bahu Nirgranthāḥ prīty" âstuvata Gomukham.

ath' âyam Ṛṣidattāyāḥ pādau gāḍhaṃ nipīḍayan
abravīt «su|prasannau me bhavantau bhavatām!» iti.

tayā tv «asya prayukt'|āśīr asmākaṃ laghu|śāsane
śrāvakasy' âpi saṃvādyā pratipattir bhavatv!» iti.
24.25 ath' ôktam Upanandena «vīṇā|goṣṭhī pravartyatām!
eṣa saṃnihitaḥ saṃghaḥ sakalaḥ suhṛdām» iti.

anyen' ôktam «an|āyāte pravīṇe Gaṅgarakṣite
a|saṃnihita|haṃs" êva nalinī nī|ravā sabhā!
tasmān mahā|pratīhāraṃ bhavantaḥ Gaṅgarakṣitam
udīkṣantām!» iti

vately enjoying the pleasure of their sight and company. The 24.15
man whose happiness is open to all is perfectly happy, but his counterpart, because he tries to conceal his happiness, is miserable. As a result your friends are angry and do not want to talk to you. You must think of a suitable way to bring your guests to us."

Go·mukha called out, "Punar·vasu will soon †arrange for us to meet you there." Then we went†* to the Jaina temple with Nanda and Upanánda.

On arriving there, I greeted the arhats, the community of robed monks and Rishi·datta, and sat down on a seat
offered by the latter. Go·mukha, his arms hanging down 24.20
and the end of his dhoti loose, stood at the door of the temple and sung a hymn to the Jinas: "Homage to all the perfected ones and homage to the virtuous and homage to Ríshabha and the other omniscients!"

Several naked monks praised Go·mukha affectionately, saying things like "Bravo, devotee! Blessed is he that pays homage to the omniscient one!"

Then he clasped Rishi·datta's two feet tightly and said, "May both of you show me favor!"

She said, "A sincere welcome and blessings to this devotee of our humble order!"

Then Upanánda said, "Let the lute concert begin! The 24.25
entire assembly of friends is here and ready."

Someone else said, "But without the master Ganga·rákshita, the gathering is as mute as a lotus pond without a swan, so you must wait for the great chamberlain Ganga·rákshita!"

tataḥ samprāptaḥ Gaṅgarakṣitaḥ.
taṃ dṛṣṭvā nāgarair uktam «ārya|jyeṣṭhasya v" âsya vā
ākhyāta nipuṇaṃ dṛṣṭvā kataraḥ rūpavān» iti.

āsīc ca mama «yat satyaṃ satyam ev' âsmi rūpavān
Gaṅgarakṣita|rūpeṇa rūpaṃ me sa|dṛśaṃ yataḥ.
24.30 yadīyam etadīyena rūpeṇ' âpy upacaryate
upamānam upādeyaḥ so 'pi rūpavatām» iti.

vanditvā Jinam A|granthān Ṛṣidattāṃ ca māṃ ca saḥ
upāviśat punaś c' ôktam Upanandena pūrvavat.
tataḥ pravrajit" āha sma «śreṣṭhini Priyadarśane
an|āyāte sadaḥ sarvam idam a|priya|darśanam.
ataḥ pratīkṣyatāṃ śreṣṭhī kṣaṇam» ity udit'|ēkṣayā
«ayam āyāta» ity ākhyan nāgarāḥ Priyadarśanam.

āsīc ca mama taṃ dṛṣṭvā «n' âiv' âyaṃ Priyadarśanaḥ
eṣā puruṣa|veṣeṇa bhūṣitā Priyadarśanā.
24.35 strainībhir gati|saṃsthāna|vāṇībhir vyaktam etayā
kṣipta|trailokya|saundaryam ākhyātaṃ strainam ātmanaḥ.»
sā tu vandita|dev'|ādiḥ s'|ādaraṃ mām avandata
«ciraṃ sundari jīv' êti» may" âpi prativanditā.

tataḥ krodh'|āruṇ'|âkṣeṇa Gomukhen' âham īkṣitaḥ
citraṃ nāgarakaiḥ kaiś cid lajjitaiḥ kaiś cid ambaram.
Ṛṣidattā punaḥ s'|âsraṃ sa|vikāsa|cal'|ēkṣaṇā
sa|Gomukham apaśyan mām ā|śiraś|caraṇaṃ ciram.
atha prapañcam ākṣeptum etaṃ sapadi Gomukhaḥ
abhāṣata suhṛd|vargaṃ «goṣṭhī prastūyatām!» iti.

Then Ganga·rákshita arrived. When they saw him, the townspeople said, "Look carefully at the great nobleman and this man, and say who is the more handsome."

I said to myself, "I must truly be handsome if my looks
are similar to those of Ganga·rákshita. If one is used as a 24.30
term of reference by which to compare handsomeness such as his, then one must be counted among the handsome oneself."

He greeted the Jina, the naked monks, Rishi·datta and me, and sat down. Upanánda repeated what he had said before. Then the nun said, "Without the head of the guild, Priya·dárshana, the meeting is unpleasant to behold,* so let's wait a moment for the head of the guild." Then the townspeople looked up and announced the arrival of Priya·dárshana.

When I saw him I said to myself, "This is not Priya·dárshana; it's Priya·darshaná, a beautiful girl dressed as a man.
With her ladylike walk, figure and voice, she is proclaiming 24.35
clearly her feminine beauty, which surpasses anything in the three worlds." She greeted the gods and so forth before greeting me politely, and I returned the greeting, saying, "Live long, beautiful lady!"

His eyes red with rage, Go·mukha looked at me; some of the embarrassed townspeople looked at a painting, others at the sky. But Rishi·datta, her darting eyes wide open and tearful, looked me and Go·mukha up and down for a long time. To stop the situation developing further, Go·mukha quickly said to the assembled friends, "Let the entertainment begin!"

24.40 Upanandas tataḥ pūrvaṃ tathā vīṇām avādayat
yathā vigata|rāg'|ādyair Nirgranthair api mūrchitam.
Upanandāt tato Nandaṃ Nandād api Punarvasum
Punarvasor agād vīṇā kramāt taṃ Gaṅgarakṣitam.
Upanand'|ādikānāṃ ca jita|Nārada|Parvatam
parājayata dūreṇa pūrvaṃ pūrvaṃ paraḥ paraḥ.
krama|prāptā tato vīṇā Gomukhaṃ Gaṅgarakṣitāt
Sarasvat" îva vitt'|āḍhyād īśvarād dur|gataṃ gatā.
Gomukhas tu tato vīṇām avādayata līlayā
yathā nāgarikair dīnair īkṣitaḥ Gaṅgarakṣitaḥ.
24.45 Gomukh'|âṅkāt tato vīṇā yāti sma Priyadarśanam
ku|laṭ" êva priy'|ôtsaṅgāt kāminaṃ priya|darśanam.
tataḥ pravādite tasmin pragīte c' âti|mānuṣam
vailakṣyād Gomukhasy' āsīd abhiprāyaḥ palāyitum.
kiṃ tu «Nārada|śiṣyo 'yaṃ suto vā Tumburor» iti
yat satyam aham apy āsam adbhuta|śruti|vismitaḥ.
mukta|vīṇe tatas tatra śanair māṃ Gomukho 'bravīt
«adhunā prāpta|paryāyaṃ vādanaṃ bhavatām» iti.
hasitvā tam ath' âvocam «ady' âpi hi śiśur bhavān
yo māṃ yatra kva cit tucche pravartayati vastuni!
24.50 nagna|śramaṇakānāṃ ca kirāṭānāṃ ca saṃnidhau
vīṇāṃ vādayamānasya mādṛśaḥ kīdṛśaṃ phalam?»
iti śrutv" êdam ukto 'ham anena kṛta|manyunā
«Campāyāṃ kīdṛśaṃ kāryam abhavad bhavatām?» iti.
tatas tam uktavān asmi «śrūyatām yadi na śrutam
prāptir Gandharvadattāyās tatra kāryam abhūd» iti.
ath' âyam avadat tatra «devī|prāptiḥ phalaṃ yadi
ih' âpi Gomukha|prāptiḥ phalam uttamam iṣyatām.
‹yuṣmad|anyo na māṃ kaś cid vīṇayā jitavān› iti
idaṃ me śreṣṭham āgamya śreṣṭhin" âpahṛtaṃ yaśaḥ.

Upanánda played the lute first, in such a way that even 24.40
the impassive naked monks were spellbound. From Upanánda the lute went to Nanda, from Nanda to Punar·vasu
and from him in turn to Ganga·rákshita. As Upanánda and
the others played in succession, each far surpassed the one
that had played before, each of whom had surpassed Nárada and Párvata. From Ganga·rákshita the lute went in
turn to Go·mukha, like Sarásvati going from a rich lord
to a pauper. But Go·mukha played the lute so gracefully
that the players looked with pity at Ganga·rákshita. Then 24.45
the lute went from Go·mukha's arms to Priya·dárshana, like
an adulteress going from the arms of her husband to her
handsome lover. When he played it and sung divinely, Go·
mukha was so deflated he wanted to run away. But in fact
I, too, was astonished by the amazing recital and wondered
whether he might be a pupil of Nárada, or Túmburu's son.
When he had handed the lute on, Go·mukha whispered to
me, "Now it is your turn to play." I laughed and said to him,
"You are still a child—that is why you get me involved in any
old silly business! What does someone like me have to gain 24.50
from playing the lute before naked monks and merchants?"

Taking umbrage, he replied, "What was there for you to gain in Champa?"*

I said to him, "Listen, if you don't know already: the aim there was the winning of Gandhárva·datta."

He replied, "If winning a queen was the reward, then now you should want to win Go·mukha, the best of rewards. Having heard my boast that other than you no one has ever surpassed me on the lute, the chief of the guild has come

24.55 so 'yam asmad|yaśaś|cauro yadi n' āśu nigṛhyate
tyajāmy eṣa tataḥ prāṇān duḥkha|bhār'|āturān!» iti.
mama tv āsīd «a|saṃdigdhaṃ sarvam atr' ôpapadyate
maraṇ'|âbhyadhika|kleśo māna|bhaṅgo hi māninām.
śāstr'|ârtha|jñāna|mattasya nigṛhītasya vādinaḥ
kāntayā ca vimuktasya duḥkhaṃ ken' ôpamīyate.
tasmād etad iha nyāyyam» iti niścitya sādaram
vyavasthāpayituṃ tantrīr ārabhe dur|vyavasthitāḥ.
tataḥ pṛthulitair netraiḥ pulak'|āliṅgita|tvacaḥ
anyonyasya niraikṣanta vadanāni sadaḥ|sadaḥ.
24.60 tantrīṣu kara|śākh"|âgraiḥ parāmṛṣṭāsu te tataḥ
«hā! hā! kim idam?» ity uktvā pusta|nyastā iv' âbhavan.
ath' âitasyāṃ avasthāyāṃ mayā vīṇā ca saṃhṛtā
taiś ca mukt'|āyat'|ôcchvāsair jīva|loko 'valokitaḥ.
harṣ'|âruṇa|parāmṛṣṭaṃ vikasad|viśada|prabham
abhrājata tataḥ sadyaḥ Gomukh'|ānana|paṅka|jam.
jita|Gomukha|darpas tu jito 'pi Priyadarśanaḥ
jita|dur|jaya|vād" îva prītimān mām abhāṣata.
«śreṣṭhī jyeṣṭhena vīṇāyāṃ jagad|vijayinā jitaḥ!
iti me prasthitā kīrtir ā|payodhi vasuṃdharām!
24.65 pūrṇā hi vasudhā śūdrair na ca tān veda kaś cana
Rāghav'|ôtkṛtta|mūrdhnas tu Śambūkasy' â|malaṃ yaśaḥ!
kiṃ c' âdy' ārabhya yuṣmabhyaṃ may" ātm" âiva niveditaḥ
vīṇā|vād'|ârthinaṃ śiṣyaṃ parigṛhṇīta mām» iti.

along and stolen my glory. If the thief of my glory is not 24.55
defeated soon, I shall give up my life, afflicted as it is by the
burden of sorrow!"

I said to myself, "Of course, everything he is saying is
true. For the proud, humiliation is more painful than death.
What can compare with the sorrow of a man intoxicated
by his understanding of the scriptures being beaten in a
dispute, or of a man separated from his sweetheart? So, in
this case, it is the right thing to do." Deciding thus, I carefully started to tune the out-of-tune lute strings. Their skin
tingling all over, the members of the assembly looked with
wide eyes at one another's faces. As my fingertips plucked the 24.60
strings, they said, "Ah! Ah! What is this?" and became like
waxwork dummies. They were still in that condition when
I put down the lute. Letting out long sighs, they returned
to the land of the living. Touched by the rising sun of joy,
Go·mukha's lotus-face suddenly shone with a blossoming
brilliance. Priya·dárshana, the man who had humbled Go·
mukha, had been beaten. Even so, he spoke to me affectionately, as if he himself had beaten an unbeatable musician:
"The head of the guild has been beaten at the lute by the
world-conquering master! Thus my fame has spread across
the earth as far as the ocean! The earth is full of shudras and 24.65
nobody knows who they are, but because Rama cut off his
head, Shambúka's fame shines forth! What's more, from
today onward I offer myself to you. I want to learn to play
the lute; please accept me as your student."

asyām eva tu velāyām avocad Gaṅgarakṣitaḥ
‹ayam eva mam' âpy arthaḥ sa|phalī|kriyatām!› iti.
tatas tau Gomukhen' ôktau «bhavantāv āgam'|ârthinau
an|āyās'|ôpadeśau ca yat tad evaṃ bhavatv» iti.
sa mayā śanakair uktaḥ «kṣipram eva tvay" ânayoḥ
prārthanā pratipann" êti» Gomukhen' ôditaṃ tataḥ.
24.70 «śarīraṃ Kāśi|rājasya rājyam antaḥ|puraṃ puram
yac c' ânyad api tat sarvaṃ Gaṅgarakṣita|rakṣitam.
yasya ca svayam ev' âyaṃ dāsyām abhyanugacchati
tasy' āpadbhir a|saṃkīrṇā hasta|sthāḥ sarva|saṃpadaḥ.
a|śeṣa|śreṇi|bhartā ca śreṣṭhitvāt Priyadarśanaḥ
sa yasya kiṃ|karas tasya kiṃ|karā sakalā purī.
etat phalam abhipretya may" âitābhyāṃ pratiśrutam
na hy an|ālocya|kartāraḥ kiṃ|karā bhavatām» iti.
praśaṃsya tasy' êti mati|prakarṣaṃ
Nand'|Ôpanand'|ādi|suhṛt|samagraḥ
namas|kṛt'|ârhad|vrata|cāri|saṃghaḥ
Punarvasor veśma gatas tato 'ham.

. . . Priyadarśanā|lābhe.

At that very instant, Ganga·rákshita said, "I have the same wish. Please make it come true!"

Then Go·mukha said to them both, "You are keen to learn and it will be no trouble to teach you, so he will do it."

I whispered to Go·mukha, "You accepted their request very quickly," and he replied, "Ganga·rákshita protects the 24.70
person of the king of Kashi, his kingdom, his harem, the city and everything else. The man to whom he is subservient has nothing but success in his hands with no chance of misfortune. As head of the guild, Priya·dárshana is in charge of all the merchants: the man who has him under his control has the whole city under his control. It was with this end in mind that I gave them my consent. Your servants do not do things indiscriminately."

I praised his excellent judgment and, after paying homage to the congregation of arhats and monks, went to Punar·vasu's house with Nanda, Upanánda and all my other friends.

. . . in the Winning of Priya·darshaná.*

CANTO 25
GO·MUKHA'S WEDDING

Tatra Nand'|ādibhir mitrair ārādhana|viśāradaiḥ
a|kṛtrima|suhṛd|bhāvaiḥ saṃgataḥ sukham āsiṣi.
ekad" āhāra|velāyāṃ dṛśyate sma na Gomukhaḥ
atha nītam an|āhārair asmābhir api tad dinam.
asau tu sāyam āgatya n' âti|svābhāvik'|ākṛtiḥ
tad|a|nātha|mat'|ôdvignaṃ māṃ vinītavad uktavān.
«rāja|mārge mayā dṛṣṭaḥ paura|saṃghāta|saṃkaṭe
bhṛtyo Hariśikhasy' âiva loken' ântaritaḥ sa ca.
25.5 tad|gaveṣayamāṇena may" âdya gamitaṃ dinam
kārye hi guruṇi vyagraṃ jighats" âpi na bādhate.
sa c' â|vaśyaṃ may" ânveṣyaḥ suhṛd|vārtt'|ôpalabdhaye
tasmān mā mām a|paśyantaḥ kṛdhvaṃ duḥkhāsikām» iti.
mayā c' âyam anujñātaḥ kṣipta|sapt'|âṣṭa|vāsaraḥ
mada|manthara|saṃcāro bahu|jalpann upāgamat.
ath' âinam aham ālokya krodha|kṣobhita|mānasaḥ
sthitvā kṣaṇam an|ālāpaḥ paruṣ'|ālāpam abravam.
«īdṛśas tādṛśaḥ prājñaḥ prekṣā|kārī ca Gomukhaḥ
iti paṅgos turaṃgasya kṛtā Garuḍa|vegatā.
25.10 pūrvaṃ brāhmaṇam ākhyāya samastāyāḥ puraḥ puraḥ
adhunā madhunā mattaḥ kathaṃ paśyasi mām?» iti.
atha mām ayam āha sma «na madaḥ pāramārthikaḥ
sa|doṣaṃ tu vaco vaktuṃ may" âyaṃ kṛtrimaḥ kṛtaḥ.
mattasya kila vāg|doṣāḥ pāruṣy'|ân|ṛtat"|ādayaḥ
dūṣayanti na vaktāram ato 'yaṃ kṛtrimo madaḥ.»
tatas tam uktavān asmi «saṃbhāvita|guṇasya te
mada|pracchādan'|ôpāyaḥ kiṃ nv a|doṣo 'pi vidyate?»

I STAYED THERE HAPPILY in the company of Nanda and my other friends. They served me expertly and their friendship was unforced.

One day Go·mukha failed to appear at lunchtime and we did not eat all day. He arrived in the evening, not quite his usual self. I had been worried about not having him to look after me, and he humbly said to me, “On the main road, in the midst of a crowd of citizens, I saw Hari·shikha’s servant. He then disappeared into the throng. I have spent 25.5
the whole day looking for him; hunger does not trouble a man busy with an important task. I must find him in order to get news of our friend, so do not be worried if you don’t see me.”

I gave him my permission. After seven or eight days had passed, he arrived stumbling drunkenly and babbling. When I saw him, my mind was perturbed by anger and I stood speechless for a moment before addressing him harshly: “Here’s Go·mukha, such a wise man, who acts with such deliberation—the swiftness of Gáruda has been bestowed upon a lame horse! You declared yourself to be 25.10
a brahmin before the entire city. How can you now show yourself to me in this drunken condition?”

He replied, “This is not real drunkenness; I have faked it in order to speak offensively. The offensive words of a drunk—insults, lies and so forth—have no ill effect on their speaker. That is why I have faked this drunkenness.”

I said to him, “Your virtues are celebrated, but how can this trick of hiding behind drunkenness not be sinful?”

ath' ânen' ôktam «ast' îti» «katham?» ity udite mayā
ayam ārabhat' ākhyātuṃ lajjā|mantharit'|âkṣaram.
25.15 «śrūyatām Ṛṣidattā me yatra netra|pathaṃ gatā
ārabhya divasāt tasmāc ceto|viṣayatām iti.
niravagrahatāṃ buddhvā cittasy' âtha mam' âbhavat
kasmād a|viṣaye cakṣuś cetasā me prasāritam.
jñāta|dharm'|ârtha|śāstratvāt sthānāt sādhu|sabhāsu ca
rāg'|âdhīnaṃ na me cakṣuḥ pravṛttaṃ gaṇikāsv api.
nūnam eṣā parigrāhyā mama pravrajitā yataḥ
saṃkalpena mam' âitasyāṃ dur|dānta|turago '|yataḥ.
tasmād ‹asyām an|iṣṭasya saṃkalpasya nibandhanam
jijñāsye tāvad› ity enām agacchaṃ draṣṭum anv|aham.
25.20 nān"|ākārair vinodaiś ca deś'|ântara|kath"|ādibhiḥ
dvi|trair eva dinais tasyā viśvāsam udapādayam.

ekadā prastut'|ālāpaḥ pṛṣṭo 'ham Ṛṣidattayā
‹ke ke deśās tvayā dṛṣṭāḥ krāmatā pṛthivīm?› iti.
‹samṛddhiḥ sa|śarīr" êva Kauśāmbī yatra pattanam
Vatsa|deśaḥ sa dṛṣṭaḥ prāṅ mam' êti› kathite mayā.
tay" ôktam ‹alam ālāpair aparais tava dur|bhagaiḥ
kriyatāṃ Vatsa|Kauśāmbī|saṃbandh" âiva punaḥ kathā.
atha jānāsi Kauśāmbyām ākāra|jita|Manmatham
Gomukhaṃ nāma niṣṇātaṃ sa|vidyāsu kalāsv?› iti.
25.25 ath' âcintayam ‹ātmānam etasyai kathayāmi kim?
atha vā dhig a|dhīraṃ mām evaṃ tāvad bhavatv› iti.

tato 'ham uktavān ‹ārye jānās' îti kim ucyate?
ātmānaṃ ko na jānāti? sa hi me paramaḥ suhṛt!
atha vā na viśeṣo 'sti sūkṣmo 'pi mama Gomukhāt
tena māṃ paśyatā vyaktaṃ dṛṣṭo bhavati Gomukhaḥ!›

"It is not," he replied. When I asked how, he started to tell a story, his voice heavy with shame.

"Listen. I fell in love with Rishi·datta the day that I saw 25.15
her. Knowing my heart's lack of restraint, I wondered why it had set my sights on something unobtainable. Because I knew the treatises on religious and practical behavior and had lived among virtuous men, my sight was not in the sway of my emotions, even when it fell on courtesans. I just had to take this nun for myself, for the untamed stallion of my heart was set on her, let loose by desire. Thinking that I might discover the reason for my unwanted desire for her,
I went to see her every day. Using various different ways to 25.20
entertain her, such as tales of foreign lands, it took me just two or three days to win her confidence.

One day, when we were talking, Rishi·datta asked me, 'What countries have you seen during your travels across the world?' When I replied, 'I have seen the country of Vatsa in the east, whose capital, Kaushámbi, is the embodiment of prosperity,' she said, 'Don't talk of anywhere else—I'm not interested. Tell me more about Vatsa and Kaushámbi. Do you know a man from Kaushámbi called Go·mukha, who is more handsome than the god of love and an expert in the sciences and arts?'

I thought, 'Shall I tell her who I am? Wait—foolish me 25.25
for being so impatient—I'll just tell her this. . .'

I said, 'Madam, how can you ask if I know him? What man does not know himself? He is my best friend! Anyway, there is not the slightest difference between me and Go·mukha. The person who sees me has without doubt seen Go·mukha!'

ath' âsau locan'|ântena bāṣpa|stimita|pakṣmaṇā
s'|ânurāg" êva dṛṣṭvā māṃ ciraṃ mantharam abravīt.
‹Gomukhaḥ kila rūpeṇa kalā|kauśala|cāriṇā
Vatsa|rāja|sutaṃ muktvā n' ânyena sadṛśaḥ kṣitau.
25.30 yadi c' âsau tvad|ākāras tvat|kalā|jāla|peśalaḥ
vidyā|dhara|kumāreṇa Gomukhaḥ sadṛśas tataḥ.
yas tvad|ākāra|vijñānaḥ sarvathā puṇyavān asau
Gandhaśailo 'pi hi ślāghyas tulyamānaḥ Sumeruṇā.›

ity uktvā cīvar'|ântena mukham āvṛtya nīcakaiḥ
asau roditum ārabdhā s'|ôtkampa|stana|maṇḍalā.
Ṛṣidattām ath' âvocam ‹ārye kiṃ kāraṇaṃ tvayā
rudyate mṛta|paty" êva Gomukha|śravaṇād?› iti.

tay" ôktaṃ ‹śrūyatām! asti vidvān Rājagṛhe vaṇik
Padmo nāma dhanaṃ yasya padmasy' êva mahā|nidheḥ.
25.35 kuṭumb'|ācāra|cature priye patyuḥ pati|vrate
Sumanā Mahadinnā ca tasya bhārye babhūvatuḥ.
tayor abhavatāṃ putrau mātṛ|nāma|sa|nāmakau
putrābhyāṃ dayite pitros tathā duhitarāv api.
tatra yā Sumanā nāma tasyāḥ Sumanasaḥ sutā
nagaryāṃ pariṇīt" âtra śreṣṭhinā Kāliyena sā.
duhitā Mahadinnāyā yā ca mātuḥ sa|nāmikā
Cedi|Vats'|ēśa|mitreṇa pariṇīta'|Ṛṣabheṇa sā.
Ṛṣabhān Mahadinnāyām utpannaḥ kila Gomukhaḥ
na kutaś cin na kasyāṃ cit kaś cij jagati yādṛśaḥ.
25.40 ahaṃ tu Mahadinnasya tanayā guṇa|śālinaḥ
Him'|âdrer api niyānti saritaḥ kṣāra|vārayaḥ.
s" âhaṃ bāl" âiva gurubhir Gomukhāya pratiśrutā
kaṃ hi nāma na gacchanti kanyā|pitror mano|rathāḥ.

She gave me a long and seemingly affectionate look out of the corner of her eyes, their lashes wet with tears, and said slowly, 'I'm told that other than the son of the king of Vatsa there is no one on earth comparable to Go·mukha in looks and artistic talent. If he looks like you and is as talented as 25.30
you in all the arts, then Go·mukha must resemble the prince of the sorcerers. A man with your looks and intelligence is truly blessed; even when compared with Mount Suméru, Mount Gandha·mádana is still to be praised.'

After saying this, she covered her face with the end of her robe and started to sob gently, her round breasts trembling. I said to Rishi·datta, 'Madam, why do you cry like a widow on hearing about Go·mukha?'

She replied, 'Listen. In Raja·griha there is a learned merchant called Padma, whose fortune is like Kubéra's great lotus treasure. He had two dear devoted wives, Sumanas and 25.35
Maha·dinna, who were skilled at running the household. They had two sons who had the same names as their mothers, and two similarly named daughters, who were more dear to their father than his sons. The girl called Súmanas, Sumanas's daughter, was married to Káliya, the head of the merchants in this city. Maha·dinna's daughter, who had the same name as her mother, was married to Ríshabha, a friend of the king of Chedi and Vatsa. Go·mukha was born to Ríshabha and Maha·dinná, and no father and mother in the world had ever had a son like him. I am the daughter 25.40
of the virtuous Maha·dinna: salty rivers can flow from even the Himálaya. As a child I was promised to Go·mukha by my parents; there is no limit to the desires of a girl's mother and father.

kāle kva cid atīte tu taṃ guṇair jana|vallabham
hima|kāla iv' â|sādhuḥ kālo 'dmam anāśayat.
tat|kuṭumbaṃ tatas tena dhārakena vinā|kṛtam
unmūlita|dṛḍha|stambha|mandir'|âvasthāṃ gatam.
Vārāṇasyāṃ tataḥ pitrā svasuḥ Sumanaso gṛhe
sthāpit" âhaṃ pitṛ|svasrā duhit" êva ca lālitā.
25.45 saṃtat'|ādyaiḥ krameṇ' âtha jvaraiḥ pañcabhir apy aham
pīḍyamānā babhūv' ândhā pratyākhyātā cikitsakaiḥ.
atra c' â|gādha|Jainendra|śāstra|sāgara|pāra|gā
āsīc Chrutadharā nāma śramaṇā karuṇāvatī.
etaṃ vācā samānīya mantr'|âgada|viśāradā
mām asāv a|cireṇ' âiva tasmād vyādher amocayat.

svasth'|âvasthāṃ ca māṃ dṛṣṭvā Sumanā gṛham ānayat
atha krodhād iv' âgṛhṇāt s" âiva jvara|paraṃparā.
tataḥ Śrutadharāyai mām arpayat Sumanāḥ punaḥ
sa ca yātaḥ punar vyādhir mantr'|âgada|bhayād iva.
25.50 śravaṇām avadad dainyād dur|manāḥ Sumanās tataḥ
«pravrajyā|grāhaṇen' êyaṃ bālikā jīvyatām» iti.

tathā c' āgrāhayat sā mām arhat|pravacanaṃ yathā
sakalaḥ śramanā|saṃghaḥ siṣyatām agaman mama.
kevala|jñāna|dīpena dṛṣṭvā saṃsāra|phalgutām
nirvāṇasya ca sāratvaṃ niṣṭhāṃ Śrutadhar" âgamat.
nirvṛttāyāṃ tatas tasyāṃ saṃhatya śramaṇā|gaṇaḥ
gaṇa|nīm akarod asmin vihāre mām an|icchatīm.

dhyānaṃ yad yat samāpadya devat"|ālambanaṃ niśi
balād ālambanaṃ tatra Gomukhaḥ saṃnidhīyate.
25.55 yadā yadā ca go|śabdam adhīyānā vadāmy aham
mukh'|ôttara|padas tatra jāyate sa tadā tadā.

After some time had passed, like a cruel winter taking a lotus, death took Padma, whose virtues had made him dear to the people.* Deprived of its mainstay, his family became like a house whose supporting pillar has been uprooted. My father sent me to the house of his sister Súmanas in Varánasi, and my aunt looked after me as if I was her daughter. But 25.45
then I suffered from the five fevers in succession, starting with the steady fever, and became blind. The doctors gave up on me. A kindly nun called Shruta·dhara, who had crossed the ocean of the unfathomable treatises of Jainéndra, was living here. Skilled in spells and medicines, she drew the fever out with her voice and quickly cured me of the illness.

When she saw that I was well, Súmanas took me to her house, but then, as if enraged, that series of fevers held me in its grip again. Súmanas brought me to Shruta·dhara again, and the disease departed once more, as if in fear of the spells and medicines. Súmanas was downcast and said to the nun 25.50
sadly, "In order to survive, this girl must become a nun."

Shruta·dhara taught me the doctrine of the arhats so well that the entire community of nuns took me as its teacher. Having used the lamp of absolute knowledge to see the insignificance of worldly existence and the importance of liberation, Shruta·dhara went to her final resting place. After her death, the community of nuns met and, against my will, made me the abbess of this convent.

Whatever deity-based meditation I practiced at night, Go·mukha would force his way in as its object. Whenever 25.55
I uttered the word *"go"* ("cow") in the course of my recitations, it would be followed by the word *"mukha"* ("face"). If during a conversation I used the word *"mukha"* ("face")

jalpantī mukha|śabdaṃ ca prayuñje yadi kevalam
gaḥ|śabda|pūrva|padatāṃ balāt tatr' ôpagacchati.
«Gomukhena parāmṛṣṭaṃ ślāghanīyaṃ tṛṇ'|ādy api»
iti cintā|parādhīnā mahāntaṃ kālam akṣipam.
tāvac ca na mayā tyaktā praty|āśā Gomukh'|āśrayā
āgatā yāvad any" âiva vārttā datta|nir|āśatā.

Campā|sthasya prabhor mūlaṃ prasthitaḥ sa|balaḥ kila
Gomukhaḥ sa|suhṛd|vargaḥ Pulindair antare hataḥ.
25.60 yac c' âsmi na mṛtā sadyaḥ śrutvā Gomukha|vaiśasam
vicāraṇa|samarthāyāḥ prajñāyāḥ sā samarthatā.
āsīc ca mama «jīvantī jīvitasya mahat phalam
ramyām ākarṇayiṣyāmi Gomukhasya kathām» iti.
api c' âparam apy asti jīvit'|ālambanaṃ mama
hataḥ pravāda|mātreṇa Gomukhaḥ śabarair iti.
tena Gomukha|saṃbandhām ākarṇya ruditaṃ mayā
a|mṛt'|âbhyadhikatve 'pi duḥkha|hetuṃ kathām› iti.

mama tv āsīd ‹yath" āh' êyaṃ sarvaṃ tad upapadyate
yuṣmad|dāsāḥ kathaṃ kuryuḥ pāpa|saṃkalpam anyathā.
25.65 svair iyaṃ gurubhir dattā madīyair api y" ârthitā
kumārī s'|ânurāgā ca tasmān na tyāgam arhati.›
ity|ādi bahu nirdhārya tat svī|karaṇa|kāraṇam
a|duṣṭaṃ grahaṇ'|ôpāyam aham etaṃ prayuktavān.
svādunā piṇḍa|pātena vandanena cikitsayā
mardan'|âbhyañjan'|ādyaiś ca laghu saṃgham atoṣayam.
vyagreṇa c' âtra vṛtt'|ânte dattaṃ vaḥ kṛtak'|ôttaram
‹mitra|vārtā|vidā|vyagraṃ pratīkṣadhvaṃ na mām› iti.
Ṛṣidattām ath' âvocaṃ ‹sva|śilpe labdha|kauśalāḥ
śrāvakaiḥ saṃnidhāryantām anna|saṃskāra|kārakāḥ.

on its own, it would automatically be preceded by the word *"go"* ("cow"). "Even something like a blade of grass is praiseworthy if Go·mukha has touched it"—I spent a long time obsessed with this thought and I did not give up my longing for Go·mukha until news arrived that made me lose hope.

It seems that Go·mukha set out with an army to meet his master in Champa and he and his friends were killed on
the way by the Pulíndas. That I did not die immediately on 25.60
hearing of Go·mukha's murder is because of the intellect's capacity for reflection. I said to myself, "Alive, I shall be able to listen to delightful tales about Go·mukha, an ample reward for living." And there was another reason for me to stay alive: it was only according to hearsay that the tribals had killed Go·mukha. Thus I have told you why I wept when I heard tales of Go·mukha: despite being better than the nectar of immortality, they are also a cause for sorrow.'

I told myself that what she had said all made sense. How
otherwise could your servants have sinful desires? She had 25.65
been given by her parents and asked for by mine, and she was young and in love, so she was not to be shunned. After much such deliberation I employed the following blameless ruse to make her accept me as her husband. I quickly ingratiated myself with the community by giving them delicious food, respectful salutations, medicine, massages, ointments and so forth. It was when I was busy doing that that I lied to you by telling you not to wait for me because I was busy trying to get news of our friend. I said to Rishi·datta, 'Have the
lay followers assemble some expert cooks. I want to worship 25.70
the arhats with scents, clothes, garlands and so forth, and give a feast for the sages and nuns. The sin accumulated

25.70 arhatām arhaṇaṃ kṛtvā gandha|vāsa|srag|ādibhiḥ
ṛṣibhyaḥ śramaṇābhyaś ca dātum icchāmi bhojanam.
mithyā|dṛṣṭi|sahasrāṇi bhojayitvā yad arjyate
tad ekam arhataṃ bhaktyā sadyaḥ pāpaṃ pramārjyate.
tena sant' îha yāvantaḥ priya|sarva|jña|śāsanāḥ
sa|śrāvaka|gaṇān āryāṃs tāṃs tad āmantryatām› iti.

sarvathā sādhitaḥ sūdair āhāraḥ sa tathā yathā
jita|jihvair api prītaṃ Jina|śāsana|pāra|gaiḥ.

ath' âham Ṛṣidattāyāḥ puraḥ sa|kṛtaka|jvaraḥ
patitas tuṅga|romāñcaḥ sa|vepathu|vijṛmbhakaḥ.
25.75 tādṛśī ca mayā vyaktā jvarit'|ânukṛtiḥ kṛtā
duṣ|karaḥ paritāpo 'pi yathā saṃbhāvitas tayā.
‹kim etad?› iti c' âpṛcchat sā mām ujjvala|saṃbhramā
danta|kūjita|saṃbhinnaṃ may" âpy etan niveditam.
‹ṣaḍ|rātr'|â|bhakṣaṇa|kṣāmo gṛhīto vāta|hetunā
jvareṇ' ânubhavāmy etām avasthām īdṛśīm› iti.

tataḥ sva|svapan'|āvāse śramaṇā|gaṇa|saṃkule
mām asau karuṇ"|āviṣṭā saṃvāhitavatī ciram.
atha saṃghaṭṭayan dantān uktavān asmi tāṃ śanaiḥ
‹mahā|jana|vivikto 'yam āvāsaḥ kriyatām› iti.
25.80 Ṛṣidattā|kṛt'|ânujñās tāś ca pravrajitā gatāḥ
tad|abhiprāya|jijñāsur atha tām idam abravam.
‹ārye virudhyate strīṇāṃ pitṛ|bhrātṛ|sutair api
vrata|sthānāṃ viśeṣeṇa sthātuṃ saha rahaś ciram.
ahaṃ ca kitavaḥ pānthaḥ saṃbhāvy'|â|vinay'|ākṛtiḥ
pṛthag|janā janāś c' âite tena nirgamyatām› iti.

by feeding thousands of heretics is wiped out immediately by devotion to a single arhat, so please invite all the noble devotees of the doctrine of the omniscient ones that are here, together with the lay followers.'

The food prepared by the cooks was so utterly delicious that it was loved by even those who had subjugated their tongues and mastered the Jaina doctrine.

Then I collapsed in front of Rishi·datta, feigning a fever: the hair on my body stood on end and I convulsed and retched. I faked the fever so well that she believed it to be a 25.75
serious illness. In a beautiful panic she asked me what the matter was. My voice punctuated by the chattering of my teeth, I said to her, 'I am like this because I am in the grip a fever brought on by a wind imbalance due to my being weakened by six days without food.'

Filled with pity, she massaged me for a long time in her bedroom, which was crowded with nuns. Making my teeth chatter, I whispered to her, 'Please make all these people leave the room.'

At Rishi·datta's command, the nuns left. Keen to find 25.80
out her intentions, I said to her, 'Madam, it is forbidden for women, particularly those who have taken religious vows, to be alone for long with a man, even if he is their father, brother or son. I am a vagabond—from my appearance one would surmise that I am ill-mannered—and there are laymen here, so you must go.'

tay" ôktaṃ ‹kṣaṇam apy ekam a|śaktā svastham apy aham
muktvā tvāṃ sthātum anyatra kiṃ punaḥ saṃtata|jvaram.
saṃbhāvan" âpi ramy" âiva mādṛśyās tvādṛśā saha
ślāghyā kiṃśuka|śākh" âpi vasanta|saha|cāriṇī.
25.85 dhanyo jvaro 'pi yen' êdaṃ tvad|aṅgam upayujyate
Kālakūṭam api ślāghyaṃ līḍha|Śaṃkara|kaṃdharam.›

evam|ādi bruvāṇ" âiva prakhalī|kṛta|sādhunā
sā mahā|graha|caṇḍena gṛhītā Bhāvajanmanā.

mama tv āsīd iyaṃ cintā ‹satyam āhuś cikitsakāḥ
«sarve saṃkrāmiṇaḥ rogāḥ spṛśatāṃ prāṇinām» iti.
madīyaḥ kṛtrimo 'py enāṃ yatra saṃkrāmati jvaraḥ
kathaṃ nāma na saṃkramet tatra yaḥ param'|ârthikaḥ.
tathā hi sveda|romānca|bāṣpa|kampa|vijṛmbhikā
jvarasya parivāro 'yam aṅgam asyāḥ prabādhate.
25.90 sarvathā Smara|śāstreṣu yad iṅgitam udāhṛtam
lāvaṇyam iva gātreṣu tad asyāḥ prāsphurat sphuṭam.›

tatas tām uktavān asmi ‹dhik tvāṃ niṣ|karuṇ'|āśayām
śīta|jvar'|ārtam aṅgair yā na pīḍayasi mām!› iti.
ath' āśliṣyat tathā sā māṃ n' âdṛśyata yathā pṛthak
viral" êv' âruṇ'|ālokaṃ niś'|ânta|śaśi|candrikā.
tatas tāv āvayoś caṇḍau tath" āśleṣa|cikitsayā
apāyātāṃ muhūrtena kṛtrim'|â|kṛtrimau jvarau.

She replied, 'Even if you were well, I could not bear to be apart from you for a single moment, let alone when you have a steady fever. The coming together of a girl like me and a man like you is to be enjoyed: because it accompanies spring, even the branch of the *kim·shuka* tree is celebrated.
And the fever is lucky to be in contact with this body of 25.85
yours; because it lapped at Shiva's throat, even the Kala·kuta poison is celebrated.'*

As she said all this, she was seized by that fierce and febrile fiend who makes villains of the virtuous: the god of love.

I thought to myself, 'The doctors are right when they say that all diseases are transmitted by people touching one another: if even my faked fever can be caught by this girl, why shouldn't a real one do the same? In the same way that the symptoms of fever—sweating, horripilation, crying, con-
vulsions and retching—are afflicting her person, the signs 25.90
mentioned in the treatises on erotics have all manifested in her body as clearly as her beauty.'

I said to her, 'Shame on you for being so cruel-hearted that you won't press your body against me, stricken as I am with a feverish chill!' Then she embraced me so tightly that there was no difference between us, just as there is no difference between faint moonlight at the end of the night and the glow of the dawn. Our two fierce fevers, one fake, one real, were cured in an instant by the medicine of our embrace.

yātāyām atha yāminyāṃ buddhvā vṛtt'|ântam īdṛśam
saṃghaḥ saṃhatya tāṃ svasmān nivāsān niravāsayat.
25.95 atha pravahaṇ'|ārūḍhām Ṛṣidattāṃ mayā saha
anayan muditaḥ śreṣṭhī gṛhaṃ maṅgala|saṃkulam.
tatr' âvayoḥ sa|Sumanāḥ su|manāḥ Priyadarśanaḥ
prīta|nāgarak'|ânīkaṃ kara|graham akārayat.
tad evam Ṛṣidattā vaḥ saṃvṛttā paricārikā
atha vā kiṃ vikalpena? svayam ālokyatām!» iti.
tath" âpi kathitaṃ tena n' âiva saṃśayam atyajam
duḥ|śraddhānaṃ hi sahasā kākatālīyam īdṛśam.
māl"|âlaṃkāra|vastr'|ādi gṛh'|ôpakaraṇāni ca
prasthāpya prāk tad" ârhāṇi tāṃ didṛkṣus tato 'gamam.
25.100 tatra c' âsau mayā dṛṣṭā citr'|âṃśuka|vibhūṣaṇā
nānā|puṣpāṃ hasant" îva vasant'|ôpavana|śriyam.
pratimāḥ kāṣṭha|mayyo 'pi śobhante bhūṣitās tathā
lajjit'|âsura|kanyāsu tādṛśīṣu tu kā kathā?
pravrajyāyāṃ punar yasyāḥ kāntir āsīd a|kṛtrimā
dur|labhāṇi kva cit tasyā vācakāny akṣarāṇy api.
āsīc ca mama «duḥ|śliṣṭaṃ kānta|rūpa|virūpayoḥ
alaṃkāra|kalāpasya guru|sārasya dhāraṇam.
alaṃkār'|āvṛtā tāvat kānta|rūpasya cārutā
na śakyā sarvathā draṣṭuṃ janair lol'|ēkṣaṇair api.
25.105 virūpasya tu vairūpyaṃ yat pracchādanam arhati
prakāśayati tad loke paṭu|maṇḍana|ḍiṇḍimaḥ.»

When the night was over, the community learned what had happened. After convening, they expelled the girl from her residence. Then the head of the guild put Rishi·datta 25.95
on a carriage with me and gladly brought us to his house, which was full of festivity. The gracious Priya·dárshana, together with Sumanas, had our marriage performed before rows of happy citizens. Thus Rishi·datta has become your servant. But anyway, enough dithering: you must see her for yourself!"

Despite his telling me like this, I still had my doubts, for when something as unexpected as that suddenly happens, it is hard to believe. After sending ahead things like garlands, ornaments and clothes, together with the appropriate household utensils, I set out to see her. When I ar- 25.100
rived I found her wearing wonderful clothes and jewelry; she seemed to surpass the beauty of a garden in spring with its many flowers. Even wooden statues look beautiful when decorated; what can one say about ladies like her, who put the daughters of the *ásura*s to shame? But that girl had a natural beauty even when she was a nun, and words to describe her are hard to find anywhere. I said to myself, "It is wrong to adorn either the beautiful or the ugly with a host of precious decoration.* When concealed under decoration, there is no way that the beauty of the beautiful can be seen by anyone, even those with keen eyes. Meanwhile, the ug- 25.105
liness of the ugly deserves to be covered, but the drums of excessive embellishment proclaim it to the world."

ath' âdhiṣṭhita|paryaṅkam Ṛṣidatt" ôpagamya mām
avandata prahṛṣṭ" âpi pravrajyā|tyāga|lajjitā.
tatas tām uktavān asmi «sakhyāḥ kiṃ kāryam āśiṣā
sa|rāg" âiva satī yā tvaṃ vīta|rāga|gatiṃ gatā.
mokṣaḥ kāruṇikair uktaḥ siddhair duḥkha|kṣayaḥ kila
kṣīṇa|duḥ|saha|duḥkhatvān mokṣaṃ prāpt" âsi sarvathā.
sarvathā su|bhagatā|mah"|ôddhataḥ
    kiṃkaro bhavatu Gomukhas tava
yoṣito hi jita|dṛṣṭa|bhartṛkās
    toṣayanti jananī|sakhī|janam.»

Priyadarśanā|lābhe Gomukha|vivāh'|ākhyānam.

I sat down on a sofa and Rishi·datta came up and greeted me. Despite being overjoyed, she was embarrassed at having given up being a nun. I said to her, "What is the point of blessing a friend like you who has attained a state of passionlessness while still impassioned? The compassionate perfected masters have declared liberation to be the end of suffering. You have rid yourself of an unbearable suffering, so you have definitely attained liberation. Go·mukha has most certainly been uplifted by his good fortune—may he be your servant. Women who win their husbands simply by being looked at delight their mothers and friends!"

Thus ends the story of the Wedding of Go·mukha
in the Winning of Priya·darshaná.

CANTO 26
A GLIMPSE OF BREASTS

26.1 ITY|ĀDI|kuṭil'|ālāpa|kalāpa|gamita|trapām
tām āmantrya svam āvāsam agaccham saha|Gomukhaḥ.
ekadā punar āyātas tay" ânuṣṭhita|sat|kriyaḥ
vipaṇer gṛham āyātam apaśyam Priyadarśanam.
kañcukam muñcatas tasya mayā dṛṣṭaḥ payodharaḥ
payodhar'|ântar'|ālakṣyaḥ śaś" îva parimaṇḍalaḥ.
āsīc ca mama «yoṣ" âiṣā yatas tuṅga|payodharā
stana|keśavatītvam hi prathamam strītva|lakṣaṇam.
26.5 lokas tu yad imām sarvaḥ pratipannaḥ pumān iti
bhrānti|jñānam idam tasya kim cit sādṛśya|kāritam.
atha vā kim vikalpena mam' â|timira|cakṣuṣaḥ
na hi dṛṣṭena dṛṣṭ'|ârthe draṣṭur bhavati saṃśayaḥ.»
ity|ādi|bahu|saṃkalpam a|nimeṣa|vilocanam
apaśyad Ṛṣidattā mām paśyantam Priyadarśanam.
ath' âsau gadgad'|ālāpā prīti|bāṣp'|āvṛt'|ēkṣaṇā
«ātmānam cetayasv' êti» Priyadarśanam abravīt.
asāv api tam uddeśam prakāśya jhagiti tviṣā
taḍid|guṇa iv' âmbhodam prāviśan mandir'|ôdaram.
26.10 Ṛṣidattām ath' âpaśyam krodha|visphārit'|ēkṣaṇaḥ
yay" âpakramitaḥ śreṣṭhī mama locana|gocarāt.
utthāya ca tataḥ sthānāt sa|kāma|krodha|Gomukhaḥ
Punarvasu|gṛham prāpya paryaṅka|śaraṇo 'bhavam.
tataḥ kramam parityajya kām'|âvasthā|paramparā
tumul'|āyudhi|sen" êva yugapan mām abādhata.
ath' â|cir'|āgata|śrīko yathā bālaḥ pṛthag|janaḥ
tath" ājñāpitavān asmi Gomukham rūkṣayā girā.
«api pravrajitā|bhartaḥ! priyā me Priyadarśanā
a|kṛta|pratikarm" âiva kṣipram ānīyatām!» iti.

AFTER I HAD REMOVED her embarrassment with my artful words, I said goodbye to her and went home with Go·mukha. 26.1

One day when I went there again and was welcomed hospitably by her, I saw Priya·dárshana, who had come home from the market. As he took off his jacket I caught sight of a breast: it looked like a round moon seen through clouds. I said to myself, "He must be a woman: he has prominent breasts. The primary mark of womanhood is the possession of breasts and long hair. Everyone who thinks she is a man 26.5
has been misled by her passing resemblance to one. But my eyes see clearly and I am in no doubt; when something is seen the seer does not doubt what he has seen."

While I was having these thoughts Rishi·datta noticed me staring unblinkingly at Priya·dárshana. Her eyes filled with tears of happiness and in a faltering voice she said to Priya·dárshana, "Watch yourself!" Like a streak of lightning going into a cloud, Priya·darshaná lit the place up with her beauty before darting into the house. My eyes bulged with 26.10
rage as I looked at Rishi·datta, she who had made the head of the guild leave my view. I stood up and, accompanied by love, anger and Go·mukha, left there for Punar·vasu's house, where I took refuge in my bed. Abandoning their usual order, the progression of manifestations of desire assailed me all at once, like a chaotic army of warriors. In the manner of an ignorant and vulgar parvenu, I harshly ordered Go·mukha, "Hey, nun's husband! I'm in love with Miss Priya·darshaná. Quickly, fetch her, and don't let her make herself up!"

26.15 sa tu mām abravīt trastaḥ «kā nāma Priyadarśanā
tyājitāḥ stha yayā sadyaś cetasaḥ sthiratām?» iti.

may" ôktaṃ «tava yaḥ syālaḥ puruṣaḥ Priyadarśanaḥ
ayam eva jagat|sāraḥ pramadā priya|darśanā.
yac ca vakṣyasi ‹sarvasyāṃ Vārāṇasyām ayaṃ pumān
bhavataḥ katham ekasya pramad" êti› tad ucyate.
‹Ṛṣidattā virakt" êti paricchinnā purā tayā
adhunā bhavataḥ kāntā jāt" êty› atra kim ucyate.
gat'|ânugatiko lokaḥ pravṛtto hi yathā tathā
param'|ârthaṃ punar veda sahasr'|âikaḥ pumān» iti.

26.20 ten' ôktaṃ «janatā|siddhaṃ viruddham api na tyajet
kriyate chagalaḥ śv" âpi saṃhatya bahubhir balāt.
tena yuṣmad|vidhaiḥ prājñair na vācyaṃ sad ap' īdṛśam
a|śraddheyaṃ na vaktavyaṃ pratyakṣam api yad bhavet.
śrūyatāṃ ca kathā tāvad arthasy' âsya prakāśikā
pramāṇaṃ hi pramāṇa|jñaiḥ purā|kalpe 'pi vartitam.

babhūva Kauśiko nāma Veda|Ved'|âṅga|vid dvijaḥ
satya|vratatayā loke prasiddho Satyakauśikaḥ.
kadā cid abhiṣekāya tena yātena Jāhnavīm
sa|śiṣya|parivāreṇa tarantī prekṣitā śilā.
26.25 mahat" âsau prayatnena śiṣyān anvaśiṣat tataḥ
‹n' âyam artho mah"|ân|arthaḥ prakāśyaḥ putrakair› iti.

ath' âikaś capalas teṣāṃ baṭuḥ Piṅgala|nāmakaḥ
vipaṇau mantrayāṃ cakre kasya cid vaṇijaḥ puraḥ.
‹śreṣṭhi kiṃ na śṛṇoṣy ekam āścaryaṃ kathayāmi te
tarantīṃ dṛṣṭavān asmi s'|ôpādhyāyaḥ śilām!› iti.

Frightened, he asked me, "Who is this Miss Priya·dar- 26.15
shaná that has made you suddenly lose your composure?"

I replied, "Your brother-in-law, that man Priya·dárshana, is in fact the finest thing in the world, a beautiful young woman. If you ask how he can be a man to all Varánasi and a woman to me alone, then I shall reply that Rishi·datta was deemed to be a celibate ascetic by the city and now she has become your sweetheart! What do you say to that? People follow the beaten track in everything, but one man in a thousand understands how things really are."

Go·mukha replied, "One should not ignore popular opin- 26.20
ion, even if it is absurd. When many people act together, they can even force a goat to become a dog!* So clever men like you should not say such things, even if they are true. Even something seen with one's own eyes is not to be reported if it is unbelievable. Listen to a story that illustrates this point, for even in days of old a standard was established by those who understood such things.

There was a brahmin called Káushika who knew the Vedas and their auxiliary disciplines. Because he observed a vow of truthfulness, everyone knew him as Satya·káushika. One day when he had gone to take a bath in the Ganga with
a group of students, he saw a floating rock. He took great 26.25
pains to admonish the pupils, saying, 'Boys, this matter does not bode well; you must not publicize it.'

One amongst them, a naughty lad called Píngala, said to a merchant in the market, 'My good man, you should listen to me—I'm going to tell you something amazing. My teacher and I have seen a floating rock!'

ath' ântaḥ|purikā dāsī kim api kretum āgatā
etad ālāpam ākarṇya rāja|patnyai nyavedayat.
tay" âpi kathitaṃ rajñe sa tāṃ pṛṣṭvā paraṃparām
baṭun" ākhyātam āhvāyya pṛṣṭavān Satyakauśikam.
26.30 ‹«satyaṃ brūh' îti» no vācyaḥ satya|vādi|vrato bhavān
«mithyā brūh' îti» no vācyaḥ kāmī mithyā|vrato hi saḥ.
kiṃ tu yat Piṅgalen' ôktam etad yuktaṃ parīkṣitum
pramadāt satyam apy ete vadanti baṭavo yataḥ.
sa|śiṣyaiḥ kila yuṣmābhis tarantī prekṣitā śilā
kim etat satyam āho svin mṛṣ" êty ākhyāyatām!› iti.

āsīc c' âsya ‹dhig etāṃ me ninditāṃ satya|vāditām
duḥ|śraddhānam an|iṣṭaṃ ca yan mayā vācyam īdṛśam!
«na satyam api tad vācyaṃ yad uktam a|sukh'|āvaham»
iti satya|pravādo 'yaṃ na tyājyaḥ satya|vādibhiḥ.
26.35 tasmāt satyam idaṃ tyaktvā mṛṣā|vāda|śat'|âdhikam
a|satyam abhidhāsyāmi satya|vāda|śat'|âdhikam.›

ath' âvocat sa rājānaṃ ‹rājan mithyā baṭor vacaḥ
agniṃ paśyati yaḥ śītaṃ plavamānāṃ śilām asau.
kaḥ śraddadhyād baṭor vācaṃ nisarg'|â|dhīra|cetasaḥ?
capalasy' ôpamānaṃ hi prathamaṃ baṭu|markaṭāḥ!›

viṣaṇṇam iti viśvāsya rājānaṃ Satyakauśikaḥ
viruddha|vādinaṃ kruddhaḥ Piṅgalaṃ niravāsayat.
tad evaṃ loka|vidviṣṭam anuyukto 'pi bhū|bhṛtā
satyam satya|pratijño 'pi n' âvadat Satyakauśikaḥ.
26.40 yuṣmākaṃ punar a|jñāta|śīla|cāritra|janmanām

A servant from the royal harem who had come to buy
something overheard this and reported it to the queen. She
then told the king and he asked her where she had heard it.
He summoned Satya·káushika and asked him about what
the boy had said: 'There is no need to tell you to speak 26.30
the truth because you have taken a vow of truthfulness, just
as there is no need to tell a lover to lie for he has taken a
vow of mendacity! But we should check what Píngala has
said, because young men can also tell the truth by mistake.
Apparently you and your students have seen a floating rock.
Is this true or false? Tell me!'

Satya·káushika said to himself, 'Damn this cursed truthfulness of mine for making me have to say such an unbelievable and undesirable thing! "Even something that is
true should not be told if it will then bring about unhappiness." Those who are truthful should not ignore this saying
about the truth, so in this matter I shall part from the truth, 26.35
which is worse than a hundred lies, and tell a lie better than
a hundred truths.'

Then he said to the king, 'Sire, the lad's words are untrue.
Only the man who sees cold fire sees a floating rock! Who
would believe the words of a young lad; their minds are
naturally excitable. Boys and monkeys are prime examples
of fickleness!'

Having thus convinced the disappointed king, the angry Satya·káushika had the quarrelsome Píngala expelled.
So, even on being questioned by the king, Satya·káushika,
despite having taken a vow of truthfulness, did not speak
the truth because it would have been unpopular. Moreover, 26.40

viruddham idam īdṛk kaḥ śraddadhyād vadatām?» iti.

sa may" ôkto «bhavān eva duḥ|śraddhānasya bhāṣitā
yasy' âsmin pramadā|ratne pumān iti viparyayaḥ.
kiṃ c' ânena pralāpena strī|ratnaṃ Priyadarśanām
a|cirāt svī|kariṣyāmi krośatāṃ tvādṛśām!» iti.

evaṃ ca mama vṛtt'|ântaṃ vijānann api Gomukhaḥ
vaidya|rājaṃ samāhūya vaidya|rājam upāgamat.
sa mam' ālāpam ākarṇya kāya|chāyāṃ vilokya ca
pradhārya c' âparair vaidyaiḥ śanakair idam abravīt.
26.45 «mānaso 'sya vikāro 'yam īpsit'|â|lābha|hetukaḥ
ten' âsmai rucitaṃ yat tad āśu saṃpādyatām» iti.

atha Nand'|Ôpanandābhyāṃ saṃskāry' āhāram ādarāt
māṃ Punarvasu|hastena Gomukhaḥ prāg abhojayat.
sa c' āhāraḥ su|saṃskāro lobhano 'py amṛt'|āśinām
tri|phalā|kvāthavad dveṣān mam' âṅgāni vyadhūnayat.
tato Nand'|Ôpanandābhyāṃ bhojyamānaḥ krameṇa tau
sa|viṣādau karomi sma viṣa|dāv iva vairiṇau.
teṣu vandhya|prayatneṣu Gomukhaḥ Priyadarśanam
lajjā|manda|pada|nyāsaṃ namit'|ānanam ānayat.
26.50 sa māṃ samāna|paryaṅka|madhyam adhyāsitas tataḥ
grāsān agrāsayat ṣaḍ vā sapta vā Gomukh'|ājñayā.

your character, conduct and birth are unknown: who would believe you if you said something so absurd?"

I replied, "It is you that is saying something unbelievable, perversely asserting that this jewel of a girl is a man. But enough chatter! I shall make Priya·darshaná my own precious wife before long, while people like you make your laments!"

Even though he understood what I had told him, Go·mukha asked after the best doctor available and went to him. When he heard me speak and examined my body, the doctor consulted some other doctors before saying quietly,
"He has a mental derangement caused by his not getting 26.45
something he wants, so he must quickly get whatever it is that is dear to him."

Go·mukha made Nanda and Upanánda carefully prepare some food, and then had Punar·vasu feed it to me before anyone else. The food was so well made that it would have been tempting even to the gods, who eat ambrosia, but like a decoction of *tri·phala* it made my body shudder with disgust.* Nanda and Upanánda took turns to feed me and I made them feel as unwanted as if they were enemies giving me poison. When these attempts were unsuccessful, Go·mukha fetched Priya·dárshana, who shuffled in embar-
rassedly, hanging his head. He sat down on my bed and, at 26.50
Go·mukha's command, fed me six or seven morsels of food.

ye tat|pāṇi|saroja|saṅga|su|bhagā
grāsā mayā svāditāḥ
taiḥ sadyas tanutām anīyata sa me
saṃkalpa|janmā jvaraḥ
śail'|êndrāḥ śuci|śukra|bhānu|dahana|
pluṣṭ'|ôpal'|âdhityakā
mandair apy uda|bindubhir navatarair
ujjhanti saṃtaptatām.

Priyadarśanā|lābhe
Priyadarśanā|stana|darśana|sargaḥ 26.

The morsels that I ate were blessed by the touch of his lotus-hand and they instantly relieved my love-induced fever. When stony mountain plateaus are scorched by the burning of the dazzling summer sun, even gently dripping drops of fresh water remove heat from the huge rocks.

Thus ends the Glimpse of
Priya·darshaná's Breasts Canto
in the Winning of Priya·darshaná.

CANTO 27
THE WEDDING TO PRIYA·DARSHANÁ

27.1 TATAḤ SAMĀPIT’|ĀHĀRAḤ suhṛdām eva saṃnidhau
Priyadarśanam āliṅgam An|aṅg’|ônmūlita|trapaḥ.
atha krodh’|âruṇa|mukhaḥ Gomukhaḥ Priyadarśanam
pāṇāv ākṛṣya tvaritaḥ sva|gṛhān pratiyātavān.

sa may” ôktaḥ samāyātaḥ krodha|vistīrṇa|cakṣuṣā
«pāṇḍity’|ândhaka mitr’|âre mā sma tiṣṭhaḥ puro mama!
pipāsor madhu|śauṇḍasya madhu|śuktiṃ haret karāt
yasya yas tasya kas tasmād arātir aparaḥ paraḥ?»

27.5 ity uktaḥ sa viṣādena tyājitaś campak’|ābhatām
Rāhuṇ” êva tuṣār’|âṃśur agamad dhūma|dhūmratām.

taṃ ca dīrgham ahaḥ|śeṣam āyatāṃ ca vibhāvarīm
pravṛddhair gamayāmi sma niṣād’|āsana|caṅkramaiḥ.
suhṛd|vṛnda|vṛtaḥ prāyo dveṣy’|â|śeṣa|vinodanaḥ
Priyadarśana|saṃprāpter upāyam agaveṣayam.

evaṃ|prāye ca vṛtt’|ânte dhaval’|ôṣṇīṣa|kañcukau
vismitau ciram ālokya sthavirau mām avocatām.
«kiṃ|nimittam api brahman Brahmadattaḥ praj”|ēśvaraḥ
bhavantam icchati draṣṭum iṣṭaṃ ced gamyatām» iti.

27.10 idam ākarṇya yat satyam īṣad|ākula|mānasaḥ
Gomukhasya smarāmi sma vicāra|caturaṃ manaḥ.
«kiṃ gacchāni na gacchāni? gacchataḥ kiṃ bhaved?» iti
vitarkya kṣaṇam āsīn me saṃdeha|chedanī matiḥ.
«yo bandhavyo ’tha vā vadhyo na sa kañcuki|dūtakaḥ
sa hi śṛṅkhala|nistriṃśa|pāṇibhiḥ parivāryate.
ye ca ke cij janā yeṣāṃ viṣaye sukham āsate

AFTER I HAD FINISHED the food, love removed my shame 27.1
and I embraced Priya·dárshana right in front of my friends. His face red with rage, Go·mukha grabbed Priya·dárshana by the hand and hurried home.

When he came back, I was wide-eyed with anger and told him, “You are blinded by your learning and an enemy to your friends—get out of my sight! There is no greater enemy of a thirsty wine drinker than the man who takes a glass of wine out of his hand!”

On being spoken to like this, sadness made him lose his 27.5
golden complexion, like Rahu making the moon take on a smoky hue.*

I spent the rest of that long day and drawn-out night repeatedly lying down, sitting up and walking around. Surrounded by a group of friends but finding all diversions despicable, I spent most of the time trying to think of a way to get Priya·dárshana.

Thus things stood when two old men with white hair and robes looked at me in amazement for a long time before saying, “Brahmin, for some reason King Brahma·datta wants to see you. Please come.”

When I heard this, to be honest I was slightly worried, and 27.10
I thought of Go·mukha and his shrewd mind. “Should I go or not go? What will happen if I go?” After deliberating like this for a moment, I thought of something that cut through my doubt: “When a man is to be imprisoned or executed, he is not summoned by a chamberlain, he is surrounded by men with chains and swords. Furthermore, how are those who live happily under their kings to continue doing so if they disobey them? My right eye is quivering quickly

rājñām ājñām avajñāya teṣāṃ jīvanti te katham?
a|manda|spandam etac ca kāṅkṣitām akṣi dakṣiṇam
ākhyat' îva priyā|prāptiṃ mahyaṃ tad gamanaṃ hitam.»
27.15 niścity' êty|ādi nirgatya gṛhāt pravahaṇaṃ bahiḥ
kañcuky|ānītam adrākṣam ārukṣaṃ c' â|viśaṅkitaḥ.
paura|saṃghāta|saṃbādhaṃ rāja|mārgaṃ vyatītya ca
rāja|dvāraṃ vrajāmi sma citra|maṅgala|maṇḍalam.
Gomukh'|ākhyāpit'|âbhikhyaṃ
tad adhyāsya kṣaṇaṃ tataḥ
prāvikṣaṃ prathamāṃ kakṣāṃ
dvāḥ|stha|vṛnd'|âbhinanditaḥ.
samṛddhiḥ srūyatāṃ tasyāḥ kṛtaṃ vā tat|praśaṃsayā
ko hi varṇayituṃ śakto naraḥ Meror adhityakām?
tām atikramya pañc' ânyāḥ prakṛṣṭatara|ramyatāḥ
saptamyāṃ dṛṣṭavān asmi mah"|āsthānaṃ mahī|pateḥ.
27.20 Śruti|Smṛti|Purāṇ'|ādi|grantha|sāgara|pāra|gaiḥ
dhanur|ved'|ādi|tattva|jñaiḥ kalā|dakṣaiś ca sevitam.
viruddhāṃ bibhrataṃ mūrtyā candramaḥ|savitṛ|prabhām
sukha|sevyaṃ dur|īkṣaṃ ca tapt'|âṃśum iva haimanam.

svasti|kṛtvā tatas tasmai jāta|rūp'|âṅgam āsanam
adhyatiṣṭhaṃ nṛp'|ādiṣṭaṃ nirvikār'|âmbar'|āvṛtam.
nṛpas tu māṃ ciraṃ dṛṣṭvā sneha|snigdh'|āyat'|ēkṣaṇaḥ
tataḥ Tārakarāj'|ākhyaṃ senā|bhṛtāram aikṣata.
sa tu mām abhitaḥ sthitvā kārya|mātrasya vācakaḥ
avocad vacanaṃ cāru vispaṣṭa|madhur'|âkṣaram.

and seems to be saying that I will get what I want—the acquisition of my sweetheart—so it will be good for me to go."

After deciding thus, I emerged from the house and saw 27.15
outside the carriage that the chamberlains had brought.
I climbed aboard without hesitation. I crossed the palace
road, which was packed with crowds of citizens, and reached
the royal gate with its many and various auspicious markings. Go·mukha had told me of its beauty and I stopped
there for a moment before entering the first hall, where I
was greeted by a group of doormen. Let me tell you how
magnificent it was... but wait, enough of its praise: what
man is capable of describing the heights of Mount Meru? I
went through it and five other even more beautiful rooms.
In the seventh I saw the king's great assembly hall. It was 27.20
frequented by scholars who had plumbed the depths of
the Vedas, the traditional teachings, the Puránas and other
scriptures, as well as experts in the disciplines of archery and
so forth, and skilled artists. It appeared to have the contrast-
ing luminosities of the sun and the moon; like the winter
sun with its warm rays it was agreeable but hard to look at.

I greeted the king courteously. He pointed to a golden seat covered with a plain cloth and I sat down on it. The king stared at me with eyes made wide and moist by affection. Then he looked at his general, who was called Táraka·raja. The general stood in front of me, and, getting straight to the point, he made a delightful speech, its tone clearly friendly.

27.25 «ārya|jyeṣṭha manas tāvad a|vikṣiptaṃ kuru kṣaṇam
rājā man|mukha|saṃkrāntair vākyais tvām eṣa bhāṣate.
y" êyaṃ Bhāgīrathī|śubhrā Kāśi|bhū|pati|saṃtatiḥ
sā kim ākhyāyate tubhyaṃ prathitā pṛthiv" îva yā?
asyām asya prasūtasya Brahmadattasya bhū|pateḥ
ye guṇās te 'pi te buddhāḥ śiśir'|âṃśor iv' âṃśavaḥ.
asy' āsīt Kāliyo nāma śreṣṭhī prāṇa|priyaḥ suhṛt
sa|phalair draviṇair yasmād Draviṇ'|ēśo 'pi lajjitaḥ.
antarvatyām asau patnyāṃ nītaḥ puṇyais tri|piṣṭapam
atha sā gṛhiṇī tasya kāle putraṃ vyajāyata.
27.30 tasmiñ jāte mahā|rājaḥ sv'|âtma|jād api harṣa|de
pure s'|ântaḥ|pure ramyaṃ mahā|maham akārayat.
saḥ kṛt'|â|śeṣa|saṃskāraḥ śiśur gacchan kumāratām
aṅgair vidyā|kalābhiś ca sakalābhir alaṃkṛtaḥ.
evaṃ|prāye ca vṛtt'|ânte dvāḥ|sthair vijñāpito nṛpaḥ
‹dvāre vaḥ Kāliyaḥ śreṣṭhī tiṣṭhat' îti› sa|saṃbhramaiḥ.
tataś citrīyamāṇena sa nṛpeṇa praveśitaḥ
‹kas tvaṃ? kasya? kuto v" êti› pṛṣṭaś c' êdam abhāṣata.
‹dev' âhaṃ Kāliyaḥ śreṣṭhī devena sva|śarīravat
lālitaḥ pālitaś c' āsaṃ śikṣitaś c' â|khilāḥ kalāḥ.
27.35 so 'haṃ su|caritair aṅgaiḥ sukhād yuṣmat|prasāda|jāt
cyāvayitvā divaṃ nīto na hi nāśo 'sti karmaṇām.
ath' âsau bhavatāṃ dāsī dur|manāḥ Sumanāḥ sutām
jātāṃ «putr' êti» khyātim anayad lobha|dūṣitā.
mṛṣā|vādena ten' âsyāḥ sura|lokād ahaṃ cyutaḥ
bhāryayā hi kṛtaṃ karma patyāv api vipacyate.

"Noble sir, focus your mind for a moment: it is the king 27.25
that is speaking to you in words coming from my mouth. The dynasty of the king of Kashi is as glorious as the Ganga and as well known as the world: what need be said to you about it? King Brahma·datta here is born of it; you know of his virtues too, just as you know of the rays of the moon. He had a friend called Káliya, the head of the guild, who was as dear to him as his own life and who was so munificent that he put even the lord of wealth to shame. When his wife was pregnant, his good deeds took him to heaven. In
time she bore his son. The boy's birth made the king even 27.30
happier than the birth of his own son, and he had great celebrations held in the city and the palace. The infant had all the ceremonial rites performed, and as he grew up he was embellished by a healthy body and all the sciences and arts.

Thus things stood when one day the king was informed by his perplexed gatekeepers that his friend Káliya, the chief of the guild, was standing at the gate.

The surprised king had the man come in. On being asked who he was and what family and place he came from, he replied, 'Sire, I am Káliya, the chief of the guild, whom Your Majesty cherished, brought up and had instructed in
all the arts as if he were his own self. That is who I am. 27.35
When I was alive, my good deeds had me removed from the happiness that your kindness had created and taken to heaven: actions never fail to come to fruition. Then that wicked servant lady of yours Sumanas was corrupted by greed and made it known that the daughter to whom she had given birth was a son. Her lying had me cast out of heaven, for the actions of a wife have consequences for her

kule ca kula|putrasya jāto jāti|smaraḥ punaḥ
etam īdṛśam ākāraṃ vahāmi jana|ninditam.
asau ca yuvatir jātā kānt'|ākārā ca dārikā
kasmai cid abhirūpāya varāya pratipādyatām.

27.40 aham apy etam ātmānam aṅga|vaikalya|ninditam
Prayāge saṃnyasiṣyāmi prasthāpayata mām› iti.

evam|ādy uktavān ukto vismitena sa bhū|bhṛtā
‹pūrvaṃ yad āvayor vṛttaṃ tat kiṃ cit smaryatām› iti.

anen' âpi vihasy' ôktaṃ ‹yad yad devāya rocate
a|saṃdigdhaṃ su|viśrabdhas tat tat pṛṣṭatu mām iti.›

ath' â|dhyāya ciraṃ rājñā yad yat pṛṣṭaṃ cirantanam
a|śeṣaṃ tat tad etena sa|viśeṣaṃ niveditam.

‹ath' âty|adbhutam!› ity uktvā jāta|saṃpratyayo nṛpaḥ
āh' âinaṃ ‹dārikā kasmai jāmātre dīyatām?› iti.

27.45 ayaṃ tu paritoṣeṇa skhalad|akṣaram uktavān
‹rocate yo varas tasyai tasmai sā dīyatām› iti.

tato 'ntaḥ|puram ānāyya sā sārdham Ṛṣidattayā
pṛṣṭā devī|samūhena hriyā kūrm'|âṅgan'|ākṛtiḥ.
‹asau c' âsau ca jāmātā kula|rūp'|ādi|bhūṣaṇaḥ
bhavatyai «rocate n' êti» māta ākhyāyatām iti.›
ath' âruṇa|kara|chāya|kapol'|ēkṣaṇay" ânayā
puṇḍarīkam iv' â|vāte mantharaṃ calitaṃ śiraḥ.
ath' ārya|jyeṣṭh' êty ukte prasann'|âkṣi|kapolayā
sved'|ārdr'|âṃśukayā prāgvan na tad vicalitaṃ śiraḥ.
27.50 tad bhavān rucitas tasyai nṛpāya ca yatas tataḥ

husband, too. I was born once more, into the family of a nobleman, and remembered my previous life. I now have this revolting appearance. As for the girl, she has become a beautiful young lady. Please have her married to a suitable husband. My life, meanwhile, has been made despicable by 27.40
my deformity and I shall give it up at Prayága. Please give me leave to go.'

After he had said all this, the astonished king told him, 'Remind me of something that happened between us in the past.'

He laughed and replied, 'Your Majesty is free to ask me whatever he likes in complete confidence.'

Then, without having to think for long, he described in detail everything from the past that the king asked him about.

The king, now convinced, said, 'How very amazing!' and asked him to whom his daughter was to be married.

His voice faltering with delight, he replied, 'She should 27.45
be given to whomever she chooses.'

Then she and Rishi·datta were brought to the inner apartments, where, with her shyness giving her the appearance of a she-tortoise, she was asked by the ladies to say whether or not she liked this or that prospective husband who was adorned with nobility, good looks and so forth. With cheeks and eyes the hue of the rising sun, she slowly shook her head, which moved like a lotus in a place sheltered from the wind. When you were announced, my lord, her eyes and cheeks brightened and her clothes became wet with sweat. She did not shake her head as before. So, since both she and the 27.50

ady' âiva śreṣṭhi|kanyāyāḥ pāṇim ālambatām!» iti.

tato manda|spṛheṇ' êva may" ân|ādara|mantharam
bhīt'|ântaḥ|pura|dṛṣṭena cirād idam udīritam.
«Avanter aham āyātaḥ saha bhrātrā kanīyasā
Veda|śāstr'|āgamāy' âiva na yoṣit|prāpti|vāñchayā.
kiṃ tu bhū|bhartur ādeśo dur|laṅghyaḥ pura|vāsibhiḥ
yoga|kṣem'|ârthibhir bhavyais tasmād evaṃ bhavatv» iti.

etasminn antare mandraṃ sa|tāla|tumula|dhvani
pratidhvāna|dhvanad|vyoma prādhvanat tūrya|maṇḍalam.
27.55 yaś ca saṃvatsareṇ' âpi duḥ|saṃbhāro nṛpaiḥ paraiḥ
vivāh'|ârthaḥ sa saṃbhāraḥ rājñā saṃbhāritaḥ kṣaṇāt.
tataḥ s'|ântaḥ|puraḥ rājā sa sa|dāra|suhṛd|gaṇaḥ
rāj'|âjire mam' ôdāraṃ kara|graham akārayat.
dattvā tataḥ śreṣṭhi|padaṃ nagaryāṃ
    vittaṃ ca bhū|maṇḍala|mūlya|tulyam
samṛddhim anveṣya ca Kāliyasya
    prāsthāpayan māṃ mudito nar'|êndraḥ.

āsīc ca mama «lok'|ôktir iyaṃ mayy eva saṃprati
‹vardhamāno yathā rājā śreṣṭhī jāta› iti sthitā!
atha Nand'|Ôpanand'|ādyaiḥ pravṛddha|prīti|vismayaiḥ
Priyadarśanayā c' âsmi saha kṣipta|Śacī|patiḥ!»

27.60 aho|rātre tv atikrānte sa Gomukham a|paśyataḥ
mahā|vyasana|saṃkīrṇa iv' āsīn me mah"|ôtsavaḥ.
āsīc ca me vilakṣasya «vilakṣaṃ Gomukhaṃ balāt
vidagdha|suhṛdāṃ kaś cid api nām' ānayed» iti.

king find you agreeable, take the hand of the merchant's daughter this very day!"

Then, under the gaze of the anxious women of the harem, I pretended not to care and took a long time before replying slowly and indifferently, "I have come from Avánti with my younger brother for the sole purpose of studying the Vedas and scholarly treatises, not out of a desire to get a wife. However, those who live in a king's city and want to safeguard their livelihoods for the future should not disobey his orders, so I give my consent."

A host of musical instruments together with tumultous applause immediately rang out, and the air reverberated
with their echoes. In an instant, the king made preparations 27.55
for a wedding that other kings would have had difficulty arranging in a year. Together with his harem, his wives and his friends, the king had my marriage ceremony performed with great pomp in the palace courtyard. After bestowing on me the rank of chief of the guild in the city and giving me riches that would cost the earth, the overjoyed king sought out Káliya's property for me and sent me on my way.

I said to myself, "The proverb 'On succeeding to the throne he became chief of the guild' is now particularly suited to me! In the company of Nanda, Upanánda and other friends full of affection and admiration, and together with Priya·darshaná, I put Indra to shame!"

But a day and a night had passed without my seeing Go· 27.60
mukha and to me the great festivities seemed mixed with great misfortune. Upset, I thought that Go·mukha would be upset, too, and hoped that one of my clever friends might make him come to me. Then I saw him paying his

tataḥ saṃmānayantaṃ tam ānatān pura|vāsinaḥ
adrākṣaṃ bhṛtya|vargaṃ ca saṃcarantam itas tataḥ.
cintitaṃ ca mayā «diṅ māṃ vilakṣakam a|kāraṇe
balād ānāyayāmy enaṃ kiṃ duḥkhāsikayā mama.»

atha Nand'|Ôpanandābhyām asāv ānāyito mayā
āsīnaḥ smayamānena s'|ôpālambham iv' ôditaḥ.
27.65 «kiṃ Gomukhaḥ sakhā yasya prājñaṃ|manyo na vidyate
tasya sādhyāni kāryāṇi na sidhyant' îti»

so 'bravīt,
«sarva|prāṇa|bhṛtām eva purā|kṛta|kṛtaṃ phalam
na tu tat|kāraṇair yogyair vinā sidhyati kasya cit.
yad ap' îdaṃ mahat kāryaṃ yuṣmābhiḥ kila sādhitam
tatr' âpi Gomukhasy' âiva prājñaṃ|manyasya kauśalam.
prabhavaḥ prabhavanto hi doṣ'|ābhāse manāg api
bhṛtyān udvejayanty eva teṣāṃ kiṃ kriyatām?» iti.

«kim asmin bhavatā kārye kṛtam?» ity udite mayā
ākhyātum ayam ārabdhaḥ «śrūyatāṃ yan mayā kṛtam.
27.70 asty ahaṃ bhartsitaḥ kruddhair yuṣmābhiḥ sva|gṛhaṃ gataḥ
tatra prāvṛtya mūrdhānaṃ patitvā śayane sthitaḥ.
tatas trasad|druta|girā pṛṣṭo 'ham Ṛṣidattayā
‹kim etad?› iti tasy" âiva na mayā dattam uttaram.
sā yadā dṛḍha|nibandhā pṛcchati sma punaḥ punaḥ
yuṣmad|vṛtt'|ântam a|khilaṃ tadā kathitavān aham.
s" âtha pramoda|bāṣp'|ârdra|kapol" âpṛcchad ādarāt
‹Vats'|ēśvara|sutaḥ kaś cid ārya|jyeṣṭho bhaved?› iti.

respects to some bowing citizens, and a group of servants running hither and thither. I thought to myself, "Shame on me for being unnecessarily upset. I'll have him brought to me; there's no point in my wallowing in sorrow."

I had Nanda and Upanánda fetch him. He sat down and
with a smile I said, seemingly in reproach, "So without the 27.65
friendship of Go·mukha, who thinks himself so clever, a man cannot do the tasks he needs to do?"

He replied, "All living beings' destinies are the reward of their past actions, but without the appropriate means to bring them about they happen for no one. Even in this great work which you apparently accomplished one finds the skillful hand of none other than Go·mukha, 'who thinks himself so clever.' For, when masters are lording it about, if there is the slightest semblance of a problem, however trifling, they strike terror in their servants, and something has to be done for them."

When I asked, "What did you do in this matter?" he
proceeded to explain. "Listen to what I did. When you 27.70
were angry and scolded me, I went home, covered my head, collapsed and lay on my bed. Then, in a shaky and indistinct voice, Rishi·datta asked me what the matter was. I did not answer her. When she insistently asked me over and over again, I told her everything that had been going on with you. Her cheeks wet with tears of joy, she asked keenly, 'Might his lordship be the son of the king of Vatsa?'

śapathaiḥ pratiṣidhy' âināṃ tvad|vṛtt'|ânta|prakāśanāt
‹āma su|bhrū sa ev' âyam› iti tasyai nyavedayam.
27.75 ath' âsau ‹sthira|dhīratvaṃ Gomukha śrūyatām› iti
s'|âsūyā sa|pramod" êva mām uktv" âkathayat kathām.
‹āsīt Sumanasaḥ k" âpi priyā vidyā|dharī sakhī
divya|jñānā marud|vegā nāmnā ca Priyadarśanā.
sā yadṛcch'|āgatā c' âināṃ prasaṅge kva cid abravīt
«tvaṃ māṃ āpadi kaṣṭāyāṃ vartamānā smarer» iti.
tataḥ śreṣṭhini Kālena nīte Vaivasvata|kṣayam
śreṣṭhinyāḥ kanyakā jātā śok'|ânala|ghṛt'|āhutiḥ.
asyās tv āsīd a|putrāyā «draviṇasy' âti|bhūriṇaḥ
sārasy' âsy' âsmadīyasya pālakaḥ ko bhaviṣyati?
27.80 uktā c' âsmi purā sakhyā ‹vyasane māṃ smarer› iti»
tataś cintita|mātr" âiva dadṛśe Priyadarśanā.
tāṃ c' âsau dārikāṃ dṛṣṭvā prakarṣa|pramada|smitā
avocat «sakhi mā bhaiṣīr janayitv" ēdṛśīṃ sutām.
eṣā vidyā|dhar'|êndrasya bhaviṣyati bhaviṣyataḥ
priyā priyatamā tasmāj jṛmbhantāṃ tūrya|paṅktayaḥ.»
ath' âsāv oṣadhī|garbhaṃ baddhvā tasyāḥ sphurat|karam
kanyāyā hāṭakaṃ dṛṣṭvā kaṇṭhe gaṇḍakam abravīt.
«prabhāvād oṣadher asyāḥ striyam enāṃ satīṃ janāḥ
drakṣyanti puruṣaṃ muktvā bhaviṣyac|cakra|vartinam.
27.85 a|mal'|ân|anta|puṇyatvāt sarva|jñāś cakra|vartinaḥ
paśyanti hi yathā|bhūtam arthaṃ divyena cakṣuṣā.

I made her promise not to tell anyone about you before saying to her, 'Yes, beautiful lady, they are one and the same.'

Then she said, 'Go·mukha, listen to to a tale of steely 27.75
determination,' and half jealously, half happily, she told the following story. 'Sumanas had a dear friend who was a sorceress. She had divine knowledge and was as swift as the wind. Her name was Priya·darshaná. One day she arrived unexpectedly and while talking about something or other said to Sumanas, "You must think of me when you are in trouble." When death had taken the head of the guild to the afterworld, a daughter was born to his wife, an offering of ghee into the fire of her grief. Because she did not have a son, she said to herself, "Who will look after this vast and
valuable fortune of mine? Some time ago my friend told 27.80
me to remember her in times of trouble." Merely by being thought of, Priya·darshaná appeared. When she saw Sumanas' daughter, she was overjoyed, and smiled as she said, "Friend, there's no need to be worried after giving birth to a girl like this. She shall be the beloved sweetheart of the future emperor of the sorcerers, so let the ranks of musical instruments ring out!"

Then she tied a glittering golden locket containing a magical herb around the girl's neck. Looking at it, she said, "By the power of this herb, everyone who looks at this lady
will see a man—except for the future emperor. Because of 27.85
their pure and infinite merit, emperors are omniscient and with their divine sight they see things as they really are, so the man who sees her as a woman is sure to be the emperor, the ruler of all the sorcerers, and her husband. The herb

tena yaḥ striyam ev' âināṃ draṣṭā saḥ bhavati dhruvam
cakra|vartī patiś c' âsyāḥ sarva|vidyā|dhar'|âdhipaḥ.
oṣadhir yā ca kaṇṭhe 'syāḥ sā nāmnā Priyadarśanā
idam eva ca nām' âsyāḥ praśastaṃ kriyatām iti.»
tena yo 'yaṃ pura|śreṣṭhī puruṣaḥ Priyadarśanaḥ
vidyā|dhar'|êndra|yogy" êyaṃ pramadā Priyadarśanā.
kiṃ ca vīṇā|samasyāyāṃ yad uktaṃ cakra|vartinā
«ciraṃ sundari jīv' êti» ten' âiva viditaṃ mayā.
27.90 «na hi śaktaḥ striyaṃ draṣṭum enām avani|gocaraḥ
yas tu paśyati sma vyaktaṃ cakra|vart" îty» abhūn mama.
tvaṃ ca Gomukha ev' êti tad" âiva jñātavaty aham
sa|rūpaḥ sa|vayāś c' ânyo n' âsti yac cakra|vartinaḥ.
rūpaṃ ca yuva|rājasya tava c' ānāyitaṃ mayā
Kauśāmbītaḥ paṭe nyastaṃ tac ca niścaya|kāraṇam.
ity|ādibhir mayā cihnair «ayam a|vyabhicāritaḥ
cakra|vart" îti» vijñātaḥ paścimaṃ stana|darśanam.
yaḥ punar ghaṭan'|ôpāyaḥ kāryaḥ sa bhavat" ânayoḥ
ghaṭane dur|ghaṭasy' âpi caturo hi bhavān› iti.
27.95 evam|ādi tataḥ śrutvā spṛhayāmi sma mṛtyave
yasmān niścitavān asmi trayaṃ maraṇa|kāraṇam.
mayā satyaṃ bruvad bhartā ‹mithyā brūt' êti› kheditaḥ
atra jīvati yas tasya mṛta ev' âmṛt'|ôpamaḥ.
‹pāṇḍity'|ândha suhṛd|vairi mā sma tiṣṭha puro mama!›
iti yaḥ svāmin" ādiṣṭas tasya mṛtyur mah"|ôtsavaḥ.
na c' âsti dur|ghaṭasy' âsya ghaṭane mama kauśalam
tasmān maraṇam ev' âstu dhik prāṇān duḥ|sthitān iti.
niryātaś ca purī|bāhyaṃ maraṇ'|ôpāya|lipsayā
kasy' âpy a|dṛṣṭa|rūpasya vācam aśrauṣam ambare.

around her neck is called Priya·darshaná and she is to be
known by that name."

Thus the man Priya·dárshana, the chief of the guild in
the city, is the lady Priya·darshaná, a bride worthy of the
emperor of the sorcerers. It was during the lute contest,
when the emperor said, "Live long, beautiful lady," that
I found out. I thought to myself, "It is impossible for an 27.90
inhabitant of the earth to see her as a woman; he who sees
her as she is is the emperor." I realized then and there that
you had to be Go·mukha: there is no one else with the same
looks and vigor as the emperor. Then I had a picture of
you and the prince brought from Kaushámbi to confirm
it. These and other clues made me realize beyond doubt
that he was the emperor. The last was when he saw her
breast. Now you must put into action a plan to bring them
together, for you are skilled at making even difficult things
happen.'

When I heard all this from her I wanted to die, because 27.95
I realized I had three reasons to do so. I had offended my
master by telling him to lie when he was speaking the truth.
For a man living in such a situation, being dead is like being
an immortal god. And when a man is told by his master,
'You are blinded by your learning and an enemy to your
friends—get out of my sight!' then his death is an occasion
for great joy. Finally, I thought I was not clever enough to
bring about this difficult union, so there was nothing for
it but to die; I cursed my wretched life. I went out of the
city looking for a way to kill myself, when I heard in the
sky the voice of some invisible being: 'You misguided man, 27.100
turn back from your disgraceful decision to die. Dying is

27.100 ‹viparyasta nivartasva nindyān maraṇa|niścayāt
na hi duḥkha|kṣay'|ôpāyo mṛtyur iṣṭaḥ satām› iti.
tataḥ śithilit'|ôdvego girā khe|caray" ânayā
puraḥ puruṣam adrākṣaṃ skandh'|āropita|dārakam.
asau ca dārakaḥ kuṇṭhaḥ khañjaḥ kubjaḥ pṛth'|ûdaraḥ
iti saṃtakṣitaḥ pitrā karkaśair vacana|kṣuraiḥ.
‹mriyasva dharṣiṇī|putra! preta|khādita|mātṛka!
na vahāmi na puṣṇāmi bhavantaṃ niṣ|prayojanam.
eṣa tvāṃ gāḍham āveṣṭya grīvāṃ bhittv" âtha vā śiraḥ
mārayiṣyāmi tad gaccha Vaivasvata|purīm!› iti.
27.105 tatas tena vihasy' ôktaṃ ‹mā vākṣīr mā ca māṃ puṣaḥ!
etāvatā hi te kāryaṃ na madīyena mṛtyunā.
may" âpi kila kartavyaṃ mahat kāryaṃ mah"|ātmanām
tad bhavān māṃ sahasreṇa vikrīṇītāṃ mah"|ātmasu.
sahasraṃ yac ca tad|dattaṃ paryāptaṃ jīvanaṃ yataḥ
mā sma tasmād vinā kāryān mārayan māṃ bhavān› iti.
mama tv āsīn ‹mah"|ātmānaḥ ke 'nye yuṣmaj jagat|traye
kutaś c' ânyan mahat kāryaṃ yuṣmaj|jīvita|rakṣaṇāt.
sahasraṃ te na yat kiṃ cit koṭy" âpi yadi labhyate
tuccha|mūlyas tath" âpy eṣa tṛṇa|muṣṭi|samā hi sā!›
27.110 tat tad ity|ādi niścitya gṛham ānāyya taṃ tataḥ
krīṇāmi sma sahasreṇa cintā|maṇim iv' âśmanā.
Ṛṣidattām ath' âvocaṃ ‹yāvat smarasi kiṃ cana
pracchannaṃ śreṣṭhino vṛttaṃ tāvan me kathyatām› iti.
Kāliyena ca rājñā ca yad yat kāryaṃ rahaḥ kṛtam
tat tat Sumanase bhartrā kathitaṃ dhīra|cetase.
yac ca śruta|dharā kāryaṃ rājñaḥ śrutavatī guru

not the right way for virtuous men to put an end to their sorrows.'

My anxiety was tempered by this voice from the sky and I saw before me a man carrying a boy on his shoulders. The boy was deformed, lame, hunchbacked and potbellied. His father was cutting him down with spiky barbs: 'Die, you whoreson! Your mother has been devoured by ghouls! I shall neither carry you nor bring you up—there's no point! I am going to kill you, either by strangling you or smashing your skull. Go to the city of the god of death!'

With a laugh the boy replied, 'You needn't carry me or 27.105
bring me up: you should just do the following, and it doesn't involve killing me. It happens that there is an important task I must do for some nobles, so you should sell me for a thousand pieces to the noblemen. The thousand pieces that they give will set you up for life, so don't kill me pointlessly.'

I asked myself who in the three worlds was more noble than you and what task was more important than protecting your life. A thousand pieces is nothing for you; even if he cost ten million the lad would still be cheap—the ten million
would be like a handful of grass! After deciding this I took 27.110
him home, where I bought him for a thousand pieces. It was as if I were buying the philosopher's stone with a piece of rock! I then asked Rishi·datta to tell me about any of the chief of the guild's private deeds that she could remember. Káliya had told his shrewd wife everything that passed in private between him and the king. She had a good memory and told Rishi·datta the important secret affairs of the king that she had heard about. The two ladies told me, I told the hunchback, and the hunchback told Brahma·datta. You

tayā tad Ṛṣidattāyai duṣ|prakāśaṃ prakāśitam.
tayā tayā ca tan mahyaṃ kubjāya kathitaṃ mayā
kubjena Brahmadattāya śeṣaṃ pratyakṣam eva ca.
27.115 tad ‹yuṣmābhir yad ādiṣṭaṃ yad atra bhavatā kṛtam
tad ācakṣv' êti› kāryaṃ tad etad atra mayā kṛtam.»
ity|ādy ākarṇya tat tasmād indra|jāl'|âdhik'|âdbhutam
prāśaṃsaṃ caritaṃ tasya praśasyā hi guṇ'|âdhikāḥ.
kā vidyā|dhara|cakra|varti|padake
tucchā ratir mādṛśaḥ
su|prāpaṃ dharaṇī|carair yad aparaiḥ
krodh'|ādi|vaśyair api
prajñā|dhik|kṛta|deva|dānava|gurur
yeṣāṃ suhṛd Gomukhaḥ
te yat piṣṭapa|saptak'|āpti|vimukhās
tat|karmaṇāṃ jṛmbhitam.

iti Priyadarśanā|vivāhaḥ.

know the rest. You told me to tell you about my involvement 27.115
in this matter; I have thus done so."

On hearing all this I praised his actions, which had been more miraculous than witchcraft. Those who are excessively talented should be praised. How trifling is the pleasure that a man such as me takes in the position of emperor of the sorcerers: other inhabitants of the earth, even those in the thrall of anger and other emotions, can easily attain it. Go·mukha puts the gurus of the gods and demons to shame with his wisdom, so if those who have him as a friend fail to obtain the seven heavens, it is the result of their past actions.

Thus ends the Wedding to Priya·darshaná.

CANTO 28
PRIYA·DARSHANÁ WON

28.1 Evaṃ Vārāṇasī|sthaṃ māṃ dāra|mitrair upāsitam
upātiṣṭhanta Kāśikyāḥ śreṇayaḥ paṇya|pāṇayaḥ.
tāṃś ca bhāṣitavān asmi «sarva|vṛtt'|ânta|kovidaḥ
ayam ārya|kaniṣṭho vaḥ śreṇi|śreṣṭhī bhavatv» iti.
atha yāte kva cit kāle saudhe sa|Priyadarśanaḥ
sopāne tāram aśrauṣaṃ haṃsānām iva nisvanam.
mama tv āsīn «na haṃsānāṃ nūpurāṇām ayaṃ dhvaniḥ
pada|manthara|saṃcāro yac c' â|vicchinna|saṃtatiḥ.
28.5 na c' âiṣaḥ kula|nārīṇām upapattyā virudhyate
utsav'|âbhyudayeṣv eva tā hi bibhrati bhūṣaṇam.
ten' ântaḥ|pura|saṃcāra|vāra|strī|caraṇ'|ôcitaḥ
kim artham api sopāne caraty ābharaṇa|dhvani.»
evaṃ ca vimṛśann eva tār'|ābharaṇa|śiñjitāḥ
citr'|âṃśuka|dharā nārīr apaśyaṃ rūḍha|yauvanāḥ.
tāsāṃ Kumudikā nāma loka|locana|kaumudī
pragalbh" âpi vinīt" êva vanditvā mām abhāṣata.
«ārya|jyeṣṭha yaśo|bhāgin bhavato bhartṛ|dārikā
vijñāpayati vanditvā sādaraṃ rāja|dārikā.
28.10 ‹mayā vratakam uddiśya pūjitā devatā|dvijāḥ
vaṇṭakas tasya yuṣmābhiḥ sa|dārair gṛhyatām› iti.»
atha mahyaṃ su|saṃskāraṃ sā sa|mudraṃ sa|mudgakam
vāsaḥ kusuma|gandhāṃś ca hāri|gandhān upāsarat.
ath' ôdvṛtya jagat|sārān asau mahyam adarśayat
dvi|prakārān alaṃkārān nara|nārī|jan'|ôcitān.
may" ôktaṃ «dvayam apy etad arhati Priyadarśanā

WHILE I WAS STAYING in Varánasi with my wife and 28.1
friends, the guildsmen of the city came to me carrying their wares. I said to them, "My noble younger brother
is an expert in every eventuality. Let him be the chief of
your guilds."

After some time had passed, I was in the palace with Pri-
ya·darshaná one day when I heard from the staircase a shrill
sound like the call of swans. I said to myself, "This is the
sound of anklets, not swans: it is an unbroken succession of
soft footsteps. And it cannot be coming from ladies of the 28.5
court, because they wear ornaments only on festival days or
at celebrations. So for some reason the sound of ornaments,
which normally comes from the feet of the courtesans who
wander the inner apartments, is coming from the staircase."

Just as I was thinking this, to the shrill tinkling of their
ornaments I saw some girls in the bloom of youth wearing
colorful dresses. One of the girls was called Kumúdika and
was like the light of the moon to the eyes of the world.
Though proud, she seemed demure as she greeted me and
said, "Noble and glorious sir, your master's daughter, the
princess, greets you respectfully and makes the following
request: 'In observance of a vow, I have made a worshipful 28.10
offering to the gods and the brahmins. Would you and your
wife please accept a share of it?'"

She placed before me a beautifully decorated sealed box,
clothes and delightful incense scented with flowers. She
opened the box and showed me priceless treasures of two
kinds, suitable for both men and women. I said, "Priya·dar-
shaná should have both: they have been sent by a woman,
so it is a woman that should have them." When they heard

preṣitaṃ yoṣitā yat tad yoṣid eva yato 'rhati.»
idam ākarṇya tāḥ prekṣya vismitāḥ sa|smitāś ca mām
tasyai dattvā ca tad dravyam agacchan kṛta|vandanāḥ.
28.15 «yaśo|bhāginn» iti śrutvā tay" ôktaṃ pīḍito 'bhavam
an|abhyastaṃ hi yad yena tena tad vastu duḥ|saham.
mam' āmantrayate yāvāt puruṣaḥ pramadā|janaḥ
sarvo 'sāv «ārya|putr' êti» muktv" âitāṃ puruṣām iti.
kiṃ c' ânyat kula|kanyānāṃ k" êyam īdṛk|sva|tantratā
y" êyam asmad|vidhaiḥ sārdhaṃ loka|yātrā nir|aṅkuśaiḥ.
kiṃ tu kāmayamān" âpi kāmini kāmini priye
na dhanāyaty api sv'|âṅgaṃ kim aṅga dhanam a|dhruvam.
tad «asyāḥ ko bhaved bhāvo may' îty» etad vitarkayan
andha|kāra|mukhen' âhaṃ Gomukhen' êti bhāṣitaḥ.
28.20 «ārya|putra dur|ant" êyam īdṛśībhir bhavādṛśām
loka|yātr" êty.»
ath' âvocam enaṃ parihasann iva,
«dur|antā v" âtha vā sv|antā na h' îyaṃ prastutā mayā
atha vā saṃkaṭāt trātā mam' âsty eva bhavān» iti.
iti tasminn aho|rātre gate Kumudik"|ādikāḥ
āgaty' êdam abhāṣanta sa|vrīḍā|vinayā iva.
«ārya|putr' ārya|duhitā vanditvā rāja|dārikā
asmad|doṣe kṛta|vrīḍā vijñāpayati s'|âñjaliḥ.
kṣamaṇīyo 'yam asmākam ācār'|âti|kramo yataḥ
mūḍha|bhṛtya|kṛtā doṣā na grāhyāḥ svāminām» iti.
28.25 may" âpy uktaṃ «na paśyāmi doṣam ācaritaṃ tayā
asti cet kṣānta ev' âsau tath" âpy ākhyāyatām» iti.

this, the ladies looked at me with smiles of surprise. Then they gave Priya·darshaná the treasures, paid their respects, and left.

When I had heard the lady address me as "glorious," I 28.15
was troubled, for it is difficult to take something to which one is unaccustomed. Whenever any man or woman other than she addressed me, they would all use "Noble sir." And there was another thing: how could respectable girls be so free in their interactions with unfettered men like me? But, when lusting after a lover, in respect of her dear sweetheart a girl counts for nothing her own body, let alone an unfixed asset like her reputation.

As I was wondering what her feelings toward me might
be, a somber-faced Go·mukha said to me, "Noble sir, inter- 28.20
action between girls like these and men like you will turn out badly."

Chuckling, I said to him, "Whether it turns out badly or well, I did not start it, and, anyway, I have you to get me out of trouble."

A day and a night passed and then Kumúdika and the other girls came and said, somewhat shyly and humbly, "Noble sir, our mistress the princess greets you and, embarrassed at our misconduct, joins her hands and requests that you forgive us for overstepping the line. Wrongdoings by foolish servants should not be imputed to their masters."

I replied, "I was not aware that she had done anything 28.25
wrong. If she did, it is completely forgiven. Nevertheless, please tell me what it was."

tataḥ Kumudik" ācaṣṭe «mām apṛcchan nṛp'|ātma|jā
‹ārya|jyeṣṭhas tvay" ālāpān bhāṣitaḥ kīdṛśān?› iti.
‹ārya|jyeṣṭha yaśo|bhāginn› ity|ādau kathite mayā
s'|âsūyā sa|viṣād" êva vepamān" êdam abravīt.
‹ayi vairiṇi! bhartāram evaṃ vadati k" âṅganā
yath" ôkto mandayā jyeṣṭho ‹yaśo|bhāginn› iti tvayā?
na ca tvadīyam ev' êdaṃ vacaḥ saṃbhāvayaty asau
para|saṃdeśa|hārī hi pratīto gaṇikā|janaḥ.
28.30 yaḥ śreṣṭhi|duhitur bhartā so 'smākam api dharmataḥ
Priyadarśanayā sārdham a|bhinn" âiva hi me tanuḥ.
ārya|putras tvayā tasmād ‹ārya|putr' êti bhāṣyatām
tathā vijñāpyatāṃ c' êdaṃ yath" âvajñāṃ na manyate.
asmad|arthaṃ mayā c' êyam ucyatāṃ Priyadarśanā
vratak'|ôtsavam āsevya sāyāhne pratiyāsyati.›»

iti śrutv" êdam āsīn me «ko 'nyaḥ paribhavaḥ paraḥ
etasmād yad asāv āha ‹bhāryā prasthāpyatām› iti.
yā vadhūs tāta|pādānāṃ mama bhāryā ca sā katham
kuṭumbi|jana|yoṣ" êva gacchet para|gṛhān?» iti.
28.35 atha māṃ Gomukho 'vocat «kim a|sthāne viśaṅkayā
n' êdaṃ para|gṛhaṃ devyās tathā viditam eva vaḥ.
maṅgalaṃ hi vivāh'|ântam asyās tatr' âiva kāritam
tac c' âitac ca gṛhaṃ tasmād a|bhinnaṃ dṛśyatām» iti.

tatas tad|vacanān nyāyyād anujñātā satī mayā
prāsād'|âgrād avārohat samaṃ tu Priyadarśanā.
atha prāsāda|pṛṣṭha|stho dāntair ujjvala|maṇḍanaiḥ
gobhiḥ pravahaṇaṃ yuktam apaśyaṃ rāja|vartmani.
rāja|kañcukibhir vṛddhair an|antair vetra|pāṇibhiḥ

Kumúdika said, "The princess asked me what I had said to the noble sir. When I told her that I had started by saying, 'Noble and glorious sir,' she seemed angry and upset, and, trembling, she said, 'Oh, you are against me! What lady speaks to her husband like you did, foolishly calling sir "glorious"? He will not believe that the words come from you alone, for courtesans are known as the bringers of messages from others. The husband of the guild chief's daughter is by 28.30
rights my husband, too, for there is no difference between Priya·darshaná and me. As a result, you should address the noble sir as "Noble sir." Tell him this, so that he does not take offense. And another thing: tell Priya·darshaná from me that she is to attend the celebration of the end of the fast; she will return by evening.'"

When I heard this, I said to myself, "She is ordering my wife about—what greater insult is there than that? She is the daughter-in-law of my revered father, and my wife: how could she go to another man's house as if she were a woman from his household?"

Then Go·mukha said to me, "There is no need to worry. 28.35
You know very well that for her ladyship it is not the house of another man: the concluding rites of her marriage were performed there, so there is no difference between that house and this one."

What he said was right, so I gave her my permission and she went from the roof terrace down to the ground floor. Then, from the roof terrace, I saw in the royal highway a carriage yoked to some beautifully decorated oxen. It was surrounded by several elderly royal chamberlains carrying canes, and crowds of people, mainly women and eunuchs.

nārī|varṣavara|prāya|jana|vṛndaiś ca saṃvṛtam.
28.40 tac ca rāja|kulād dṛṣṭvā gacchat pravahaṇaṃ tataḥ
tad dinaṃ gamayāmi sma dīrgha|bandhana|dur|gamam.
sūryo 'pi tad ahar manye bhagn'|âkṣa|syandano bhavet
daity'|ôcchinna|turaṃgo vā yen' âstaṃ katham apy agāt.
atha prāsādam āruhya rāja|mārgaṃ nirūpayan
tad eva yānam adrākṣaṃ dīpik"|āvalay" āvṛtam.

avatīrya ca harmy'|âgrād dīpikā|candrikā|sakhīm
sopāne dṛṣṭavān asmi śrāmyantīṃ Priyadarśanām.
tām ādāya tataḥ pāṇau mada|pramada|bādhitām
cirād āropayāmi sma harmy'|âgra|śayan'|ântikam.
28.45 kṣaṇaṃ ca tatra viśrāntāṃ tām āliṅgam asau ca mām
tataś «caṭ» iti vicchinnaṃ tat|kāñcī|guṇa|bandhanam.
śarāṭi|kurara|śreṇiḥ pulinān nalinīm iva
śiñjānā raśanā śayyāṃ tan|nitambād ath' âpatat.
tāṃ ca bhinna|maṇi|chāyāc chatra|chādita|dīpikām
dṛṣṭvā pṛṣṭā mayā tasyāḥ saṃprāptiṃ Priyadarśanā.
«bahu śrotavyam atr' âsti krameṇa śrūyatām» iti
uktvā ruṣṭ" êva tāṃ dṛṣṭvā s" ācaṣṭa sma kathām imām.

«asty ahaṃ yuṣmad|ādeśād gatā kany"|âvarodhanam
na ca tatra mayā dṛṣṭā mārgayantyā nṛp'|ātma|jā.
28.50 tataḥ parijanas tasyāḥ prāha māṃ ‹rāja|dārikā
gṛh'|ôpavanam adhyāste tatra saṃbhāvyatām› iti.
praviśya ca mayā dṛṣṭā tasminn udyāna|pālikā
vasanta|su|manaḥ|kḷpta|māl"|ābharaṇa|dhāriṇī.
sā ca pṛṣṭā may" âvocad ‹yo 'yaṃ saṃdhyā|vad āruṇaḥ

After I had watched the carriage leave the palace, the day 28.40
seemed like a long imprisonment, and I got through it with difficulty. That day I thought the axle of the sun's chariot must have broken or its horses must have been cut loose by a demon, it had such difficulty in setting. Then, when I climbed onto the roof terrace and looked out onto the royal highway, I saw the carriage returning, surrounded by a ring of lanterns.

I came down from the roof of the house and saw the weary Priya·darshaná on the staircase, accompanied by lamplight and moonlight. I took her by the hand. She was overcome by fun and excitement, and it took a long time to help her
up to her bed at the top of the house. After she had rested 28.45
there for a while, we embraced one another and the thread tying her girdle snapped. Like a line of herons and ospreys falling from a bank into a lotus pond, the girdle fell from her hips onto the bed with a jingling sound. The light from its various gems made the lamp appear as if shaded by a parasol, and when I saw it I asked Priya·darshaná how she had got it. "It's a long story. Listen to it in stages," she said. Seeming angry, she looked at it and told the following story.

"At your instruction, I went to the inner apartments. I
looked about but could not find the princess. Then one of 28.50
her servants told me that she was in the garden and I could find her there. I entered the garden and saw a lady gardener holding decorative garlands made from spring flowers. On being questioned by me she said, 'The princess is sitting in a quiet place over there in that copse of *ashóka* trees as red as the dawn. The safe way to her ladyship is via this winding path that goes through the *priyángu* thicket. Farther on there

aśoka|ṣaṇḍas tatr' āste vivikte rāja|dārikā.
anena c' ārya|duhitur vakreṇ' âpi tathā vrajaḥ
yo 'yaṃ priyaṅgu|ṣaṇḍasya yāti madhyena nir|bhayaḥ.
dūrāt kurabakānāṃ ca [.....] kānanam
mādhavī|sahakārāṇām aṅkolānāṃ ca varjaya.
28.55 bhrāmyan|madhu|kara|stena|senā|saṃbādha|pāda|pam
bhṛṅga|daṃśa|bhayāt kas taṃ n' â|pramattas tyajed› iti.
tena ca prasthit" âdrākṣaṃ kadamba|kuṭajān api
mālatī|saptaparṇāś ca mañjarī|channa|pallavān.
mama tv āsīd ‹aho śaktir dohadasya varīyasī
an|ṛtāv api yen' âite jṛmbhitāḥ pāda|pā› iti.
s" âtha paṅka|jinī|kūle Himavat|kaṃdha|rājate
śilā|pṛṣṭhe mayā dṛṣṭā sāndra|candana|kardame.
sama|śīt'|ātape 'py asmin vasante śārad" îva sā
madhyaṃ|dine jvareṇ' âiva khedyamānā balīyasā.
28.60 saṃtatais tāla|vṛntaiś ca candan'|āp|ārdra|mārutaiḥ
vījyamānā vacobhiś ca sāntvyamān" âti|komalaiḥ.
atha tasyā mayā gatvā samīpaṃ vandanā kṛtā
tay" âpi kṣipta|cetastvān na kiṃ cid api bhāṣitam.
tataḥ Kumudikā tasyāḥ pādam ālambya niṣṭhuram
pratibuddhām avocat tāṃ ‹bhaginī dṛśyatām› iti.
tataḥ Kumudikā|hastam ālamby' ôtthāya māṃ ciram
āliṅgitavatī sv'|âṅgair dhvānt'|âṅgār'|âgni|duḥ|sahaiḥ.
sukh'|āsīnāṃ ca mām āha ‹bhartā te sukha|bhāgini
satataṃ kuśal"› îty|ādi ‹tath" êti› ca may" ôditam.
28.65 punar āha ‹sa te bhartā chāttratvād dur|janaḥ kila
āhār'|ādyair dur|ārādhas tvayā tad iti me matiḥ.›
‹prītyā Nand'|Ôpanandābhyāṃ yen' āharati sādhitam
tena n' âiv' ôpacaryo 'sau may" êti› kathitaṃ mayā.

is a grove of red amaranth, *mádhavi*, *saha·kara* and *ankóla*;
stay away from it.* Its trees are thronged by an army of 28.55
treacherous buzzing bees. Out of fear of the bees' stings, anyone with their wits about them steers clear of it.'

So I started on my way and saw *kadámba*, *kútaja*, *málati* and *sapta·parna* trees, their twigs covered in blossoms. I said to myself, 'See the great power of desire: it has made the trees flower even out of season!'

Then, by the bank of a lotus pond as silvery as a Himalayan cloud, I saw her on a flat rock that was thickly covered in sandalwood paste. Even in this temperate spring season, for her it seemed to be autumn and at noon she
was suffering from a strong fever. She was being constantly 28.60
cooled with a moist sandal-scented breeze from palm fans, and soothed with the sweetest words. I approached and greeted her, but she was distracted and said nothing. Kumúdika grabbed her roughly by the foot and, once she had got her attention, said, 'Your sister is here.' Holding Kumúdika's hand, she got up and gave me a long embrace, her body as unbearable as a smoldering fire. When I was sitting comfortably, she said to me, 'Lucky lady, is your husband keeping well?' and I replied that he was.

She continued, 'He is a student, so I expect he is bad- 28.65
tempered and difficult for you to keep happy in matters of food and so forth.'

I replied, 'He gladly eats the food that Nanda and Upanánda prepare, so I do not have to serve him.'

punar uktaṃ tayā smitvā ‹n' êdaṃ saṃbhāvyate tayoḥ
rājy'|âṃśo daśamas tābhyām abhimānāt kil' ôjjhitaḥ.
tau tvad|bhartur a|vittasya pānthasy' â|jñāta|janmanaḥ
dāsyam abhyupagacchetāṃ kathaṃ nām' êti dur|ghaṭam.›
may" ôktaṃ ‹sarvam asty etat kiṃ tu tau divya|cakṣuṣau
yad ev' ādiśataḥ kiṃ cit tat tath" âiva hi sidhyati.
28.70 jyeṣṭhasya ca guṇā jyeṣṭhās tābhyāṃ kasy' êti mānuṣāḥ
ten' âṅgī|kṛtavantau tau mad|bhartur bhṛtyatām iti.›
Bhagīrathayaśāḥ śrutvā niṣkamp'|âkṣī kathām imām
tanū|ruha|vikāreṇa s'|âśruṇ" āliṅgitā balāt.
evaṃ ca kṣaṇam āsīnām āha māṃ rāja|dārikā
‹aṅgaṃ pravahaṇa|kṣobhāt khinnam abhyañjyatām› iti.
‹āstām āstām› iti may" ân|icchantyā yāvad ucyate
tāvad balād balā|tailaṃ nyadhāt Kumudikā mayi.
sarvath" âkṣi|nikoc'|ādyair uktvā Kumudik"|ādikāḥ
sā me 'bhyaṅg'|âpadeśena vivṛty' âṅgāni paśyati.
28.75 etat tvat|kara|śākhābhir likhitam [...] bhakam
madīyam aṅgam ālokya rāja|dārikay" ôditam.
‹aho sakhe sa|lajj" âsi bālikā kula|pālikā
yay" êha duḥ|sahā soḍhā komal'|âṅgyā kadarthanā.
atha vā tvaṃ par'|ādhīnā bhart" âiva tava nirdayaḥ
yena prabala|darpeṇa kṛtaṃ vaiṣamyam īdṛśam.
ko 'nyo niṣ|karuṇas tasmāt tvaṃ yen' ôtpala|komalā
dantin" êva mah"|ândhena mathitā puṇḍarīkiṇī?
mat|saṃdeśaṃ ca vācyo 'sau «kim a|sthāne kṛtam tvayā?»

With a smile she said, 'It is hard to believe that those two gave up a tenth of the kingdom, apparently out of pride. Your husband is a man of no substance, a traveler of unknown birth: why on earth would they become his servants? It is most unlikely.'

I replied, 'That is all as you say, but they have divine sight
and everything that they predict comes true. The qualities 28.70
of the noble sir are pre-eminent—no man surpasses him and Go·mukha in human virtues—and thus Nanda and Upanánda became servants of my husband.'

Bhagíratha·yashas heard this with unmoving eyes, then shuddered violently and started to cry.

I sat there for a while and then the princess said to me, 'You must be aching all over from being bumped about in the carriage: have a massage.' I did not want one, but, while I was refusing, Kumúdika put *bala* oil on me against my will. With winks and so forth, the princess gave instructions to Kumúdika and the others: under the pretext of a massage my body was uncovered and she looked at it.

When she saw that it had been scratched by your fin- 28.75
gernails, the princess said,* 'What a demure and well-bred young lady you are to have borne this insufferable abuse on your tender body. Or perhaps you are under another's control and it is your pitiless husband who in his overweening arrogance has performed this outrage. You are as tender as a lotus; who else could be so cruel as to hurt you, like a senseless elephant destroying a lotus pond? Ask him from me why he has needlessly done this. One should not say, "I am in charge," and then tie one's crest-jewel to one's foot.

na hi cūḍā|maṇiḥ pāde «prabhavām' îti» badhyate.
28.80 idaṃ hi karkaśāḥ soḍhuṃ śaktā rājanya|kanyakāḥ
chāyā|komala|gātryas tu nāhi vānija|dārikāḥ.›
ity|ādi bahu jalpitvā sā mām udvartan'|ādibhiḥ
sat|kārair anna|pān'|ântaiḥ saṃmānitavatī ciram.
tasyāś ca kṣaṇa|saṃkṣiptaṃ mama saṃvatsar'|āyatam
yuṣmat|kathā|prasaṅgena s'|ârkaṃ gatam idaṃ dinam.
ath' â|cala|nitamb'|âbhāt sva|nitambād vimucya sā
āmucan mekhalām enāṃ man|nitambe laghīyasi.
bahur visraṃsamānāyāṃ granthir asyāṃ tayā kṛtaḥ
sva|hasta|vilatair yatnān mṛṇālī|tantu|sūtrakaiḥ.
28.85 tataḥ prasthāpitavatī mām ity|ādi vidhāya sā
mekhalā skhalitā c' êyaṃ chittvā tat|tantu|bandhanam.»
iti tasyās tayā citre prapañce 'smin nivedite
Saṃkalpa|janman" āmṛṣṭaḥ saṃkalpayitum ārabhe.
tayā yad guru saṃdiṣṭam upalabdhaṃ ca yat tayā
etad eva su|paryāptam anurāgasya lakṣaṇam.
yat punar mekhalā baddhā niḥ|sārair bisa|tantubhiḥ
satsv apy anyeṣu sūtreṣu tatr' êdaṃ cintitaṃ tayā.
nir|day'|āliṅgana|kṣobhād idaṃ vicchedam eṣyati
ath' êyaṃ mekhalā srastā śayyāyāṃ nipatiṣyati.
28.90 lambāṃ c' êmām asau dṛṣṭvā man|nitamba|viśālatām
anayā [...] prītim ādhāsyaty api kām iti.
ek'|âikato 'pi vṛtt'|ânta upapanne tayā kṛte
mayā tu jñāta|kāryatvād utprekṣ" êyam upekṣitā.

Hardy princesses can put up with this, but not merchants' 28.80
daughters, whose bodies are as soft as shadows.'

After saying this and much more, she spent a long time honoring me with treatments like shampooing and so forth, culminating in some food and drink. For her, the day passed in an instant and for me it stretched out like a year as we talked about you until the sun went down. Then, from her hips, which looked like the flanks of a mountain, she removed this girdle and put it on my slender behind. When it kept slipping, she tied several knots in it with fine lotus
fibers that she had carefully picked herself. After dressing 28.85
me up with that and other clothes, she sent me on my way. Here is that girdle; it slipped off when the thread holding it together snapped."

When she reported the lady's curious behavior, I felt a twinge of desire and started to reflect. The laboured message that she sent me and the things that Priya·darshaná had found out were clear indications of affection. Moreover, she had tied the girdle with flimsy lotus fibers when other threads were at hand, so she must have been expecting the girdle to break from the pressure of a passionate embrace,
then slip and fall onto the bed, and that I would see from 28.90
its length how huge her hips were, which would make me feel somewhat attracted to her.* Every one of her actions fitted the pattern of events, but, realizing what she was up to, I pretended not to have noticed.

ath' âham abravaṃ «śyāmā Bhagīrathayaśāḥ sphuṭam»
«kathaṃ vetth' êti» s" âpṛcchad ath' êttham aham uktavān.
«gaurāṇām a|sit'|ābhāsam a|sitānāṃ sit'|âdhikam
śyāmānāṃ maṇḍanaṃ taj|jñaiś citra|varṇaṃ tu varṇitam.
pārijāta|srag|ābhā|bhā yad iyaṃ mekhalā tataḥ
bālā dūrvā|dala|śyāmā niyataṃ rāja|dārikā.
28.95 kiṃ ca n' ânyā tataḥ kā cid darśanīyatamā yataḥ
darśanīyatamā śyāmā nārīṇām iti darśanam.»
tay" ôktaṃ «dhig dhig astv eṣāṃ ratna|lakṣaṇa|kāriṇām
janaḥ pracchādanīyo 'pi khyāpito yaiḥ śaṭhair api!»
ity|ādyā kathayā tasyāḥ kṣapāyāḥ prahara|dvayam
prāpty|upāya|vicāreṇa tṛtīyaḥ prerito mayā.
mama tv āsīd iyaṃ cintā «kiṃ mam' ôpāya|cintayā
devatās tat kariṣyanti yena śāntir bhaviṣyati.
Vegavaty|ādik'|â|prāptāv upāyaḥ kaḥ kṛto mayā?
yathā tāḥ prāptavān asmi tathā rāja|sutām» iti.
28.100 atha mām ekad" āgatya sāyaṃ Kumudik" âvadat
«Bhagīrathayaśā yuṣmān vanditvā yācate yathā.
‹ye may" āropitāś cūtā mādhavī|campak'|ādayaḥ
te jātā mañjarī|bhāra|bhara|bhaṅgura|pallavāḥ.
ataḥ śvas tatra gatv" âhaṃ mādhavī|sahakārayoḥ
kartrī vivāha|saṃskāram apareṣāṃ ca pūjanam.
tena yuṣmad|gṛha|dvārād gṛhītvā Priyadarśanām
prāta eva prāyāt" âsmi tad eṣā mucyatām› iti.»

I said, "Bhagíratha·yashas clearly has a dark complexion." "How do you know?" asked Priya·darshaná, and I replied, "Experts in the matter have prescribed black ornaments for those who are pale, white and the like for those who are black, and multicolored ornaments for those who are dark. This girdle resembles a garland of *parijáta* flowers, so the young princess must be dark, like a blade of *durva* grass.
What's more, there can be no lady more beautiful than 28.95
her, for she who is dark is held to be the most beautiful of women."

Priya·darshaná said, "Curses on the men who fix the characteristics of jewelry—the scoundrels expose even those who should be kept hidden!"

Two-thirds of the night passed in talking about her like this. I spent the last third thinking of ways to get her. But then I said to myself, "There is no point in my worrying about a plan: the gods will arrange a happy outcome. What plan did I use when I was unable to get Végavati and the others? I will have the princess just as I had them."

One day Kumúdika came to me in the evening and said, 28.100
"Bhagíratha·yashas greets you and informs you that the twigs of the mango, *mádhavi*, *chámpaka* and other trees that she planted are now about to break under the weight of their many blossoms, so she is going to go there tomorrow to perform the wedding of the *mádhavi* and mango trees, and to worship the others. She plans to collect Priya·darshaná from the door of your house in the morning and continue on her way, so please let her go."

atha tasyai pratijñāya «gacchatv evaṃ bhavatv» iti
draṣṭavyā rāja|putr" îti khidyamāno 'nayaṃ niśām.
28.105 prātaḥ Kumudik" āgatya bhāṣate sma sa|saṃbhramā
«Bhagīrathayaśāḥ prāptā gacchatv ārya|sut" êti» mām.
atha tāṃ dṛṣṭavān asmi prasthāpya Priyadarśanām
prāsād'|âgra|sthito dvāḥ|stha|svaccha|pravahaṇ'|āsthitām.
āstāṃ ca mama tāṃ dṛṣṭvā kṣaṇaṃ mānasa|cakṣuṣī
suṣupty" âvasthitasy' êva naṣṭa|saṃkalpa|darśane.
sarvathā puṇyavantas te sur'|âsura|nar'|ôragāḥ
asāv a|kāla|mṛtyur yair nārī|rūpo na vīkṣitaḥ!
tayā c' ānanam unnamya dṛṣṭaḥ saṃdṛṣṭavān aham
Sahasr'|âkṣaṃ svam ātmānaṃ tac|cakṣuṣ†kādika†ujjvalam.
28.110 māṃ ca mad|dayitāṃ n' âsau saṃmānitavatī samam
mayi dṛṣṭim adāt tasyāṃ gāḍha|hasta|grah'|ârhaṇām.
atha sva|yānam āropya sā priyāṃ Priyadarśanām
kañcuky|ādi|camū|guptā nagar'|ôpavanaṃ gatā.

aham tu tad dinaṃ nītvā kṛcchrān mandira|niṣkuṭe
harmya|mūrdhānam ārohaṃ rāja|putrī|didṛkṣayā.
atha pravahaṇen' âsau nabhasvat|paṭu|raṃhasā
mad|gṛha|dvāram āgacchad dūrād unnamit'|ānanā.
sā ca māṃ tatra paśyantī saṃtataṃ Priyadarśanām
gāḍhaṃ niṣpīḍayantī ca ciram aṅgaṃ nyapīḍayat.
28.115 vandanā|chadmanā paścān māyy ātmānaṃ nidhāya sā
ceto|vinimayaṃ kṛtvā pravṛttā śibikāṃ iti.

I gave her my consent, saying, "So be it: she may go," and spent the night troubled by the thought that I had to see the princess.

In the morning, Kumúdika hurried in and said to me, 28.105
"Bhagíratha·yashas has arrived. Her ladyship must leave." After sending Priya·darshaná on her way, from the roof of the house I saw Bhagíratha·yashas in a gleaming carriage by the door. And that was enough! For a while after seeing her, it was as if I was in the deepest of sleeps—my mind and eyes were devoid of thought and sight. Lucky indeed are the gods, demons, men and snake-people who have not beheld the untimely death that is womanly beauty! She raised her head and saw me, and then I saw myself as thousand-eyed
Indra,* resplendent in the light from her eyes. She did not 28.110
show me and my wife equal respect: she fixed her gaze on me and treated Priya·darshaná to a firm handshake. Then she sat my wife Priya·darshaná in her carriage and went to the city garden under the protection of a troop of chamberlains and others.

After struggling through the day in the garden of my house, I climbed up to the roof terrace in the hope of seeing the princess. Then, with her face raised from a distance, she arrived at the door of my house, her carriage moving as swiftly as the wind. Once there, looking at me all the while, she pressed Priya·darshaná in a tight embrace, squeezing
her body for an age. Finally, in the guise of a greeting, she 28.115
gave herself to me in exchange for my heart and returned to her carriage.

ārādhayāmi nṛpa|sūnu|kṛte nu Gaurīṃ
kiṃ khānayāmi caturais tvaritaṃ suruṅgām?
ity|ādy|upāya|śata|cintana|tānta|cetāḥ
kṛcchrān niśām anayam a|pratilabdha|nidraḥ.

iti śrī|Bhaṭṭa|Budhasvāminā kṛte Śloka|saṃgrahe
Bṛhat|kathāyāṃ Priyadarśanā|lābhaḥ
samāptam
śubham!

Am I to propitiate Gauri in order to win the princess ... Am I to have some skilled men quickly dig a tunnel? ... My mind wearied by thoughts of hundreds of such stratagems, I struggled through the night without getting any sleep.

Thus ends the Winning of Priya·darshaná
in the Abridgement into Sanskrit Verse
of the Big Story by Bhatta Budha·svamin.
The End
Good!

NOTES

Bold *references are to the English text;* ***bold italic*** *references are to the Sanskrit text. An asterisk (*) in the body of the text marks the word or passage being annotated.*

18.1 **Rati** is the consort of Kama, the god of love, and **Vasánta**, the personification of spring, is Kama's friend.

18.5 Mítravati means "having friends."

18.7 **Vardhamána** was the given name of the last of the Jaina *tīrthaṅkaras*.

18.8 **Ríshabha** was the first of the Jaina *tīrthaṅkaras*.

18.10 **Sanu·dasa** means "servant of Sanu."

18.40 ***Karṇikāra*** flowers are very rough.

18.43 The word for **nectar**, ***madhu***, is also the word for "wine."

18.52 The **six flavors** are sweet, sour, salty, pungent, bitter and astringent.

18.94 Budha·svamin is making a pun on the substantive ***prasanna***: as an adjective, it means "pleased" or **happy**, and as a feminine noun it refers to an alcoholic drink.

18.115 ***Triphalā*** is a medicine made from three fruits: *āmalaka* (Phyllanthus emblica Linn.), *vibhītaka* (Terminalia bellerica Roxb.) and *harītakī* (Terminalia chebula Retz.).

18.167 The comparison implies that Sanu·dasa ate the grains that had been used to remove the foul-smelling oil from his body.

18.190 The travelers will not eat before their guest has eaten.

18.206 The **Vaitárani** is the river that the dead have to cross before reaching the afterlife.

18.248 Budha·svamin is making a play on the word ***nātha*** which can mean both "patron" and "parent."

18.255 The song is found at *Mahābhārata* xii, 47.41.

18.286 Budha·svamin is making a pun on the word ***sāgara***. As well as being the name of Samúdra·dinná's father, it also means "sea."

18.313 The **self-born god** is Kama, the god of love.

18.379 **Vishva·karman** is the divine architect of the universe.

18.479 The half-verse is found at *Mahābhārata Śāntiparvan* 136.173cd.

18.505 *Titaü* A rare Vedic word meaning "sieve", the *aü* indicates that this is not the diphthong *au*.

18.503 **Jatáyu** was the king of the vultures and fought against Rávana when helping Rama to rescue Sita.

18.554 Budha·svamin is using three meanings of *vara*: **boon**, **finest** and **husband**.

18.589 The witnesses add a half-verse here that translates, "It is the manifestation of the power of the asceticism of Vishvásu and Bharad·vaja." As suggested by LACÔTE (1908:274), this half-verse is probably a gloss on 589ab. There are no one- or three-line verses elsewhere in the text.

18.638 The **four sciences** are the Vedas, logic, government and business.

18.702 There appears to be at least one verse missing here: all the other cantos end with a verse in a meter that is not *anuṣṭubh*, and at the beginning of Canto 19 Nara·váhana·datta is the narrator, not Sanu·dasa.

19.63 **Mano·hara** means "charming."

19.65 **Vasánta**: Cf. note to 18.1.

19.103 Indra is said to have cut the mountains' wings, rendering them immobile.

20.27 This is an allusion to the legend of the sage Agástya drinking the ocean.

20.69 The realm of the gods is to the north, while to the south lies the land of the dead.

20.180 **Shashi** is the moon and **Róhini**, "the red lady," is his consort, the lunar asterism that contains Aldebaran, a red star.

20.212 Nara·váhana·datta is imagining this conversation; cf. 20.216.

20.278 **Durvásas** is a notoriously irascible sage.

20.282 The ***chátaka*** bird is said to live off raindrops.

20.289 I have not attempted to translate ***ubheṭī***, the meaning of which is obscure.

20.310 Because of Ámita·gati's closeness to Nara·váhana·datta, the king describes him as the latter's brother, and (313) says that Nara·váhana·datta's mothers are Ámita·gati's mothers.

20.387 The rat is addressing the element fire.

20.391 The **restless one** is the element wind.

20.422 Rumánvat is the general; Hari·shikha is his son.

20.426 Yaugan·dharáyana's son is Maru·bhútika.

21.2 Budha·svamin is making a pun on the name **Avimúkta** (a sacred site near Varánasi), which means "inseparable."

21.3 These cities are situated at the extremes of India, in the cardinal directions (east, north, west and south, respectively).

21.57 **Dridhódyama** means "He who tries hard."

21.118 **The man in Sindh** is Tamo·bhédaka.

21.137 **Bhinna·tamas** means "He who has cast darkness asunder."

22.21 **Kunda·málika** means "garland of jasmine."

22.24 I have found no other instances of the word ***kurubhaka***, which I have translated with "freak."

22.39 In the *Mahābhārata*, the Pándavas caused Drona to surrender and be killed by telling him this lie.

22.89 **Álaka** is the city of Kubéra, the god of wealth.

22.167 As will become apparent, Kunda·málika has dressed as a male *Kāpālika* ascetic.

22.224 The doctrine of the *Kāpālika*s was called Soma·siddhánta.

22.240 **Náimisha**, where the *Mahābhārata* was recited, is modern-day Nimsar, near Lucknow. **Ganga·dvara** is modern-day Hardwar. The country of the **Kurus** is the region around Kuru·kshetra, to the north of Delhi.

22.241 The location of **Mahálaya** is uncertain.

22.264 Kunda·málika is now dressed as a female *Kāpālika* ascetic.

22.291 The verse, which is called *Mānastoka* because it begins *mā nas toke...*, is found at Ṛg Veda1114.8.

22.305 In the *Mahābhārata*, the Pándavas spent a year in disguise at Viráta's court.

23.54 Nala, Yudhi·shthira, Púshkara and Shákuni are renowned dice players in the *Mahābhārata.*

24.17 The sense indicates that there is a lacuna between 17b and 18c (it is not marked in the witnesses). It must have meant something like '**Punar·vasu will soon** arrange for us to meet you there." Then we went **to the Jaina temple**.'

24.32 Budha·svámin is making a pun on the name **Priya·dárshana**, which means "lovely to look at."

24.51 This is a reference to Nara·váhana·datta's playing of the lute at the contest described in Canto 17.

Col. 24: The colophon of this canto is incomplete.

25.42 Jana·vállabha, which means **dear to the people**, is also the name of a type of lotus (*padma*).

25.85 Shiva drank the *kālakūṭā* poison when it emerged at the churning of the ocean of milk.

25.103 ***Duḥśliṣṭa***, which has been translated with "wrong," also suggests "bad poetic practice." Thus verses 103 to 105, as well as being an attack on excessive personal ornamentation, are also denigrating poetic ornamentation. "Poetic ornamentation" is another meaning of *alaṃkāra*, which has been translated in these verses with "decoration."

26.20 The reference is to the popular story of a brahmin being convinced by thieves that his goat is a dog. See, e.g., *Hitopadeśa* 4.10.

26.47 ***Triphalā***: Cf. note to 18.115.

27.5 Rahu is the demon that causes eclipses.

28.54 There are five syllables missing from the second foot *(pāda)* of this verse.

28.75 There are three syllables missing from the second foot *(pāda)* of this verse.

28.90 There are three syllables missing from the third foot *(pāda)* of this verse.

28.109 Indra, caught trying to seduce Ahályа, was covered in a thousand eyes by Gáutama, her husband.

INDEX

Sanskrit words are given according to the accented CSL pronuncuation aid in the English alphabetical order. They are followed by the conventional diacritics in brackets.